D1521074

The First Book of Kalendeck

THE FIRST BOOK OF KALENDECK

BY
DAVID W. SHERWOOD

Laure
Thank you so much
Please enjoy.
David Sherwood

This book is was edited by the author. There will be mistakes, I know this guy. If you could bring these to his attention it would be greatly appreciated. As well as a review of his work on Amazon. 1-5 stars, he just asks that you be honest. You may find him on Facebook if you search for 'David Boo Sherwood' it should take you right to him. Thank you so much for purchasing his work. Other stories he has written include.

The First Book of Kalendeck – Young Adult Fantasy
The Second Book of Kalendeck. - Young Adult Fantasy
The Red Queen's Gamble – Sci Fi Fantasy
Hopscotch – Serial killer / Thriller / Female Detective
Darken French Road – Paranormal Romance
The Short Stories of David W. Sherwood. - Contemporary Fiction

The incredible cover artwork has been done by Lincoln Renall. This gentleman does an amazing job. If you like it, let him know. If you need help he is the one to go to.

All his work is Vampire/Zombie/Werewolf free.
Again, thanks!! Please enjoy.
To my friend and editor Lynda Moreno. A faire child.
Thank you.

I would like to thank everyone who has helped me with this project. Some are friends I have lost touch with over the years. I hope they find their way back someday. I miss their friendship.

It has been a very long journey that began some time in the mid 1980's. It is odd to see that some ideas, which had started so simple, quite literally a spark of imagination, grew as if they had a life of their own. The main character I have modeled after many people, but then, no one in particular.

      I have penned this story for a very long time. The characters I have created are like friends to me. I like to visit from time to time and often wonder what they are up to now, now that my involvement in their lives is over.

      It was once my story, it is now yours. Enjoy the journey.

      Thank you.

Chapter #1

Alone, I stood on the platform and waited for the six-thirty train to arrive. The heavy downpour that had started well over an hour ago continued. Lightning sparked brightly in the distance while thunder spoke softly in echo over the hills holding time in its voice, age in its sound.

I sighed and sat my small black case on the covered platform near my feet. I had not planned on the weather being this foul. Even with my collar up my clothing gave little help in keeping out the wind and rain. Sunny and warmer when I left, I cursed the heavens more than once.

A wooden bench behind me creaked as it took my weight. The sound of the rainfall, combined with the growing darkness relaxed my senses.

Lost in my thoughts, I heard the man's shoes scuffle on the wet sidewalk a moment before I saw him round the corner.

He held his open coat over him to shield the rain. When he lowered this, under the protection of the roof, and put it on, his appearance gave me a start. I was expecting someone clean shaven and meticulous. He was not. I nodded to him respectfully, apparently a farmer by way of his attire, and he nodded back in kind.

He leaned on a post and put his hands in his pockets and waited as well.

Before long the farmer cleared his throat and spoke. "Hey, son. Are you waiting for the seven p.m. Mills?"

"No, sir." I touched the brim of my hat minding my manners. "I'm taking the six-thirty from here to Franklin," I replied politely.

He nodded and looked back at the tracks. He kept whistling a tune, a little ditty, under his breath as he stood there and tapped his foot nervously. By his manner he waited impatiently.

"Expecting someone?" He asked me. "No, wait," he held his hand to his chin. "By the black case you have and your clothes you're a traveling man."

I nodded and he smiled.

"My turn to guess for you," I said, being drawn into his simple game. Talking with someone kept my mind off things and helped pass the idle time away. "Your clothing is that of a farmer. You are waiting for someone you care about, someone special, to come from Mills and you have not seen them in a while."

"Close, mostly, I am heading to Mills. May I?" he asked and I moved over, sliding my case with me, so he could have room enough on the bench to sit. "I'm on my way to Mills to get my wife. It's been awhile since I've seen her and she's not expecting me. I find it hard to wait," he rubbed his hands together and placed them on his lap. He fidgeted restlessly and kept tapping his fingers on his legs.

His clothing looked new, as if he had purchased everything for this occasion alone. The common shirt he wore, and his work pants were ironed. His grooming was in stark contrast with his clothing, however. He wore his hair in a long braid much like an Indian of the West might, a single braid, not two. His hair was brown, not black, and he didn't look like an Indian. I had seen some on the movie screen at the local theater. I had to listen intently as his accent made it hard to place his origins. I admit that I am not the worldly gent I tried to make myself seem. I thought he probably came from the old country and let it be. He was a burly man, bearded, tall, broad-shouldered and heavy-handed. I pitied a man who ever crossed him.

"I just came from Mills. My mother is in a hospital there," I said.

"Ah, I see." He folded his arms across his chest and stroked his thick beard. "She hurt?" I heard his concern, but knew his thoughts were absent.

"A sickness actually. Hopefully she'll be better soon."

"The cancer?"

"At times I wish it was a cancer. Not that I want to wish that kind of death on anyone, but at least then they would know for certain."

"A terrible thing, cancer is. What could be worse, you say?"

"There is this sickness," I began, taking a deep breath, "that is making her grow old. I mean, she is getting older faster than anyone normally would. She's my mother, but to look at her you would believe that she is my grandmother. She is in her mid-forties but already her hair is white and the aches have her and won't let go. She's been in the hospital off and on for all but a half a year now."

"My word," he said. He had stopped fidgeting. He no longer tapped his fingers or toes. Talking calmed him and seemed to take his mind off things. We sat there under the green slate roof of the train platform and watched the rain fall just a few feet away.

"Do they have a name for that disease?"

"Um, accel...decryption. Just a moment." I reached in my pocket and pulled out a paper. "Here it is. Accelerated decrepitude. The doctor wrote that down. They say she may have had it since birth and it may have only surfaced after I was born. Probably has something to do with her glands; an imbalance of her humors." I folded the paper and put it back in my pocket.

"Going on war medicine," he said rubbing his hands together, "these doctors seem to know everything now. Amazing what they can do. Almost lost my fingers in an accident years ago, but they fixed me up just all right." He quickly flashed his hand and I saw an old scar running across his palm. It was a thing that people kept to themselves. I did not pry further and he did not offer any more.

I nodded in agreement. "They say if they can't do a thing for her then they will bring a specialist down from Boston. If he can't help her, I'll find a rest home closer to home and she'll stay there."

"Family could could take care of her," he offered, turning the collar up on his own denim jacket. The wind had picked up again, not blowing the rain on the platform, just making itself known. "Your father?"

"He's gone." my voice quieted. I leaned forward with my elbows on my knees and combed my hair back with my fingers. "Went to the war and never came back. Just ma and me at the house, growing up." In most ways, and most days, I was always grateful to leave the crowded turmoil of the city and get back to the country and its openness. However, today, leaving my mother at the hospital made me feel incredibly lonely. I was glad this farmer was here to help take my mind away from my worries.

"Do you remember him?" he asked.

"No. I was too young when he left. Ma has no photographs."

He looked me over as if judging my age and nodded. "War's a terrible thing. Does your mother miss him?"

"Oh yes," I held my bowler in one hand and traced the edge of the brim with the other. "There was this old rocker that she had by the upper bedroom window. She'd spend her days sitting there watching and waiting for his return. Suppose he had left in that direction and that was the way she expected him to return. Neighbors thought his absence had driven her to senility. His name is on a plaque in the town square. She just won't accept it." Only death had kept my father away. I had known this for the longest time.

"You've plenty of work to do when you get home?"

I shrugged my shoulders. "We have a barn with a forge in it, my father's business; it's not been fired up in years. I can learn that trade, I guess. We shall see. What do you do?" I suddenly felt as if I were steering the conversation.

"Hmm?" he looked up as if I had interrupted him from his own thoughts. He might have dozed or listening to the rain. He raised his eyebrows and thought for a moment. "Well, I guess you could say that I am between jobs. Having just been let go from the burdens I had before, I am now free to do as I feel. For once in my life I have no path before me."

"I see, and these burdens have kept you away from your wife?"

He chuckled. "Yes, yes they have. She will be very surprised to see me tonight. I'll . . ."

He stopped when we heard a clock inside the building chime seven times. Instinctively, I looked at my watch. It was seven o'clock. My watch was four minutes slower from the one I heard and I had to reset it. I did so, winding the spring as I did every evening.

Late trains were not rare in this part of the country. If the scheduled train had been on time, I would have been twenty minutes closer to my destination by now. By ten I had hoped to well and away from here in a town called Franklin many miles to the east. That would put me at my front door at close to midnight.

This little delay was natural and for the most part I have come to expect it. For some reason, this part of the rail line was more prone to delays and setbacks. The rain made it worse for some reason. Awful as it might be, the thought of getting stranded here tonight started to become real. I didn't want that. I did not welcome a night, damp and cold, here at the train station.

If this train arrived within the next few minutes my trip would work like clockwork, as it sometimes did, and I would sleep comfortably at my home in a few hours.

"Late again," the farmer grumbled. Slapping his hands on his legs, he was clearly agitated. "I have no time for this, not this day. She waits."

He stood and began to slowly pace back and forth across the platform. I stood likewise and leaned against one of the timbers supporting the roof.

On the other side of the tracks a long hedgerow of briars lay. Beyond this was a large plot of pastureland, and there in its center, a giant solemn oak stood. Its branches dipped and swayed as if positioned for conducting some vast orchestra as wind pulled through its limbs.

Then from the darkened clouds, a whip of lightning struck down. So sudden and unexpected was this that it startled both of us. Its bristled tip engulfed the whole of the tree. The limbs and trunk didn't crack or splinter; the tree just merely stopped all movement as if the wind meant nothing. For an instant bright blue light glowed all around its silhouette. A limb fell to the side and I was sure, for that moment only, I saw someone standing by the trunk of the tree, hands flung upward as if to stop the falling branch. I blinked and there was no one--just a trick of the light. The lightning disappeared as quickly as it had come.

I closed my eyes. The brightness was still there, etched in the darkness in the back of my mind. I saw the negative. In my mind's eye, the tree seemed brighter than the lightning.

A drop of rain struck my cheek.

And only then, as if to judge its distance and to triumph over striking the tree; thunder came, low and hollow.

Behind me I heard a set of rusted hinges creak as a door opened. Turning around I saw an elderly man looking out. His glasses perched on the rim of his nose, his hair was thinning and resembled the down of a goose so light with time and age that when the wind moved through its strands it seemed to have a mind of its own.

The farmer and I both went to the window.

"I thought I heard people out here. Are you all waiting for someone?" The elderly man asked, his voice so low and he could hardly be heard above the wind of the storm.

"Oh no. No I'm just waiting for the next train to Franklin to come. I'm trying to get home," I said holding one of the doors open. I held my ticket half crumpled in my hands.

"I'm trying to get to Mills this evening," said the farmer.

"Well, you know, I just received a call about twenty minutes ago from the station on the other side of the county. Your ride to Mills might still be coming along, but the train heading east to Franklin ran into some trouble. They say Central is going to close the section down. The storm must have been really bad over there, doing a lot of damage I suppose. Power is out here and along the whole line."

"How soon do you think the next train will be coming through?" I asked tucking my ticket away in my pocket.

"Like I said; to Franklin, there is nothing; the Mills run still may pull through."

"Nothing tonight, then. I don't want to go back to Mills," I tried to hide the disappointment in my voice. I didn't have the money to stay with mother one more night. I needed the two dollars to see me through the week.

"Not any time tonight, tomorrow noon at the earliest. The Franklin run should resume then. They won't be able to get the horses up there to clean the tracks until sometime after sunrise. That's if the weather clears. If it's still storming in the morning, it will be even later."

"Well, this is not good," I thought aloud as thunder clapped distantly. "Would you know of any place, a hotel, or someplace where I could stay the night?"

"Shaye's," said the farmer nodding obvious familiar with the town.

"Yes sir. There's Shaye's Hostel 'bout four blocks up the street. Should have enough room for you to stay the night. It's been rather slow these days. Don't expect much though. It's a simple place."

"Good luck," I said to the farmer.

"Good luck to you too. Hope your mother gets better."

"Thanks," I said and tipped my hat to the gentlemen. Picking up my case from the bench, I raised my collar once again to the wind.

The train station and tracks were on the edge of town. Heading up the street, towards the hostel, I could see the town was dark and quiet. I felt odd walking up a street with no street lamps to show the way. With no electricity to power the lamps on the sidewalk, darkness descended full and complete. Most of the shops had closed and locked up, waiting for the morning with grim faces of wood, glass, and tile.

At the first corner I came to I noticed a candle flickering in a window of the store across the street. "Alvinston's Books" read the name of the store painted on the large glass window. Catching my interest, I made my way across the street and peered in.

A woman sat at the front counter reading a large book on a podium by candlelight. Her hair had fallen over her shoulders and covered her face as she read.

Shelves of books all of various sizes lined the walls. Smiling, as if greeting old friends after an absence, I laid my hand on the glass and my breath misted around my fingertips.

The books I had read in life would never leave me. Since I was young, I loved to read. Books had kept me company when friends and family had failed. I would read everything I could get my hands on. Although this passion for books had subsided somewhat over the last few years, I still loved a good story.

I went to the door and walked in removing my hat. A cowbell on the inside handle clanged against the door, and the woman looked up with a start.

"Oh, my goodness it's really dark out. What time is it?"

"Just after seven," I said walking to the counter.

"I should have closed an hour ago. That's what happens when I get into a good book, just can't put it down."

"Do you want me to go?" I asked half turning.

"No it's fine. What can I help you with?"

"I'm just looking for something to read, I guess." I sat on a high stool and looked around the shop. The musty smell of old paper, and glue hung in the air around me.

"What do you like to read?"

"Well, I enjoy adventure novels most. Nothing too modern."

"I see; would it bother you to read a second-hand book?"

"No, not really. It's better if they're broken in. Shows somebody liked it before."

"This book I'm reading right now is very adventurous. I'm almost at the end, just the last few pages of the last chapter and I will finish. If you give me a couple of minutes, it's yours."

"Okay."

She pushed her glasses back on, picked up the book, and instantly forgot about me.

I turned my attention from her to the books on the shelves behind me. It was hard to see the titles in the dim candlelight, but in moments I discovered several familiar authors and smiled. Most of these authors I had not read in a long time. I picked up a book here and there, flipped through some pages, read a few passages, then returned them to the shelf. It was like revisiting old friends.

I heard a sigh behind me, and so I turned. She held the book closed between her hands and was looking at the candle, her thoughts very distant from this small shop on a rainy night. Waking from a dream it always took a moment to return to the here and now.

She sat there for a few seconds before she gave me a sidewards glance.

"Here you go," she said as she handed the book over to me. He smile was broad. "You can have it."

"How was it?"

"Very interesting, I think it will raise your spirits and make you look at life a little differently. The author creates a whole world that feels so real. It's very hard to come back to this one. I wish I could have stayed even though the journey is over. I'd love to see how the people fare as time goes on. You said you like a good adventure, right? You should enjoy this story," her smile was infectious and I smiled back at her. If she found this book so exiting, then I could afford to spare fifty or seventy-five cents for it. With a good book to sustain me, I could live on bread.

"How much do I owe you?" I placed my case on the stool and began to fumble in it for my billfold.

"Nothing, just take it. It's a treasure, but I can't take money for it."

I gave her a quizzical look. Few things were free in this day, let alone a book. Her smile was unwavering and I saw no hint of deception in her eyes.

"Thanks," I said as I looked down at the book in my hands. It was old and looked much like an old family bible. The well-worn cover was made from simple brown leather with three slender strips of brass binding the pages together. Hand-made. This was almost unheard of with the printing practices of today. I turned it slightly so the candlelight played over the surface and I could read the title. The single word "KALENDECK" stamped in gold relief across the cover gleamed as I ran my fingers gently across the letters.

"This is my name," I said so softly at first it was almost a whisper. Turning it again I had to be sure of the name. I almost laughed, thinking it was a joke of some kind. I cleared my throat and said it again louder so she could hear. "Well my last name, that is."

"It is? How odd."

I nodded. "Do you know who wrote it?" I asked.

"If I remember correctly, in the back, it says something about the author. He's a man named Ravenstein lives in Jackson, Massachusetts. Close to Boston. I've never seen anything else written by him."

"It was good though?" I asked. Setting the book down I thumbed through the pages. The musty scent of old paper and glue rose around me anew.

"Very. He's a good writer. I like his style."

"Are you sure you want to just give this to me?" I asked taking a step back and watching her face to read her expression. "It looks quite expensive and very old?"

"Listen, if you are ever in town again, you can stop by and return it to me, and tell me how you liked it. As you can see, it has been around. I was not the first owner and I think you will not be the last," she said taking her jacket off of a wooden peg behind her chair.

"I travel through this area often. I'll find some way to repay you. Thank you very much," I said placing the book on top of my other possessions in the black case.

"Just enjoy the story. And have a safe journey."

"Good-bye," I said and left. The cowbell rang again as I closed the door behind me.

Walking up the street, I continued into the night. With every step my case slapped against my thigh. A sense of contentment filled me and the night grew more tolerable. It seems I would have a friend tonight. The book would keep me company.

With a few more minutes walking I saw a rusted chain supporting a sign. The words "Shaye's Hostel" could be read on its weathered surface.

I entered a small foyer lit brightly by candles. Warmth enveloped me, along with the aroma of cedar. The air was noticeably drier here. This place would be a lot more comforting than any seat on an east-bound train.

I closed the door shutting out the damp, and then opening my case I reached for my billfold I kept inside the inset pocket.

It wasn't there.

Taking the book out I searched the bottom. Standing, I slapped the pockets of my jacket, checked my pants, front pockets, back pockets, and the breast pocket of my jacket. Nothing. Searching through my clothing in the case, I came up empty once more.

I cursed in the candlelight. How was I going to pay for a room? I had my train ticket, but I needed it to get back home.

I stood there in the foyer and thought for a second. Footsteps could be heard as someone came from the room inside to the foyer door. Quickly, I picked up my book and case and was about to turn and leave when the inside door opened up.

"Good evening, can I help you?" The man asked.

"I was looking for a room for the night?"

"Well you've come to the right place, come on in." I went in reluctantly as the clerk closed the door behind me. Trapped now, I could feel the room get notably warmer. Candles of all sizes were in place wherever there was an empty space on a shelf. The room was better lit with the candles than it would have been with the electric lamps. The heat became suffocating. I looked out the window at the night and wished I were still out there looking in.

"Now then," he said going behind the counter and picking up his pen. He handed me a blank registry card. "Do you have a reservation?"

"No, no I don't" I could not think of anything to say, so stalling for a moment I said. "At least I do not think so. I do have a friend coming. He'll arrive here later this evening. I'm sure he has made a reservation."

"Is his last name . . . Kalendeck?" The desk clerk asked as his finger scrolled down the registry. My breath caught in my throat and I took a step backwards almost dropping the card. Wind was blowing a branch against the side of the wall outside. The man cleared his throat. I could not have heard him right.

"I asked if his name is Kalendeck?"

"No, no that's not it. M - my last name is Kalendeck."

"Well then you're the only one registered to stay here tonight. I see nothing for your friend."

"Did the man from the train station tell you I was on my way up?" I asked. It was the only thing I could think of and I was sure we did not exchange names.

"No, our power's been out for sometime now. You'll notice the candles. I was about to lock the place up for the night when you arrived."

"I see." I wondered who had known I was going to get stranded here tonight and could think of no one. As I thought on this, another one came to mind.

"I think my wallet was lost on the train tonight. I am sorry, but I have no way to pay you for this room."

The manager fumbled under the counter for a moment and brought out a receipt. On it was my name, just my last, and also my complete address. At the bottom, stamped in dark blue ink, were the words 'PAID IN FULL' with today's date. Beside this there were two signatures.

"Who signed it?" I asked.

"The first was Avery's, that's the morning clerk. As for the other signature, I cannot tell you. What I can tell you, is that a room is paid for, and under your name. You can take it or not. It's damp and chilly out tonight," he stifled a yawn with the back of his hand.

"Can I wait a bit?" I asked. The room was closing in on me. I had to get back outside.

"To see if your friend comes along?"

"Yes, that's it," I said snapping my fingers. "I'll just wait outside for him. Thanks."

"We have a lobby," the man suggested with a wave of his hand.

"I'll just wait outside. So he doesn't miss the place in the night." Grabbing my case I hurried out before the man could say more.

As I closed the door, several of the candles that lit the foyer blew out.

Once outside, I leaned against a dark lamppost to gather my thoughts. The cool, damp air felt good against my skin and I realized I was sweating. I waited for my heart to slow down, and then, started back towards the bookstore.

How odd, I thought, as my foot went into a puddle, to run into my name twice in one night. I was sure no one knew I would be in this town tonight. My being here was a direct result of the storm, something purely incidental. Should I trust these events and take the room for the night, or stay away and see what the night brings? I was not sure.

By now I was standing outside the window of the bookstore. It was just as dark as the other shops. I retraced my steps back down to the railway station, but found the lock was in place on the front door. I went around the back only to find all the entrances barred and tightly secured.

I sighed as I returned to the platform by the tracks. I sat on the same bench I had sat on earlier. It was very dark and sheltered here and I tried to rest. I sat the case beside me and pulled my light jacket closer seeking what little warmth it would give.

I shivered, my stomach growled, my feet and pants were wet. It was very quiet as the little town slept. I jumped when I heard the clock inside the station strike half past eight.

Even with my thoughts all jumbled, it would be better to return to the hostel before I froze to death on this autumn night. Maybe by unknown circumstances someone did prepare a room for me tonight. It would be a lot warmer than the platform. I would search the room completely and lock it from the inside. If it were a prank, I would not be fooled.

As I neared the building once more, I hesitated for a moment. The cold numbness I felt in my fingertips and toes urged me to go on. I stomped my feet again on the steps and went to the door.

The man was sleeping with his chair leaning back against the windowsill. As the door closed, he woke with a start and his chair came forward with a bang.

"Your friend didn't make it?" He asked wiping his eyes seeing I was alone.

"Ah, no. Trains are down. They will have to get the horses out tomorrow and clear the tracks up," I said as I shuffled up to the registry with my hat and my case in hand.

"Well, your room is at the top of the stairs two doors down and on the left. Business is pretty slow so I am going to lock the front door. If you need anything though, I'll still be here. I have a cot in the back."

"Is there something I need to sign?"

"Just when you leave in the morning. Here's your key and also a candle so you can find your way. Will you be wanting anything else this evening?"

"No, I'll be fine, thank you. Good night."

"Good night to you, then. The furnace is gas. So electricity is not needed except for the blowers. You might be lucky and feel some heat coming through the floor vents," he said as he came from behind the counter and began to snuff out the candles.

Taking the candle given, I found my way upstairs to my room.

The room, being at the far side of the hostel, was as cool as the night, but with no wind and no rain it was definitely a blessing. Once inside, I found a kerosene lamp sitting on a simple desk. I brought life to the wick with the flame of the candle. I blew out the candle and set it to the side.

I slid the bolt into place and then checked it by trying to open the door. It held tightly. I went to the window and checked it also. No one would be coming through unexpectedly this night.

I placed my wet shoes over an air duct that felt warm. I undressed and placed my socks next to them and my pants nearby. My light jacket and shirt I placed on separate wooden hangers above the duct and slightly off to the side.

I began to really look at the room for the first time. The bed was higher than the bed I had at home and covered with a heavy patchwork quilt. It was a simple design; circles within circles. It looked warm and inviting. To the side against the wall, was a very large mirror that, with the help of the door, used up the wall opposite the windows.

The kerosene lamp sat on a desk with a wicker-back rocking chair in front of it. It would seem the desk was not so much for working, just relaxing.

I pushed the quilt aside and lay down between the sheets pulling the quilt up over me. I had sat my case along with the book on the dresser next to the mirror. I looked at it for a long moment. When my feet and legs warmed up some I would consider bringing the book to bed with me.

Minutes passed and my eyelids grew heavy. Feeling secure, warmer, and more relaxed, I was soon asleep. Lightning stuck nearby and the thunder startled me from a dream. I went to the lamp and blew out the flame. A heavy odor filled the air as this wick cooled. I did not mind, my mind clouded with sleep. Returning to the bed, I pulled the covers over me once more and slept.

*   *   *   *   *

For some reason, the room had become extremely warm. Even stripped down to nothing, with the quilt kicked to the floor, I was sweating.

My eyes opened slowly and I brought my head up from the pillow. The room was full of light as if it was morning. Rolling over on my side, I faced the window.

I propped myself on my elbows and rubbed the sleep from my eyes. I wasn't sure if I dreamt or if I was awake, but just outside the window a blazing blue light shone through the curtains. It was bright enough to mimic the sun, but I could tell by the shadows the source was right outside the window itself and not from the sky above.

Seconds passed and nothing happened. My heart was beating swiftly.

I stood and pulled the sheet from the bed to cover myself, securing it tightly around my waist as I went to the window. I drew the curtains open slowly. The light was so bright, even squinting with my hands over my face tears were still falling from my eyes.

The air closest to the windows was hotter than it had been near the bed. Sweat rolled down the small of my back. I could not think of an explanation for what was outside the window. It could have been ball lightning, but I wasn't sure. I had never seen ball lightning before, although I had heard people talk about it. It could be a freak from the storm.

I stepped back away from the window to the far bedside. There was the sound of an arc, an electrical snap that lasted ten seconds or so, then stopped.

Curiosity brought me back to the window to see what had happened. All I could notice from my vantage point was the ball had shrunk; its brightness was less intense.

The air had also cooled, and smelled of ash. My breathing was rapid, and shallow. I steadied myself by holding on to the back of the rocker. My lungs filled deeply with air as I forced myself to calm down. I was going to give myself a heart-attack. Only eighteen and dies of a heart-attack. Goodness, what would mother say?

I stood there and watched the object as it hovered in the night. There was movement behind it, off to the upper right, back in the hills. It was there in the corner of my eye and it didn't register until it brightened.

It was second ball of light, much like the first, rising from behind a hill like an angel in the sky to become a miniature sun on a stormy morning.

My gaze left the ball before me and I watched the one behind it. It did nothing but hover there. And then, like a stone it fell. Before it reached the earth, it began to come forward, toward the hostel.

Perhaps the ball before me drew the other closer. I judged its distance as a few miles out, but then as it fell it began to pick up speed, the distance decreased rapidly.

"It's coming straight for me," I realized with a shock. I dove backward, throwing myself across the bed and hit the floor as the two spheres met.

Their momentum carried on after the impact, and the window erupted inward. There was a brilliant flash of light followed by a rainfall of wood and glass. I was on the floor and the bed shielded my eyes from the flare.

The clap of thunder was so loud it pushed the air from my chest and drove me to unconsciousness.

* * * * *

Flame.

Something, somewhere was on fire. I didn't hear it or see it; I felt it. With recognition of the pain in my ankle, my foot jerked in reflex.

I coughed and rose to my knees quickly. Most of the far wall was gone. What remained of it, along with the ceiling and the bed, was on fire. With every breath, my lungs filled with the heat. Thick, dark smoke rolled out of the hole that had once been the window.

Flames printed abstract patterns on the aged wallpaper just before the fire consumed it. The heat was like a weight pressing against my unprotected body. It inhibited my normal functions and in turn made my reactions slower.

"I don't want to die in here."

Everything was flowing in a slower speed. Fire raced through the old timbers at an alarming rate. As I turned to the door the lamp burst, flames spread covering the desk. The door was splashed with burning oil. I felt a sharp pain in my thigh.

"No, oh mother, no," I heard myself scream over the roar. I had it in my mind to ram the door with my shoulder. My forward momentum should carry me out into the hallway, and from there I could safely leave. To bust through the fragile wall of wood and flame would be easy.

Then I saw the mirror. Or rather, I didn't see the mirror; it was gone. It wasn't moved, or shattered, it was just simply not there. In its place there was nothing but darkness. As I watched it, shades of colors began to cross its surface, changing like wind blowing across oil on water. My body froze; my gaze had room for the mirror only. My mind became divided as if there was another person occupying my skull. Part of me screamed and cursed inside begging my muscles to move. The other was completely fascinated by the fantastic colors of the mirror and would not be distracted. Again I tried to move, but couldn't. At that moment, I knew I was going to die.

Smoke clouded my eyes for a second and I finally looked away. As I hesitated the option I had, to ram the door with my shoulder, vanished as the door was now completely engulfed by flames.

In these last moments my senses sharpened. The heat behind me was the fire, and my death. The pain in my leg was a shard of glass from the lamp, and also my death. I looked at the blood running freely down my leg. It pooled on the floor with fire reflecting on its surface. Laying on the edge of the dresser next to the thing that was once the mirror, lay my black leather case, untouched. In the case was the book I would never get the chance to read.

"Would they be able to find my bones in the ashes?" I wondered.

Smoke hazed my thoughts as it did the air in the room. I began to turn, to face the fire and my death straight on, but I never made it. Death would be cheated this once.

From the corner of my eye, I saw a ceiling crossbeam fall from its resting place. With its one end still attached to another beam above my head, it fell in a sweeping motion; its arc carried it at an angle just off the center of my back.

I had no time to react. I felt the impact and it shoved me forward, into the darkness that once was the mirror. My shoulder nudged the case and it fell through behind me.

The the sudden roar of wind replaced the sound of the flame. The air was cool, damp, and refreshing. The burning odor became that of . . . of . . . hemlock?

Darkness over came me completely and I felt myself drifting as if lost.

And soon, even that was gone.

*   *   *   *   *

The darkness was present for a long time. I was drifting in nothingness, time had stopped it seemed.

I slowly began to feel my body about me again, starting at my very core, my heartbeat. It was good to feel warm blood moving through my veins again.

With every beat of my heart, the knowledge of my body around me grew. Up through my torso, down my arms and to my fingertips. As the feeling of life returned to my limbs, there was an odd sensation-like being pulled out of warm water to the colder air above. Or perhaps, it was more like wildfire spreading over virgin grassland. The effect was gently numbing. It was a pleasant sensation and for a few seconds I enjoyed it.

The side of my face was numb.

"Fire" . . . ? The thought had passed from my mind before it completely manifested.

The feeling of warmth was the same as sensation traveled downward. The burning went through my left leg, whole and complete, but went only half way on the right. There it began to build like water behind a dam. The warmth in my right leg grew, with increasing pain. I needed to fight it; to suppress the pain before it filled my body. I tried to sit up to hold the pain, to extinguish it with my own hands.

But hands held me; several hands were pushing me back down. The fire, the burning in my leg, couldn't they see. They had to see!

The pain burned higher. I forgot about the hands, there was nothing but the pain. With a surge, the dam broke, and the pain filled my body. I screamed.

With the scream, my senses left me again and I was cast back into the darkness.

Chapter #2

It was well before evening twilight when he passed the stone ruins of the keep and left the main trail. He turned on the path that would eventually take him home. It had been a short journey to the village, but this day, this day of days, there was so much he had to do. He was a healer and after mending a broken bone, several large cuts and an assortment of other illnesses, his day was over. You would think that living in such an isolated place the people would try to go about their business carefully. Such as it was, it could have been far worse.

There was a movement to the side of the path and he realized that he had been so caught up in his thoughts he had failed to notice his daughter sitting on a large rock in the shade trees.

"Father!" She exclaimed when she saw him. He bent to fold her in his arms for just a moment. She was getting too tall for him to carry comfortably anymore.

"Have you been waiting long, Kalista?" He asked as she walked in step beside him.

"No, mother said you'd be along shortly."

"Ah, she knows me well."

"Was there much to do in the village today?" Her voice was light and a skip in her step.

"I had a man with a broken shoulder. He had it in a sling for two days. There were other people I tended and they are better now," he smiled and put his hand around her shoulder.

"You feel heavy. Did it take away your strength?"

He paused a moment catching his breath; not realizing he was leaning so much on her. She stopped with him and took the pack from his shoulder and the staff from his hands.

"I'll take these, father. You ask too much of the magic you use. Mother says the broken bones do not have to heal in one day. Let them heal in their own time."

"I do get swept up in it. You and your mother know this," he straightened and stretched his back glad to be rid of the pack and its belongings. Ointments and salves out in the morning, coins back in it in the evening. There was nothing breakable in the pack now. He could let her carry it without fear. The thatched roof of his house appeared. He was almost home.

"If you hurry along and fetch mother, I'll give you a coin to spend on ribbon on market day."

"Truly speaking?"

"Aye, child. Truly speaking."

She took off as only one full of youth and life could.

"Leave the staff," he said and laughed when she turned. When in his grasp once more, she was gone again.

By time he was in sight of the doorstep, Deanna stood in the doorway wiping her hands on her apron. The worried look gave way to puzzlement when she saw the look on his face.

"What is wrong?" Deanna asked, "Do I needed to come quickly."

"Nothing is wrong." There was a pause as he looked in her eyes. "Deanna, he is here."

"Who?" She looked at the path behind him but saw no one. "Someone is coming for a meal this evening?"

He let his staff lean on the side of the house and placed his hands on her hips. Kalista stood beside them taking it all in. With a kiss on her forehead he looked into her eyes once more.

"Deanna, listen to me." Weary from the day's work and the journey home, his breaths came heavy and with effort. He tried to keep the trembling out of his voice. The feelings of relief and sadness were almost overwhelming.

"He is here." The words spoken again, he looked in her eyes willing her to understand.

"He is here? You mean he he?" She asked in disbelief. The smile on her face could not be contained. Be it from excitement or happiness he was not sure, but tears welled in her eyes and she wept. It had been so long for the both of them; the waiting was finally over.

"Yes," he said kissing her on the forehead. He pulled her in his arms, holding her as she sobbed. "Just a short time ago, before I turned into the path home, I felt him cross over." And having said it, tears formed briefly in his eyes.

"So long we have waited. Do you know where he is, my love?"

"To the south, for certain or one of the territories east perhaps. For the Brothers to have him cross over in the wasteland of the north would be of no sense. On market day we will learn of it, I'm sure. The rumor of his arrival will travel fast. Now, I must go inside and sit. My legs will carry me no further. Kalista some cold water, please."

Inside he found his chair and sat down heavily.

"We have to gather so much. Ryeson, will we have time?"

"Yes we will," he said taking a drink of water that she brought. "I'll collect things to cure the snake bite before winter, and in more quantities than we need. To be sure."

Deanna sat holding her head in her hands and looked about the room.

"I am sorry for the tears," she said and laughed, dabbing away their remnants with her apron. "Kalendeck gave us so much, you see? Now the one he told us of is here. We have to repay his generosity."

"Time will bring him to us. We have one year and a day to wait and he'll be here at our home."

"Is this the one that is written of on the paper?" Kalista asked refilling his mug from a pitcher of water freshly drawn.

"Yes, yes he is. The paper was given to us by a man during the wars. We knew this day was coming, and now it is upon us. This means I will have to go to the Gathering this year, Deanna." He clapped his hands together and laughed. "Ha! They will be very shocked to see me there after so long."

"I will make new clothes for you. I will not have you go to the Gathering in thrice mended garments. And you'll have to find a new pair of boots. The ones you have won't last that distance."

"Ah, Deanna, you never change do you?" He reached for her hand and holding it in his own he kissed it gently.

The sun began to set by the time he stood and brought his staff in from outside. He placed it where it could be found easily in the morning. Taking off his boots, he went to his chair near the fire and rested once more letting his wife and daughter continue with the evening chores about the home.

*   *   *   *   *

Ryn, this day a cabinet maker, stood on the edge of the stone wall, hands on his hips, and looked down at the men laboring below. He had been strong once as they are. Days untold his sweat mixed with the soil as he worked the land. If he closed his eyes and listened, the sounds he heard would bring back memories so long forgotten they seemed as dreams--the whinny of a horse, the strike of a hammer and anvil, the rolling sounds of distant thunder, the snap of canvas in the wind. All of these brought back events and places of an earlier time; a time when he was one of the strong and one of the brave.

Someday the land would claim him. He balled his hand into a fist trying to remember the strength that was now all but gone. In his other hand he held a hammer. He placed it at his feet, not wanting to hold it for a time. His age gave him an excuse to rest.

As Ryn flexed his hands, he saw the old scar that ran across his palm. When the weather turned it would ache to his bones still. A constant reminder-that was all it was-a reminder of the different paths he could have taken, of how the actions of a man could change the land. As a farmer tills the soil, he held within his grasp for a time the ability to till men. To make them into something stronger than they were.

Not wishing to relive memories of the past, he looked elsewhere. Men brought a new load of stone earlier. People worked unloading the stones and placing them on wide strips of heavy canvas. These were then picked up by the ends and brought to the tower, whereupon the masons worked them. There were more bundles than people available and it would be some time before the wagon was completely empty.

These men, common soldiers from the five territories and Land Streth, for a time, had put aside the armor and weapons and labored together for one cause. Never had they raised a sword to one another, but together, as they worked now, their fathers had fought a common enemy. Those from the five helped rebuild and reshape the lands of the Wiladene Territory, the sixth territory, the one territory that had been lost.

They still wore the colors of their respective lands. They made alliances and friendships rebuilding what their fathers had forged all those years ago. Hopefully, their friendships would carry on after their time here was complete. Like mortar between rocks, it could only strengthen the bonds that held the kingdom together.

The sea breeze picked up, bringing with it the smells of salt and seaweed. His mind wandered further and hefting his hammer, he walked over to the side of the castle wall that was closest to the ocean.

Ryn stood there and watched the wind in the tall grass for a time.

{He is here,} said a voice over his shoulder. Knowing who spoke to him, he did not turn, only nodded. Although he showed no emotion outwardly, his chest soon filled with excitement. This day they had long been waiting for.

The hammer once again settled at his feet.

"How long until he is with us?" Ryn asked keeping his voice low.

{We have time,} said the voice again. {Duke Almonesson and Tyndall will take good care of him.}

"He has much to learn," Ryn said to the voice.

{Yes. Yes he does. Some lessons will be harder than others.} There was a pause when they were both silent. {Look below, there she is,} hearing this, the man leaned forward slightly to look down over the wall.

The castle was far from complete and the wall stood only as high as the rooftops of the village home and shops. A young girl with long sun bleached hair and a homespun dress walked barefoot towards the castle with a vessel of water from the wellspring. Ryn had known the girl from birth and had watched as she grew through the years. Now in her fifteenth year she matured very well.

"Brembry," he said and he heard the voice behind him laugh. "Should we warn her of her fate?" He asked the voice and there was more laughter. This question an old one and they brought up from time to time as they talked.

{As we warned others years ago?} said the voice and Ryn frowned remembering the inevitable. Brembry was still young and, given the chance, she might have become a beautiful woman. He saw how some of the soldier's heads turned as she walked by. He saw her smile. She knew why the men stopped in their labors.

This winter would be her last.

They were silence for a time that was common among the two. Each man content on knowing the other was there. Like brothers, the two had bonded in a way few could understand. Battle does that to a person.

"When he arrives here, I would like to see him," said Ryn.

"See who, grandpa?" asked a woman nearby. He turned and smiled.

"Ah, you've caught me," he said reaching out and touching her arm. His granddaughter had grown through the years and now stood as tall as he. Living her life happily, she had chosen to take no man as a husband and was content as such. Her long dark hair had a few telltale strands of gray, but they did not take away from her beauty. The fire which once burned inside her slowly turned to ash.

"You were talking with the voice again?" she asked.

"He was talking with me, actually," he paused until she looked at him. Catching her eyes, he went on. "He has brought news. The one we have waited for is here." And now, as he said it to her, he let down some of his guard and knew she heard merriment in his voice.

"My, my. The Writer of All has taken his time," she mumbled

looking down on those that worked. "Why does he have to travel the length of the kingdom? I hoped this would be the year that we would see him. Now you tell me we must wait till next year."

"Look at me," Ryn said holding his hands out so that she could look upon him. "I wished he had come years ago. I have aged. I can only wish I will be helpful still. Be that as it may, the Writer has his own intentions. Some other things had to fall into place first."

She sighed and looked out toward the ocean. "It took a long time for me to carve the staff, the wolf head was especially trying."

"Do not fear, it will be returned in time. Tyndall has it now and he will know to give it to him when it's proper. See, it's all fitting together like he said it would."

"Should I note his arrival in my chronicles?" Fast to pen most deeds and spoken words to paper, she was the obvious choice for a Chronicler of the village. This position she was thankful for.

"If you wish," he shrugged his shoulders and picked up his hammer once again. More for wood working than for masonry, he worked during the day with those who placed shelves in the kitchens.

"Do you think we will finish with the castle before he comes?" she asked.

"No. The king has not sent enough men. A castle here at Ihrhoven is not a task on top of his list. Yet," he pulled her close and whispered so that only she could hear his voice. "When word of the Drenthen returning reaches his ears, there will be a flood of men here."

She searched his face, but he still remained expressionless. Whistling a little ditty, he turned, his hammer now resting on his shoulder, and returned to his work.

*　*　*　*　*

Sorcerer Tyndall counted the doors as he walked down the hallway. This late at night with the majority of the servants in their quarters there were few others in the hallways and passages of the castle. Except for the occasional breeze ruffling the tapestries and swaying the hanging lanterns, his boots were all that he heard.

At the last door on the left, he stopped and took just a moment to straighten out his clothing. He coughed softly to clear his throat, muffling the sound with a closed fist. He brushed his beard smooth and quickly ran a hand through his hair. Boots tied, pants and tunic free of anything that could cause a discord with the duke; he was presentable.

The rooms in this wing of the castle were not frequently used to house anyone. Some were for storage. This one was once used before, if he remembered properly, as a simple study for one of his students. The student had moved on years ago and the room had remained empty.

When he received the summons to meet Duke Almonesson in this particular room, he had to ask the boy twice. If this was a prank, the young lad would find his hair a different color in the morning.

He raised his hand and knocked gently on the heavy door.

A servant peeked out and shut the door again.

A moment later the door opened and the servant stood aside. When Tyndall entered, the servant bowed respectfully towards Duke Almonesson and left. The door closed and the latch fell.

"What is it, my lord?" Tyndall asked stepping in the candlelight. Only then did he notice the wounded young man lying on the bed. A bandage around his head, arms to his side, the man breathed and was not dead. It struck him as odd that Duke Almonesson would be in the room with someone injured. A healer should be here attending to him. At first glance, Tyndall was sure he did not recognize the man from any at the castle.

"Come closer and have a look, will you?"

Tyndall went to the bed and knelt over the man.

"What can you tell me about him?" The duke asked.

Sorcerer Tyndall paused, looking for a place to start. "His cheeks are blushed, almost rose in color. Possibly from scrubbing?" Tyndall looked up, but the duke kept his face expressionless. "There are light gray circles around his eyes that could be the traces of ash," he turned the young mans head to one side and then the other. "And his ears are a bit off-color. He has an injury to his head, blood is the back of his head on the wrappings on, the cut is deep, but not to the bone. That must have hurt."

"Very good. Go on," said the duke urging him to speak further.

"There is an injury to his leg. Heavy blood loss there, the wound is deep. I see someone has propped it up to help slow the bleeding. I can feel the glow of a simple healing spell that someone applied. Just skin and muscle harmed, nothing vital or he would have bled to death. It is an easy area to kill a man. He was lucky the person who attacked him had little skill." Tyndall's hand moved down the sheet searching for anything misshapen. "There are no bandages on his other leg and these seem as his only injuries. I am no healer, however. Have they been called?" He asked.

"His age?" Duke Almonesson went on ignoring the question.

"Hmm," Tyndall folded his arms across his chest and stood back. "He has a little chest hair, no beard or mustache, but his height tells me he is almost full grown. I would have to say about twenty summers. He is not muscular by any means. He turned of age some time ago, but with nothing else to see I cannot tell you his profession or vocation." There was a pause as Tyndall thought of how to properly voice his question.

"Who is he?" Tyndall asked finally, taking a seat on the opposite side of the bed. This movement to the bed did not disturb the man at all. Instinctively, he reached down and touched the injured man's forehead. It was cool and dry and he felt no presence of a fever. Something he should have checked for at the start, but he was not a healer and the duke knew this. When he studied Alden, the magic of the spirit, it was not with the eagerness that others did.

"I do not know," said Duke Almonesson sitting back and folding his arms across his chest, hiding his hands in the darkness of his tunic. He paused as he spoke. When he continued, Tyndall noticed a change in his voice. "He fell through the mirror, Tyndall, in the dining hall almost on top of Fern just after he helped serve the evening meal."

"He fell through the mirror? Actual gate travel?" Tyndall searched his eyes for a hint of a smile or jest. Duke Almonesson never made light of such matters.

"Possibly yes, actual gate travel. Someone found a way. The servant Fern said he was walking to the hall when he saw this young man appear. It is as if the mirror became a door and he fell through it. I could see no damage to the mirror, and yet there were a few pieces of glass on the floor. This one," he reached over to a nearby table and carefully picked up a shard of glass that gleamed brightly in the candlelight, "Was the biggest and found lodged in the poor fellow's leg. The cause of the wound that could have killed him." The glass he held had a rosy tint to it.

"May I, your grace?" Tyndall asked as he reached one hand out for the glass. "I thought it was a knife wound and that he had been attacked."

The duke gingerly handed him the shard of glass with his thumb and forefinger. "When they first saw him, they thought he was an evil spirit. He was all but naked, smelling of smoke as if he had been in a fire, and there was blood down his back from his head wound. Spawn of the Drenthen, they thought at first sight. On his back are three or four welts where Fern took a serving tray to him."

Tyndall looked at the glass for a moment. An engraving of a small flower lay in bold relief on its surface. The glass held a deep red color and about the length of his longest finger. He placed the glass on the stand beside a candle shaking his head.

"Open wounds, smelling of smoke, shards of glass, naked and gate travel," he sat for a moment, counting these factors off one by one. There were no accounts of people having to become naked to travel through a gate. If he created a gate as a means of escape from somewhere, why would he be without clothing? The preparations to create a gate are not the simplest of tasks. It is known that many of the spells and incantations were long and drawn out. The fire, from whence he came, would have consumed him long before he got halfway though the spells. His time would have been better spent in fleeing.

He looked down at the man and wondered.

"Did he have anything with him?" Tyndall asked. "If there were things he brought with him, it would help us discover who he is. Even the colors of his home territory would help."

Duke Almonesson smiled at this. Shaking his head he spread his arms wide to show that the man arrived empty handed.

"He brought with him all I told you. The only items that we have found were the shards of glass, some smaller that others. I cannot discern their markings," he said finally. His manner was like this sometimes and Tyndall dismissed his actions. If the duke had any secrets in the matter, it would be in his best interests to share them. As a counselor, Tyndall needed to have all the facts when dealing with a situation of this importance. With this reasoning, he knew Duke Almonesson held no secrets.

"Do you think he is from the village or a neighboring one?" He asked the duke who only shook his head. Another thought came to mind. "Perhaps he is a man from the castle playing a prank."

"No, we accounted for everyone. And I have never seen him before. Had he tried to get in the castle without the proper authorization, the guards would have stopped him. I do not believe he is from anywhere around here. All who have seen him tonight say they have never seen him in Croskreye. How could an injured man just suddenly show up in my castle without the means of magic?"

"He may belong to a group of people traveling through--one of the traders or merchants. Perhaps a glass maker. This would explain the shard."

"That might be, but by what force could he appear through the mirror in such a manner? Tyndall, listen to what I have told you. Someone achieved gate travel. Only you, sorcerer, or a person that is your equal, could accomplish such a feat."

"I do not work with the medium needed to create and sustain gates. The king ordered the books away, and they have been, since the end of the war; therefore no one would now be skilled in this knowledge. The kingdom was not ready to have these particular books dusted off and used."

The duke turned in his chair and looked at him. "I am not doubting the strength of your powers in other matters of magic. You have proven yourself many times. It is also apparent that you have never deviled in gate creation. Who has the books on gate travel?"

"Yahn, I believe, my lord. Land Streth holds this knowledge. But I must tell you that I have felt no magical disturbances of the size needed to create a gate," Tyndall said shrugging his shoulders. He placed his hands folded upon his lap. "I have only just now returned from Westrick. A spell of the strength required would take time to build . . ."

"Some spells are more powerful than others, Tyndall."

"True, yes," he disliked when someone who knew little of magic told him the rudimentary rules. Without hesitation he went on. "Had I known of this incident I would have sought you out immediately. I would have felt the ripple, possibly even enough to tell you from which direction it came. Tonight all I have noticed is the magic that is always present. No one could open or close a gate in your castle, on this island, without my knowledge of it. Something magical of that size, the ripple would be very obvious. More than a candle in the darkness, I could sense it like fox-fire on a rainy night. Could it be that Fern had dipped his cup in the wine once too often tonight as he is prone to do?"

"I have already talked to him," said the duke rubbing his chin and stifling a yawn. Tyndall was silently thankful that Duke Almonesson was in control of his temper. There were times when the simplest thing caused him great anger and unrest. "He is well and sober this night. More so now it seems. Others happened along just after the man appeared. So there is truth in his story."

Tyndall shook his head. "Yahn is reluctant to open his books. Sorcerer Cinnaminson was the last to practice the magic of the gates. When Cinnaminson died he took much of his knowledge with him. Very little of his magic still lingers." Tyndall absently touched a charm that hung around his neck. If someone gained the ability to open a gate then this was good news indeed. If they, somehow, learned to do it without the magic making itself known, this would be something to cause great concern among the Territories.

"The skies," Duke Almonesson noted, interrupting his thoughts. It took a moment for Tyndall to realize what he spoke of.

"The skies did take years to recover and if people search in forgotten places, they can still find the magical remnants of war. To this day," Tyndall tapped his finger on his open palm, concentrating on keeping his voice in a low tone. "The water at Welteroth can still be found unfavorable by some. But gate travel, the magic that controls it, does not survive after the gate closes. Other traps have been found, but the gates, they are gone, my lord."

"I do not know why people take magic to such extremes." The duke almost spat out the words, not attempting to conceal his bitterness or distaste. Tyndall did his best not to flinch. "I do not share your love for it Tyndall and I never will. Someday someone will make a mistake and the cursed Drenthen will seem like children in comparison to the havoc it will cause."

Tyndall sat silently for a moment. He did not wish to get into a disagreement with his lord now. This was neither the time nor the place. Past discussions only caused frustration, mistrust, and lack of sleep. Bitterness, in any form, was a wasted emotion.

He had realized years ago when he was a young apprentice that the people of the kingdom followed several different paths. There were those to which magic came easily when needed. They could invoke the power of the Brothers with a whim and use it without harm or repercussion. These people were few.

A second group, himself included, had to deeply study the books of magic to go beyond the simplest of spells and incantations. Of the four types of magic only one or two could be learned to a degree of certainty within a lifetime.

The third group, to which he was sure Duke Almonesson belonged, knew just the commonest of spells and used them only when they absolutely had to. They preferred the wit of their own mind and the strength in their own hands to accomplish their tasks.

"Of course," Tyndall went on searching for a different path to take the conversation. Being the dukes adviser and at times he had to lead him down different paths. "You remember, it is so written, Sorcerer Cinnaminson had brought Kalendeck here at the beginning of the wars. Possibly, this has happened again."

The duke reached out, and with his hand, moved the young mans head to the left, and then to the right. He did not stir; his breathing was steady, his chest rose and fell with rhythm.

"Sorcerer Cinnaminson has been dead for seventeen years now. I remember Kalendeck, Tyndall. I fought at his side in several battles. We drank and shared many meals. We fought the Drenthen together until his death." Tyndall bowed his head knowing he had possibly opened up an old wound. "You are Jarlett's replacement. And I know you are still settling into the position of sorcerer for my territory. And I know I seek answers that cannot be found; however, the people in the castle will want an explanation for what has happened. So close to The Day of Turning," The duke looked at Tyndall and gave a bit of a laugh. "I hope the common folk do not take this as an omen."

"Ah, this is true," said Tyndall scratching his head. "I'd almost forgotten. With just over a month to go before the festival, I think they will see no connection. If he arrived a few days closer, before or after, maybe, but not with this much time beforehand."

They sat in silence for a few moments.

"Do you think he could be another?" asked the duke.

"Another Kalendeck? If the Brothers, or the Writer, saw fit to bring someone here, I cannot imagine a reason why. The kingdom is not in peril, as it was in Cinnaminson's time. It might be that there is some trouble in the upper territories we have yet to hear of, but it is doubtful."

Duke Almonesson shook his head. "If there is danger it may manifest itself in time. We will wait and see. Look at this man; he seems harmless enough. I think we are like children believing the darkness is full of things in order to scare ourselves."

"So, this is the question that you wish waylaid, my lord?"

"It is," Duke Almonesson said. Tyndall looked into his eyes and he could see the apprehension there.

"I do not see him as a threat, my lord. If there is any issue then we will know about it after he wakes. By what I have seen we cannot tell. I am sure rumor and speculation will abound, people are known to talk, to us at this time he is harmless. He looks healthy enough; his wounds should heal easy and clean. I doubt that we will have need of the healers. Who's healing spell?"

"My own." And at this Tyndall raised an eyebrow. "I learned it many years ago." The duke offered no further explanation. "When he wakes, we will see who he is and what he knows. Nayoor might be interested in him, if this man is still here when they return from the north. It would be interesting to see if he has ever had any weapons training. Looks like he's been pampered most of his life. No scars, clean-shaven, very short hair, and his fingernails hold no dirt. Possibly he is a learned man." The duke let the man's hand drop and then stood. Tyndall stood as was customary. "See to it that he's taken care of for now, sorcerer. Let me know when he wakes up."

"Aye, my lord." An order was given and he acknowledged it with a bow.

"You may wish to send notice of his arrival to those in your guild. Worded carefully, mind you. Undoubtedly, they will have a great interest in this. If this turns out that this is something larger than we think it is I shall have to notify King Trahune."

"You may wish to do so regardless, my lord. If rumor of this reaches him first, he might be curious as to why he was not in the knowing." Tyndall straightened his clothing, frowning as a lock of hair strayed.

"Rightly so," said the duke his mind elsewhere. "I shall send a message. Hopefully everything will be well. I would like you to stand watch over him tonight. I will also have a guard posted outside the door for your own protection. It is still not known what he is capable of."

"If I may fetch a book from my study to pass the time?"

"You may. I'll have Fern send someone by at the turning of the day to check you. I'll have some food brought also."

"Yes sire, and thank you. You are kind."

"Go get your book then. I'll wait here until your return."

Tyndall bowed slightly and left.

*   *   *   *   *

Almonesson sighed heavily as the latch fell. He listened as Tyndall's footfalls retreated, growing ever softer. He studied the young man's face and as he did he searched his memories for those of a man he once knew. If there was a resemblance, it was faint, not easily seen.

He turned the man's hands over and he bore no telltale scar across the palm. The familiar scars on the forearm and chest were not there. He shook his head and moved away. He was looking for ghosts that were not there. This one was too young to bare these marks.

His attention strayed from the man lying on the bed and he went over to stand near the window. He opened the shutters and looked out over his land.

The moon shone in the sky, glowing like a huge lantern over the edge of the world. Clouds had formed off to the south, otherwise the skies were clear. The night ambled well into its third hour, and most of the villagers slept. A few lights could be seen throughout the town of Croskreye.

At the bottom of the village, where it met the calm waters of the Applegate Straits, men worked loading and unloading the ships in port. Lights glowed faintly in the harbor of Denhartog across the Straits. Toward the horizon, the lights mingled with the stars. How the stars blazed across the heavens this night. He heard a slight breeze as it drifted through the branches of the trees down by the channel.

He sighed, and folded his arms over his chest. To look in his eyes one could see his thoughts indeed were troublesome.

"Kalendeck," he voiced his questions softly, though there no one could hear. "You spoke of a messenger arriving to my castle all those years ago. You said nothing about a young man arriving through a mirror with a book. The pages are blank. Nothing is written. How can there be a message if the pages are blank? Is the Writer of All supposed to write what is needs written? There is nothing these blank pages can tell us. Is there a way to use magic to bring it out?

"I was waiting for someone walking, or on horseback, a traveler, a vagabond. Never did I expect something like this. Why was he sent to us? I would like some guidance on an issue with the king. If this lad can help, then so much the better. You were always full of riddles and stories, I wonder if this is one.

"Fourteen years after I began to govern my lands a messenger would arrive. This is what you said. This is the year and I have told no one. You told me in secrecy and the secret remains still. My father is gone, and much has changed. Many think of you only in memory and songs that the young hear at gatherings.

"I doubt anyone, even one as yourself, could return from the ashes of Welteroth. Are you truly dead, are your ashes scattered in the wind? Where do you rest this night? Surely they have granted you a place at their table on the Skye Boat. Are you with the one you love? Where have you gone, my friend?"

He stood in silence for several moments letting his thoughts wander on times past and things that could not be changed.

Someone knocked at the door.

"Enter," he said turning. "Ah, that was quick?"

"I had this book lying open on my desk, Sire. I was beginning to study when the page arrived," Tyndall said as he closed the door. "My lord, your daughter has taken ill again. Englay told me the healers are tending to her now. I can send word north to the duchess by bird if you so desire."

The duke let out a sigh and shook his head in frustration. "No need to trouble Lowy. Another spell, so sudden, so soon. She has barely recovered from the last. Is there anything you can do to help the healers?"

"I have looked at all the books I have and none are for cures. The healers in Land Streth have been searching in their books. We shall find and answer, my lord. It will just take time."

"I have to find a cure soon. These spells have grown in their strength."

"I begin to fear for her safety."

"As do I. Perhaps Lowy and Farnstrom will bring good news on their return. I will leave you now. If there is any change in his condition let me know as quickly as you can," he made a slight motion toward the open windows. "The night is warm. Sleep when you are able. I'll be by Wenonah's side if you need me."

"Aye, my lord. Good night."

Taking the chair by the back Tyndall moved towards the window. Opening his book to a marked page, he began to read softly to the young man in the candlelight.

Hearing the passages laden heavily with the sing-song words of magic, Duke Almonesson turned and departed.

*   *   *   *   *

The servant woke Wenonah as she opened the shutters to the room. After rubbing sleep-sand from her eyes, Wenonah turned to her side and stretched quietly. The cool morning air replaced the stale air of the previous day. It must have rained during the night. Morning light always struck the stone of the west wall. Possibly, past the seventh hour. She watched the patterns on the curtain that divided the room as she collected her thoughts and tried to remember a dream she was in.

She watched her servant Englay for a few moments noticing how she was getting on in years. There was never a time in Wenonah's memory that she wasn't there. Over the years her hair turned gray; her form softening along with her temperament. Although Englay could still be stern with the servants that worked beneath her, it was rare that she showed this side to Wenonah.

"Morning, Englay," Wenonah said softly as not to startle her. "I am starving, have I slept long?"

"Oh goodness, did I wake you my lady? How do you feel?" Englay asked as she tried to secure the open shutters on the far side of the room while speaking over her shoulder.

"No, you did not wake me. I woke before the sun came up and lay just resting now. Has it happened again?" she asked running her slim fingers through her raven black hair. On a small stand nearby was a length of green lace and she used this to tie it back from her eyes.

Englay did not answer her, but went to the door and opened it. "Tell the healers and her father she is awake," she said to someone in the hallway before closing the door and turning back.

"Father knows?"

"He does." And at this Wenonah audibly groaned and placing a hand to her forehead, fell traumatically back into the mattress.

Englay gave her a curt look. "You have suffered one of your spells again. As you walked down the back hall near the kitchens, you collapsed. Your father stayed here with the healers from Westrick most of the night, my lady."

"How long this time? What day is it?" She asked, sighing as she pulled herself up on her elbows.

"Just this night, today is market day, and the morning is well into its seventh hour. As long as you're up, I may as well put your clean linen away for you."

Wenonah sniffed the morning air again and smiled. The flowers were beginning to bloom, and the gentle wind smelled sweet. Thank goodness the stables sat downwind from the castle.

"I've sent for the healers now that you are awake. Do you feel strong enough to rise this day?"

"Ummm yes, I feel good." She smacked her lips. "If I had a fever, it's gone."

"Let me see," Englay touched her forehead with the back of her hand. "I have noticed no fever, thank the Brothers. You may want to take it easy though. Do you wish food brought?" She asked over her shoulder as she went back to putting the linen away.

"No. I can fetch something from the kitchens for myself. I may go to the market today."

"Don't be so brave, my lady." Englay tsked several times. "You must stop pushing yourself after these spells. You need to relax and take life easy for a few days. Act responsibly, like the young lady you are." The wardrobe muffled her voice. It was a conversation they had several times and Wenonah mouthed the words as Englay spoke them and shook her finger in the air.

"I'm not as frail as you think," Wenonah said loudly with a smile. She yawned again.

"Then if you set your mind, I cannot stop you. If the healers tell you different, you mind them. Were your mother here, and not north visiting, she would tell you the same. Before you go, you may want to ask your father on the condition of our visitor. They have kept me from his room this morning. Everyone wants to know how he is," Englay said still half in and half out of the wardrobe.

"What visitor?" Wenonah swung her legs over the side of the bed. The wood of the floor was cool to the touch. As she rubbed her eyes once more, a few loose strands of her dark hair, loose of the ribbon, fell to cover her face. She smoothed her nightdress down over her knees.

"You don't remember? Oh, of course not, he came to us at the same time you became ill."

Englay came and sat on the corner of the bed with some sheets and bedclothes in her heavy hands.

"Let's see," she said and her eyes lit up as they did every time she shared something secret. Castle gossip was always entertaining. "It seems a man of about your age fell through the big mirror in the hallway into the common room. He had blood all over his head, and smelled of smoke. Naked as a baby he was. He's been sleeping for as long as you have, and still is, as far as I know. I happened a glance at him last night. A simple looking fellow he is. He didn't look that muscular at all."

"Is he all right?" Wenonah asked quizzically, her interest now aroused. She sat up straighter.

"Yes, so it seems. His head has a bandage on it, but other than that I believe he's fine. Oh, and his leg is hurt. Fern couldn't sleep a wink last night. He's the one that found him. Scared him silly. Couldn't have happened to a better fellow." Englay chucked.

Wenonah stood and raised her nightdress slightly so she could see her feet to put her sandals on. This done, she let it fall back into place to cover her long legs. She started to reach for her brush, but thought better of it. With her hair in the ribbon she was presentable.

"Take me to him, please," she begged. "This is the most exciting thing that's happened in this place in a long time. Maybe he's a sorcerer or something-or a son of a great warrior."

"Maybe the son of a fisherman or potato farmer. But you can't go child. No, no. They have a guard at the door. I doubt they would let you in. He might be dangerous. A wild man," Englay shook her finger at her.

"Please Englay. He's been sleeping all of this time; by what reason would he suddenly wake up now? I need to talk to him. I'll be sure to tell you first all that I hear," she smiled and laughed softly.

"Be reasonable child ..." Englay searched for an excuse. She watched Wenonah but did not rise from the bed. "The healers will be here in a moment to tend to you. People should not see you in the castle in your nightdress. You need the proper clothing first, after your bath, and what ..."

"Englay," Wenonah said sternly as she put her arms through her heavier robe. The word, spoken with so much emphasis, stopped all further protest. Her face was unyielding; all humor had left her. "This robe is a bit threadbare, but has covered me well enough in the past and it will continue to do so now. After I check on him I will get ready and go to the market. Please, please," As she pleaded she could not stop the mischievous humor from coming back in her eyes. "Let me have this little bit of freedom for now. I will tell you of him first and only."

Englay sighed and shook her head.

"Stay just a few moments." As Englay said this Wenonah could barely suppress a giggle. "Then, young lady, it's off to your bath and then to the market if you're able. And don't forget you must eat sometime. The healers will be upset, and if your father hears of it he must know it is not my doing. I wish only to save you from his anger," Englay said with her hands on her hips. "And I did not agree to you going to the market outright."

Wenonah was to the door with her robe and night dresses in a whirl.

"Where is he?" she asked over her shoulder. She had opened the door and looked both ways down the hall.

"Last door of the students hall. At least take a brush to your hair." But she spoke in vain for the young lady was already gone.

Chapter #3

I blinked.

It occurred to me that I did not remember the actual time of wakening. The wooden timbers slowly took form from a dark nothingness above. My mind rested and threatened to pull me back under. The rain stopped and I could no longer hear it's drumming. The thought a whisper through my head, and I wondered why I would think of rain. Of course, it was raining when I left. When I left, or when I fell asleep?

Sleep called to me again and as much as I didn't want to, I fought against falling into that abyss.

Falling. I remembered falling from somewhere. Possibly a dream, but the sensation, more than the act itself, was more vivid than any dream could provide. When a person falls in a dream they wake up. I had slept on.

Rest would have been nice, but the mattress scratched my back. It was uncomfortable and lumpy in places. I closed my eyes again for several moments and took in the sounds and smells around me while trying to remember. I really didn't feel like wakening up yet.

The air was cool and felt slightly damp; perhaps it did rain. That part I did not dream. I smiled knowing it wasn't all a dream.

A branch scratched across closed shutters and the sound of iron-shod hooves on cobblestones could be heard in the distance along with the pounding of iron upon iron. Perhaps there was an iron smith nearby. My father was a smith, or had done things with an iron smith. I tried to remember his face, or the way he talked, but the memory vanished before it completely formed. I heard the laughter of children playing in the distance and my thoughts went elsewhere.

Nearby, I heard the sound of cloth moving against cloth. Like the sails of a ship or sheets in the breeze hung out to dry. The noise came again and it seemed closer.

With a start, I realized there was someone in the room with me. I opened my eyes and slowly turned my head to look around. There sat a man. He wore dark leather boots, brown pants, and a white shirt that billowed loosely from tied cuffs at the elbows. His dark hair fell to just below his shoulders, and he had a thick full beard. I had never seen this man before. An odd thing, to have a stranger in your room while you're sleeping.

He read a book as he sat in a chair, near the corner of the room, with his feet propped on the stone windowsill. His left arm draped across the table and his left hand touched the upper corner of the book. A page held between the thumb and forefinger. The sill of the window sat low to the ground and the window itself was a tall as a man.

Two candles were lit although rays of sunlight came in from under the slats of the shutters. The walls of the room were of stone blocks. Huge stone blocks--taller than my forearm was long. The ceiling was of beams and boards more than two palms wide. I must have been in a barn or something as the floor around the bed in which I lay was evenly covered in a layer of straw.

In the corner of the room, just beneath the large wooden supports, I noticed a shelf with a polished wooden figure on it. This was the only thing adorning the walls. The sharp outline of a cat looked out over the room. So skillful was the workmanship that I believed it real at first. It did not move, however and so after watching it for a time I realized that it was a carved piece.

I turned my shoulders slightly to ease the itchy feeling a little, and in doing so alerted the man reading. His head turned, he blinked once, and then smiled.

He quickly marked his page with a large ribbon and was on his feet in an instant. Coming to the bedside he knelt. A calloused hand reached out, grabbed mine, and held it firmly. I tried to pull back, but his strength was such that I could not.

"Can you hear me, do you understand me?" The man asked in a low voice. I could tell that, although he held his voice in check, he could not mask completely the enthusiasm he felt. The words rolling from his tongue were thick with an accent I had not heard before. Though the words were familiar sounding, the accent made them seem foreign.

I nodded, not quite sure I understood him.

"Welcome to Croskreye, I am Tyndall. How do you feel?"

The effort to speak, trying to at least, made me feel the dryness in my throat. Tyndall released my hand, stood, and brought some water. The chill of the metal cup startled me and I spilled some before quickly draining it.

"What happened? Where am I?" There was a pause as this man, Tyndall he said his name was, began to cope with a dialect that was odd to him.

"You gave us quite a scare," he spoke slowly realizing the differences in our languages. "The day before this you came through one of our mirrors.

You've been asleep since." Tyndall brought the wooden chair to the bedside from across the room. It creaked slightly as it accepted his weight. I had just a glimpse of the ornate carvings on the back of the chair and its legs. Even the seat was engraved with a design.

"Where am I again?" I asked. He had spoken the words too fast for me to follow. Something was starting to seem wrong. A nagging feeling I had in the back of my mind tried to tell me something. In a moment I would be able to put my finger on it.

"You are in Croskreye, my friend," he said still speaking somewhat slower.

"Never heard of it. What state is it in?" I said speaking as slowly and with the same enunciation as he did.

"I do not understand your question. Croskreye is a one of the southern lands of the kingdom, we are at a state of peace with the other territories if this is what you ask."

My head hurt. . . it was difficult to think. Was it numb around the edges, or a bandage? I brought my hand up and felt my forehead and temples. Closing my eyes, I laid my head down hoping the throbbing would stop. I winced, biting my lip, as a sharp pain shot through the back of my head.

I felt him stand and fix my pillow before sitting back down. It helped a little, as did the cool air coming from under the shutters. A drink would be nice, something to sooth my throat once more.

"Where am I?" I thought to myself. *"Wasn't there someplace or something, a home or a station I had to get to?"* The name of the town was on the tip of my tongue, but I couldn't quite get it. Slowly my memory began to fade like smoke in the wind, or ashes on a river. My past was a flame that could not be rekindled. My memory became lost. Names slipped by and try as I could, there was no way for me to hold them.

"Maybe some fresh air would be good," Tyndall said.

I heard the man get up and open the shutters. The light from the candles extinguished as a slight breeze and cool moist air flowed into the room. For that I was grateful. The blue sky brightened the room and I had to squint as my eyes adjusted.

He brought me more of water. As I propped myself up on my elbows to drink, I felt a dull ache in my leg. I reached down to find a compress of wadded cloth.

"Was I in an accident? What happened to me?" I asked lying back carefully to not aggravate the pain in my head further.

"We do not know for sure. There was a piece of glass lodged in your leg just above the knee. We removed it and applied a bandage. We've changed it again early this morning there is no sign of disease. It will heal cleanly, though you will have a scar. You also have a wound just below the ear. You lost a lot of blood with that one. It will heal soon. Our healers have taken good care of you." As Tyndall finished speaking, he stood and placed the chair back near the table then moved towards the door.

"I will return shortly. I must get the duke; he will want to see you now that you have woken. I've stayed too long as it is. Please rest easy while I am gone, I will not take long, hopefully." With this Tyndall departed.

"Duke?" I asked, but the man was gone and left me alone.

With little I could do I waited in this room, silently. Others could be heard on the floor above and in the hallway. A boy shouted in the street and a bell rang somewhere. Closing and opening my eyes did nothing to change the scene before me. I thought perhaps if I opened my eyes fast enough I would wake up and be home. Maybe if I closed them real tight and then opened them; that would wake me up from this place. This I did several times, but to no avail. Closing one eye and looking around changed only my perception of depth, but did little else.

He left the book he had been reading on the rushes on the floor with the cover slightly open. I reached down and picked it up gently. I had loved books since I was . . . Was young. I loved books.

The leather of the cover was smooth with a small, simple design etched in the lower corner. The leather seemed old, I opened it up and began to flip through the pages. The ink had faded on the well-worn pages to a dark gray. The hand written text was penned in a style which seemed so unfamiliar, I had trouble understanding it at first. With the individual letters hard to make out, and joining them to make words became almost impossible.

Throughout the book, sketches of various items littered the pages. The meanings of some were difficult to grasp, but others you did not have to use your imagination at all. On one page was a crude drawing of a man standing beside what appeared to be an egg or a large rock that stood almost chest high. A word stood out on top of the page. 'Kear'.

Several pages later another word took up the left upper corner of a page. 'Alden,' I whispered this word silently several times. It held no meaning and I began to turn pages again. On another, arrows pointed to several places on the human skeleton--points of interest, no doubt.

I puzzled over the book for several more moments, before I returned it to the floor. My eyes and head had begun to ache from looking at the letters.

Tyndall came back shortly with, presumably, the duke. He wore dark green clothing with a purple sash from his left shoulder to his right hip. Over his heart, I caught the shape of a bear head that lay stitched into the purple fabric of the sash with a string of gold. The bear's head looked over the dukes chest and its mouth was open as if it roared. The duke also wore a thin band of gold about his head. He carried an aroma about him though, like that of stale grapes or rotted berry.

Before the door could be closed, two others came in. Their simple clothes were not as rich or as fine as that worn by the duke or Tyndall. Servants, no doubt. They cleared the table of scraps and straightened up the room. They did their work quickly and left without a word.

I tried to push myself up on my elbows to greet the duke.

"Don't get up." he held his hand out, palm downward. "You've been through quite a bit. How are you feeling?" The duke asked as he took the chair near the bed. As he got closer, I recognized the odor that followed him was the smell of wine. It lay heavy on his breath.

"I feel a bit weak and there is some pain."

"What did he say?" the duke asked Tyndall without turning his head. Tyndall repeated what I had said adding that it would be best if they spoke slowly.

"This feeling of tiredness should pass in time as your strength returns," Tyndall said to me after he had finished translating for the duke.

"He speaks oddly, doesn't he?" The duke said looking up at Tyndall. "Sounds like someone from the north, Wiladene territory, perhaps. Can you tell us where you are from?" He asked me directly.

I shook my head. "I'm sorry, sir. All I remember is smoke and the fire. Is this a castle?" Each word he spoke slowly. They looked at each other as if not believing my question. The duke smiled.

"Aye, this is a castle. Do you remember your name?" Tyndall asked.

I paused for a few seconds before I shook my head. That was something I had not thought about. "I wish I had some answers. If not for you, for myself," I smiled weakly.

"What do you think?" The duke asked looking over his shoulder at Tyndall.

As he spoke to the duke his words quickened. "I don't know what to make of it. Perhaps whatever bruised his head caused his memories to flee also. It happens when there is a strong blow to the head sometimes. I've heard of it in battle. Although I must say, I have never seen it before myself. There might be something in the books, but the subject would take days to search thoroughly."

I did not know what to say, so remained quiet. I had questions, but they seemed too complex to ask when they, we actually, could scarcely understand each other. A silence filled the room as we were lost in our own thoughts. Tyndall was about to speak again when I heard a slight commotion outside the door and a young woman entered.

She noticed the duke and Tyndall in the room and brought her hands up to cover her mouth. I could tell she thought she was in trouble. Tyndall turned and shook his head giving her a harsh look. The duke had a slight smile on his face and I saw the muscles in his jaw tighten. He chuckled.

She was a very attractive young women. Her long, dark hair fell well beyond her slender shoulders. She wore it tied loosely in the back. She stood almost as tall as Tyndall's shoulders and the resemblance to the duke could not be denied. You could see it in the eyes. The robe, blue as the sky in the window behind her, covered her thin frame well until its frayed hem reached just above her ankles. It seemed she wore her sleeping gown, but it did not detract from her beauty.

More conscious now of being naked in bed under the sheet with young woman present, I pulled the sheets up further to cover myself. I think she too, may have felt embarrassed as she turned her head and averted her eyes. Folding her arms over her chest, she pulled the robe tighter.

The duke, who had not turned when she entered, spoke first to her over his shoulder.

"It's good to see you awake, Wenonah. I did not expect you about and so spirited so soon. Why are you here?"

"How did you know it was me father?" She asked taking small hesitant steps with bare feet until she stood at her fathers' side. By the sound of his voice, I knew her intrusion did not anger him. She rested her arm across his broad shoulders and kissed his head lightly.

"Because," he said as he turned, "who else would enter a room thusly, without so much as a knock? Did you by chance not see the two men outside? They had swords and armor."

"I came to see the visitor. I didn't know you would be here," her voice remained soft and low as would a child's when speaking to an angered parent. Truly, I saw she was trying to play on his emotions.

"Oh, so you expected him alone. What a scare you would have given him," Tyndall put in.

"I meant no harm," she folded her hands before her, and bowed her head.

"Oh, come here you young fawn, you, and say hello to our visitor."

"Hello, very pleased to meet you," she solemnly extended her hand in greeting while her other arm held the robe tight to her chest. Her voice was now much suited her age. Her fathers quick anger all but forgotten.

"The same." I managed a slight smile and took her hand. I was not sure if be the proper response. She looked at me oddly and smiled.

"I hope you get better soon. We could go riding perhaps when you are well. The higher meadows are beautiful this time of year."

"A great time later. Give the man a chance to heal."

"Yes father."

I felt a slight wave of dizziness and brought my hands across my eyes to still the room. Following the conversation became difficult. Watching their faces, reading their expressions, would be a task for me under normal circumstances. With a head wound, it grew even more demanding.

"We should leave, all of us. He does seem tired. What the healers have done for him will take a few hours to work its course." With that the duke stood, and stretched slightly.

"Tyndall, he is able to recover on his own now. You don't have to stay this day. I feel a guard is not needed anymore." Turning towards the bed the duke spoke to me again. "You should eat if you are able, and then rest as you can. Everything will be for the better, son."

"The healers have placed spells on the fruit. They'll ease the pain and help you to heal. Do you wish the window stay open?" Tyndall asked. He repeated the last when I didn't respond.

"Yes, leave it open, please. The fresh air feels good. Thanks."

Tyndall moved the table closer so I could reach the water if I wished. They left quietly and I was glad for the solitude.

Not sure if I heard the man correctly, I did not touch the fruit.

*   *   *   *   *

I dozed from time to time. A bell sounding somewhere in the castle which woke me later that day. From my bed I could look across the room and out the window. The day grew brighter now with just a few clouds. The sun began to shine on the open shutters. I watched as the light lengthened. My stomach grumbled miserably. I tried a few bites of fruit from the table and found it refreshing.

* * * * *

I woke again later the same day to the smell of smoke.

A single candle lit the room creating a dim glow. Someone must have brought it as I slept. It burned bright and true, with only a very slight string of smoke coming from the flame to loop around the beams above. This, however, did not account for the distinct smell of wood burning.

Somewhere nearby there was a fire ablaze.

I quickly drew back the sheets and sat on the edge of the bed. Dizziness struck me in a wave. I paused a moment and closed my eyes. Beneath the bandage on my head I felt moisture. Be it blood or sweat, I couldn't tell. Bringing my hand away I saw my fingertips were just a bit damp with no sign of blood. It was sweat.

Some clothes lay on the back of the chair, and with great care I slowly put the pants on over my somewhat stiff limbs. The cloth was loose enough so it did not restrict the bandage. It took me a moment to realize the leather strap was a belt. With no buckle I could only tie the ends. It worked for the most part and kept the overly large pants to my waist without falling. I slipped the simple tunic over my head.

Using first the table and then the chair for support, I managed a few wavering steps and reached the sill of the open window.

Everything was peaceful, no one ran around screaming, as would be expected if a fire raging in the castle. I watched people on the cobblestones below; some with baskets, some with tools. Nothing was amiss. I soon discovered the smoke came from a nearby home beyond the wall; it might be time for the evening meal. I smelled the air again and found hints of other aromas masked in the smoke.

My view was from high up. I counted the rows of windows beneath me. The room I was in was on the third story. At the base of the castle lay a wide lane of cobblestones. Further still lay a small grassy mound with a set of small shacks one row deep. These sat against an ivy-covered wall almost the same height as my room. This wall was thick and wide. Men in uniform paced back and forth here. With the castle being the highest point on the hill, I could just see over the wall to the surrounding village. Grey tile or slate covered the tall, steep roofs. Beyond this, a large body of water lay.

All this I took in as the sun set before me. The window must face directly west to catch the rays of the evening sun. Leaning out a little I could see two towers at the corners to my left and right and there were at least two more stories above me. I could not lean out too far. The window was as wide as my shoulders, and tall. Oddly, it was just stone and shutters, there were no frame or glass to keep the weather out.

I stretched and yawned, rubbing the edge of the wrapping where my head itched. Turning, I went back to the table and took a slice of cheese and one of the small buns with honey and nuts. My leg was sore. Several times while I ate, I tested it by putting pressure on it. It throbbed dully.

Not wanting to return to bed I went back to the window, pulling the chair close to enjoy the evening air, I sat and ate my simple meal. I brought the second chair over to prop my leg upon.

The village was not silent. People were busy going about their evening chores getting ready for the night. Just up the street a noise like a hammer sounded as it beat hot metal on an anvil. Children ran, and dogs joined them, as they played a game that looked like tag. A man came around the far corner with two mules in tow. As he passed underneath, he alone noticed I was looking out the window. We waved at each other.

There was a knock at the door. I turned as a serving boy entered with a pitcher, a mug, and a small tray of food. I stood as best I could and picked up the rest of the last meal and placed it on a plate.

He was simple looking. Unlike Tyndall and Duke Almonesson who took distinction in their grooming, this servant did not. Wide-eyed, he smiled constantly. His face was clean and his hands were quick in their tasks. I could not guess at his age. He could have been about twelve to thirteen years old, and a head shorter than I.

He smiled broadly as he waited patently. "Good evening, they thought you might be thirsty. I fetched some water for you," he brushed his hair from his eyes with his forearm. It was sandy colored and cropped just below the ears. The shirt he wore was too big and the sleeves covered half his palm. Stained and soiled in several places, he wore the garment untucked from his trousers. He placed the items he carried upon the table after which he took the plate I held.

"Thank you," I said bowing to him slightly. I was not sure of the proper etiquette in this matter. He was busy and did not notice.

He gave me the mug, and I drank deeply. Was the water sweetened I wondered, or did it naturally taste this way? It cooled my throat. I sat the empty mug down on the table and he refilled immediately. I tried to wave him off, I could pour my own water, but he just smiled at me.

"Thank you," I said again. "That was good. Here, have a seat." I gestured to him the chair by the window.

"Oh, no. I should stand," he said folding his hands before him. His cheeks blushed slightly and I took that as he was not normally treated so.

"I cannot stay on my leg long. Stand if you prefer." I hobbled over to the bed and sat on its edge. The chairs remained empty.

"I have felt better," I said with a groan.

"You look well. My name is Rouke, named after a great potter to the west. You should have heard of him. Have there been many here to see you? They say you fell through the mirror a day past. Where did you come from?" He said more, but spoke the words too fast for me to follow. I believe he spoke this onslaught of words in one breath. Rouke stood with his hands folded in front of him; so many questions for a young boy. I held my hands up, palms outward, and he was silent.

"I have no memory of my home. I am quite sure this place is not where I'm from," I said as I took another bite of my bread. The rolls he brought were still warm and smelled of butter, very delicious.

"You may feel as though they have forgotten about you, but they haven't," he shook his head. He was very excited as he spoke. "Tyndall is reading through his books looking for a way to get your memories back. He has contacted his fellow sorcerers from the other territories to see if they have any answers for you."

"Why do you call them sorcerers?" As I asked the question, I saw the look on the boys face. He looked puzzled and shocked at the same time.

"I do not understand your question. Speak slower, mayhap," he said.

"You said they are sorcerers. I have never heard of this before. Magic, from my experience, is sleight of hand, nothing more."

"You must have had some bump on your head if you think such. I have seen magic work. It would be better if you try to tell me there is not water in the channel, but milk. They have their schools, one for each type of magic. It's real I tell you," Rouke stated. As he finished speaking, he pointed at a piece of cheese on the tray and with a nod from me, he grabbed it.

"The sorcerers work with potions, spells, and such?"

"Of course they do and he does. Tyndall is one of the highest in the arts, very close to the greatness of Sorcerer Cinnaminson. He replaced Sorcerer Jarlett a bit ago. If anyone finds your memories, he will be the one."

"Say your name again? Slower," I asked at last. The dialect made it difficult to understand. His speed at answering the questions I asked was not helping.

"R-o-u-k-e. They taught me how to spell it. Do you think since you don't remember your name, they will come up with one for you? Lady Wenonah was talking with Tyndall and they have found one from the old tongue. Marecrish. It could be shortened to Marc if you wish. There is some history behind it, but I am not sure what it is. She says if you don't like it you can always toss it aside and get another. She said you are like a Marecrish, a-lost-one. What do you think?" Rouke paused for a breath. Again, I had to listen closely, my ears picking up bits and pieces of words and quickly forming them into thoughts.

I sat on the edge of the bed and thought for a moment in silence. Was he saying that I should take this name? I spoke the name a few times in my head. Then I said it aloud once.

"You think I should take this name as my own?"

He nodded with a smile.

"Well, I'm not sure. Maybe I will find a name for myself soon. I don't know. Perhaps mine will come back to me." I finished my small meal of bread and cheese.

We sat in silence for a while longer as we ate. Rouke was quite fond of the cheese. Again a bell sounded somewhere in the castle, and it was to ring seven times, but at the first he was on his feet.

"I have to go. It's already the seventh hour and the hounds have not been fed. Thanks for sharing your food with me, Marc. Keep the water. Others will be by later to take the dirty crockery away so you need not worry. Well met," he raised his hand in parting. I did the same.

And the door closed before he spoke another word. The silence filled the room and left me to my thoughts, and he had given much to think about.

I sat back on the bed with my back against the coolness of the wall. I touched my skin around the bandages, testing for pain as my thoughts drifted.

I would need a name, they would have to call me something and I needed something to call myself. A name was not mandatory, but it was useful. If I grew to dislike the name Marecrish, or Marc, I could always choose another. Tyndall will be able to help there. He spoke like a learned person, and seemed very knowledgeable.

Thinking of Tyndall brought back the notion of magic. What kind of magic was it? It was something I was not familiar with and would have to ask later on its purpose. If magic were real then perhaps commonplace things would have different properties. Images came to mind as I sat quietly in the candlelight.

First, there was a woman sitting on a broom flying in the air. Next came the vision of a man sitting in a chair with a large clear ball before him on a table. Doves flew from a black hat. A wand turned into bright colorful cloth. Coins appeared from thin air behind an ear. Yes, these were types of magic I could remember. I tried to see other areas around the images in these memories, but found I couldn't. I waited a long time for other memories to come. The door closed; the page had turned. My mind for the time being, let me see no more of my past life.

I thought back to this morning and the man who had clasped my hand when I had first awoke and smiled. Tyndall would be helpful in the days ahead. Adjusting to being here would take some time.

*　*　*　*　*

Only when my chin touched my chest, did I realize I had fallen asleep. I went back to the window to close the shutters. The moon was just a sliver over the horizon. Is this the same moon as the one I remembered? In the darkness which had covered the land it was as if I were the only one awake. I stood at the window for a while before I closed the shutters, blew out the candle, and went to bed.

Dreams I could not see disturbed my sleep during the night. I could not remember them the next morning. Only in the last few hours before dawn did they leave me and I could find rest and refuge in the dark.

Chapter #4

A knock on the door brought me around as I sat on my bed lost in my thoughts. Rouke may have returned with a morning meal.

"Hello," I called out.

The latch lifted and a man entered with a young girl closely behind him. He cleared the table of the crockery and food crumbs and laid a heavy cloth on the bare wood. He worked without saying a word. His shirt was deep forest green with large sleeves tied by a loose knot just before his elbows. He wore black pants and his boots made no sound as he walked on the rushes on the floor. The dark cap he wore held one black feather.

The girl, carrying a book and a small pack over her shoulder, wore clothing of the same colors. Since they had not spoken, I assumed they were people of importance and so waited in silence.

He took the book and placed it upon the table with obvious relief from her. It looked heavy for someone her size. From her pack she brought out a glass vial with a cork stopper. He brought out a few other instruments before he was ready to talk. He took a chair and sat, bringing one boot up to rest on his knee. In his hand he fiddled with a long, slender, silver object.

"I will introduce myself and my assistant," he said speaking his words carefully and enunciating each syllable so I could understand. The effect seemed a bit too dramatic, but I found it entertaining.

"I am Thane," he went on to point to himself with the silver object. "My apprentice is Rhen. We are the Chroniclers here in the castle at Croskreye. When people visit, people of importance, we write down their dealings with Duke Almonesson and Duchess Lowy. We also scribe information on the castle on a daily basis. Can you understand me, Marc?"

"Yes," I said sitting up in the bed a bit straighter. The man spoke the name so easily, I almost did not realize he had said it. "You need to write down information about me. You feel that my being here has some type of importance."

"This is correct. When you speak, do so slowly please. I must get every word correctly for the ledger to remain accurate. Once I start writing just keep talking."

"May I ask, what is that thing in your hand?"

"This?" he held up the silver object with a look of confusion on his face. He held it out for me to see. I got the impression I could look at it, but not touch. I kept my hands down to my side.

"Yes."

"This is a pen. A simple person would not know of them. We make lines on paper and can read them back," he took a cap off the end of the silver rod. Inside the substance looked like wood which formed a blackened tip.

"Why do you call it a pen?" I asked.

"Like a farmer would build a pen to capture or to hold livestock, we use one of these and paper to keep words."

"Ah," I said seeing the relation between the two. "You pen written words."

"Yes, exactly."

"How does it work? Do you dip it in ink over and over again once the tip is dry?"

"No," he looked at me and sighed as if my ignorance on the subject was annoying. "The wood soaks up the ink and the silver keeps it contained. When I remove the cap and press the tip on paper then the ink flows back out."

"Feathers are not used?" I said and motioned to the one in his cap.

"Ha!" he covered his mouth, palm outward, to hold back his laughter. Rhen chuckled as well. "No, we do not use feathers. Now shall we continue?" he recapped the pen and placed it on the table.

"I thank you for doing this, but I do not have much to say." The look of disappointment in his eyes was obvious.

"What do you mean?"

"Yesterday I woke up here. I was in some pain, but feel a bit better now. I can tell you little else of what has happened."

"There is nothing else you can give me? Something from your origins? Your parents, brothers, or sisters? What of your beliefs and customs?"

"I am sorry. Tyndall knows all I do. I've met him," I said with some enthusiasm hoping that would grant me a few lines in his book. "The duke and some of the servants I have met. Oh, and the duke's daughter, but that is all. Should I tell you about my conversations with them?"

He stood and shook his head. Turning, he began to gather his things muttering under his breath. I caught a few words. ". . . With so much to do elsewhere . . . Waste of valuable time . . ." and realized that by coming here they took away from other duties.

He placed his items back in the pack and Rhen slung it over her shoulder. She gathered the book, still closed, in her arms and he picked up the cloth.

"May I see that for a moment? Please?"

"The cloth?" he asked.

"No, the book."

"You can read?"

"Yes. If I can understand your language, I might be able to read it."

The two exchanged puzzled looks and he nodded to her. She brought the book over, but would not let me hold it. She opened to a page marked with a ribbon. The page was in the middle of the written pages. The text was hand written, much the same as it was in the book Tyndall had left on the floor the day before.

"If you can, tell us what you read."

I looked at them both seeing the wonderment in their eyes. I cleared my throat before I went on. Not knowing where to start I began reading the first line. It was awkward because it was in the middle of a sentence.

"fought on the second day of the festival. During the tourney one horse was lost due to injuries of the neck and back. Lord Farnstrom took second place, much to the dismay of Duke Almonesson, Duchess Lowy, and many of the young ladies attending. Attending the tourney was his lordship . . ."

"Hmm, you can read," Thane said interrupting. "I shall make a note of this. Come Rhen, they need us elsewhere."

She rolled her eyes when he turned his back, winked at me, and without further question or comment they departed as quickly as they had come.

* * * * *

Tyndall came later the same morning to check my bandages, and my well-being. Several thin strands of woven leather held his hair back. His dark tunic matched his pants and both looked well-worn, but not in dire need of mending.

"I see you're doing fine. I would have been here sooner, but I did have my morning duties," he took the wrapping off of my head and looked at that wound.

"You will not need these on your head anymore. It has healed quite well. I do recommend you keep it clean for the next few days and pay a visit to the servant areas for a bath. How are you feeling? Any pain elsewhere?"

He asked as he raised the loose pant leg up over my knee and began to take the wrappings off.

"No new pain. I don't feel too bad, restless though. I need to get out of here," I said as I slapped the bare wall with the flat of my hand. "It's getting to feel like a prison in this room."

"Well, if you feel up to it you can go out. I will have to give you some restrictions, places you are not permitted to go in the castle. There was word among the servants that you took the name of Marc."

"Who told you that?" I asked thinking he would have talked to the man with the book.

"Lady Wenonah did this morning. She is always talking with the servers."

I sighed. It seems I had little choice in the name now. "I suppose I'll take it. Try not to get used to calling me by that name because as soon as I remember my real name I'll use that one. What will I be able to do once I get better? Will there be work of some sort for me to do?"

"That may present a bit of a problem." The ends of the sleeves of his tunic were loose and he rolled them back to keep them out of the way.

"Why is that?" I raised my leg a bit as he took the old bandage off. There had been very little seepage from the wound. A scab was beginning to form.

"Everyone here is born into a status. From the high king down to the lowest servant, everyone has their own position, their rank, their status. Freemen are free and may choose what they will do in life, and even that, in certain parts of the kingdom, is somewhat limited. But it's your appearance that is making us confused. You are special. You came here wearing nothing, so we are not sure what status you held where you came from. How can we judge a person so? You don't look like a servant, or a son of a nobleman. We don't know what you should do. Should you take up an apprentice craftsmanship and work with wood, metal, stone, water, wheat, meat, or magic . . ."

"You really are a sorcerer then," I said more as a statement than a question. He wore a simple band of metal around his wrist. I could only catch a glimpse at the carvings etched upon its surface and when it touched my skin it was cold. I tried not to shy away.

"Yes I am." Tyndall looked up for a moment and I saw the puzzled look on his face. "Oh, that's right. The servant boy had said that you had some confusion about magic. How odd."

I looked at him and waited for him to laugh as if he were joking with me. "I've never really dealt with it as if it were a real thing. There are people, I vaguely remember, who call themselves magicians. With a twist of the hand and a quick movement they can make a coin disappear and reappear." I made a few feign moves with my hand, flicking it back and forth, to demonstrate.

"Like a young boy, you mean, stealing a piece of fruit from a venders stall? He has to stay quick, and with practice it looks as though the apple vanishes. No magic at all, just a fast hand."

"Yes, that's it." I told him briefly of my other visions of the night before. When I finished, he shook his head.

"If you are from such a place with no magic, it is an odd place indeed. I have never heard of a woman flying on a broomstick. Don't think flight for a man is possible," he said scratching his head in thought. "For us magic is like . . . " he searched for a word. "The sun that shines, or the ground we walk upon, I suppose. I have never known life without it. Our people, the whole kingdom, have lived with magic all our lives. It was always so. From almost the moment we lived on the great land by the Writer of All, it was something we had. It grew as the years went by and man studied it; the same as farming, herding, and building. I suppose it could be called another element, such as air, water, and stone; part of our everyday life.

"Our use of magic was simply that until the wars. That's when we found that we could use it for more than our simple purposes. If the kingdom did not have magic, we would not have what we have today. Our lands would be gone, our people would be slaves. I am sorry if I am confusing you; I have never had to explain it to anyone before."

"Rouke didn't say anything about the wars." I shifted my weight upon the mattress.

"He would only know about them through the tales and songs we have. He is far too young to know of the war first hand and so the stories are not strong in him. I was just under fifteen years, about his age, when I first heard about the fighting. Men from the north, across the sea, traveled here on great wooden boats. We do not know why they traveled, why they left their lands. They may have been sea people. Some say their leader was a deceitful brother, or son, banished from his own kingdom. Who is to know why? What is certain is they were not here to trade with our people, although it would have helped all. They came to the kingdom to conquer."

Tyndall began to re-wrap the wound. This time the bandage was much smaller.

"Your magic helped you," I asked.

"Yes, oh yes, of course. Men of stone magic were able to reinforce structures to make them withstand much more than they normally would have. They used fire magic for destruction; clothes could be set afire from some distance, wagons they took from us met the same fate. Water magic made dangerous rivers look calm and shallow. These are all traits of magic we had never used before. Aspects I hope we never have to use again."

"You say this war killed many people?" I said after a moment of silence urging him on.

"Yes. Two complete territories were lost. The fighting killed or wounded more than half of the men from the other five territories. There are still whole villages in the north deserted and in ruin, and will probably remain so for generations to come."

As I watched Tyndall talk, I could see the expressions on his face mirrored the horror of what he was saying. He stopped talking as he secured the dressing.

"To live through such a time must have been difficult."

"More than you'll ever know, lad. We can only pray to the Writer of All it will not happen again. It is known throughout the kingdom if the men from the north attacked again, with the force they had, we would have to lay down our weapons and surrender. There is no way we could face a mass of soldiers, such as those, again. Maybe in two or three generations time, when our strength in numbers returns, but not now."

Another question nagged me and I paused for a moment thinking on how to word it before I asked it.

"The young woman who was here, you called her Lady Wenonah. I should address her as such?"

He looked at me for a moment with a puzzled look on his face. When he spoke again there was a hint of a smile on his lips.

"You don't know of our social structure either?"

I shook my head and he went on.

"When in her presence you will refer to her as Lady Wenonah. When you address the duke you must treat him with respect as well. If he approaches, you will go to one knee and not speak until spoken to. 'My lord' and 'sire' are acceptable greetings. Truly, you don't know about this?"

"It is not familiar. How should I address you, and that servant boy?"

"Ah, well, I am a free man. No royal title is given. I serve Duke Almonesson and hold a position here in the dukedom, but require no formality. The status I have I earned. I am a sorcerer, Sorcerer Tyndall.

Speak to me openly but do not bow before my presence. As far as the servants, they know their place, and again, with them you do not need a type of formality."

"So much to learn . . ." I said.

"Yes, I believe so. We'll have to school you as we would a child."

His hands were still as the final knot of the bandage was complete. The old dressings were left on the table for someone to take away later.

"There," he touched the bandage softly. "It's done. I am no healer, but it should do. Do you want to walk on it and see how it feels to you?"

"Yes," I said as I swung my legs over the edge of the bed. I then stood on my good leg with the aid of the chair, and was able to take a step. I was awkward and stiff with only my toes and the ball of my foot touching the stone floor.

Tyndall uttered words of encouragement as I went, and soon I was walking from one end of the room to the other with only a slight limp. It felt good to walk with both feet, and not hop from place to place like before. As these earlier excursions were short, I went only as far as the window and the chamber pot.

"May I go out?" I asked hoping for a positive answer.

Tyndall said nothing, but went to open the door and limping, I slowly followed him. With a smile on my face, I leaned on the wall and looked out at the corridor for the first time.

It was wide, about twice the length of outstretched arms. The walls in the hallway were of the same large stone blocks that made up those of my room. Footsteps were heard on the wooden floor above.

"Would you mind if I walked around on my own for a while?"

"By all means go right ahead. Some things to note however; stay on this side of the castle. These are storage rooms. For now, concerning you, a closed door is a locked door. If you can, avoid travel further inward towards the center of the castle. The Families private chambers are there and you are to only go there if someone invites you. Guards are at their posts about the area also. There is a small library down the hallway and to the right. If you are hungry go to the common room so servers will not have to bring you food. The common hall is this way down the stairs and to the left. Other than that, you can go where you please. We should assign you someone for both your protection and ours. Let me bring the matter before the duke. I cannot stay now. There is much I must do this morning and I still have my studies to attend to."

"Magic?"

"Of course. Heed my warnings. I am off then."

Tyndall nodded to me and with a wave he turned and left.

* * * * *

I walked the hall, slowly making progress. My first obstacle was a set of stairs winding their way up to the next floor. I thought it better to hop up these, the bandage was too tight to make stepping upward possible. Here the one good foot was better than chancing the awkward one.

When I got to the top, I wiped the sweat from my brow with my shirt sleeve. Twenty-one steps. I walked a few feet and sat on a bench in an alcove of the wall. My leg throbbed a little as did the back of my head. I could feel the blood pulsing in the wound beneath the bandage.

Maids were busy cleaning out the rooms at the end of the hallway. One looked my way; then whispered quickly to the others. There was more whispering as the two others glanced at me from the rooms they were cleaning.

"Hello," said the girl who first noticed me. She had risen from where she knelt brushing the wooden floor, and came closer.

I smiled back, nodded my head, and waved.

"Are you Marc?" she asked, placing her bucket and brush aside. She began to take several steps forward. The others started to follow, but with a word she ordered them back to work. They returned to the rooms they were cleaning, finding something to do near the door so they could listen and watch.

"I am Marc," I said after clearing my throat.

"Pleased to meet you. I am Elesebeth," she said as she walked toward me. Not knowing what to do, she stopped several lengths from where I sat. She was tall. Even standing this distance from me, she towered over me. Her long skirts hid her feet from view.

"Is there anything you need?" she asked. She did not look into my eyes but kept looking at the floor.

"Tyndall, the sorcerer, has granted me permission to spend time in this area of the castle. If I am bothering you or the others, please let me know and I'll leave."

"There is no trouble. It is not very often we get a visitor such as you. The gossip is mostly about you. It will be hard getting my people back to work now. They like to talk," she smiled and paused for a moment before she went on. "There are stories of you around the castle. Sorcerer Tyndall has been quiet about you, not giving up the slightest bit information, as has Lady Wenonah. Many that work here are curious of where you are from. Is it true you are not of the kingdom?"

"Yes. I do not recognize anything of your culture. Your language and manners are strange to me."

"It's hard for us to understand or even imagine. We have never known anyone outside the kingdom. All I know of is the cursed Drenthen and the fighter Kal . . . " she did not finish. Someone could be heard on the floor above walking toward the stairs. She looked up and then back at her work with concern.

"I must get back to work. I hope there is a chance we could talk again sometime later. We have a rest period after the evening meal."

"I am sure I shall see you again."

A door opened on the floor above and light filled the walls of the stairway.

Saying nothing, Elesebeth did a quick curtsy, and went back to her chores. Her long legs making her walk seem awkward. A heavyset woman came down the stairs and walked past where I sat. I remembered her from before. Her name was Englay, one of the women directly charged with the cleanliness of the castle. She walked past and smiled nervously at me but said nothing. With her came the smells of soap and a hint of wood. I sensed a happiness in her.

According to Rouke and Tyndall she has been of service since she was quite young and took her work seriously. As she immediately began to inspect the rooms being cleaned, I decided this would be a good time to leave and pay the baths a visit.

Twenty-one steps. How would I ever get back down?

*   *   *   *   *

Sweat. A small annoying bead of water, made its way down my forehead to the bridge of my nose. Slowly it pooled with smaller ones, but went no further. I refused to wipe it. In time it would drip and I could find a moment of relief.

The practice sword I held in my hand was from a light wood in color and weight. Pine perhaps. I quickly looked down at the grain of the wood, but could not identify it. Magic gave it strength Beyson said.

To me it felt much heavier now then when we had first started. I could barely lift it in my defense. The tip lowered towards the floor even as I concentrated on keeping it up. When the muscles grew too weary in one arm, I quickly took the sword with my other hand. Shaking my free hand and repeatedly making a fist, I tried to ease some of the weariness. As quickly as I could, I would wipe the sweat off my free palm using the leg of my pants. The wooden sword felt awkward no matter which hand it was in.

The area near my leg wound was still very sensitive. I know it had healed, but now it felt as though a thread or small hair was pricking it. I ached to scratch it. Just once, that's all it would take. In another two days or so it would be completely healed but that did little to ease the itch now.

Beyson, the man facing me had yet to break a sweat, he looked as if he had just stepped from his room for evening supper. There was no indication we had been in the large room above the armory, sparring for the last hour.

Tyndall had brought me here earlier to show me some of the weapons the soldiers used. The swords on a rack on the far wall were very impressive. The shields mounted around the room had carvings and characters etched upon their surfaces. I saw pike-staffs, hauberks, maces and a horseman's lethal axe; all beautiful, all well crafted and all deadly. When we met Beyson, Tyndall took the armorer aside to speak privately. Tyndall then departed leaving the two of us. It was then that I was given this practice sword and Beyson took one of his own. He spoke one sentence to me before we began.

"All you have to do is touch me with the wooden sword you have in your hand and we will finish."

There was a movement and another bruise to my ribs. I stifled a cry of pain. It wasn't a hard blow, just enough to sting. Immediately, Beyson had my attention again. He appeared in the same position I remembered him in just a second before. Could someone move so fast? I was sure I saw him move, but there was no change to his posture whatsoever. The man was holding back his blows, this was true. He could have done a lot more damage if he had wanted to.

I was beyond anger. Twice I tossed the wooden sword down. Beyson, through pokes, prods, and slaps made me think twice and I snatched it back to help in my defense. My shins still hurt from that quick lesson as did the back of my hand and shoulders. Red bruises marked my forearm, but the skin was not broken.

I gave in to the irritating drop of sweat and tried to wipe it with my shoulder. The second my arm covered my eyes, Beyson brought his practice sword in again. It slapped me slightly harder on the ribs adding to the bruises already forming there.

* * * * *

Tyndall went to the door of the armory and paused. There was no sound from beyond the door. Surely, they had not finished already. Once inside he saw Beyson standing over Marc who lay half upright on the far wall.

Beyson looked up at Tyndall, his sword still at the ready, but said nothing. As he came closer, Tyndall could see Marc holding his sides tightly. Sweat soaked his hair, and his breathing was somewhat sporadic. His hands and arms trembled slightly.

Tyndall placed his hand on Beyson's shoulder and the man backed a few steps away.

"Marc," Tyndall said slapping him on the side of the face. Marc's eyes slowly focused and he came out of his stupor.

"Why?" Marc asked looking up at Tyndall.

"Get up, if you can. Beyson, help." Together they managed to bring Marc to his feet.

"I believe you know where the servant bath house is. Bathe and change your clothes. The rest of the day is yours. You'll wish to rest."

Still, in somewhat of a daze, Marc turned. Tyndall and Beyson watched him stagger across the floor and to the door leading out. His shoulders drooped, and his arms hung in an odd way, such as those of a cripple.

Beyson was about to speak, but Tyndall held his hand up. Marc closed the door by leaning on it from the outside. It shut loudly, and his footsteps could be heard going down the stairs. Only then did Tyndall lower his hand and allow Beyson to speak.

"He is clumsy, he is."

"Does he know how to use a sword, Armorer?"

"He pokes and jabs like a child, once he figures out the business end. Old Man Fern could have sparred with him and he would have done the same."

"Could he have hidden his knowledge of the sword?"

"Not very likely. I pushed him, I did. Took him to his limit; gave him ample opportunity near the end. If he had any skill he would have shown it. Better watch him around the kitchenware he may lose a finger, I'd say. The young man is harmless."

"Thank you Beyson. I shall give the duke this information."
Beyson bowed as Tyndall turned and left.

* * * * *

Lady Wenonah knocked softly on his door, but there was no answer. Her candle flickered slightly making her shadow dance on the far walls of the hallway. This early in the morning there was no one about. The sun would rise in an hour and the servants had yet to wake. She lifted the latch and opened the door just enough to let a ray of the candles light pass through.

Peering in, she saw Marc asleep on his bed. She checked the hall again to see if anyone was about, she then went in and closed the door.

He slept deeply. She placed the candle on the table and took the chair quietly as she brushed her long hair back from her eyes. After she heard what had happened in the armory, she felt the need to come and spend some time with him. Before daybreak she would have to leave.

Her father and Tyndall had explained what they had done, and in a way it made sense. If Marc was from the Drenthen, they had to know. Tyndall was certain he knew nothing of his past life. Her father was less sure. More tests would be conducted by Tyndall in the days that followed and then they would know for certain.

There were others in the kingdom, mostly in the great guild houses in Land Streth, who showed an interest in Marc. However, if he could not remember his origins, and the means that brought him here, he was of no use to them. He would then be left alone and be allowed to find his place in the kingdom and live his life as he wished.

How much more would it take for them to realize he had no wish to harm anyone? Thank the Writer this would be the last physical test they put him through. The many-colored bruises on his arm would be seen to by one of their best healers when the morning light came. She would make sure of it if she had to bring them from Westrick herself.

Looking towards the open window she could see the night had grown much closer to the morning. She had to leave before anyone found her here. Looking once more about the room, she picked up her candle. He still slept soundly. Her intention had only been to look in on him. Having no desire to disturb him, she left as quietly as she had come.

* * * * *

Tyndall stood outside the door to Marc's room with Bischof, a healer from Westrick. He began to speak softly. The spell he wove was of comforting words and soft syllables. Bischof recognized it as one that young mothers sang to their children to quiet their fears and make them rest easy. With the spell spoken Tyndall paused a moment to let it gain strength and power from the well of magic he possessed. His hands moved suddenly, a tight quick circle and a thrust forward, palm open and facing down, and the spell was cast.

"He sleeps very soundly now," Tyndall said taking a deep breath.

"I should take no more than one half of an hour. His bruises will heal easy enough. His mind may take longer."

"Very well." Opening the door, they quickly stepped inside.

Bischof wasted no time and started his spell as soon as the door closed. He stood beside the bed and examined Marc's arms and sides.

"An apprentice could heal this. It is easy enough," he began to chant. Soon a soft healing glow surrounded Marc from head to foot. With great skill Bischof healed muscle and skin using gentle words and gestures.

Tyndall watched as the glow shifted from a golden-yellow to a bright white. The glow then faded and was gone.

Bischof renewed the spell concentrating on Marc's head. Again the spell of the healing glow was cast. This time it only surrounded his head. Bischof chanted further and the glow grew in strength until it was half a palm in width. It was white meaning there was no damage.

"Bischof, keep the spell for as long as you can. We need his mind healed. We need to know where he is from," he watched as the healer struggled with his spell.

Bischof nodded, continuing to reinforce the spell with several smaller spells.

"There is . . . something blocking me," he said. He labored in his breathing as he spoke. "I feel . . . an area I . . . I cannot reach." Abruptly the light was gone.

Bischof found the chair and sat down heavily. Sweat dripped from his sparse hair. Tyndall looked at Marc and sighed. He still slept soundly.

"I am sorry. I should not have pushed you so."

"He has a . . . a place up here," Bischof tapped his own head. "I cannot reach. Perhaps he knows of magic. I felt a strong . . . attraction to healing-spirit magic. If he were to study magic, any type, in this he would be most proficient."

"His memories?"

"I cannot be sure. I . . . I was not able to find anything wrong with his mind. It's the one area that troubles me. I sense no magic blocking me, but also it's nothing physical. As I say, it could not be reached. Also, whether it is important or not, he is not the only child in his family."

"You know this? He has brothers and sisters?"

"Yes, I can tell. He is the youngest. He will be a stubborn one. The younger ones have to constantly stay strong in the family. Always proving themselves, always fighting for their place. They get the scraps not suitable for the rest and make due with this. His way will be a strong one."

"Thank you Bischof. I shall tell the duke of our progress."

With his breath slow to return, Bischof wiped his forehead with his sleeve and stood.

"The spell of sleep should wear off soon. He'll be awake in an hour or so. If you could come to my study I'll pay you for your services."

"Thank you, Tyndall," he said as they departed.

* * * * *

I did not want the dream to end. It felt as if I was laying on a rock in a forest clearing basking in the warmth of the summer sun. Birds chirping nearby made me open my eyes and I vaguely took in my surroundings. I could hear a brook close on, but could not see it. The trees of the forest circling the clearing were tall with large trunks and big leafy branches. There was little shade on the rock as the sun was overhead.

My attention drew to a woman walking from the trees. She wore a long dress of black that accentuated her form. It was so long it hid her feet as she walked. In my dream the grasses and flowers moved aside as she came forward. Her hair was of two different colors. Her braid, which lay on her shoulders appeared a mixture of silver and copper. The light softened the colors.

"Mother?" I thought. But it couldn't be. My mother was different somehow.

She crossed the glade and came closer to the rock on which I sat.

She held out her hand as if offering it to me in greeting. And I held out my hand, but a heartbeat before we touched I felt my weight shift and my being rise into the air. In this dream I couldn't stop. Looking closely, I saw she was crying. Tears had pooled in her eyes and it was as if she knew she was losing me. She bowed her head in sadness. When she looked back up, I was very high in the air and saw only the oval of her face, I was too high to see her eyes. With great effort I tried to will myself back down, but it was no use. I relaxed my struggle and gave into what I could not control. I let myself be drawn upward.

Opening my eyes again I found myself back in my humble room.

* * * * *

I awoke well after morning. The memory of the dream lingered heavily in my mind. My stomach grumbled. Sitting, I saw someone had brought in a tray of fruit and bread while I slept. Beside this there was a pitcher of water. Taking it by the handle, not caring to pour it first into a cup, I drank deeply.

Her face. I could not forget it. She was well into her elder years, but I remembered a softness and beauty in her eyes. If possible, she gave the appearance of being young and old at the same time.

* * * * *

"I hope that you are not angry," Tyndall said calmly. He stood near the window of my room, leaning back on the sill with his arms folded. "The duke and I are testing you to see if there is any chance you might be harmful to us. These last few days have not been easy for us as well. Try to understand our fears, Marc. We truly believe that the Drenthen may return to the kingdom. So many of our books of magic were lost during the war, we fear the Drenthen may have taken them, learned our gate magic, and plotted a return. Since the wars have ended, you are the only thing out of our normal way of life that has happened.

"Some believe you might be of the Drenthen. But when you speak, it is in a language very close to our own. There were very few of our people, if any, that could even begin to speak to them. I believe that if you came from the Drenthen then your language would not sound the way it does.

"We have not been working with the type of magic needed to bring you here. The tools and instructions for gate magic have been lost or locked away. If we did not bring you here, then who did? From our point of view the only answer to this question is the Drenthen. We have not been able to make any other link. I have no idea where you come from. With your memories still gone there is no way we can tell for certain.

"What I have to say next may sound harsh, but it needs heard. We

cannot just give you a status. We could deem you a servant and leave it at
that. You'd spend your life serving the members of the Family here in
Croskreye. I will not permit that. The duke and I have yet to discuss this
matter but I believe he will name you a freeman as we cannot give you
much more than that. You are welcome to stay here as long as you wish. I
must say though, we trim fat. The more you contribute the more we
welcome you. If you wish to leave us, we will welcome you back. We will
take in consideration the circumstances of your arrival. We are not in the
habit of harboring criminals. If you choose that way of life then that is your
choice.

"You are under our laws and our customs now. We will teach you
about our common law. After such a time, you will be held accountable for
all your actions. For now there will be a grace period. We will observe you
closely. Any significant error on your part might be viewed with great
suspicion."

I sat on the edge of my bed and listened, trying to take in all Tyndall
said.

"I will be free to come and go from the castle?"

"Yes. You will tell the guards and if you wish to leave for a short
time you can. Please let someone, someone in status higher than the
servants, know where you are going and a given hour when you will be
return."

"I should agree to these terms?"

"Actually, Marc you have very little choice. You do not look like the
type to rebel. You are very calm, almost subdued. You will obey the duke's
rules. We will not harm you. Your cooperation will earn you our help in to
trying to regain your memories and finding your way home."

"Thank you, Tyndall. I shall do as you ask."

"Very well," he slapped me on the shoulder, and turned to leave.
"We are a gentle people, Marc. Please hold no grudge against myself or
Beyson for yesterday in the armory. We had to know your strengths and
weaknesses. There will be more tests I need to conduct. Simple ones. I want
to find out about your reading skills and how good you are with numbers."

"I hold no grudge with anyone. You must do what you have done." I
held up my hand and he paused. "If you think it is advisable, I would like to
learn how to use the sword. Do you think Beyson could teach me?"

"You would have to ask. Wait a while, however. I do not think the
duke would rest easy knowing you had a sword strapped to your side. I am
sure we will need help with the harvest before winter. If you wish to show

the duke he should favor you, work there as much as you can give an effort."
"I understand."

Chapter #5

Candles from past visits had dripped their wax on the small statues of the fallen warriors. The room was an offshoot of a large vault that held the casks and remains of no less than four generations of kings. The casks, traditionally, were not ornately carved or laden with gold. Except for a simple humble cloth, the kings lay in death as they had at birth. Everything, save for a few small gifts from loved ones, passed on to the living so they may better govern the kingdom. The air was stale and cool, smelling of the good earth and dampness.

Commander Sablich had sat here in the room away from the king's vault for a good part of the morning. Dressed in light armor and meaning full well to go to the drilling fields to help train men, he found this day he needed a place to think. The crypt of dead kings was not a common place for him and, truth be told, the number of times that he came here to seek solace and silent council could be counted on one hand.

In the room in which he sat men had created a large table and upon it were the small statues of his predecessors. It was these men, these silent stone effigies, that he sought to obtain an answer from. These men earned their rank and position through sweat and toil, where as with the kings it was given to them as a birthright.

The candle above his predecessor sputtered and spat. Threatening to go out completely, wax dripped on the ancient wood and the flame burned brighter. The king's champion, Commander Nathel, gone for almost twenty years and now reduced to a stone carving no bigger than a hand, had been a dear friend. His likeness bore the tarnished copper that represented the copper maille he wore when he died. Killed on the northern shore, in a battle with the foemen Drenthen, his body was never found and never returned home. He died in battle. A better passing could not be envisioned.

Behind his statute was one of Commander Jaderholm, Nathel's brother. He had died just a few years before Nathel battling the same enemy. It had taken four of them at once to bring him down. Sablich had fought along side them both. The commander before Jaderholm was too distant in memory to recall.

Placed by the side of the simple stone carving of Commander Nathel was one of another man. He had been an adviser to Nathel and a man that he trusted many times with his life. A friend, unique and like none other before or since, Sablich had wept at news of his death. Nay, at the news of both their deaths he had wept and mourned silently inside for weeks. He still missed them both.

Reaching out from where he knelt he touched the figurine and remembered. He made a promise to Kalendeck just before Kalendeck's death. A promise that he intended full well to keep.

A door opened in some hallway above stirring the air and making the candles flicker.

"Commander?" Came the voice of his captain.

"Aye?" he replied loud enough for his captain to hear him, but not loud enough to insult the bodies of the kings lain in their casks. Presently he heard footfalls on the stone steps and Elowen's familiar face appeared behind a lamp he carried.

"T'is time. The king calls." As if in echo there was the barest sound of trumpets filtering through the halls of stone.

"Aye." A second time he said and stood. "He claimed he could see spirits, but in the handful of times I have been here he has never made an appearance. I have always fancied that he would."

"Nathel?"

"Nay, Kalendeck. He told me he was quite troubled by them when they choose to show themselves."

"Bid you are the lucky one," said Captain Elowen looking about. "In a place such as this they would abound. Regardless, your king is in need of you now. The boy has that all important decision to make."

Sablich sighed. "As an adviser I will see an avenue that he will not. I have a promise I must keep."

"You will not wear formal clothing for such an auspicious occasion?" As a jest Elowen absently brushed something unseen off of Sablich's shoulder.

"It will be forgiven," Sablich said simply. "I must not make him doubt that you pulled me from the training fields. If he knew I was here seeking solitude amongst his dead brother and father he might be inclined to visit the vault early."

He pinched candles out till only Elowen's lamp shone. With naught else spoken Elowen led the way. His footfalls hastened and Sablich was unsure, as the distance between them grew, if the younger man walked faster because of his youth, or mayhap he disliked the crypt.

* * * * *

The air cooled the Great Hall in the castle of Land Streth by a constant gentle breeze coming this day from the east. Commander Sablich entered through a series of small doors and antechambers. He surrendered his sword and a dagger to a steward before he walked across the stone to the dais where the throne sat. From where he was he skirted the mosaic tiles forever inlaid upon the floor. Knowing the king's dilemma, he was not surprised to see people from various walks of life scattered about the main floor.

Going to one knee he bowed before the young king.

"Rise commander, we have work to do." Which was now one of his common greetings. Commander Sablich stood and went to his side. There was never a time that Sablich did not enjoy being around the man. King Trahune sat on the throne and when his young mind was not wondering on distant meadows, or on the heroics of sword play, or on the five wolfhound pups that showed great potential, he thought deeply.

His reign began at the age of ten at the untimely death of his brother Talmadge who had died by his own hand while on a hunting excursion in the king's woods. A wild sow had made Talmadge's horse rear and with his crossbow primed, the bolt was accidentally released through his neck just beneath his jaw. By royal decree from that day on crossbows were no longer permitted while hunting bore or deer.

Trahune did not receive the throne by greed, or by murder. He had no lust for the position or the power that it would bring. At the time he was busy behaving as any boy of ten behaves. When he learned of his brother's death and the sudden responsibilities heaped upon his slim shoulders, he visibly shook. Nevertheless, under the untainted guidance of his advisers he had taken to the part after the first few months. Were it not for the memories of the war with the Drenthen the kingdom would be an enjoyable place.

The last ten years, however, was not what the young king pondered as he sat in the Great Hall. This day was one that he had notably dreaded for some time. Being a close adviser to him, he told Sablich thus on many occasions.

There were several advisers and others gathered at his call. They came forward, gave the king their advice and returned to the place in the hall from whence they came. Commander Sablich stood to the side and as the day progressed from morning to noontide he began to fidget. Mayhap a day sweating on the training field was far better than this.

Some servants and a few peasants were still scattered about the main floor. They stood calmly where the advisers placed them earlier all the while waiting on the king.

"Wroe," he motioned to his sorcerer with a wave of his hand. "Shuffle them around again."

"Yes, my lord. Any particular order, if I may ask?"

He sighed and stood from the throne. Everyone went to one knee. One peasant, a thin elderly man who was shaking with nervousness was slow in this task. King Trahune approached him and two guards in light armor came forward. They seized the man by the arms before the king came close.

"He has done no harm. Getting old is not a crime. Please release him." The guards did thus and King Trahune sent them away with a wave of his hand.

"Yahn, it is difficult to see from there. This is something that needs done here."

"Of course." The sorcerer, a man many years his elder, bowed his head in acceptance.

"Now, people, please stand. We'll work this out and I will trouble you no more this day. Off the map." His commanding voice echoed from the rafters high above.

Without hesitation those that stood on the colored mosaic tiles on the floor moved to the edges and turned to face inward. Beneath his feet was a map of the kingdom. Isolated and alone, the island nation lay surrounded by vast oceans. Here, on the edge of the map, deep blue tiles depicted the ocean's water. Some had sea creatures drawn upon them.

"You, man," King Trahune motioned to the elderly man who had trouble kneeling. "Come forward and stand on Land Streth." His feet brought him quickly shuffling back to the very center of the map. "You will represent myself and the lands immediately around the castle."

The elderly mans smile could not be contained.

"Now turn slowly and tell me what you see."

The man did so and when he finished he spoke.

"My king, I see all that you govern. The sun rises in the east warming the morning and sets in the west bringing the cool of twilight right behind. Men toil by day and your bidding is your law."

"Wroe, Yahn, Sablich, we have the rare find of a poet among us," he clapped his hands and rolled his eyes skyward so the man could not see. All of the advisers laughed. The jest even drew a smile to Sablich's face.

"You, server, come here," he said and pointed to the area north-east of Land Streth. "Lay down, the Territory is dead. Wiladene Territory lay in waste by Drenthen." Adjusting the servers feet and hands he made the young man look as though he were laid to rest upon a funeral pyre. "I have nothing for beneath your head." His words carrying some distance. Snapping his fingers another server brought a cleaning cloth which she folded and placed beneath his head.

"You there, girl." The peasant girl came forward. She wore a well-mended, if slightly soiled, dress of deep blue that covered her feet. With difficulty Sablich looked away from the sway of her hips. Before the king spoke again Sablich looked at the tapestries that hung high above their heads with feigning a look of complete boredom. "To the south of Wiladene Territory, and to our east, is the Territory of Delfuri, the horse people. Come, you stand here. I deem you, for the moment, Duchess Bessa."

She stood upon her set of tiles and curtsied to the king.

A fourth person came forward. "To the south of Duchess Bessa lays Duke Almonesson, Kahshgrance Territory. His lands lay to our south-east. Spices are his trade." At this time the three territories on the right side of the map and Land Streth at its center stood occupied.

The fifth person on the mosaic stood on the northern area of the map where the Spruill Territory was laid out. Beside him was the young server laying on the floor. "You are north-west of us. I have chosen you because your clothing is black which is the standard color of the Spruill people. The young lass, in Delfuri's space, is in blue, the color of Duchess Bessa's standards. Yahn, these two are in agreement with each other?"

"Yes, my king," Sorcerer Yahn walked forward as he spoke. "When the order went out years ago to find someone of suitable linage to govern the Wiladene Territory which now lays in ruin, Duchess Bessa sided with Duke Tominson. They have a mutual uncle in mind. They feel he will be best."

"Being the two territories that border the Wiladene they have much to gain by allegiance to one another."

"That they do, my king."

"You man, stand to our west, Chisemore Territory, and you good sir, to our southwest, Obfelden Territory." When he did this each individual represented the six territories and Land Streth.

"Duke Lysaght and Duke Curwin, respectively, my king. Duke Lysaght has an uncle that meets all requirements. Duke Curwin sides with him on certain conditions. The agreements they are working out amongst themselves."

"They disagree with the person that Bessa and Tominson have chosen."

"That is correct, King Trahune," Yahn said and stepped back.

"As with Lysaght and Curwin, Bessa and Tominson disagree with the choice the others have made." Commander Sablich spoke up for the first time. His voice was deep and weighty. Showing that his mind was still on matters at hand King Trahune gave him a quick nod.

The king began to walk in and amongst the people standing.

"I know the decision to place a new royal family could ultimately fall upon my shoulders," he mused as he walked. "I thought that the four dukes and duchess would be able to come together and we would all have a mutual family that would govern without recourse. One territory dead, two for one family, two for another, and then there is this one."

He stopped next to the man who stood on the Kahshgrance Territory. For all his effort the man tried to appear calm and smiled a broad toothy smile at the king. Clearly nervous he did not cringe away. Under such scrutiny he was sweating profusely.

"Duke Almonesson, my lord," Sablich noted. "He and I fought side by side against the Drenthen. The others have never seen battle."

"Almonesson's advice to me on the matters is that I, and I alone, should choose who should next govern the Wiladene Territory," The king said to the foolishly grinning man.

"His advice is worthy," said Sablich stepping forward, his boots coming to rest on the very edge of the crafted stone. "The dukes, all except Almonesson, have always looked at such a prize with greed in their eyes. By their own hand they could manipulate the man who governs the Wiladene Territory for their own profit. Almonesson will not side with either. To do so would cause resentment from the others. Bessa or Curwin, having chosen two different people could harry his borders. He voiced this concern even before he knew whom the other would choose. Almonesson knew of this dilemma years before it manifested itself."

King Trahune walked between the people while still looking at the made boundaries of the map. "He speaks rightly, Wroe."

"That he does," said the counselor coming several steps closer to the inlaid map. "What is your opinion, commander?"

Sablich breathed deep. "You both had asked before and, like Duke Almonesson, I will not sway. It is council you ask and you have heard many this day. May we bide our time a little while longer? Not to postpone the outcome, but to give us more time to reflect. I believe we need to hold meetings with Duke Tominson and Duchess Bessa firstly, Dukes Curwin, Lysaght, and Almonesson thereafter. It is not a decision we should take lightly."

Commander Sablich bowed slightly and stepped backward.

"Sorcerer Yahn, you feel thusly?"

"It is one path to take, my king," he said after a moment's hesitation. Arms crossed, forefinger on his chin he began to pace around the circle. "Although there are promises you have made to Duchess Bessa, my king. The men will complete the castle in her governing village of Carfrae by this winters end. You stated to her that you would visit when she finished it. To pull her from there to come here, when it is nearly finished, only to go to her territory a month later would not sit well. She, and the dukes, are beneath you, but they can make things difficult."

"Your proposal?" asked the king motioning to Sablich with his hand.

"Visit her on her lands in her newly completed castle as you stated you would. She will be very happy and things may go smoother. How long can it possibly take?" Commander Sablich asked.

Turning to him Sorcerer Yahn spoke with the rustle of robes. "Her castle is due to for completion mid-winter to early spring. She would be angered if we did not fulfill this promise. We could visit there and come back, King Trahune would be able to send for the others just after the next Day of Turning."

"It would seem that the conclusion to this riddle will last almost a year longer," said the king rubbing his chin thoughtfully. "The dukes may not wish it, but they will have no choice."

"If the dukes become disruptive we may have another uprising." There was a collective gasp as these words sunk in. Yahn raised his hands palms outward. "I am simply stating, before the king, that we must quell any acts before they have time to manifest."

"People, be gone," said King Trahune and everyone moved towards the doorways. They had to rouse the man lying on the space of the Wiladene Territory. He picked up the cloth and hurried away.

"Sorcerer Yahn, I feel that you have spoken too openly," King Trahune waved his hand and stopped him from speaking. "Such truths are not for the common people to hear. Rumors could spread; people in positions of power could get the wrong ideas. The people of the kingdom could tear it apart far faster and with the cruelty of the Drenthen horde.

"Send out the message Bessa. We will listen to her arguments at her castle and then the others." Sorcerer Yahn and the others turned to do the king's bidding. Commander Sablich saw the king start to leave by a side entrance as his majesty continued to speak closely with others. He nodded in the king's direction and inwardly smiled.

*   *   *   *   *

Standing near the window in his sleep clothes, Duke Almonesson waited until the servant Fern gathered the days other clothes, and left. This was the same servant who had been in the hallway when Marc arrived. He was a frail man who had been in service at the castle for as long as Almonesson remembered. Age had slowed him a little and as time went on he tended to dip his cup a more and more frequently. The ale soothed his joints and eased the burden. A favorite of his fathers, he let the man be and was content that he still served without complaint.

The latch fell as Fern backed out of the room and still Almonesson waited.

He was alone. Finally, after a long day of assisting his people he could now rest and collect himself for tomorrow. One by one he pushed his thoughts and concerns of the day away until he thought only of what mattered most to him.

Memories of his wife, Lowy, were first and foremost in his mind. Tasked by the king himself, she was in the north with Lady Bessa. She would return in less than half a year. When the snows left the land, she would be back to her home. Granted, there was much to do in the north, but this would be the last separation he would suffer. The people of the Kahshgrance Territory have given enough to help rebuild the kingdom. More than some, less than others. A simple letter to the king would see that she remained where she belonged from hereon.

His son Farnstrom and Commander Nayoor would remain behind as well. The territory needed a sense of normalcy. A time that Almonesson only remembered as a young man. Before the Drenthen.

With bare feet, he walked to a small table. Under a black cloth was a book like no other. He removed the cloth, tucked it under his arm and gently picked the book up in his hands. He ran his fingers lightly over the letters in gold relief. The book had seen a lot of use. The leather of the cover was well-worn, but the name still held a certain luster. It was inlaid with gold and gold never faded.

Placing the book on a larger table he sat and placed the cloth to the side. Here, in the candle light, he opened the book and began to study.

The style of writing was a curious thing. The lettering was thin and quick. There were no decorative characters, no fanciful animals. The words themselves painted a picture that was easy to see.

There were only a handful of pages with any text upon them. The rest had remained blank. He looked to see if the pages had anything else written upon them, but there was nothing new.

Returning to the first he began to read a story that was the same this night as it had been previously. The words read the same and invoked the same images, but he felt the need to read it once more.

The story began with Marc coming to the kingdom much the way he had. It was the young server, Rouke, who had found Marc in the hallway. The tale portrayed Tyndall as being a bit older with hair and beard completely gray. Wenonah was slightly younger and with beauty that would rival the sun rising in the morning. Almonesson's name was in the lettering also and he was the most perfect and just ruler of people who could exist. In the story, Marc had lost his memory, but without the wounds and the pain. It was simply explained that this is what happened by traveling through mirrors. In the story Farnstrom was younger than Wenonah. If the description was correct, he would have looked much like the serving boy, Rouke.

Reading to the end, the words stopped in mid-sentence and spoke to him no more.

Sighing, Almonesson closed the book.

The words had not changed. The Writer added nothing new and had taken away nothing.

The book was waiting.

* * * * *

Tyndall heard his name called and placed the papers down. It was rare that people called on him such. He went to the door and lifted the latch.

"Is someone there?" he asked down the spiral stairway.

"I need to speak with you," It was the heavy voice of Duke Almonesson.

"I will be down, my lord."

"No need. I would like to see my way, please," he said.

Instinctively, Tyndall spoke the command and the candles in the recessed sconces lit. Already almost halfway up, the duke would be there in a moment. If Tyndall tried to ready a place for him, he would have to release the door. It would be a grave insult if the door closed as the duke reached the top. If he used a slight wind to hold the door open, it would blow out the candles. This was also not acceptable and so he waited.

"My grace, this is truly unexpected. If you wished to talk, we could have met in the Gathering room," he said as he saw the dukes hand on the wood railing.

"This might be your keep, but it is my castle. I have not been up here in years and I believe our privacy is better here." By now the duke was at the top of the stairs. Even though the years were slowly catching up to him, he was not winded from the exertion. Tyndall held the door for him and he entered.

"Your advice is what I seek now," he said taking one of the few chairs Tyndall kept in the place. Duke Almonesson's eyes searched the mantel above the fireplace and Tyndall saw they stopped when he saw the likeness of a face etched in the stone. It was something that Duke Almonesson had done when he was a young lad. There was a second in the rooms that were once his bedroom when his father ruled. These are the same rooms Lady Wenonah now used. A third one, rumor spoke of, Almonesson engraved in the mantel above the fireplace of his parents rooms. The duke looked upon this place every time he was in the tor.

"I shall give you all the advice I can, my lord," Tyndall took another chair and brought it around the table.

"It feels much cooler up here."

"With the four windows open the heat of the warm days does not stay."

"Maybe I'll start conducting court in the eastern tower."

"It is downwind of the stables, my lord. The idea would not sit well with the others."

"Anyway," Duke Almonesson cleared his throat. "My thoughts stray from my purpose. Marc has been on my mind. To bring it out forthright, I must say that the similarities between his arrival and the arrival of Kalendeck cannot be denied. Such is something that we cannot over look. I have watched him off and on since he has been here, and although I do not see any resemblance between him and Kalendeck, there might be something there. They could not have brought him here to just live out his days in Croskreye."

"I understand what you are saying, my lord. Your thoughts mirror my own. Have there been any disturbances?" Tyndall asked.

"There have been none. When Cinnaminson brought Kalendeck through the mirror, they heeded his warning and rushed off to Glenhelen. This young man brings us nothing. We have watched the seas around my lands, I have ordered more men on patrol, I have sent messages back and forth to King Trahune, but nothing."

"You are waiting."

"Yes," said the duke clasping his hands on his lap before him. "I do not wish to have my guard down like Duke Shindle and Commander Caddoan. They were great men; however, had they listened they may have lived longer."

"I agree."

"I must ask you to give me an oath of secrecy," Duke Almonesson looked into his eyes.

"It is given, my lord," Tyndall nodded. "I have never swayed in my loyalty to you. But . . ."

"What I am about to tell you must tell no one. You cannot send notes off to those in the guild houses, my daughter must not hear of it, and I will not have Marc tainted. I will not have his decisions influenced by what I now say."

"Understood. One moment," said Tyndall. He spoke a simple spell, let it build for several heartbeats and then released it. A noise was heard down the stairwell and at the door at the top. "I have locked the tower," he said simply.

"Good. I have two reasons for visiting you," Duke Almonesson cleared his throat. "I received a letter from Duke Lysaght. Our neighbor in the Obfelden Territory wishes to affect our decision in the king's choice for the new ruler of the Wiladene Territory. He believes that if I tout Marc before the king, as another Kalendeck, people will be behind me. King Trahune will want his people happy and so grant the dukedom to whomever Marc, I, or Duke Lysaght, chooses."

"Who would you have control the territory, my lord?" Tyndall asked leaning back.

"I still believe that King Trahune should place there whom he feels will best govern the area. We can advise the king to a point, but I feel that my hands are free. It is not our decision."

"Marc, or his influence, could change that," said Tyndall.

"His influence would wear thin when they find out the truth about him. They may believe he is a second Kalendeck, when actually he is not. I bet my coffers he never raised a sword in his life before he arrived here.

Should I parade him before the king? The man would see right through him. My credibility would wane. No, I will not have him be a pawn in this game." Duke Almonesson sat back. Tyndall heard the tension in the duke's voice.

"Will they send someone, an emissary to our lands? Truly, they will see how Marc behaves. The stories of Kalendeck's deeds and triumphs are well known. As you say, I do not see Marc doing such."

"I doubt Marc would have the influence to have anyone follow him even to the market," Duke Almonesson laughed and slapped his knee. "He is a good lad, he is really. Of the fight for control of the Wiladene Territory, I do not wish him involved. These are kingdom matters, and not his."

"If they do come, if they send someone, they will want to see him."

"They will," said the duke. He placed his foot upon his knee and began to work at a loose grommet on the leather. "We shall have to prepare him for them. Which leads me to the second reason for my visit," he sighed deeply, looked at Tyndall a moment, and began to speak.

"Kalendeck, in the lulls between warring, would spin stories. He told me one night when I had drunk too much and slept very little, that I should expect a messenger. Bah, in my mind it was a trivial thing, something that did not surface until this mirror thing happened. I believe it was this year, or the next, that such a messenger was to arrive. All his other predictions have come true, I expect the same of this one."

"You believe that Marc is the messenger," said Tyndall tapping the tabletop with his finger.

"I know Marc is the messenger, how can he not be? He could be the harbinger of another war, but his secrets stay locked away in his mind. Others will desire the knowledge they believe Marc has. We cannot let them have him. I, and I alone, must know the message that the messenger carries."

"We have tried to undo what the Writer has done, but we could not, my lord," said Tyndall leaning forward. "Bischof from Westrick wove his best magic. I have never seen the healer work so hard. On the island he is the best healer. We would have to find a better one in the kingdom. Ryeson, perhaps."

"You miss my point," said Duke Almonesson waving his hand in the air, his voice barely a whisper. Leaning forward he placed his hand upon the table. "I believe that it is not for us to bring it out of him, but he must find it himself. Akin to yelling at a rock to give up the diamond that it holds. All we have done, and all we will do, is useless."

"How do you propose to coax him to bring it to light?" Tyndall asked leaning backward.

"There is a teacher from Taberham who might be of assistance."

"I received schooling in Taberham," said Tyndall.

"You know of Davlyne then."

Immediately, Tyndall smiled. "I know her. She is one of the best, but she always has a full complement of younger students. To bring her here would be costly."

"I have a debt to Kalendeck I feel I have to repay. How much is one man's life worth?" Duke Almonesson folded his hands across his chest and Tyndall knew he would speak no further on the matter. Rarely would he speak of his conquests.

"Marc is already being taught."

"They instruct him on the simple things of our life. How to behave before royalty; how much does a bundle of brembry wood cost in the north, proper dining habits. It's all trivial nonsense. I wish him to know more. If Marc is not ready, then we must prepare him. Do you, Tyndall, believe this is the correct course of action to take with him?"

Tyndall drummed his fingers on the table slowly.

"At his home he may have been a properly learned young man. He has his wits about him and is always alert and open to what is around him. I believe that to release him to menial work about the castle would truly be a waste. If it was on your mind to release him, I was going to ask if I could take him on as an apprentice after a time. Time with Davlyne would be an excellent start."

Duke Almonesson was quiet for a time before he spoke.

"The thought of him doing crockery or scrubbing floors brought me around. A freeman he would be, but to earn a wage he would have to start out somewhere. And to think this was all the higher I would let him climb. I will bring Davlyne here to teach him. I would send him there, but I wish to keep a watchful eye on him. Lysaght or Curwin could send their men in and he could be taken from our lands."

"Davlyne, it is known, has a broad base of magic in all areas. She will set him on the proper path. When can she be here?"

"The next new moon," said the duke. "Right after the Day of Turning. I am going to ask the castle staff not to speak of Kalendeck to Marc. My daughter is taking him riding tomorrow. I will call a meeting with everyone. We will gather in the dining hall when they are gone and I will have them swear an oath. Again, I do not want him tainted and believing he is something he is not. I do not want this opportunity wasted," said Duke

Almonesson standing.

"May I indulge in one request, my lord?" Tyndall went on when the other nodded. "Marc has asked that he be trained with weapons. We could give him to Beyson to have him learn just the basics. If there is a war coming then he must know at least this."

"You wish to send him in the ranks?" Duke Almonesson asked.

"No, he could be an adviser as Kalendeck was. It would not harm him to know how to defend himself," Hearing this, Duke Almonesson thought a moment and then nodded.

Chapter #6

I left the building used as the living quarters. After holding the door open for a maid bringing in two pails of water I crossed the courtyard. The open sunlight was bright compared to the light filtering in through the castle windows. I squinted and raised my hand to shade my eyes. The intensity of the light bothered me some. I still had the headaches that would come and go, but even these were fewer and less strong.

My stomach fluttered. It wasn't due to the fact that I did not have food this day, I was nervous and tired. I slept just a little last night. She had asked her father and he had given her permission to take me riding with her today. No escort, no servants, no chaperone. Just her and I.

My stomach knotted again and for a moment I was light headed. If I could do so, I would have run across the courtyard to the stables. I walked at an easy pace hiding my excitement.

Duke Almonesson himself warned me that I should use caution. There were men from the other territories that may wish to harm me or take me away. I knew that many saw me as something that I was not. With me under their wing they could gain in power and prestige. Duke Almonesson had let me know that he was not about to do this. And I was grateful.

The courtyard was a busy place this day. Maids were bringing in buckets of water drawn from a wellspring at the courtyard's center. Through the main gate a wagon appeared with a load of stone. They were adding to a tower on the eastern side of the castle.

I spoke to no one as I walked. They looked up at me when they passed and a quick nod or smile was enough. More than once I received a reprimand for talking to the cleaning maids. When they had free time they could talk, but not during their chores. This free time was mostly during their meal hours and that always depended on their duties. Even then, they always had to hurry to get back to their chores. I saw Elesebeth once or twice more. If she was among those at the well I was just going to wave, but I did not see her tall figure so she must have been elsewhere.

The blacksmith worked with raw metal at his place near the wall. I timed my steps with the beating of his hammer on the anvil.

As I got closer to the stables the wind changed and for a second I caught the smell, the rotting pungent smell, of dung. Flies buzzed around me like miniature dragons that could not be held at bay.

I was whole again in a broad sense of the word. If I thought about it hard enough, I could almost create a childhood from the lives I saw around me. I could have lived as any one of the boys splashing about the streams and water front. In my mind I tried to think of a noble profession for my parents. Blacksmith, perhaps for my father, strong and sure with a hammer, forge, and anvil. My mother would bake and sew. It was a simple life, this one I dreamed for myself, and a hard one. One we would live with satisfaction.

But I knew, deep down, the life I now lived was not mine. The emptiness was still there at times and the loneliness that came with it. At the end of the day everyone else had their own place to return to. Here they had their own lives and I was just a convenient interruption to the daily sameness they endured. I tried not to let myself reflect on this much. My past life lay in a chasm that could not be crossed no matter how I willed it. I was still a hollow nameless being in a world full of life and energy. I had to keep myself distracted, not let the dread seep in, so I worked and studied as much as I could.

My thoughts were suddenly interrupted as a stable hand brought two mares from the stables through a large doorway. Lady Wenonah was next to him wearing dark breaches and riding boots. A riding cloak graced her shoulders, its hood lay on her back. The clothing she wore was not what I expected of someone of her position. However, she was prone to wear old clothing. The robe she wore the very first time I saw her was a bit tattered. The boots she wore today were of hardened leather that had chaffed and cracked in places. They had obviously seen a lot of wear. The riding cloak, which was several faded shades lighter than the traditional green common in Croskreye, had a patch over the elbow and a fray at the shoulder. It might be her style to wear clothing that made her look like a commoner.

I greeted her with a formal bow, and she smiled.

"Good morning, Lady Wenonah, and how do you fare this morning?"

"I am good, Marc. You are learning well. And yourself, are you well?" she asked as she took the reins from the stable hand. Her voice was light and cheerful.

I took in a deep breath of air letting it out slowly. Besides the odor coming from the stables, the morning air was crisp and clean.

"I feel wonderful," I said and could not keep the excitement from my voice. Her smile was contagious. "The sky is clear, and we have a full day of riding ahead of us."

"It is nice out, isn't it? It's good to see you in such a mood. I will not have you brood about today. Well let's be off, I want to get to Westrick and back before dusk." She put her foot in the stirrup, and with one swift motion she was on the horse. She clicked her tongue and pulled the reins to the right. Her horse did a circle and she stopped where she started. She waited where she was, looking down at me with a smile.

I felt foolish for just a moment. I had no memory of ever riding a horse before. The brown mare shifted her weight and for an instant I was afraid she was going to step on me. Quickly I held up my hands and backed away.

Lady Wenonah saw me hesitate and came to my rescue.

"Help him. His leg is not fully healed," she commanded the stable hand. Seeing no way to back down I stepped forward. One moment I was standing on the ground with my foot in the stirrup beside the horse and the next I was in the saddle on its back. I held tightly with my legs almost too afraid to move.

The stable hand looked up at us and smiled.

"You will return them around dusk, my lady?" he asked.

"Yes, Rayne. I'll bring them back with all four shoes on their hooves. You must remember the horse Rada?" She openly laughed at this. "How will the weather be today?"

The man took the cap off of his head and turned his face skyward, eyes closed. After a pause he spoke. "Like this all day. Storm will be coming in from the west early tomorrow morn. It won't last long though, over well before sun up."

"You do good work. Tell your wife and the children I send greetings and wish them well," Lady Wenonah said with a smile.

"I shall," Rayne said as he bowed.

There was a commotion in the courtyard, and we turned to see Rouke running toward us. Chickens scattered in his wake.

"Hold! Wait a moment," Rouke yelled over the din of chickens as he drew nigh. He walked the last few paces careful not to spook the horses. He rested against the neck of my horse as he caught his breath.

"Are you going to Westrick, my Lady Wenonah?"

"Yes we are," she answered.

"Can I trust you with a message? Last year at the Day of Turning I met a girl and we danced. Remember? Tell her I miss her greatly. She . . . Is my true love."

I saw Rouke blush as he spoke the last. His eyes darted back and forth between us.

"I know whom you are speaking of. I shall tell her," Wenonah said.

"Thank you," he said as he bowed. Before he raised his head, we were on our way.

*   *   *   *   *

At the main gate the guardsmen stopped us.

"Commander! They are leaving," A young soldier at the castle gate yelled to the guardhouse on top of the wall.

"Marc," Wenonah whispered so that only I could hear. "I must warn you what we say next will be in jest. Do not take us seriously."

"Well, well, well." I looked up to see a grizzled man in helm and leather armor leaning over the stone of the wall. He tipped his helm back. "What do we have here? What are your names and where are you bound? Quickly, now, before I have your heads on a pike." Being warned by Lady Wenonah I could hear the hint of humor in the mans voice.

"Oh, please great Sir, we mean no harm." Lady Wenonah looked up at him with an odd look in her eyes. "I am known in the seven territories as the hag of the woods with dark hair and few teeth. My companion is Harold Cornsniffer, a direct descendant of the great and mighty Willem Cornsniffer, the cow dancer. Do not let his warts and lack of hair fool your eyes. Look beyond his, and even mine own ugliness, and see us for whom we really are. Poor and wretched. We are deeply humbled by someone as great as yourself. Please, let us pass with no trouble." Her arms were covering her head protectively.

"Hmm, why should I do that?" He held up a club that must have leaned beside him against the castle wall and began to tap it menacingly on the stone. "I thought I could smell the foul stench of you two from well beyond those trees." Pointing with the club he went on. "If I release you from this prison where will you travel?"

"I will be honest and tell you that we have heard of a great treasure that lays many months away from here. We will have to fight a dragon and hoard of harpies to claim it as our own. If you release us, this is where we shall travel. Eastward, me thinks, then mayhap to the north-west."

He considered this by rubbing his chin. "You'll give your most humble word that you'll harm no one whilst you are gone?" The commander scowled down at us. He spat noisily and missed the horses by a great deal.

"I must say that we are not capable of doing anyone any harm. Since

Harold has lost his last tooth, he has become quite broken in." As she said this I gave a weak smile, much like the village idiot.

He mulled it over. "Any proof of your honesty you can give me would be greatly appreciated. Think not of it as a bribe, for bribes are forbidden for one as noble and trustworthy as myself." At this he puffed his chest out.

Lady Wenonah spoke up. "This mere stone I carry may look like a simple field stone, and you may look on it as such," She held her hand up so he may see better. Opening her palm she revealed a pebble from the courtyard. "But it is a diamond of the most highest quality. I shall give it to you after you open the gate and draw the portcullis."

He scowled. "You may keep your stone, Hag of the woods with dark hair and of few teeth, buy yourself a fish for supper and be well on your journey. May we not see you again for many days and many more nights. Your beauty drives the very stars from the sky at night. The moon fears to raise this evening less you gaze upon it. Open the gate," he yelled to the soldiers and they did his bidding without hesitation.

Lady Wenonah bowed her head deeply and I did the same. When we were through, she turned and smiled at me.

"Commander Terchey has known me all my life. He enjoys the game."

I could only smile. The interaction between these two seemed like a quite well rehearsed play.

*   *   *   *   *

We exited the castle proper and entered the village that surrounded it. The castle walls that loomed over us were slowly hidden as we traveled through the village streets. From the main gate the roadway lay at a steep angle. Cobblestones made obscure patterns beneath the hooves of our mounts.

There were many small shops along the main thoroughfare in Croskreye. A man was sweeping in front of his shop, but stopped as we passed. Everyone bowed to us and moved out of our way. Lady Wenonah called out names, and waved to many of the townspeople. A baker rushed out with two small loaves of bread for us to try. It was warm, delicious, and hinted of the flavor of butter and ginger.

I was somewhat overwhelmed by the number of people here. The castle was all but deserted compared to the village. Several children raced behind the horses, careful not to get under their hooves in the narrow street. A cat watched contentedly from its perch on the second floor window sill of a home as we passed. A wall built around the village of Croskreye protected the village in times of trouble. A second gate rose before us. This one was open and unmanned.

We crossed over a bridge that covered a small stream, and suddenly the village with its noise and congestion was left behind. I came after her as best I could as she went forward at a fast trot. My horse followed hers with little encouragement or persuasion. There were just a few people walking on the road before us. They moved quickly aside as they saw Lady Wenonah on horseback.

On a small hill stood the chimes. A stone foundation formed a base for the four large wooden beams. Standing upright they supported a roof from which tubular chimes hung from thick chains. The tubes of metal appeared large enough for a man to place his whole arm in. It would have taken a strong wind to make them sound.

Surprisingly, she did not stay on the road that wound its way along the shoreline, but found a well-worn path that ran beside the stream that came from inland. Here we slowed the horses to a walk. Thankfully it was wide enough that we could ride side by side.

"This way is a little shorter," she explained pointing to the dirt path. The forest soon rose on either side to hide us. The day was cooler here beneath the large canopy with just a bit of mid-morning sunlight filtering down.

"The road takes the easy way to Westrick for the wagons, and it's also much longer," she said. "If we went that way by horseback, we would be back tomorrow morning. This way is better for those walking or on horseback. It goes a bit higher on the mountain and you can see the island better once you get to the meadows beyond the trees."

"Ah," I said. "I did not know whether to believe you or not when you said this was an island. I guess it is. For some reason, I thought it was much bigger that it is. From the room I stay in trees in the village block much of my view of the Straits, it looks like it is only a river." I did not feel embarrassed about my ignorance about places to them that were commonplace. I realized that I only could only learn so much from the classes I attended. There were so many names that I asked to cease that line of schooling. From that day they went on with economics and treaties.

"There is a tale about a man who lived several generations ago. When men of the kingdom first set foot here they thought as you did, that this place is much larger than it is. Among the group was an ill-tempered young noble. His name was Rossmoyne. He was the first to realize this was an island."

"How did he find out? Climb to the top?" I asked as my horse shifted.

"No. There was a dispute on who would gain control over the rich land. He was quite upset when they told him that the king selected another family to rule. It a fit of anger he mounted his horse and galloped off. By the next morning he still had not returned. A search group found his remains and the remains of his horse at the bottom of the cliffs. He rode his horse so fast he couldn't stop it. Over the cliffs' edge he went."

She held her arm outward and made a diving motion with one hand.

"He didn't?" I said. She grinned with a half smile and I could not tell if she was jesting or not. I watched her for several moments and all she did was raise her free hand, palm outward, and nodded, as if making a vow.

"Albeit, realizing this was just an island the interest and disputes died down. Shortly thereafter spices were found here in the lower areas, and minerals in the caves on the mountain. Settlers moved in and founded the three villages. My ancestors were of the royal family in Land Streth. They built a castle on the island and the village of Croskreye arose. My father has control over the affairs of this area. He governs wisely. As did all his fathers before him."

"Is the island big?" I asked.

"Rossmoyne, the poor fellow, found the shortest distance from one side to the next. His journey was roughly north to south. Ending at the southern cliffs. That way it takes only a few hours. Traveling in this direction, east to west, from one tip to the other would take three days on horse. To the village of Westrick it will take just a few hours."

"That's good," I said to her, and mumbling loud enough for her to hear I added, "I am not familiar with horses. The sooner we get there the less time I spend on this beast."

She turned in her saddle and smiled at me.

A breeze raced through the trees and brought with it the scent of the sea and hints of sage and thyme. If there had been any low fog this morning it was surely gone by now.

"So how do you like it here?" she asked.

"I enjoy it, you have a very beautiful village here. The people are friendly and courteous. Your society works well. I have seen nothing unpleasant yet." The incident in the armory with Beyson was all but forgotten.

"You are taken care of by our servants, however."

"Yes, this is true. All of my clothing has been given to me."

"You are being schooled at no cost to yourself. It gets expensive if you must pay."

"All of my meals cooked for me. I must hunt or forage for nothing."

"You have no memory of the society you left to compare ours to."

"It's rare that I leave the castle and enter the village. Yes, I see what you're saying, but the people are generally happy. You can look at them and see. Why, there was that man two nights ago. Did you hear him by chance?"

"I'm not sure. Continue please," she maneuvered her horse around some roots from a very large tree. This brought her closer. I was a bit uncomfortable not knowing how my horse would react. My worries were for nothing. In a moment the normal distance separated us. When she looked back at me she smiled not knowing of my concern.

"It was late in the evening," I went on. "And I heard this man singing almost at the top of his voice. He was obviously drunk, surely, and the song I could not understand at all. Probably a war song or something because it was very rhythmic. He went on for some time and no one paid him no mind and just let him sing. Your people are very happy. It surprised me no one joined in."

A group of five people were on the trail before us. I reined back and let Wenonah take the lead. They recognized her and bowed deeply, speaking well of her and the family. We moved past them and I moved back beside her. I happened a side-ward glance at Wenonah. She was looking at me and her face was turning red. She was smiling, and with great effort it appeared as though she was holding something back. I thought for a moment that she was going to pass out.

"Are you well?" I asked. "Have you been stung?"

She stopped her horse and began laughing uncontrollably. Almost doubling over, I had to hold her arm to help her keep her balance. I laughed with her, not sure of the source of her mirth.

"You are amusing," she said trying to regain her breath.

"How do you mean?"

She chuckled more and urged her horse on with her heels.

"You know my father likes to sing when he drinks his wine." As she said these words I could feel a cool chill creeping down my back. Regardless, I started to sweat and feel light-headed at the same time. She turned and saw the look on my face, and began to laugh more.

"I'm sorry," I stammered searching quickly for words. "I mean, I had no idea it was your father. Please understand I would never belittle the duke."

"Oh, no need to apologize. I have heard some others do worse," she wiped tears from her eyes. "Singing that is. He, ah . . . gets in these moods when he drinks. Sometimes he's kind, other times he gets in a real dark mood. My grandfather and an uncle died in the fight against the Drenthen. He hasn't stopped grieving for them. If you look closely, sometimes you can see it in his eyes."

"I see. I shall not speak of his singing again. A great man he is," I said but still could not help smiling.

"That would be wise. He upsets easily enough."

We continued on and for a while I could still hear her mutter to herself and giggle. I searched for another topic to change the subject.

"Have you lived here long?" I said quickly, seemingly to blurt out.

"I have . . . been here all of my life of course. I am not permitted to go farther than Westrick without an official escort. I have not traveled as much as I would like to. I have to almost beg my father to let me go to Westrick. He says that I go there too much."

"What's in Westrick anyway?"

"It's a popular trading village. There are cliffs there as well and the water is shallow. Ships will not port there. Ships can only dock here in Croskreye and on the other side of Mount Suburi in Hathersage. Because the channel is shallow, it is easier and faster to bring to bring goods over land. We have the spices, you know, ginger, nutmeg, sage, and cinnamon to trade with the many things that come through each season for commerce. Thyme lines the banks of the river near the village. Hence its name."

"Which is?" I prompted her.

"Thyme River," she gave me a questioning look, but said nothing more about it.

"Is that why you are going there this day, to get spices?"

"No, there is very little going on Croskreye. I told my father that today I was going to teach you about how our commerce works. What better place to see it work then Westrick? After being stuck in your classes for the past two weeks I think you need a break from your teachers. It's a day well spent away from Croskreye. Before you arrived, my father had kept me to my studies as you are now. He is trying to have me learn every subject he can think of." She groaned loudly. "I need a break as well."

"What is your best subject?"

She silent as she thought, and I began to think that she did not hear me when she answered.

"Life, I think," she said with a smile, "If you can keep a secret I'll tell you one. There is a young man who works as an apprentice blacksmith in Westrick that I am fond of. We visit when we are able."

"Does anyone know?" I asked caught off guard.

"I do not think so. We have been very quiet about it."

"I shall keep your secret. If I break it may Tyndall perform some more of his tests on me."

We both laughed.

"He has been that difficult with these tests on you?"

"At first yes. As of late, he puts me under a spell, and next thing I know I wake up on the floor and several hours have passed. I believe that he's done just about everything except knocking me in the head to get my memory back. Please don't give him that idea. Twice now I've looked in the coals of a fire made from brembry wood to see if anything could be found of these memories. Nothing has, well nothing that I can remember," I smiled at this. "I wish that I could remember something, anything would be good. My name to start. You may have solved this for me."

"Yes. It's rather hard to talk to someone if you do not know what their name is. You needed a name so I gave you one. I hope you don't mind," said Lady Wenonah. I though a few moments on how to word what I was going to say next. I did not want to upset her.

"I don't mind the name of Marc. It is a name. Besides what's in a name? If my memories return I will still keep it, but possibly as a second name. Perhaps just as a name those in Croskreye will know me as. May I ask what made you think of that particular name in the first place?"

"Oh I don't know, just an impression you gave me when I first saw you. You were a person in need of something and I gave it to you. I enjoy helping people. Besides you look like a Marecrish, which means one-that-is-lost. Hence, Marc."

"It is a good name. Thank you."

*   *   *   *   *

The sun was directly above when we broke from the trees and saw Westrick in the valley that spread out below us. She stopped her mount and I came forward and moved mine abreast of hers. Flies had gathered around the horses with the warmth of mid-day and smell of their sweat. Their tails swished constantly and they shook their heads to free them of flies if only momentarily.

"Our people construct most of the villages in the same manner as this one. The large stone building in the center, the one with the tower and standard, is where the governor lives and works. Just out from this is the Market Street. With Westrick, the streets are very wide to accommodate a large number of wagons. You can see from even this distance that having been built so they are still crowded. There is talk of expanding the stonewall curtain around the village. Some want to remove it altogether, but if there is another war they may need the protection."

"They could expand it like they did at Rivenburch," I said remembering the lessons I was given. "Just build a second stonewall wide enough for homes and shops."

"You did learn."

"The governor's place here is much smaller than the castle at Croskreye," I noted.

"True. This man looks after the affairs of just this village. My father has his whole dukedom he must govern and needs more room for royal visitors from other territories. The dukedom is not just Ross Island, mind you, our territory, named Kahshgrance, covers ground well into the heart of the kingdom. Clear to the borders of Land Streth."

"I have seen maps. Like a pie with a hole in the center. Each wedge of pie is a dukedom. The center is Land Streth."

"Very good. Impressive. You have learned well."

I could not help but smile. Leaving the hilltop, we continued on.

Lady Wenonah stopped her horse just short of the village. Leaving the dirt path, she entered a small copse of young birch, and dismounted. I followed her, unsure what she was doing. I waited for her just short of the tree line.

"Why do you stop here and not in the village?" I asked.

She tied her mount to a sapling. Turning to me, she spoke. "I didn't want to enter the place on horseback. There is a limit to the number of stables and it is rather cramped in there. I have never seen the place when it is not busy. To take the horses in would be an inconvenience. Anyone seeing these horses will know them immediately as the duke's own. Besides, they will like it better out here."

"Someone may take them?" I said dismounting as well, although with my muscles stiff from the ride I was not as graceful as she was.

"Not with you here guarding them. Don't worry," she must have seen the look of sudden disappointment in my eyes. She had brought me this far only to guard horses.

"I will only be a short while. When I return you may go explore the town if you wish. I'll give you some coins to spend."

"Thank you," I said as I tied my mount to a branch close by. He neighed softly and began to eat nearby leaves.

She ran a brush quickly through her dark hair and dusted her breaches off as best she could. After she returned the brush to a pouch in the saddlebag, she came to stand next to me. I was busy undoing the straps under the horses' belly. I felt jealous and shame at being brought as a horse sitter and for these reasons I did not want to look upon her. Her eyes.

"I am sure the horses would like to eat some grass instead of those tree leaves. They can drink from the stream. How do I look?" she said catching my glance at her.

"Very well," I said as I took the saddle off of my horses back and set it to the ground. "I'll do as you ask, but what if you need help? Shouldn't I come watch over you?" I tried one last time.

"Thank you for offering, but no. I need you out here more. This place is peaceful enough."

I felt abandoned. I wanted to see the new places and explore. I may need her here with me in case of trouble, she may have needed me there for the same reason. She brought me along as a horse sitter and nothing more and there was little I could do. She, of noble birth, I had to obey. Who knew what someone else who had lived their lives in the kingdom would do at this time and what their feelings would be. She gave her reasons, however. Knowing this, I did not want to give her the impression that if I didn't get my way I would whine about it. I accepted defeat.

"I will do as you ask."

"I thank you for your concern," she said softly. She stood on her toes, hands on my shoulders and brushed her lips softly across my cheek. Her hair, was lightly scented with something reminiscent of lilacs and roses, her face washed and cleaned with soap hinting of bee honey. What I felt when she kissed my cheek was more than the physical feelings, I sensed emotions and an inner excitement within her.

For a heartbeat I felt drained. I was not expecting the close physical contact and I stepped backward almost losing my balance. I blushed slightly and at once my frustration was gone. The world became solid around me once more. Had she entranced me?

Although the day was warm she pulled the hood over her head.

"None must know who I am. I must enter secretly," she explained.

For some reason her voice was just above a whisper even though we were so far from people it would have been difficult for anyone to hear us even if we yelled. "I'll be back shortly."

With that she turned, and was gone. She had gone only a few steps when I wished her good luck. She turned, waved, and continued on her way.

*   *   *   *   *

I looked on as the horses drank deeply from the stream. They loved the flowers in the field near the bank. Mostly the purple ones. I hoped they were not harmful to them.

I sat at the trunk of a young birch tree at the edge of the copse. My legs were aching too much from the ride to stand comfortably. Watching the wagons that would come and go from the village, I noticed that I almost never saw one that was not full of goods.

I watched for half an hour, but quickly grew bored. Finding nothing better to do I began to split leaves of grass with my thumbnail. Doing so I failed to notice a servant with the basket until she was only a few paces away. She carried the basket in her one hand and with the other held her long blue dress up a bit so it would not snag in the grass. It was not clean, but soiled with flour and grease spots. It was clothing designed for the working class. I thought at first she might be looking for mushrooms, but she came straight towards me smiling.

"A lady said that I could find a man here tending to two horses," she said as she drew near. She was young and just beginning to take the shape of a woman.

"You have found him. What else did she tell you?"

"She wanted me to give you this basket of food, and to keep you company if you wanted any," she said as she placed the basket in the grass at my feet. She sat there also. She tucked her bare feet under her and they were hidden with the dark blue fabric. To quiet the pains in my stomach I reached in and brought out a small loaf of bread that was still warm from the oven. She cooked spices in the loaf and it smelled and tasted delicious.

"Do you wish that I would stay? Will you have any need of me?"

"If your task was to deliver the food to me then your task is complete. If you want your basket back, you'll have to wait."

"I must wait then. I have to return the basket to the kitchens where I work. I did not have a chance to talk with Lady Wenonah at length. How has she been lately? I heard she had another spell."

I stopped eating my bread and looked at her suspiciously.

"How do you know Lady Wenonah is here?" I asked.

"Well . . . ah . . . everyone knows that Lady Wenonah comes when she is able, sometimes with the royal traders, sometimes alone. If she thinks she is keeping it a secret, then do not let on otherwise. We are deeply honored by her presence. You see, she loves a man who works with one of the smiths. It is so romantic, he is a handsome pauper, she is the daughter of Duke Almonesson. It is love that he wants, not position or power."

"And she brought me here this day to guard horses," I said. My fingers found another small loaf of bread and I ate. My concern for Lady Wenonah was still there, however she must know what she's doing. I was the stranger here. Like the scene at the castle wall with the captain of the guard she must have played this game before, I would leave her to it. I was sure she could take care of herself.

"May I ask your name?" she asked looking at me slyly.

"I am Marc."

"Marc! Oh my, Marc?" I watched as she blushed and half stood. Her hands were suddenly busy working her hair and smoothing out her dresses. She bowed before me. "I am sorry for my boldness. Please forgive me, I beg of you."

She puzzled me at first. The people of Croskreye had openly stared at me, some shunned me completely, most had whispered behind my back, and I had grown accustom to this over time. This was something totally different. Never before had someone held me in such awe. I was not ready for it. She trembled slightly. If Lady Wenonah came by at this moment, I would never live it down. I took her by the shoulders and brought her up from her kneeling position.

"None of this, please. I am not of royal lineage. I am a commoner, a freeman. Just sit and speak with me."

She regained herself slowly and when she ran her fingers through her hair a third time I saw her hands were still shaking. With effort, she held tightly to the cloth of her apron as if willing them to remain still.

"Is what they say about your arrival true?"

"Yes," I said rolling my eyes upward in exaggeration. "The mirrors brought me here and I have no memories. All true."

"And the woman with wings singing?"

"What woman?" I asked and saw the puzzlement in her eyes.

"I have heard when you fell from the mirror they saw a very bright light and a woman appeared for just a moment, singing one high pure note. Her wings carried her back through the mirror."

"I do not think there was any of that. I did startle one of the servants, but this is all. Please, you don't know how many times I've had to explain what happened."

"I have spent too long away from my work. We are always busy. I have to leave or they will scold me," she stood wiping stray strands of grass from her skirt. "Before I go, do you know any of the servants in Croskreye?"

"I have met a few. Why?"

"If you see someone by the name of Rouke . . ."

"I know him," I smiled.

"Tell him that I send my love and give him this," she held out her hand and in my palm she dropped a small heart made of gingerbread with a pleasant smell. She had baked it in the oven until it was very hard. Possibly something that may have otherwise been thrown out. "I will be looking for a return favor on the Day of Turning."

"I will give this to him. He told us to find a girl here that he knew."

"And you have," she did a quick curtsy.

She smiled at me and departed with her basket. Through the field she skipped in the high grass. She paused at the gate to let a wagon pass and then went inside. The whole time she did not turn around once. It was not long after that Lady Wenonah emerged from the depths of the town with a man beside her.

His dark hair, that matched hers, blew in the breeze created by his long strides across the field. His white shirt was almost gray with soot and ash.

I stood as they approached. Lady Wenonah was smiling. He whispered something in her ear, and she giggled.

"Marc this is Clendenin, and Clendenin this is Marc."

"Glad to meet you." We said almost together as we shook hands. I noticed the strength and thickness of Clendenin's hand. The time he worked in the smiths' shop had served him well. He was in very good physical shape.

"I am glad to meet you Marc," his voice was deep. "Wenonah has told me all about you. I have heard rumor that someone had fallen through one of the mirrors at the castle. Now I see you and know that it is true. Wenonah told me that you do not have a memory of your past life. is this correct?"

"Unfortunately, yes," I said simply. Clendenin was so familiar with her that he dropped all formalities when he spoke her name.

She extended her hand to me, palm downward. "Here are some coppers that I had promised you. Spend them wisely."

I bowed slightly accepting her offer. The coins were heavy as I took them into my hand. I looked at them for a moment before I placed them in my pocket.

"I will see you shortly then. I won't stay long, we must go soon. is there anything that you need?"

I saw her squeeze Clendenin's hand.

"No I have all that I want," she said with a smile. "I believe that I saw Rosemary pass us as we came out. If you see her again tell her I send my greetings. She works in the Boar and Sow, just down the street from the Boot and Dagger."

"Rosemary?"

"The young woman who Rouke is courting."

"I shall. With your leave . . ." With that I turned and left. Before I entered the gates, I turned to see the two sitting in the grass in the shade of the trees.

*   *   *   *   *

I found a joy in just walking through the busy streets of the village of Westrick. There was activity everywhere I looked, as it was market day once again. There was twice as much here than in Croskreye. They say that in Westrick every day is market day. Vendors beckoned to people as they passed by, hoping to sell or trade their goods. Many had interesting items, but nothing that I wanted.

I did not stray far from the main thoroughfare. New to the village I did not wish to get lost. I searched for a brief time for the inn of the Boar and Sow, but was not able to find it. Regardless, there was still plenty to look at.

I spent my coppers in a stall where the vendor sold paper items. I searched over what she sold, and found a book I fancied. A simple one with a leather cover and backing with glue bindings which held the pages in place. The pages were blank and I felt that I could use this sort of book as a diary to keep with me. It reminded me of a book I had seen before. Not the one I had seen Tyndall with the first day I woke, but another one. I gave the elderly lady all my coins and she gave me back two. She also gave me a metal pen. Similar to the silver one that Chronicler Thane had, this one was old and had odd writing on its shaft that I could not make out.

I walked the streets a bit more and decided to leave. It was getting late in the afternoon. I left the village and went back to the knoll where I had left Lady Wenonah and Clendenin. We spoke very little as it was late for both parties. Clendenin had to get back to the forge, and we had to get back to Croskreye before dark.

They saddled the horses while I was in the village, and I mounted as soon as I reached them. Lady Wenonah had a puzzled look on her face when I showed her the blank book.

"I wish to keep a journal."

We said our good-byes. Clendenin shook my hand again, and whispered to Lady Wenonah some more. He kissed her lightly on the forehead, and then left. She watched him until he was through the gate.

She turned to look at me, to see if I was ready, and gave me a quick smile.

"He-yaa," she yelled snapping the reins on the horses' neck.

We galloped off the knoll away from the copse of birch trees, and were on our way back to Croskreye.

Chapter #7

A man led a bull down the streets of Croskreye. His massive hooves making clopping sounds on the cobblestones. There were very few people on the streets and the sound was louder than it normally would be with the echoes it created. The man led him out of the gate and across the wooden bridge to the grassy field. Here the townspeople gathered and waited. Anyone on the island who could be spared was here to mark the beginning of the festivities to celebrate the start of a new year and the upcoming months of harvest. The changes of the leaves and the winter that followed were still months away, but they were always on the minds of the people of the kingdom.

"Turnout is bigger than most," remarked a village man near me.

"It will be a great harvest this year, I'll wager," said another and others spoke their approval.

"Peaceful Day of Turning," someone said in greeting.

"Peaceful Day of Turning," I, and others, echoed.

People parted and made a path to let the bull and his handler by. The wall of people closed in behind them like tide water as they passed. The bull sensed something, and its ears twitched with nervousness, but the mass of people remained quiet. I had heard a story that has passed from one generation to the next of the year the bull broke loose and trampled several people. Since the Bone-Rite was not completed on time that year, the harvest was poor and people suffered. The lesson learned, silence was now common for the bringing of the bull for the Bone-Rite. This was The Day of Turning for the kingdom. Similar ceremonies were taking place in almost every one of the great providences.

In the center of the gathering, the destination for the bull, were four posts driven in the ground at the edges of a large sheet of canvas. The handler brought the bull forward. The animals bowels loosened once near the edge of the canvas and the town folk waited.

Four ropes secured to rings on the four posts, were then placed around the animal's head. As the last one drew taut, the bull snorted and pawed the canvas, but could not move left or right, forward or back. It was trapped.

Tyndall came out of the crowd followed by a man with a sledge-hammer.

He raised his hands and all strained to hear.

"Good people, I thank you for being here. Once he strikes the bull, we begin the chant, no sooner. We must all chant as one. We must wait till the half day hour. If luck is with us and we have a successful Bone-Rite, then this years harvest will see us to the warmer times. A new year begins today. The Day of Turning is finally at hand," he made a motion and the man with the hammer stepped forward.

He whispered to the man and only the closest could hear.

"One clean blow to the center of the forehead between the eyes. Stand here and wait with your hammer raised. The blow has to come while the sound of the bell is still in the air."

The man, bare to the waist, took his position and stood before the bull. He brought his sledge in close to the bull's head to judge the distance, nodded, and brought it back so the handle was a hand span from his shoulder. In the mid-day sunlight sweat rolled over his muscles, forearms and chest covered in hair.

The sound of the bell being struck in the tower in Croskreye made me jump. The long pure note hung in the air as the handler swung the hammer in one smooth arc. The bull dropped like a stone. Tyndall and the man stepped back, sure not to stand on the canvas, and the chanting began.

A spell was being cast.

I, having just learned the words a week ago, chanted with the others. Twelve words, from a time long forgotten, we spoke and we all paused as one, the spell gathered strength, and with a motion from Tyndall we spoke the final word.

The hammer blow had not killed the bull. Its thick skull had possibly cracked and given the chance now it would have lived. The man had merely driven it to unconsciousness. As the spell took hold, it let out a bellow and its legs twitched. If it had been able to, I was sure it would have stood and ran. It thrashed for a moment and bellowed again. The sound carried well over the silent crowd. They all watched hardly daring to breathe. It made the hairs on the back of my neck stand on end. Morbidly fascinated, I could not face away from this sight.

The bull began to lose form. It's tail no longer moved although the muscles could be seen twitching. Steam rose from its hind quarters and the bull's legs lost their form and rigidness. The hooves began to smoke. As close as I was, I could see small sparks of fire on the bone. Internal fire singed the hair away, leaving bare skin. Blisters formed rapidly.

The spell worked on.

The backbone was now gone and the ribs consumed as well. The animal burned as it still lived from the inside. The spell devoured the bones one by one. It was a bone fire. The heat partially cooking the meat. With no backbone to support it, the head drooped and soon all lost form.

In a few moments it was all over. Where once a bull stood tethered, now lay a formless pile of skin, muscle, and organs slightly cooked.

A great cheer welled up from the people of the island. The harvest gatherings would see them though the winter with ease. The spell of Bone-Rite had been very successful.

Strong men gathered at all edges of the canvas and in one motion raised it in the air. The remains of the bull pooled in the middle. There was a large pot being heated in the village. They would dump the remains there, add water until it was full, and this evening after much dancing, drinking, and singing, they would feast on soup until the early hours of the morning. Everyone would get their share.

A new year had begun.

*　*　*　*　*

I had my book open to the pages that were all but empty. I laughed loudly and rubbed my eyes. Looking at it in the light of the full moon as it lay upon my table, my book was no different from when I worked on it in the daylight. A few lines of text darkened the upper left hand page. This was all.

Come on, think. Hmm, what to write, what to write? So much to get down on paper while the day was still fresh in my mind. Should I wait until tomorrow when my head clears? Ah, the fermented cider and honey mead spun the world about me and left an aftertaste that begged for more. I held on to my chair as tightly as I could as the castle heaved around me.

It had been my habit to write a little each day, with no excuses, but today it seemed as if I was not going to pen a word. The food, the singing, dancing and of course there were the drinks. Everyone who knew me, made certain my mug was never empty no matter how quickly I drained it.

There it was again. The castle lurched violently to the side and almost unseated me. I closed my eyes and clenched my teeth. When this spell was over, I closed my book and put it out of harms way lest I cause it damage.

Some music could still be heard from the village. I was debating on going back down when I suddenly heard a whisper. My door remained locked and there was no one in the room with me.

"Oh, it's you cat. It's 'bout time you did something." I could see him there, being in shadow I knew it could only be him. It was then that I began to have a conversation with the carved cat figure in the upper corner of my room. Surely this was important for he has never spoken before. I wonder why he picked tonight of all nights to speak to me. Truly, some other night would have been better when I wasn't drunk on hard cider. It was right of me to put my book aside this night and listen to him. I sat on my bed with my arms wrapped around my knees that I folded to my chest and listened.

* * * * *

Tyndall arrived at my door early two mornings later.

I was planning to travel about the village this day. Although the celebrations were over, the people were still enjoying the gaiety of the festive atmosphere.

Tyndall's arrival early that morning changed all of my plans in a good way. He brought some clothing that I was to change into. It was loose fitting and more comfortable than any of the clothing I was given before. The boots were painstakingly made of leather worked so thin that it felt like cloth.

He then directed me to go to the armory. When I was hesitant to go, he mentioned that Beyson would be there to train me, not to test me.

"This is very unexpected," I said to him lacing my boot nervous in anticipation.

"It will keep you busy for a time."

"How long will this last?"

"Normal training is almost half a year, but that is if you were working at it for full days. Six days of training and a day of rest. For you, it will last almost a year. In a short time a woman will be arriving from Taberham. She will school you on the ways of magic in the mornings. He will teach you weaponry after midday."

"Truly?" I looked at him fumbling with the laces. "Why don't you train me?" I asked.

"Because, I am too knowledgeable in the ways of magic to start off with someone as novice as yourself. My apprentices have already worked with Davlyne and I am able to teach them easier. It has been a year or so since I have taught someone, however. I now use my talents to help others.

"Come," he raised a hand and opened the door. "Beyson waits."

*   *   *   *   *

I had thought at first his classes would be exciting. In my mind I saw myself and other students in a room full of weapons battling it out until the sun's light left us. We would return before dawn and start all over again. Dressed in full armor our strength would build and before the winter we would become these hulking men with unbelievable strength, prowess, and power.

This was only in my mind.

We, just Beyson, his assistants, and I, spent days on the various types of armor. Chain-mail was common amongst them all. It came in all different shapes and forms. The hauberk looked like a large night shirt made up of thousands of links. There were several sets of chain-mail interwoven with magic that made it lighter than normal. It offered slightly less protection due to the fact that it was lighter. A heavier chain-mail usually offered better protection.

They showed me how hardened leather with links applied near the shoulders and at the pits of the arms to add to the protection. In one way or another, almost all of the armor I saw held the same theme. It was either all leather, a mixture of each, or all chain-mail. There were a few that had small plates riveted to the leather.

Generally, a soldier wore a gambeson underneath the armor. The material, as thick as a quilt, softened the blows delivered upon the armor. They wore normal clothing beneath it all.

For three days they showed me the various types of weapons. They demonstrated, time and time again, their proficiency with all the weapons they had in the armory. I grew bored at times, but tried not to show it. It was like being a guest of honor at a tournament and having to sit, hour upon hour, watching the others try to best themselves.

At the end of the week I was given my practice sword and it did not leave my side. By the middle of the next week I was sore from head to toe. Not only did my arms ache, but so did my legs, chest, and stomach. I did not mind the limits that they pushed me to. I enjoyed it. My fingers hurt too much during this time to pick up my pen.

When they said that my teacher Davlyne had arrived from Taberham I was slightly disappointed that I would only be spending half days with them. But only slightly.

* * * * *

They directed me to a room where I had never been to before. Davlyne was already there patiently waiting for me. Sitting beside a table in simple clothing I watched her as I walked across the floor to the table. She was not an overly tall woman. She sat with her thin hands clasped before her. Her clothing was light and loose around her. She wore a green sash from shoulder to the opposite hip with an embroidered figure that I could not make out. This, I knew from earlier schooling, was to show allegiance to Kahshgrance Territory.

She pulled her hair back from her face and held in place by two strips of leather and a few metal pins.

"Pull your chair away from the table and sit in the open. I need to look at you, to get a visual image of you in my mind to show me where to take you when I teach."

I did as she told me to. She pulled her chair away and sat down so there was nothing between us. Folding her hands upon her lap, she bowed her head.

I waited and waited. I heard the bell ring signaling an hour had all but passed. Worn from my time in the day before in the armory, I folded my hands upon my lap and bowed my head as well.

"Don't," she said not looking up. "You must not fall asleep in my class. It would be bad for you."

I sat straighter and after a time she raised her head and nodded.

"Alden prefers you, and there is a slight pull towards Helfrick. Alden, however . . ." she let the thought hang in the air for a moment. "I know who you are. I know your past as much as you do. I am not here to find out your origins. I am just here to help bring out what is inside you."

"My memories?" I asked letting the question hang in the air between us.

"Your memories are gone. A vine from the kear tree has many tendrils. If we cut it from the tree, but the vine is still rooted, a new tree may grow from where the tendril holds its ground.

"This is what we will to do with you. Forget where you have been, we will give you a new beginning and see how you flourish." When she finished, she placed her hands upon her lap.

"If you know my past, you must know that I am ignorant of magic. You speak of Alden and of Helfrick as if . . . Well, as if they were living."

"No one has told you of them?" she asked in awe.

I shook my head. "I have heard of them only vaguely. In the spell of the Bone-Rite I spoke the name of Helfrick, but other than this I do not know its meaning. I saw what it did."

"I see I have a story to tell you then. Get comfortable and listen." And without further delay she told me of the magic in the kingdom.

* * * * *

"The common name for each magic is fire, stone, water, and spirit," she began. "Also, for each there is the learned name. Those that know magic use them. It's the proper name to use when you wish to use magic. Helfrick is the name of fire and smoke. Neither of the earth or of the sky, but between. Tymchak of stone and wood. His magic is from the earth. Stirewalt magic of water and air. The magic that is not earthbound and free to go where it will. Alden the magic of healing and death. The magic of man. Mankind lives between the realms of the others."

"If you invoke the name of a magic, you have to use it or cancel it out. Henceforth, do not utter a name and part of a spell unless you are ready to cast the spell."

"The elders from one generation to the next pass down a story of four brothers who found they had certain powers unlike any imagined. Helfrick was not as calm as the others and felt as though he had to use his talent often. He loved fire. Throughout the day as he walked along, Stirewalt, his brother, would follow. There were many times Stirewalt needed his skill to extinguish what his brother had started. In time, because of this struggle, each developed his skills more and more.

"If he could burn it, Helfrick did. Or at least attempted too. Everything was either covered in a light layer of ash, or damp. The townspeople soon grew angry. This was something they could not understand. Some feared it and passed their fear on to others. The village banished them, all four mind you, after Helfrick heated a chamber pot to boiling. The stench didn't leave until the next spring.

"At their last meal together, Alden, the oldest and wisest of the four, asked each to put their skills and knowledge to pen and paper. Something such as this should not pass unnoticed. Early the next forenoon they left the village, never to return, each in separate directions.

"Years passed before Tymchak and Helfrick met again. By now their hair had turned gray. It was a time for reflections of the past. Old feelings of anger and resentment vanished, and they sought out Helfrick and Alden.

"By pure chance, or fate, they found the others in the village we know as Land Streth. From their packs, they each brought forth what they had learned about their special traits during the years. The collection was quite impressive, twenty books in all."

"In a local tavern they bought a room and returned downstairs for drinks, a meal, and conversation. After some time the conversation came to the weather. All noted that it had been a bad year. To the south the sun had baked the ground with no mercy, no crop could push through the hardened soil. To the north, week after week of rain carried the seeds from the ground. To the east strong winds bent and snapped the young sprouts before they could yield a harvest. And to the west stone troths used to carry water from stream to field crumbled as if they were dust. They made a decision that night. With their power they controlled they could heal the land.

"The brothers rested for a night. And at noon the day following, when they had gathered on a knoll in the center of the village, they saw the sky had filled with massive dark storm clouds.

"It is a good sign.

"Standing back to back, facing out in the four directions, each began to speak a spell that would mend the land he faced. Stirewalt faced south to bring rain. Helfrick faced north to dry the land. Alden faced east to cure the young harvest, and Tymchak faced west to repair the damaged stone troths.

"As the sensation of their spells gathered around them, it did something they had not expected. It began to meld from four spells into one. The spell didn't go outward over the land as they had expected. Instead it turned inward to envelope the four brothers.

"Tymchak's spell was the first to take effect. Their legs grew heavy and thick as if they were of clay. Helfrick thought he could break the spell with a burst of heat. He was wrong. His spell strengthened the clay until it was hard as stone. Alden tried to react by healing their legs back. By now they were stone to their stomachs. Alden's spell only formed a protective shield around the stone that has not been broken to this day. Stirewalt had no choice, but to finish his spell. As he spoke his last words, water rose from their stomachs, through their throats and out their open mouths."

"Their spell did seem to heal the land. As the water from the fountain flowed from the knoll to the village and kingdom, it changed the ground. Mixing with the streams, the rivers and the rain, life in the kingdom flourished as it never had.

"The books they wrote were found and studied with great detail. The spell of the four brothers brought magic into the kingdom. Magic seemed to flow, like water, from Land Streth. Their spirits now wander. Held to this world as long as their forms remain in stone. If you call upon them to do something, they are bound to do it. However, it does not go without a price. You must give them part of your energy in return."

"This is our magic."

*   *   *   *   *

As she finished, I was on the edge of my seat, literally.

"These men are still there?" I asked.

"Yes, Marc. The statues are in the center of Land Streth. I have seen them on two occasions."

"Can people drink this water?"

"They can. The water has always been clean and pure. They take water from the wellspring and use it for cooking or cleaning. You've seen water drawn from the wellspring here in the castle? There, it is the same."

"Has the water ever stopped flowing?" I asked knowing the chill of winter may ice over a well and make it difficult to draw water.

At this question she paused. She was about to speak as if the response was on the tip of her tongue. She smiled and shook her head.

"Most of my students know this history before they come to me. Such questions I do not expect. This is why I hesitate to answer you. Now," She said standing looking away. She changed the subject with my question still unanswered. "I have brought several sets of books. You will have your copy and I will have mine. You and I will read them together, slowly, so you can fully take in what they say."

She brought from the table two books with faded blue colors. I was given one and, as she sat, I opened the cover. She placed hers comfortably on her lap and with a smile she opened hers.

"Please start reading aloud to me. If you have any questions do not hesitate to ask."

*   *   *   *   *

"How is his progress?" Duke Almonesson asked Beyson and Davlyne as they sat in the gathering room. Tyndall was there and listened as well as he could. Dust still clung to his boots from a journey to Eilenburg and back to assist with stonework in their mill. He was weary and in much need of a bath and a change of clothes. Rest, in his own chambers, would have been nice.

Thane, the Chronicler, sat at his place and wrote feverishly even though the only words that anyone spoke so far was the single question asked by the duke.

"My lord," Beyson spoke up. "He has worked with me longer than with Davlyne and I believe that his progress has improved. There has been nothing exceptional about his work. I have had other students who progressed further than he with less tutoring. There is something about him, however."

"Do you care to elaborate?" asked the duke when Beyson did not speak further.

"He has a way about him. I can feel something, just a sense I have, that he is different."

"I have watched him with others," said Duke Almonesson sitting back. "A person can tell there is something different about him."

"It is not just something physically, my lord," Beyson said. "It is something in his head. I was using the warrior weave, a spell from the copied Book of Harms, when he was near me it enhanced the spell slightly. Mayhap, being not of the kingdom his being heightens the magic that we use."

Thane did not notice, but he had placed a spare pen on the table awkwardly with the tip resting about a quarter of the way off of the table. Tyndall watched Beyson's eyes as the armorer brought his hand down quickly and quietly. A blur of movement in the room lit with candles. His fingers struck the tip of the pen which then flew through the air. Beyson deftly caught the pen with his other hand.

Davlyne spoke up, her voice slow and measured. "Your grace, I have noticed the same." Placing her elbows on the table, fingers interlocked beneath her chin, she leaned forward. "His reading is better than most I have seen. We began with a simple book of magic, to see what he knew, or what he would remember, and in just two weeks we were complete."

"Could he become a sorcerer himself?" Tyndall asked. His weariness kept the sound of excitement from his voice. Beyson now sat with the pen tip on his finger. With small movements of his hand he was able to keep it vertically in the air. Thane was too busy writing what they said to notice his spare pen was gone.

"It is my belief that everyone has the potential to better themselves in that way if they so desire," said Davlyne nodding in Tyndall's direction.

"But?" added Tyndall when she hesitated.

"But he has a difficult time realizing what he has read. We finished whole sections written about the basics of water. For a day or so afterward he could quote from the passages that he read, but not put them into any practical use.

"As Beyson was saying, there is something about him that is different in his mind. Think of magic as water flowing in a stream. Rocks or sticks in the stream are people bending the will of magic to their own use. Marc is the wind blowing on the water. He makes ripples in all he does without realizing it. Ripples in the magic that is already there."

Duke Almonesson sat back and looked at each. "Is what he does safe for those around him?"

"I believe it is so," said Davlyne and Beyson nodded.

"Could this have caused his creating of a gate?" asked Tyndall.

"You are the sorcerer," Beyson said. He flicked his finger making the pen spin in the air. In an instant, he judged its speed and spin, and was able to catch it on the fingertip of the other hand.

"I shall have to think about this. My lord," Tyndall spoke up. "We have taught him in the skills of the sword for three months and two in the skills of magic. Let us continue on this course. He has lived away from our magic for all of his life. Perhaps this feeling we get," he nodded to the others, "Is magic seeping into his being. To use Davlyne's example; if a bit of wood has always been in the stream, it has water throughout its being. A dry piece of wood, that is brought in the stream, will push aside the water, and eventually soak it up. I feel this is what is happening to Marc.

"He is safe, my lord. I feel that his magic will be a learned magic and not a natural magic."

"But, can you say, with certainty, that his magic will all be learned?"

"I cannot say that. He may have some magic that is natural, I have felt the same as the others have. It is something slight. Your castle, the village and everyone in it are safe, for the most part. There is no danger." It was not long afterward that Duke Almonesson dismissed them. When Beyson rose from his seat he neatly replaced the pen. Thane, so busy in his work, did not even miss its absence.

Chapter #8

I think my studies have come well. I know I was slow in the beginning. Their words penned on the pages were a bit difficult to comprehend at first, but with some effort I was able to read them.

The summer festival, the Day of Turning, had been a joyous time and there was another celebration in autumn signaling the completion of the harvest. This merriment started a day after the first notable frost in Croskreye. After the four days of celebration I returned to my studies. The trees had now lost all of their leaves and the still the weather was warm enough to keep the snow at bay.

I helped on two occasions, on my days of rest, with the hunting of wild boars in the deep woods of the upper part of the island. It was the end of the second hunt that Sorcerer Tyndall met our group of hunters just inside the portcullis of the main gate. The points of steel hung above his head as if ready to fall. It was under this metal gate that everyone had to pass to get into the castle.

As the guild leader of this dukedom his presence in the castle was not at all uncommon. Many of the men did not notice him and truth be told, we had grown distant lately. Davlyne and Beyson had occupied most of my time. I saw Rouke often. Lady Wenonah and I chatted every few days. Although she was beautiful and very alluring her heart was securely with Clendinen. I believe that because of our friendship other women shied away from me.

I only cast Tyndall a casual glance and a nod, but stopped suddenly when he motioned to me. I saw that the man's hands were pale with cold. He stood with them uncovered from his cloak.

"I see that you're cold. Wouldn't it be wise to conjure up some heat?"

"I am not here trying to get cold, Marc. I have waited for you to come back. Besides, I am not proficient in fire."

"Waiting for me?" I asked suddenly curious. "Why, has a way been found to get back my lost memories?" I asked. I reached out expectantly and touched his hand. It was cold to the touch. He must have stood there for some time.

I had silently accepted my fate, and my past life did not seem as important as time went on. As Davlyne once told me that my roots will be from here now. Tyndall had said before that my memories would return in the natural course of time. The urgency of the matter grew more obscure as the days and months went on. There still might be an answer locked away on a faded parchment in the ancient books in Tyndall's study or elsewhere. It might take several seasons to find the right one that held the answer.

I would just have to wait until it was found or the task forgotten. Priorities had changed over the summer. As the sorcerer on the island herdsmen called upon Tyndall to look into a disease that killed some cattle in the upper meadows. He also had his regular studies to attend to. There was a meeting, the Gathering, he went to each year in Land Streth. He had to have time to prepare for that. I heard from others around the castle that he would leave within a week. He had told me he would always keep my problem in mind.

"No, this is more important than finding your lost memories. Could you come inside with me?" It was more a demand than a request so I followed without question. I noticed that the others had not stopped when I did, and were now on their way to the skinning post with the boar we killed.

I studied the back of the man as he walked before me. He wrapped his heavy cloak tightly around his solid frame to help keep in the warmth. In his right hand he held an ever present walking staff, although he used it little for walking. A wisp of bark brown hair caught in the breath of late fall wind. I saw the glimmer of a few gray streaks running its length.

"I'm sorry for my impatience, Tyndall. I can see that you are cold as it is. It is only proper that we should go inside."

"If the matters were not so I would not take you from your skinning. I can remember bringing in a boar from the hunt also, you know. My head was not always buried in the pages of books," Tyndall remarked over his shoulder.

"I helped kill this one," I could not keep the pride from my voice. "It's a great feeling. Your blood is pumping you can almost feel fire in you veins."

Entering a door on the side of the main building, we came to a small foyer. The warmth felt comfortable as I took off my cloak. My ears and nose, having been in the cold for so long, felt the bite from the heat. The stone walls were so thick it was difficult for cold to penetrate their thickness. We had entered the castle near the common room that was next to the kitchens and a slight warm breeze was felt coming from that direction.

Tyndall muttered a few words softly, and with a flick of his hand closed the door from across the room.

We didn't go to the common hall like I expected. Tyndall took to the first set of stone stairs when we reached them, and then turned again at the top. Here the air was warm. The hallway must pass right over the kitchen.

We walked down the hallway in silence. As we neared the door at the end of the hall, I recognized it as the one leading to the room Lady Wenonah used. Two of the dukes soldiers stood at attention to either side of the door. Their backs straightened as Tyndall came near. He was not challenged, nor did he stop to knock, but walked straight in not missing a step.

This was very uncommon. No one was to walk into any private room of the families without first knocking and announcing oneself. It was just unheard of. That the guards were there also made me wonder. What had happened to Lady Wenonah to warrant guards posted at her door?

I hesitated a moment before I entered. I searched the guards eyes, but they continued to stare straight ahead. I followed Sorcerer Tyndall expecting Wenonah to denounce this intrusion, but nothing could be heard. All was quiet.

The room, I noticed as I entered, was about ten paces square with a curtain dividing it in the middle. A fireplace and mantel were on the inner wall. A dresser sat to the side with a chair and a mirror of polished metal. The privy with a chamber pot was on the opposite side of the room concealed with a set of painted wooden panels. The area on the other side of the curtain was lit with several of the large candles. Their incense was strong, and slightly irritated my nose, but was not all that unpleasant.

Tyndall went to a part in the curtain and entered. He held the curtain aside for me, and I entered also. I removed my cap and held the leather and fur so it covered my hands.

The duke was there, and the servant Englay, and several nurse maids. The duke was reading out loud from a large book he held in his hands when we walked in, he now stopped, marked the page and lay the book to the side.

Beside him, his only daughter, lay on the bed with her hair about her head in a dark halo, her hands lay at her side, motionless and still. She had a bandage on her forehead and cheek. She was hurt, or worse; I feared she had died.

Was the wraith of death standing in a dark corner of the room thanking the body for the soul it had given him? Did death smile?

No. death was not here this night. I saw the shadows on her chest move with the slow, gentle rhythm of her breathing. I was holding my breath and only now let it out in a long sigh.

Why were my hands shaking?

I was in the presence of royalty. I bowed, as they taught me, and did not look the duke directly in the eyes. I stared at the embroidered bear on his chest.

Englay was crying, her face pale in the candlelight. The duke looked at us as if we were just spirits and he could only see a distant outline. Then slowly, his eyes focused and he smiled.

"I see you found the lad. Good."

"He was hunting sire, There have been a lot of boar this year in the upper reaches." Tyndall had taken off his outer cloak. He went to the dukes side and they shook hands in greeting. He then took the book from the duke and began to read where the other had left off. The duke came to me, placing his heavy hand on my shoulder he spoke softly.

"Another spell has happened upon her. It would seem that she collapsed again this day. Walking down stairs she used ten times a day. How could this have happened? I was wondering if you knew anything about it? Marc from nowhere."

I could smell the ale on his breath. Strong and potent, it almost over powering. I felt the blood drain from my face and the hairs on the back of my neck cried warning. I was sure I had a look of puzzlement in my eyes. I looked at the duke wondering if I had heard the tone of his voice correctly. Of course, he would be very irrational in a drunken state and with his only daughter suddenly taken ill. Did the duke actually think that I had something to do with this? I quivered slightly, and it was as if a blow had struck at my very soul.

I quickly glanced into the eyes of a man who I had held in the highest respect ever since I had known him. This man, with his large brow, full beard, and those soft silent eyes, had now directed his anger towards me. Why would he make accusations without any type of proof?

"Of all the people in the kingdom that could do this, I was the last one here who they should suspected of anything." I thought.

"I did not push her or make her stumble. How could I have known, my lord, I was hunting? I know, little, almost nothing, of the magic in this world." I chose my words carefully not wishing to anger the man further. Once more I lowered my eyes and bowed my head in respect. Here, in his dukedom, he was the ruler. I had to abide by his wishes completely.

"I know you were hunting, but you see, before you came here she had spells, but not like this, not this damaging. She would grow faint at times, but she would never completely succumb to the beast that stalks her soul. On the same night that you came, almost to the same moment, she collapsed. Now, again, this day during the hunt. I can remember the times I hunted boar running from hillside to stream bed, hither and yon. I know, young man, what it feels like to drive that shaft into the chest of a boar screaming for it's very life!"

The duke was breathing heavy now. The veins that pulsed against his temples brought droplets of sweat to his forehead. His hands came to rest on my shoulders.

"Sire, I swear to you, I have done nothing, my lord."

"What magic do you posses to do such a thing?" the duke screamed at me.

I couldn't say anything, I just stood there. The duke's grip tightened as he grabbed me by the shoulders and shook me so that spittle came from his mouth.

"This can not happen." I thought to myself. Where was Tyndall, surely he did not think the same of me? Any action against the duke to break from his grip might be seen as hostile. I let my body go limp. He threw me sideways, awkwardly landing on my back and shoulder on the other side of the curtain.

The fall took the wind from my lungs. My head hit the stone, and I saw stars. Shaking my head, I tried to clear my vision. I sensed a presence nearby.

It took me just a second to realize that it was the duke who now stood over me. The first thing that I saw as my eyes focused was a broadsword suspended in the air by a thick and powerful arm. Where the duke had found the weapon, I had no idea. Its tip almost touched the rafters in the ceiling, but it was on its way down now. A spark of light from each candle found its razor edge. Bracing myself for the sharp pain that would soon come to rip open my stomach, I clenched my teeth.

But when the pain did come, it wasn't like I expected. It was the side of the blade that hit my chest and ribs, and not the sharpened edge. It hurt, again it was hard to breathe, but did no more than bruise my ribs.

"Get out of here, you insulting pup. Leave me now." The duke threw the blade aside and it clattered across the floor. With a scowl, he turned back to his daughter.

I scrambled to my feet and was gone before another word could be said.

*   *   *   *   *

I ran blindly at first, not realizing where I was, until I reached the hallway in outer part of the castle where my room was. I ran to my door, and with a shove inward, I flung it open.

In my fear, I stopped. The room was cold this night, no one had brought a brazier to warm the place while I was out. I latched the door in fear. However, if the duke, or his guards wanted in, I could not stop them.

This cannot be happening to me. The brunt of the duke's anger was a dull pain in my side. Still out of breath, I lay upon the bed and tried to cast the latter events of the day out of my mind.

Fatigued from the hunt, and confused from the shift in the duke's emotions, I pulled the simple blanket over me and tried to hide deeper. The last thing that I wanted to do was sleep. I could feel my blood pumping through my veins from the run. Not of my own intention, my eyelids began to close. Perhaps a spell had been cast. Sleep crept to me like the chill of the night. I fought to stay awake, but it was in vain. With a turmoil of thoughts that would match my dreams this night, I slept.

*   *   *   *   *

The dream was vivid.

The sound of the beating of my heart slowed. In my ears it became muffled, the sound changed somehow. Instead of a heartbeat, it began to sound more and more like water dripping. No wait, waves on a shore. Having no idea of movement in mind, I opened my eyes. Before me, stretched the largest body of water that I had ever seen. From where I sat, the ocean that lay before me, seemed endless. I was sitting cross-legged, in this dream, upon a snowy cliff over looking this vast beast with the waves pounding out its heartbeat with every break on the shore. Large chunks of ice rose and fell in the surge. These swayed back and forth like tiny ships. In the sky directly above me the moon, full and bright, sat perched in the night sky. Behind me I heard the sound of the wind passing through the leafless trees. Even with the chill of the winter night, I was not cold. I breathed deep and felt suddenly an inner peace.

I smiled. I had never thought about it before, but if I ever had the choice of where to die, this would be the place.

No sooner had I thought this thought when I heard something to my right, and turning to look, I saw a man sitting beside me, looking at me.

"Don't think such thoughts young man, you never know what may happen," the man said, his voice was full of warmth and held the tone of youthfulness. I was not puzzled by the fact that he knew my thoughts. As he turned his head and looked back out to the ocean, I did note some lines of silver in his hair and beard which brightened slightly by the light of the moon. The lines on his forehead and around his eyes, told me he had seen much suffering and hardship. His build was of good size and for some reason he wore clothing more appropriate for summer. Like me, the chill did not affect him. The moon was bright, and shone so strongly on the man that he appeared to almost glow in the night.

"Who are you?" I asked this man in my dream.

"My name, if it means anything, is Nathel."

"Nathel," I repeated.

"Yes. Remember that name please. I have brought you here through magic. There is so much I wish to talk to you about, but not this night, there will be time later."

I looked at him in an odd way and then shrugged my shoulders. This was a dream and in a dream anything could happen.

"We must not waste our time here tonight. Tyndall and Almonesson will know who I am. Tell Tyndall that I have the key and it will open the door to the room below the west tower. It is the room with a horse with no nose. Repeat this for me please."

I did and he smiled. This was not the most outlandish dream I have ever had, but it was one of the most lucid.

"Do you know how long you have waited to find me?" he asked looking back across the ocean. "I have been here waiting for you for a very long time as well, longer than you'll know. We have been searching for each other, you and I, though you feel lost. Don't worry we'll make it all right."

"You know of my troubles then?" I asked.

"Marc," he paused, "you believe your troubles as great demons when they are not. There are troubles ahead of you that you cannot even comprehend. The dukes' anger is nothing. There will be an end to it all. They have made sure of that. Happily and for the better of all."

In the distance a bell chimed four times.

I was going to speak to him again, but he spoke before I could.

"So soon," the disappointment was apparent in his voice. "That is the bell from the town of Ihrhoven. I have to send you back. You cannot stay longer, good-bye my friend."

As everything began to fade, I noticed blood, velvet black, flowing from a wound in Nathel's chest. I tried to stop myself from leaving, but found I had nothing to grasp on to. Smoke billowed before my eyes, and then suddenly there was fire.

* * * * *

My mind saw the fire once again, close at hand, and I tried to move. It was as if I was reliving my earliest memories of the kingdom. As before, the hands held me down.

"Easy Marc, easy." My vision cleared further and I saw Rouke leaning over me, pinning my shoulders to the stone floor.

"You're in Tyndall's study, please be still, or you'll knock something over and then we will be in trouble. He'll return soon."

"Well, get off of me you oaf, I want to sit up." Had so much time passed? It was just moments ago I was in my room fighting sleep.

Rouke put his hands under my shoulders helping me sit up. I had very little sensation in my feet, I rubbed my hands together trying to bring feeling back into them. I shivered as I sat before the fire that burned in the hearth of the study.

Few books lay on the shelves that dominated two walls of the room. Scattered around were glass containers of all sizes that could have held any number of magical items. Vials sat several rows deep upon other shelves. These contained different colored liquids. There was a simple neatness to the room even though dust and cobwebs gathered high in all corners. Where the shelves ended the beams of the roof came inward to a peak some measures above our heads. In one of the upper corners of this room a carving of a dog-shaped animal sat on a shelf similar to the one in my room. Perhaps a fox, perhaps not. I coughed and looked soberly at Rouke, both of us trying to avoid the obvious.

"You know that if we had not been able to undo the latch in your room, chances are you would have been frozen by morning," Rouke said at last breaking the silence.

"Thanks for bringing me here, but you shouldn't have. I think the duke wants to do away with me. I cannot be sure if his true thoughts are coming out or the ale making him say such," I said as I huddled close to the fire. I was now beginning to feel pain in my toes as they warmed up. As the pain grew, I clamped my teeth tightly together.

"I heard what happened in Lady Wenonah's room. Um, the news is all over the castle. You must understand that Duke Almonesson does have little tolerance when he is out of sorts. If we can, we try to avoid him. With the duchess gone there is very little to stop him from drinking his ale. He always so when she is gone," Rouke whispered with haste. If any one of any higher status heard him he could be whipped for what he had just said.

He was sitting on a stool with his feet near the fire to keep warm. When he finished talking he went to the fire and pulled a pot from near its coals. After pouring part of the contents into two mugs he handed one to me. I could smell the warm apple cider even before I tasted it.

I saw, carved in the stone mantel of the fireplace, a face. This seemed not as though it was part of the mantel originally, but added by someone recently. I had seen another one like it and it took for a moment to realize there was one similar in Lady Wenonah's room on the mantel above her fireplace. My thoughts came around and realized Rouke had mentioned about Lady Wenonah's mother.

"Where is she?" I asked.

"Who?"

"The duchess."

"It's been the custom of the family since the end of the wars to spend time with King Trahune each year in the north. They help the people there repair the damage from the wars. This year was the last. She will return with many men from Croskreye and then we will not have it as hard during planting and harvest times. The duchess wants to stay there until winter ends, and then return for good. Her sister and family are there. The duke decided to stay here and work on matters of state."

We sat in silence for several moments. The pain in my feet was all but gone. The hot apple cider warmed me inside faster than any fire could. Footsteps echoed in the stairwell outside. Rouke scrambled off of the stool and on to the floor. Presently, Tyndall entered with his cloak in one hand and his walking staff in the other.

"My apology's Marc," Tyndall said, his breathing uneven from the climb up the circular steps of his keep. He put his things away and knelt beside us. Age and wear in his knees made this awkward.

"I am one of his advisers and he asked me to wait in the cold for you to arrive. He gave me no foreknowledge of his actions. If he had, I would have taken you to see him in the morning when he was sober. At least then he would have a clear head. He is sleeping in his quarters now. Lady Wenonah has not moved in her sleep in hours," he felt my hands and forehead for fever. Finding none, he stood. "Are you feeling better now? How is the cider?"

"Yes, I am fine, the chill has begun to leave my bones."

"I believe that I have to make the apology to you because the duke never will. At least not openly," I could tell that he had to keep his anger under control as he spoke. "You must understand that he is still a very good man when he wants. Not one word of what I say will leave this room. Do you both understand? Rouke you know the punishment,"

Rouke nodded.

"What is the punishment?" I asked in a whisper.

Rouke looked at me and shook his head. "You do not upset a sorcerer." To this I nodded. I sat very still while I hugged my knees to my chest. It was no secret that Duke Almonesson and Tyndall didn't see eye to eye from time to time. I knew that there was a sorcerer before Tyndall. When Jarlett died on a summer day of age, Tyndall was the next chosen sorcerer.

"I have told you before, Tyndall, and I am sure of it, I arrived here knowing nothing of your magic . . ."

"I believe you if others don't," Tyndall said as he took a seat on the stool that Rouke had occupied just moments before. His manner seemed less formal, more relaxed. "The way you looked when you came to us tells me that wherever it was, your home is far different from here. The style of your hair and other things about you has shown us that. Your people may truly not know about magic. I see no reason to believe otherwise. I am not saying you are Drenthen, but they were ignorant of it. If the Drenthen did not know of magic, perhaps there are other peoples who do not know.

"Even with the majority of the people in the kingdom, magic is at times a difficult concept to grasp. With some the skill of magic is learned quickly, with others there is just no hope for learning. If they cannot see it or feel it, then it is not real.

"It troubles me still, however, that you have no way of getting back to your people. The duke's actions tonight trouble me even more so. Yes, he does lash out at his help from time to time, and he singled you out for his anger this night. You may always stand out from the rest of us. If you do not feel welcome here, should we try to send you back to your people? Although I have grown distant from you during these past few months I would hate to lose you. I'm sure you'll agree that your death is not wanted.

"I have asked others of my profession to search for an answer. The only idea that they came up with so far would be to make a gate and then send you through. This is a good theory, but we do not have an anchor. A gate must have somewhere to go before it can exist.

"Your studies with Davlyne are of the simplest forms of our magic. You must know then that the creating of a gate is no simple matter. We know that we used gates in the past, but most of that knowledge was lost during the chaos of the wars."

Tyndall stood and put another piece of wood on the fire. He went to the wall and fixed a tapestry keeping the cold air out. Presently he returned to his seat lost in thought.

There was a long pause in the conversation. I was the one who broke the silence with a question that I had thought about since I first woke from my dream.

"Not to get too far from what we were talking about, but would either of you know how far is Ihrhoven from here?"

"I see you've heard of the town. From Davlyne?" he asked and sat back slightly when I shook my head. He scratched his chin and thought for a moment. "I cannot think of how far it actually is, but I would say about two and a half months riding horseback, almost six and a half to seven walking. It is deep in the Wiladene Territory, past the Kear. The first town and the first territory to fall to the Drenthen. How did you come about this name?"

I told them briefly about the dream I had that night. "... and he said his name was Nathel," I concluded.

"He actually told you about the door with the horse with no nose?"

"Yes and that he has the key."

"Did he say what I would need in the room?" Tyndall asked rubbing his bearded chin.

"No, just that. You mean to say there is such a door?"

"Yes, it exists. Why would he have that key?" Tyndall asked more to himself than to us. He looked long in the fire before he went on. "There is a room that we have not been able to enter since the end of the wars. I am not native to Croskreye, but they say there is a mirror there that was once used as a gate. The place had not been used in years, I think it was a storeroom at one time. One day during the wars, someone tried to open it and found it locked. None could gain access. It remained sealed with a spell and none knew how to counter-spell the magic. If he has the key, then he will have the counter-spell.

"The room is deep in the castle, no looking for it Rouke, a forbidden area for most people. On the door was, at one time, a knocker. A horse holding a steel ring in its mouth. Someone had taken an axe to it and the nose, ring and all, was apparently cleaved off. Very hard to find this room and hallway by accident. You have to actually know where your going first.

If he has the key, he can open it. Pity he didn't tell you the counter-spell. We may have had a key fashioned and be able to open it."

"What would be so important as to keep it so?" I asked.

"I cannot even begin to guess," he drank again from his cup. He took his boots off and placed them by the hearth. There was a second pair there and I recognized my boots. Rouke must have taken them off my feet when they brought me.

"That's odd," Rouke said. "Wasn't Nathel the commander who died near the northern shore?"

"He was. He was the king's commander, his champion. They say that he was the last one of the kingdom to die at the hands of the men from the north. Some soldiers saw him fighting with two of the Drenthen. They fought the last battle on the ocean side of Ihrhoven as the Drenthen were retreating.

"That's where I talked with him!" I said loudly. "I was sitting beside him near the oceans' and he cliff."

"That is near the place that the ships first landed when they entered our kingdom. It would seem only right that the last battle would be fought there on the cliff." Tyndall stood and began to pace back and forth rubbing his beard with one hand, his drink held in the other. This helped to focus his thoughts. He drank a little from his cup before he went on.

"Nathel killed them both, but they wounded him so that he fell from the cliff to the ocean below. The waves washed his body away. What you saw, be it true enough, was his ghost."

"No, this cannot be. I talked with a man. No ghost. There was blood on his side however," I thought a moment and shuddered making a face. "You believe I talked with a dead man?"

"Yes. Possibly. Your dream is a strange one. You may believe it is just a dream, but from what you have said this dream might be more than that. Dreams normally don't take you someplace. He more than likely used magic. If that is the case, it's not really the dream itself that is strange, it's the type of the magic that he used. I have not heard of it being practiced since before the wars. So much has been lost. The lore of spirit-dream was among many arts lost.

"Let me try to explain briefly how such magic works. It is part of the spirit magic which falls under healing magic. If I were to die, and my spirit was to stay on this earth, and did not go to the heavens, I still might be able to do some types of magic.

"Spirits have been known to talk with the living by finding their living souls while they sleep. Some loved ones, or friends of those departed, have claimed to have experienced this. Visiting them in their dreams. Of course, the one that has died must have had a good understanding of the magic of the spirit-dream. It is a hard spell to learn, but is easy and simple to do once you know how. It's generally taught to adepts after they finish their apprenticeship.

"Nathel was not the type of man who used magic. He was a commander of troops. If I remember correctly, he was one that scoffed at magic. He knew some, of course, very little actually, but commanding was his calling and what he loved best. King's champion he was for a time."

"Can a ghost learn to do magic?" Tyndall asked himself as he began to pace again. "I have never thought on it, but I would have to say no. I do not believe so. Perhaps it was something he had picked up from his travels, but that is doubtful also. Again, magic such as this is a subject for students in guild houses. He would have to do almost two years schooling in order to learn the basics of such spells."

"Perhaps he learned it from his blood-brother," Rouke put in. Tyndall stopped and looked at him. He shook his head and continued.

"That could be so, but they traveled so much, in one territory and out the other. And they were always fighting. There was very little time to sit and study. During the winters when they rested, I doubt he would even convince Nathel to pick up a book. It was a shame that he couldn't have inspired Nathel with some of his own magic. However, if anyone could have taught Nathel, it would have been his blood-brother," Tyndall said as he folded his arms across his chest. Cradling the cup as he did so.

"Who was his blood-brother?" I asked not sure of the story they were speaking of. Davlyne had never spoken to me of such.

Tyndall drained the last of the cider from his mug and Rouke spoke before he could answer.

"Kalendeck, of course."

Chapter #9

I didn't move. Sitting before the hearth, with my legs in the warmth, I stopped with my drink half to my mouth. I looked at the fire over the rim of my cup and felt a chill up my spine.

"I remember that name," I said softly as a log snapped in the fireplace. When I noticed that none of the others heard me, I said it again. This time a bit louder. There was a definite look of unease as Tyndall glared at Rouke.

"I remember that name, it was on a book I had once. Before I came here."

"Are you sure?" There was a bitterness in his voice and he tried to catch Rouke's eye to no avail. The boy had his head bowed as if he had just broken a treasured vase.

"I am. If there is anything that I remember of my past, it is this name." Closing my eyes I spelled the name out for them and Tyndall nodded.

"You know of Kalendeck then."

"No, it's just his book."

"Describe it to me," Tyndall said taking his seat and leaning close, his cup held tightly in his hand. Rouke drew nearer also.

I covered my eyes and brought my hands to my forehead. I pressed the flat of my palm against my eyes and looked at the flashes of light I saw there. Frustration creased my brow, as images shimmered in the darkness of my eyes. In the desperation that followed I felt helpless because I had no control over these images that came to me.

I found that my mind was unable to grasp on to anything and hold it for any length of time, the visions would come and go like leaves caught in a dust devil. The outline of a huge oak tree suddenly flashed in the darkness, as if struck by lightning, and quickly dissolved to nothing. Was it better to let the images come and go at random? I had to find something solid to hold on to. Somewhere to start. I searched my mind, but found nothing.

I thought back to that name, Kalendeck. Slowly an image began to form in my mind and held on to it tightly. Suddenly the book was there. I studied the book I had only seen a few times and picked out the details the best I could.

"In my mind I see a book. It's thick, over three hundred pages, bound with worn leather and brass, I believe. On the front the word 'KALENDECK' is inlaid in the leather with gold. That is all that I see."

"Where is this book?" Tyndall said intently.

"I see it in candlelight and also in fire, not in a fireplace, but fire all around the room. The room is on fire. There is ivy on the walls. The book is not burning. There is blackness before me, and I fall through. The book came through with me, but I no longer have it. It is lost."

When I finished, my brought my hands down to rest them on my knees. I trembled slightly as if I were cold, and moved closer to the hearth. Blinking, I brought sight back into my eyes. I quietly looked back and forth between Rouke and Tyndall with calm eyes.

"Do you remember where you were at when this happened?" Tyndall asked.

"No. All I remember is the fire." As I finished somewhere in the castle a bell rang only once signaling the first hour after the beginning of a new day.

Tyndall let out a sigh. "Rouke," he said, and Rouke straightened where he sat near the fire. "I know the timing could not be worse. I did not get an evening meal with Lady Wenonah being taken ill. Go to the kitchens and get some food and bring it here. Hurry back. This might be a long night."

Rouke jumped to his feet, bowed quickly to Tyndall, and departed. With his boots left behind, warming near the fire, he would have to run down the stairs of the keep and across the frozen cobblestones of the courtyard barefoot.

"I am not sure what we have here, but it is very mysterious. A book written about Kalendeck you say? Who would do such? Most books we scribe in Land Streth, where guild masters teach our magic. No one has, of yet, undertaken the task of writing thoroughly about the wars. It's mostly common knowledge. Everyone knows what happened. Each royal household has their own Chronicler, someone to keep a record of the day's business and important events. There would be very few people away from Land Streth who had the time or resources to create such a book.

"Now, your seeing the book could mean a lot of things. It may even help in finding out who you are and where you are from. I might be able to make you see what is around you with more clarity. You have remembered that instant, perhaps this is the beginning of your memories returning. A crack in the wall, an anchor to hold on to."

Tyndall brought his hand up to his chin and thought deeply for many moments.

"You described . . . falling through blackness. I believe that could only mean that you have fallen through a gate, because you left the place that you started and ended up falling from the mirror in the hallway here. That is, we are assuming that the vision that you have seen is the last one you had before you came here. Gates were for travel, but it was always dangerous so we've stopped. Gate creation is a branch of stone magic. The mirror is a created mostly from sand. Putting certain spells on it creates a stable passageway that can link one mirror to another. Unstable at best and very hard to control. Also, gates have to remain balanced. If something comes through something of almost equal size and weight has to return, usually. There might be ways around this, but it is what we believe.

"The only person known to make such a gate work with any kind of accuracy, in my lifetime, was Sorcerer Cinnaminson. He's been dead for a number of years now. He saw the end of the wars and perished the next spring. Since then, there is no one of his caliber to create such a thing and make it work successfully."

"How did you get here?" Tyndall shrugged his shoulders. He sat back in his chair lost in a conversation seemingly carrying it on by himself. "I don't know. Perhaps one of my colleagues has perfected a gate and made it work. But if they did, why would they not tell the others about it?"

Tyndall stopped because Rouke entered. Rouke placed the tray with slices of steaming meat, cheese and bread on the floor before us, and beside this he placed another flask of cider. He took seat back on the other side of the hearth. I grabbed a biscuit from the tray and began to eat. My hunger returned with the warmth. Tyndall helped himself. Lost in thought he only spoke again once he finished what he held. Rouke looked back and forth between us. I held a finger to my lips for silence, but still his questioning looks remained.

"Not only would the making of the gate be some great and notable event, but also a book on Kalendeck. There has been no such talk of its creation. All of the scribes have been busy of late. Usually, when there is a grand work, such as this book would be, it is not a task lightly considered. There is research to conduct, questions asked. All sorts of things have to go on before the work is actually started. I've heard no word.

"There is something else there, that none of us can identify. I have talked with those in Land Streth and they agree that if someone created a gate, it would send a ripple that is felt through magic. In the past few months nothing of this nature has been felt. Perhaps, you arrived by a gate, but not by one that we are familiar with. I could never do such. The power needed is more than I can give."

The sorcerer was quite for a moment and mulled on his thoughts as he ate a piece of bread.

"Would you be able to tell me about Kalendeck?" I asked. "If he lives close enough to Croskreye I might be able to see him. is it possible for me to visit him someday? With the duke's permission, of course."

Tyndall began to smile, but frowned as I finished.

"I must not tell you any more," he held up his hand and stopped me as I started to protest. "I have sworn an oath to Duke Almonesson. I talk away like women cleaning crockery. How could I have forgotten? Whether I disagree with him or not, I cannot deify him so openly. Marc, I am sorry. I may have said too much already."

"Tyndall, you can't."

"I can, I'm afraid. There is information Duke Almonesson wanted. He said that just by giving you the name of Kalendeck it could taint the message," he abruptly stood. He found his boots and began to slide them on.

"Marc, gather your things." I did as he asked. Rouke did the same. He waited as we laced our boots and put on our cloaks.

"I will take you to your room. It is warm now and you will be comfortable. You will have no classes in the morning or in the evening. When the duke grants you an audience then you will see him. Only then will someone speak to you of this matter. You will not leave the room."

"Tyndall?"

"MARC!" And for the first time I saw his anger. I lowered my head in shame. "I could lose everything. Duke Almonesson and his family have provided for me for a very long time. They have been more than gracious. You have a name you can remember. Know only for now that Kalendeck was a great man. I will talk with Duke Almonesson and he will decide what to do. That is all I can say in this matter.

"Do you understand?" he asked. Seeing no further course to take, I simply nodded.

"To your room then. Rouke, find the commander of the watch. I will post a guard to see you have no visitors. You will not go hungry or cold. When Duke Almonesson is sober, he will learn of this." With no other words spoken we departed.

It had begun snowing during the night. A dusting of snow lay on everything. Rouke did not stay with us as we crossed the inner courtyard. With his boots sounding out on the cobblestones, he ran towards the building that housed the soldiers and Commander Terchey.

I walked to my room as if Tyndall was my captor and I were a prisoner. He was about to say more. I shook my head and mumbled a thank you.

It was not long before I heard a knock. I opened the door and a guard entered. He looked about the room and when he seemed satisfied, he left. The latch fell and the door secured from the outside.

Tyndall returned a short time later. He placed a book in my hands and without speaking a word, he turned and left. It was a thick book and from what I could tell it was about the properties of spirit magic. Taking it to the table, I drew the candle close and began to read.

I lay on the bed sometime later and slept no more that night. Oddly enough, the cat in the corner of my room had changed position. Leaning back in the corner it had a frightened look on its face. Eyes wide, back arched, mouth agape, its posture was different from when I last noticed it.

* * * * *

On the second night of my captivity as I slept, I dreamt.

Again, it was the waves that startled me to wake in my dream. Sitting up from the sleeping position, I looked at the ocean and smiled. I was thankful the ghost was quiet for a time and I could enjoy the dream. Where I sat, my feet dangled over the edge of a cliff. Snow, still unbroken or unblemished, was well over my waist. I reached to touch it, but my hand went right through the surface and it was not cold.

I heard the ghost beside me and did not turn to him as he sat, his feet also dangling over the edge.

"I've been brought here again," I said before he could speak.

"You have, but in a sense it is not all my doing. You search for something now. More than ever you feel that you do not belong."

"You, of all people, can help me with this?" I asked. Tyndall had said I should remain wary if I were ever to have a meeting with the ghost again. Like the men of the different territories of the kingdom, the ghost may also lure me into false beliefs or make me do deeds harmful to others.

I studied his form for a moment. In life he must have been a very solid man. He wore a brown tunic of simple design. His pants were of a style that was common among the living people who I have seen. No cap or covering, his long hair curled slightly at the ends. His beard and mustache, although not neatly trimmed, were not altogether unruly. He had broad shoulders, thick arms and heavy hands. About Clendenin's size.

"Marc, I note something in your voice. A bit of sarcasm is it? Do you think that they would let just anyone be the king's commander? I am a good judge of people, I had to judge them. I had to know who would turn and run in a fight and who would stay and stand. If you feel that I am not able to help you then please let me know now and I will stop."

"When you lived, was trust something so freely given?"

He leaned back slightly and looked at the stars above.

"There are few things given freely in this world, in my time and now. Trust, sadly, was usually something that you earned."

"I know that what you have done is truly remarkable," I said. "You, a ghost of a dead warrior, have brought me here, as I sleep, though magic." Uncomfortable with sitting to close to the edge of a cliff, I moved back until my legs and feet no longer reached the edge. He moved backwards and sat near with his legs crossed and his elbows on his knees. The light blue of his form shone on the snow. Here the wound was low enough on his stomach that the snow hid it from view.

"But in your mind," he said, "this does not warrant trust?"

I had to shake my head. "It does not. If you were in league with one of the other dukes, I would not be amazed. Duke Almonesson said once the others would go through many lengths to reach me. Still, not knowing the scope of magic available, this could be a hoax. If you pulled Tyndall here, he many see through the veil."

"Do I have to prove my trust to you, or to the ones that found you?" he said and in that instant my confidence faded.

"Well," I stammered, "You must convince me that you are who you say you are."

"And how will you know that? Hmm?" he sat back slightly and smiled. His teeth, almost blue in color, shone in the night. "I will tell you something about me, things that happened while I lived, some things that only I would know. When you see Lord, I mean, Duke Almonesson again tell him what I tell you and see if this earns his trust."

I thought this over for a moment and nodded agreement.

"On the night we found the Drenthen sacked the castle and village of Carfrae, I ordered the men with me to search the place, room by room, hall by hall. There was no one left alive in the village. With so few bodies of Drenthen around, it was my belief that they might be hiding deep in the castle. Hiding there, they could rush out and slay small groups of men as the men searched. Such a ploy would work for a very long time and a small number of men could, in fact, be the end of a large number of men.

"Almonesson was a young lord at the time. His father and uncle still lived and governed the lands that now hold you in its heart. He had met a young woman while visiting Carfrae one winter years prior. Her name was Lowy and she lived with her sister, Duchess Rachael, in the castle that was now empty of life. When we found the castle in this state it devastated him.

"Without haste he ran to their quarters and searched, but did not find her. When I came upon him, he was weeping for her loss. There is a locket he took that was one of hers. I told the men, before we even reached the bridges leading in, that nothing would be taken from the castle. I did not want them to profit from Duchess Rachael's sacrifice. This single piece, I let him keep. He was the only one granted to take anything from there. He wore this piece of woman's jewelry about his neck hidden beneath his tunic. Only he and I know of this.

"If you speak to him of it, he will know whom you speak to."

I could only nod my head. "Did he find the woman he loved?"

"He did. She became his wife and is Lord Farnstrom's and Lady Wenonah's mother. Duchess Lowy had left her sisters care just before the battle and eluded the Drenthen."

"What you speak of maybe common knowledge among the dukedom." Davlyne and Tyndall had spoken little of the stories in the kingdom. This would be one that was widely known.

"It would be my guess that when you speak of this to Duke Almonesson do so in private. If others knew of his break down of emotions, even in such a matter, he might be a bit upset. You've seen his temper before."

I hesitated again looking at his form.

"I will tell the duke this information. If he discredits the whole thing as hearsay then please do not pull me to this place again. I do not enjoy being deceived."

"Fare enough. The winds that speak tell me that you have heard his name."

"Whose name?" I asked.

"Whose name? Whose name indeed. Kalendeck. It is difficult to believe that you have spent this whole time in the castle of Croskreye and have not heard his name but this once." Nathel's voice was light and excited. He smiled and I could not help but to smile with him.

"Duke Almonesson has had Tyndall swear the name off or something as such. Are these people against me?" I asked half jesting. "It is the only name I remember from my past and they keep it from me. Like a hound having to find a bone that he has gnawed on before."

Nathel laughed at this and slapped his knee. "I see your humor in this, but I find it upsetting. Behind everything that happens there is a reason. He will explain it to you in due time."

"Could you tell me of him?" I asked.

"I could, but we will not have much time tonight," said the ghost of Nathel with another smile. "It would be best to listen to the living. They will tell you what you need to know."

The ghost was silent for a time. "He was the worst enemy and best friend that I ever had. Tell no one, but you see this scar?" The ghost raised his hand and I could see the jagged scar running from his forefinger and across his palm. "He has a matching scar. I did this once when his mind was in turmoil. It was to try to calm him down. Nothing could have stopped him once he got a notion in his head. Like you, he is not of this kingdom. He thought, at times, he was not bound by our customs and hierarchy. Treating a king like a peasant and a peasant as royalty. He was too good for all of us. Do not follow his same folly."

"Am I from his home?" I asked. The question burned in my mind.

"Where is your home?" he asked in return.

"I live in Croskreye."

"Well then, this is where you are from. If you cannot remember, search no further." For all his wisdom and knowledge he sounded much like Tyndall. I was starting to believe that learned people were just better at confusing others. He looked to the sky and found the moon. "The bells with be rung shortly. Then you will go. If you have more to say be quick."

"I have had another dream," I said thinking back to one I had when I was still bedridden with the injury to my leg. "There was a woman with two different colored braids in her hair. She wore a black dress and was very beautiful. I saw she had very dark eyes and seemed sad."

The bells began to ring. Their peal breaking the stillness of the night.

"That was not a vision of a woman," he said. "It was a sword." And the night faded. Try as I might I could not wake my body and slept on.

* * * * *

The following morning, when I woke to the sound of the hourly bell in the castle, Duke Almonesson granted me an audience. A page brought fresh clothing and I dressed quickly. Without saying a word he waited until

I finished. I followed him down the hallway.

As I entered the room, I saw Davlyne, and Sorcerer Tyndall were present. Davlyne stood and gave me a quick hug. Obviously she was concerned over my well-being. Tyndall nodded, but did not come near. Chronicler Thane and his young assistant Wren sat behind a desk upon which the large book lay. Pen in hand he began writing when I walked in. Wren sat still with wide eyes.

The snow outside was two hand-spans deep by now. Tapestries over the windows kept out the cold and the days light. A fire was burning in the hearth and the room lit with candles. When Duke Almonesson arrived a short time after I took my seat, we all knelt in his presence.

"My daughter is awake," he said simply. The room was warm and he removed an over cloak before he sat.

"Marc," he said looking at me and then glancing at the others. "Everyone here will drop all formalities while this discussion is taking place. I do not want anyone to feel that they have to hold back because of my status. We are here today to resolve this, to give Marc the knowledge he needs," he turned to me.

"I have kept his name and his deeds from you for a reason," he said straightaway. "I knew of your coming to the kingdom. Kalendeck told me of it the night after we discovered that the Drenthen destroyed the castle of Carfrae. He said there would be a messenger arriving this year and this year you are here. If you still say that you have no message then I must abide by this. He knew of your arrival, but I doubt he would know of your condition."

"May I ask what type of message are you looking for?" I asked.

"We have six territories and Land Streth in the kingdom. My territory, is Kahshgrance, westward of us is Obfelden, Chisemore, Spruill, Wiladene, Delfuri and then back to the northeastern edge of my lands. During the wars the Drenthen decimated the people of the Wiladene Territory and killed the ruling family. Delfuri Territory to our north suffered a near similar fate. Luckily, Lady Bessa, sister to Duchess Rachael lived and has since returned to rule.

"To this day there is no one ruling the Wiladene Territory. We wait for a decree by King Trahune. His word will be law. A new family will govern the area."

"Such a prize is much sought after," said Davlyne. She held an earthen mug before her with broth of some type which steamed. She wore her hair pulled back loosely. She listened to the duke eagerly.

"Yes," said the duke. "I have tried to stay out of the arguments. Duchess Bessa has sided with Duke Tominson to place a mutual uncle on the seat. Duke's Curwin and Lysaght are in league with each other. All are steadfast in their choices. Whoever I side with will sway the outcome. I make enemies either way, it seems."

"But I thought the king's word was rule," I said.

"The king wishes to make his people happy. In this he cannot decide."

"Is this the message you think I have?" I ask.

"It is," he clasped his hands before him on the table. "I had hoped for a way out. A messenger that would know the solution to what ails the kingdom. Kalendeck knew of the Drenthen arriving and forewarned the kingdom, you might be able to do the same."

Davlyne spoke up. "With your memories gone, we had hoped that in teaching you about our society it would jostle your mind and everything would come back. That was my task. To give you more instruction than would be given to the commoner. As of yet, you still have no message."

"Maybe if I knew of Kalendeck, and what he as done, I would remember," I said. At the corner of my eye I saw Duke Almonesson nod giving his consent to speak of him.

"Of all present, I am the only one to have met him." Duke Almonesson spoke before the others. "It was a rumor that he was not of the kingdom. Brought here by Sorcerer Cinnaminson through a gate, as much the same way you arrived. He warned the kingdom of the pending arrival of a race of people named Drenthen. The warning came too late and when the king's men reached Glenhelen there was not enough time to rally enough men to save it. The Drenthen swept westward destroying all they came into contact with. By winter much was lost.

"It was at the beginning of the third year of the Drenthen onslaught that I met him. As was common with young noble men, I served with the king's commander. He would train us and after a time we would return home. This is how it has always been done. I just happened to serve him when there was an invading army to destroy.

"Kalendeck was a great warrior. Well versed in different types of magic, he was as strong in muscle as he was book worthy. He fought, as if he knew, in his heart, that he would not die. Attack and retreat, attack and retreat. He would catch the enemy that could not catch him, he eluded them at every turn. Though they tried to kill him, they never did. He enraged Valaith-Chryn to such an extent that, some felt, the leader of the Drenthen changed his focus from conquering the kingdom to attempting to capture or destroy Kalendeck.

"I saw him in battle. Commander Nathel would, at times, try to hold him back, to rein him in, but it was to no avail. He was headstrong and resistant. Having the gift of seer magic he was able to know where the enemy would strike and usually he had a plan ready.

"You must understand that we have never been in contact with another kingdom. Ages ago, there were only the clans who lived in the land that is now the kingdom. For the longest time, there were small wars fought between families, and the Uprisings. One brother trying to usurp the other. Always bloody and messy. Our weapons are from those days. The discovery of magic was the catalyst that brought us together. We hold on to our swords and spears in the event the need arises. We teach the young men of your age how to handle the weapons to a certain extent. The kingdom has been at peace for generations.

"Until the Drenthen." said Davlyne before taking a sip of broth.

"It was toward the end of the war, five years after its beginning, when Commander Nathel took us to Welteroth. The Drenthen were weakening slowly. At four hundred strong we could have taken almost any of them. They were elusive and we were searching for them. Upon our arriving, the water came down with a foul stench that could not be removed even by boiling. It left a bad taste in the mouth." Duke Almonesson held a finger up. "It made more than one man retch. Outriders told us that an army of Drenthen were near. If they would have besieged the castle, we would have died of thirst. Reluctantly, the lord gave the order and we abandoned the town and castle."

"Kalendeck stayed," Davlyne pipped in obviously enjoying the story.

"Alone," said Tyndall.

"Yes, Kalendeck stayed. Valaith-Chryn swarmed down upon Welteroth and found it empty, but for one man. Finally, without struggle and further loss of life, he had the enemy that eluded him at every turn. Kalendeck did not resist them.

"Later that afternoon, well after the Drenthen entered the castle, an explosion destroyed, not only the castle, but half of the village as well. Kalendeck, regrettably, was never seen again. They say that he created the explosion and died in its fire."

I wasn't sure I heard him correctly. When I did understand I bowed my head.

My heart sank. For a time it seemed as if my hopes were not in vain.

If I could find, and talk to, Kalendeck there might be some way he could bring out the message inside of me. Perhaps he would know how. The only thing that I could remember from my past life was a book I held briefly written of a man named Kalendeck. The man was dead, the book I vaguely remembered was presumably burned.

All seemed lost.

Again.

"I saw, talked to, Nathel's ghost," I said. "I had a dream, a second one just last night and talked with him on the shoreline at Ihrhoven. He never mentioned anything of Kalendeck's death."

"Many men died there, some say there is a curse upon the shoreline. Whether it was Nathel may, or may not, be determined. Tyndall has told me what happened on that night."

"Marc," Tyndall leaned forward. "If this dream happens again, please ask for something else to verify that it is Commander Nathel. For us to believe we need to know with a grain of certainty."

"He told me of a place that the Drenthen attacked." I looked between them all and did not know if I should speak further. They all leaned forward as if trying to hear my words better. I would speak of the locket and say nothing else. If they did not believe me then I would reveal all I knew.

"The name, you spoke of it, Carfrae? I think. I cannot remember, but he said the whole village was dead. Duke Almonesson, he said your wife and her sister lived there, and the Drenthen had attacked, killing everyone. He had told the men with him to take nothing from the castle. You had rushed to her room to see if she lived and found nothing. There was a locket of hers that he allowed you to take. You wore it under your clothing so none could see."

I stopped speaking as I saw the effect it had on Duke Almonesson. His face was pale and his hands were gripping the edge of the table.

"Did he say anything else on the matter?" he asked through clenched teeth.

I shook my head. "Only that she was found alive. She had left a short time prior to the attack and eluded the enemy."

Davlyne sat back in obvious relief. She knew that Lowy had lived to become duchess. She enjoyed the story as she heard it first hand.

"Is this what happened, my lord?" Tyndall asked.

Duke Almonesson nodded his head. "No one else knew of the locket. For a time I did not believe what they said. I thought she had died. More than once I was ready to end it all. It was madness for a while and anything could have happened. Kalendeck is the one that gave me hope. The man who took the lives of so many Drenthen could not let a man of the kingdom take his own life over the loss of a love. This is the debt that I have to repay. If he still lived all that I own I would gladly give him."

* * * * *

Servers brought a meal at midday and I ate better than I had in a long time. With each passing hour my mind became more and more at ease. Duke Almonesson's manner lightened. He waved off the wine and ale, remaining content with chilled water.

I learned as much as I could from those gathered. Davlyne, no longer reined in by the duke's command, spoke very openly about the kingdoms history. Her whole manner changed as if she lifted a veil. She was very happy and excited. The stories she told were loud and light-hearted. Obviously, she enjoyed the heroic, romantic, and humorous side of Kalendeck's life. There was never any mention of a woman who Kalendeck was romantically involved with and I did not ask.

Tyndall spoke often of the magic that Kalendeck new. Many knew he was well versed in the Book of Harms, he used its fighting spells often. Beyson only had a few pages that were old copies from the book. The complete book was lost during a battle at a place called Tannahill.

They spoke of Kalendeck solving a riddle called "Cinnaminson's Lament". This was a riddle the sorcerer had given his students to try to solve. It involved a bit of a poem:

"In a forest none have seen,
Under a sky of blue and a glade of green,
Droplets form on a rose petal from morning dew,
This is the last gift she gave me.
And I know this gift to be true."

Davlyne grew silent when Tyndall said the poem. The answer was, presumably, the last breath of Cinnaminson's true love captured in a crystal. It seemed simple enough, but Davlyne was deeply saddened by its remembrance.

I was anxious to return to my room to write down what I have heard in my journal. Thane, did not want me to copy from what he had written. It would mean that I would have to touch his book. Tyndall and Davlyne said they would sit with me as I wrote the tales down in detail.

It was after the meal that Duke Almonesson dismissed himself to spend time with his daughter. This spell had been one of her longest yet. She was taking soup and regaining her strength. The effects of her spells did not last long once they were over. She would be walking again soon.

* * * * *

Duke Almonesson was weary and upset as he climbed the stairs to his private chambers. Although his daughter was awake and healthy once again his thoughts were dark. In frustration at the turn of events, he growled deep in his throat.

Against his wishes the serving boy spoke to Marc the name of Kalendeck and now all that he planned was gone as if it never was. The message, when and if, it came, would be muddled. Tainted by a name he wished on some days that he had never heard.

How could a friend such as he stir the waters causing unknown ripples in his life still? So long dead that many thought him as a legend yet his influence reached well beyond the land upon which his ashes lay.

Almonesson could have the serving boy lashed. The thought crossed his mind more than once. As explained to him by Tyndall, it was an accident, a slip of the tongue. The serving boy, upon saying the name seemed to instantly regret it. Tyndall did not build it up, as was his way, and as Tyndall told him of this he could see no wrong doing on the serving boys part.

His servants were busy elsewhere this evening, he had made sure of it. For the moment he had found peace. A drink would dull the activities of the day away and ease some of the burden from his shoulders. Too many memories of days past came to new light.

Almonesson was alone on the stairs and let himself into his own chambers. The candles were always lit as was the fire in the fireplace. His place, the rooms that gave him serenity, were thankfully empty.

He closed the door silently and drew the latch tight. He needed this solitude.

The cloth over the book lay untouched. He removed it cautiously. He had not looked upon the thing in over a month. He should give the thing back to Marc and have it over with. All secrets free, all shadows gone.

Taking the book to a recess that offered candlelight and a place to sit comfortably, he opened the cover. On the marked page, the page where the words had once ended abruptly and continued no further, there was more writing. The strange neat writing filled five more pages. Placing the green ribbon aside, he read.

* * * * *

My classes did not resume and the pattern that developed since the Day of Turning was forever broken. The next morning when I arrived in the teaching room, Tyndall was there with Davlyne. She placed her books to the side in an open chest. She would be leaving soon before the ice in the Applegate Straits stopped the ships from traveling.

In the winter the island of Rossmoyne was effectively cut off from the rest of the kingdom. Later, as the weather grew colder, people could travel by foot or by sleigh across the solid ice.

On this day, and the next, they told me in as much detail as they could, of the tales of Kalendeck. Tyndall had a list of notable events broken down for each year.

I wrote quickly, knowing the importance of the information I was given. By evening when we stopped, my hand hurt, and before I slept I placed it in a bucket of snow to help ease the pain.

The next evening, when they finished with the tale of Welteroth and Nathel dying in Ihrhoven, I placed my pen down and rubbed my hand.

"And there you have it, Marc," said Davlyne sitting back in her chair slightly. Her hand tapped mine. "All that Tyndall and I know of Kalendeck and Nathel is now penned in your book."

"I have spoken with Duke Almonesson and I believe that what you have is the most written pages about his life."

"And death," I added somberly.

"Yes, and his death," Tyndall echoed. "Think about what you have now. In your mind try to remember what you can, and possibly the answers you seek will come forth."

I nodded and looked between the two.

"What have you learned in your studies?" Davlyne asked.

"You have taught me much in the time we have spent together. I will not forget the lessons."

"Have you learned any spells?" Tyndall asked.

Without hesitation, I began a spell. Calling forth the aid of Helfrick, in the words and syllables that they taught me, I asked the magic to remove the light from the room. Before I gave the word of execution, I let the spell build in strength around me. When I spoke the word, as the last sound left my lips, the room became dark.

"Very good," said Davlyne in the silence. I heard her sniff a little as the smell and smoke of the unlit candles bothered her nose. "Can you bring them back?"

I spoke a second spell and when the word of execution was given, the room brightened once again. I felt the tingling in my chest and brought my hand to my head. The pain in my head and chest pulsed with the beating of my heart.

"The price has been given," I said.

They looked at each other and nodded. Davlyne could not help but to smile.

"You're on your way then, I see."

"There are other spells I know, almost. The one with the candles I have had the most success with."

"Do not let your spells build to a great extent," said Davlyne holding her hand up, palm outward. I noted the caution in her voice. "If you are not going to use the spell, speak the word to cancel it out. There was a man in the Chisemore Territory who let his spell build for too long. The price given was too great, and he died."

I nodded.

She stood, went to a table, and brought back him two pens and a book. She placed them on the table before me. Resting a hand on my shoulder, she squeezed softly.

"You enjoy writing. These are for you. I believe you are to journey far in the years to come. Write in this book all the tales of your time about the kingdom. In years after you have settled I would love to read them. I would enjoy seeing our world through your eyes."

"You will be a missed presence in my life," I said.

"I will listen to the winds. They will bring me news of you." And it was not long after saying this she left.

*　*　*　*　*

Tyndall stayed behind after she had gone which was odd. Usually there was always something else that occupied his mind. We sat and talked for a time.

"I am leaving also," he said finally.

"You said you have the Gathering to go to." This was common

knowledge around the castle.

"Yes, I normally leave by now, but my time with you has held me back. No, I've had no regrets," he said when he saw I was about to speak up. He held up his hand and I was silent. "I will begin to prepare this evening. I must tell you that several masters of the guild houses would be very upset if I did not take you with me. Usually the Gathering lasts two weeks. I will be late, but they will have other things to discuss."

"Honestly?" I half stood from my chair. "You want me to go?"

"Yes. For those living here the curiosity of your origins may have worn off, but there are many others who would want to see you. Duke Almonesson has no issue with you going as long as you stay under my care and protection. I believe that he expects you to swear an oath to him that your loyalty will remain to the Kahshgrance Territory. If you do take such an oath, you may not take allegiance with any others. Chances are others will try to lure you away with offers of gold or status."

"I do not desire such."

"Possibly, but the pull might be strong. I say if you give an oath do not break it. I will watch over you."

"So, do we go?"

"You will need some heavier clothing."

I slapped the table loudly with my hand and he laughed.

"We will leave in three days. You should spend the time wisely. There are those about the castle that will not wish to see you leave. I know that Lady Wenonah will be most troubled when she hears of this."

At the mention of her name I knew he was right. Rouke would miss me too. To the rest I felt no close connection to. Just these two.

"In the morning seek out the tailor and he will fit you with what you need. There will be no charge for this. Courtesy of the dukedom."

"If you see Duke Almonesson before I do tell him that I am in his dept."

Tyndall nodded and stood. Filled with excitement I slept little that night. Reading the book he had loaned to me I would pause every few passages and smile.

Chapter #10

The page walked a few paces before her carrying a lantern. He did this needlessly, she knew the way to her parents quarters and the way was well lit with candles in the scones. Except for their foot falls, it was quiet in the empty hallway. He lifted the latch and the large oak door opened quietly on oiled hinges. She entered the room and the page bowed and left.

Other servers were setting a meal in her parents room. Roast duck, corn, wheat bread with a hint of dill, and pastries dipped in honey. The braziers along with the fireplace brought warmth to the room. Candles gave light to the early winter darkness. Her father was already sitting at the large oak table, reading a parchment. A measure of cloth screened off the doorway to the sleeping chamber. She had forgotten how large this room was, how it always held the scent of cedar. For a moment she was a little girl again, running down the hallway and into the room to greet them in the early morning, or to find safety from a thunderstorm.

"Ah, Wenonah," he stood and helped her to her chair. He wore a soft leather tunic that he was fond of when he was younger. Beneath this was a heavy white shirt worn to keep the chill off. She had not seen him wear this particular garment in years. His beard and hair were freshly trimmed and combed.

"Father, this is quite unexpected," she said searching his face for reasoning.

"Yes, I know. It has been some time since you and I have had a chance to sit and eat quietly together. The last time, if memory is true, was when we had a picnic in the north woods."

"Ah, I remember. A picnic you call it? The outing lasted two days," she picked up her knife and fork and waited for her father. Once he sat, he began to eat his meal.

"The horse Rada."

"What?" she thought back. "Oh, yes," she burst out in laughter at the memory. Her father smiled and chucked as well. Seeing laughter in his eyes was sincerely a blessing. It seemed so long since he had known happiness outside of the wine bottle.

He bade the servants a goodbye with a silent nod and once the latch fell again, they were alone.

She started to eat her meal.

"How are things with you, father?" she asked between bites when the small talk could no longer contain the silence between conversation.

"I am well," he said taking a sip of water, wincing at its chill. "Your mother is coming home. I received word by courier just this morning."

"She is? How soon?" This was welcome news indeed. Their time north would finally be complete. She would have her mother and her brother back home and it would seem much like it was when she was younger. The castle was always a lonely place without them.

"A week, perhaps two. We must get the castle ready for their return. Tyndall is leaving soon or I would have him freeze the Straits."

"Is the task complete? Winter has just started, spring is far from arriving."

"Yes, she is home early. There have been some complications as of late."

"What kind, if I may ask?"

With the cloth napkin he wiped the corners of his mustache.

"Since the wars have been over the Wiladene Territory has sat empty and vacant waiting for King Trahune to appoint a governor. A full and ripe fruit for harvesting. Although there are a few people eligible for such an appointment they cannot decide on an outcome. Duke Lysaght and Duke Curwin have a close relative who could be lifted to this position. The story is the same with Duke Tominson and Duchess Bessa. Equally viable they could be asked to hold this position. Who should it be?"

"King Trahune must have someone in mind."

"He does, but others do not agree with him. Of the five governed territories Delfuri and Spruill want their chosen man to govern. As does Chisemore and Obfelden. I alone could defy them all and toss my lot with the king's choice. If there was a survivor, someone of proper linage, of the Wiladene Territory there would be no issue. I alone remain undecided."

"It shouldn't matter, father. The king's word is rule."

"I understand this, but if I side with the others it could sway his decision the other way. He would be forced to go with whom we choose to avoid bloodshed."

"I have never known you to go against the king before," she said and knew this is where his heart lay. He looked to a window, but a heavy tapestry held out the view.

"It is where my loyalty stands. Without his graciousness we would not be as well off as we are. Not just us as a family, but the whole territory would suffer," he said after a moment's pause.

"And the consequences if you stand against the others?"

"Then I would have their wrath to deal with. Subtle as it could be, they could put a stranglehold on us that might be worse. Shipments of goods could be delayed. Small raids of men could produce more chaos and disruption. The people hoard their spices more than I can hoard my gold."

"I see," she said laying her fork and knife on the tabletop.

"We are in a difficult position at this point and time. Things around the kingdom may become unsettling soon."

"So, mother is returning from Land Streth to avoid harm."

"Yes, if people of another territory captured her then my hands would be tied. I would have no choice, but to concede my vote for her safe return. However, she is safe within my borders under heavy guard. We need not worry."

He ate more, but she could clearly see the food had lost most of its flavor. He finished his duck and pushed his plate aside. Wiping his mustache once more he sat back and picked up his water.

"There is someone else I worry about. Someone dear to you. That might be used as a pawn in the time ahead."

She thought for a moment, but no one came to mind.

"Marc," he said for her.

"Marc, but . . ."

"Word of his arrival has reached far beyond here. To others, the importance of his arrival is beyond compare."

"His mind was blank when he fell through. He knows nothing. Not of our culture, our customs, let alone our politics "

"I know this. Beyond our borders his image has grown. You know how rumors and hearsay are. They say that he is Kalendeck reborn. Some say he is Drenthen and is the first of many. I look at him and see they are so far from the truth. Simple people and commoners they all are.

"I must reply to the people in the western territories, Duke Lysaght in particular, as soon as possible. He feels Marc could help him against the king. He feels that if Marc were on his side then none would dare to oppose us. There might be some hidden talents Marc has that have not been awakened. He could use this, for a time, to sway others against King Trahune thereby forcing him to concede. Lysaght's uncle, and his lineage would rule Wiladene territory hereafter. Lysaght would like Marc in his castle in Shirrow at his earliest convenience."

"What will you say to them? That he is harmless, that all he enjoys is reading and writing," she sat back in her chair, the remnants of her meal forgotten.

"I shall say that he is harmless, yes, but they want me to send Marc to them so they may see and judge his worthiness with their own eyes."

"Will you send him?"

"No. I shall not. I will tell them that upon hearing his fate he slipped away sometime in the middle of the night and as of yet we are unable to locate him. I will not bring myself to lie to them," he cupped his chin in his heavy hand. He swirled the water in his mug around and around as if it were a fine wine.

"If he lives here how can you say that you cannot locate him? Either way it is a lie," she looked into his eyes searching for truth.

"Tyndall leaves in a few days for his Gathering. I have asked that he allow Marc to journey with him. Marc will swear an oath to me before he departs. The oath will be binding and under law he cannot side with anyone else. I can hold off their answer for only so long. It can wait till he is gone."

She lowered her head, her long dark hair covering her eyes.

"So we will lose him? Toss him to the wolves. A banishment," she could not keep the distaste of his decision from her voice.

"Please keep your tone down," he scolded her. She could hear his anger was held check in his voice. She looked at him and knew she was wrong in her words to her father.

"For the better of Kahshgrance Territory I feel this is best," he wiped his hands on his napkin and stood. Walking to the fireplace with his glass, he absently tossed two more logs on the blaze to warm the room further.

"Father, it is the beginning of winter. We cannot just leave him out."

He came near and went down on one knee beside her chair. Taking her hand in his, he kissed it gently. In that moment she felt his strength and his tenderness.

"You misunderstand me. Marecrish, this man that they have built up in their minds, is leaving in the morning. Marc, the young man, will be leaving with Sorcerer Tyndall to go to the Gathering. Upon arriving those that are knowledgeable in magic will judge him, as the king may. They will see him for who he is and his influence will be no more.

"I understand you are fond of him, and rightly so. Mayhap, I was wrong about him as well. I could have misunderstood the magic he has. If he was born of noble birth, he would make a good husband for you. He will be well cared for when he leaves, subtly, for I shall let it be known that I have no hand in his assistance. Tyndall will see to it.

"Fortune is on our side, they know him only as Marecrish in the other territories. Here he is known as Marc. Very few people know what he looks like. He will be just another traveler with Tyndall until he reaches the Gathering. No one would try to best the sorcerer afterward, or on the trip there for that matter."

She looked in his eyes and could find no hint of deception or betrayal.

"His leaving will be best?"

He nodded. "Lysaght's people may be in the village already watching us here in the castle. He will no longer be on the field of play, as it is, if his whereabouts are unknown. I wish the man well. I really do. If he can avoid trouble and recognition then all will be well."

She looked into his eyes once more and then slowly nodded her consent. He brushed a stray lock of her dark hair aside and as he stood he kissed her gently on the forehead. It brought back memories of younger days.

"This meal was to sway my agreement?"

"No. I gave you this meal to make you understand. Your acceptance I was counting on once you saw things through."

He went to the mantle of the fireplace, picked up his drink and returned to his seat. Clearly more at ease now, he searched his plate for forgotten morsels. His smile had returned.

"There is another matter," he said. When she remained silent he went on after a long silence. Twice he was about to speak, twice he stopped as if unsure how to voice the words. "At a smithy, in a nearby village, there is a blacksmith."

Her food caught in her throat and she had to drink least she choke.

"Father . . . I . . ." she stammered.

He held up his hand and she was quiet.

"Certain things I can change and there are certain things I cannot. I will not have your heart broken. He will . . ."

"Father, he is a good man! No matter his status. I love him . . ."

He scowled at her until she stopped. Her face reddened and she looked at the tabletop stubbornly refusing to look into his eyes.

"If you would let me finish, daughter, I was telling you that I do not wish to have your heart broken. If, and I say if, I and your mother sent you away to the Chisemore or the Spruill Territories to marry some noble man, this is exactly what would happen.

She gave him a quizzical look not certain of his meaning. He looked intently over her shoulder to something that lay along the far wall.

Turning his gaze back to her he still frowned.

"The care for you runs deep in my soul. Although you are not as physically as strong as your brother I do not consider you any weaker." His gaze went to something over her shoulder again. He was about to say something further when he cleared his throat and bowed his head.

"There are things underway that we are not meant to comprehend," he twisted and released his napkin several times. "Your love for this commoner is known by me. I do not condemn it, but I am in no position to encourage it. From here on there will be no more unsupervised excursions. You may visit him, but these visits will be closely watched. I wish to meet this man so I may judge him for myself. There may . . ."

He said nothing further. She had stood quietly and embraced him with as much strength as she had.

*   *   *   *   *

As she made her way out of the village, she saw that he had stood where Rouke had said he could be found; at the wind chimes on the crest of the hill. The snow muffled her footfalls as she crossed the bridge. With her hood up her ears were warm and her face shielded from the wind. Snow fell from the edges of the bridge to the small brook that had almost frozen in the winters chill. She noticed that the Thyme River was starting to ice also.

Few ships dared to brave the currents of the Applegate Straits this late in the season. Soon it would be so clogged with ice that travel to the rest of the kingdom would be all but impossible. For a time, the island of Rossmoyne would be isolated from the rest of the world. In heart of winter the Straits would freeze over completely and the brave, or foolhardy, would cross.

A snow hawk sat in the upper branches of a tree nearby watching for any field mice that may appear. Its white feathers with their black tips stood out against the melancholy turmoil of the winter skies above it.

Traffic along the road from the town was light. The people of Rossmoyne Island tended to stay in when snowfall was this heavy at the beginning of the season. Many chose to stock up on food for the winter and only venture out for fresh game. Two separate wagon tracks could be seen, and several sets of footprints marked the near virgin snow. Traders will wait until the snows have set a month or so before they come from Westrick or Hathersage.

For the past few days, as she recovered, a heaviness was felt in her heart over what had happened while she was ill. Her meal with her father put her mind at ease on many things. Marc had busied himself about in the castle. This was the first chance that she was able to see him. She had waited for him to find her and they could talk as they normally would, but he had stayed behind closed doors.

She followed his steps up the hill to where he stood.

He must have heard her and turned to greet her.

His hair was a shade, dark against the snow and sky, that softened only because of the light brown cloak that he wore, and the lightness of his eyes. His cheeks and the tip of his nose were reddish with the sting of the winter chill.

When she drew close, they both smiled, he bowed to her.

"Please you do not have to do that when we're alone," she said as she scolded him softly and slapped him playfully on the arm. "All of the people here in my father's land all are lower than myself except those in my family. Even the young ladies of the village dare not talk to me, heaven knows why. I have no one that is my equal, my friend. Please be my friend. Talk to me as such."

"That I shall," Marc said and she smiled inwardly.

"I am sure you know that what my father did, he should not have. If you have not received any apologies yet I want you to know that any action against you was not intended. You are our guest here. Even though you were an uninvited and an unexpected one, we will not turn you away," she made her voice sound as strong as she could. With cold fingertips she brushed some windblown hair back beneath the hood she wore.

He gave her a look, bending down slightly to look into her eyes, and she saw mirth in his eyes. It was an easiness that he always had. "I understand what has happened. What is past is past. As I look back now all I see is a fathers' love for his daughter. Your father is a very great man. I do not question his actions. Your illness has him confounded, as we all are, and he is apprehensive about my being here."

He looked at her for a moment and when he finished he turned his back to her and the village. She moved forward to stand at his side as he looked out over bleak winter countryside. The overcast skies brought news of more snow to come.

"My father says that the sorcerer will be taking you to go with him to the Gathering. This pleases me. I am hesitant to see you go, but pleased that you are happy. You are happy, aren't you?" She thrust her hands into the folds of the cloak to get them warm.

"I am, but you are sad," he said. She knew she could not hide it from her voice.

"It is always sad when people leave. I can say that I will miss you. With you gone, my father will find some other means to vent his anger when it rises," She jested and he chuckled at this.

"I could search for a cure for your spells," he made his voice sound noble and compelling. "I promise you that when I return I will bring a cure for you. The Gathering is a trivial thing."

She looked at him and saw he wasn't serious.

"Do you believe that if they cannot find a cure for me in Land Streth, you will be able to pull something from your journeys?"

He placed his hand on his chest and looked skyward.

"On my honor, fair lady." He spoke as if taking an oath.

This made her smile on the inside again. He had a way with lifting her spirits.

The wind picked up. A strong breeze came from across the Straits and over the village. The chimes startled her. It was odd to hear them sound.

"Did you hear that?" he asked her.

"Yes. When I was younger, I would come here to listen to the chimes as they rang in the summer wind. With each passing year the chains that hold them grow thick with rust. The smith will have to replace them soon."

He just nodded and remained silent.

"So, you have seen my room?" she asked.

"I have." he pipped up smiling. "There were candles about and it was warm after being out for our hunt. I saw something carved in the mantel, a face or something."

"My father did that, actually," and at this Marc had to suppress a chuckle. She looked at him and laughed as he did. "Oh, he was not always so prim and proper. He says that he was a devious young man. There are several such carvings around the castle. One in my room, which was his at one time, one in the Sorcerer's Tor, and one in my parents own room. I believe he likes scarring mantels. He told me that my grandfather caught him with the chisel and mallet as he was finishing the one in the royal chambers. He was so angered by the defacing, he pushed my father to the side and has a scar on the back of his head where he hit the stone."

Marc chuckled once more.

"Why are you out here?" she asked him forthrightly. "It's frigid and twilight is nigh."

"I have almost finished the fifth chapter in the book Tyndall gave me to read on spirit magic. He brought it to me after you became ill and they banished me to my room. I will have to return it before we leave. I need some time away from that room, and the book, to sort it all out." She heard him sigh. Five chapters. He was a fast reader. It had only been a short number days since he started.

As he turned to her, she could see the hollowness in his features that had not been there before.

"I will help you, when you return, as much as I can," she said trying to sound excited. "If you need gold, I will give you what you need. If you need men to do your bidding, I will assign the best to you. I want to help you, I feel I am in debt to you, for what my father has done."

He was silent for another moment.

"I thank you for your kindness, Wenonah." It seemed he consciously had to pause to not say 'lady'. "I see your offer as an offer out of kindness. Do not take me wrong if I do not accept it at this time. If I need any help, I will let you know. What you have given me is a generous offer. Thank you."

"It is the least I can do."

There was another pause and she could feel the chill creeping in through her boots. Underneath the heavy cloak she shivered. "I have to go back. I don't want to get sick again," she said.

He looked at her as if the thought of someone being chilled in this weather had only just occurred to him. "Would you want to go in?" he asked.

"Yes, please," she turned and without hesitation followed the steps back. She heard him follow her as she made her way down to the village.

There were few people out. Smells of wood smoke played with her nose and she was about to sneeze once. In some of the homes she heard the laughter of children through the closed shutters and panes of glass.

She said nothing more to Marc and their conversation was thus until they reached the castle of Croskreye.

* * * * *

Tyndall stood at the top of the westernmost tower of the castle in Croskreye. Of the four, five including his tower, it was the tallest. He listened to the wind a few moments before bringing the bird in a cage up to rest on the stone. The snow was deep on the ledge and as some entered the cage the little bird hopped and piped loudly.

"Sing it to me again," he said kneeling beside the cage. He listened as the bird chirped a message he had taught it earlier in the day.

"Good," he said. Feeding it well, he fattened up the small bird for the last few days, it would need the strength for the journey.

He straightened and searched the skies. There was a storm to the south, caught inside the circle of winds that tightly embraced the kingdom. He could feel the moisture there. It was something he could draw upon. It was something he needed.

He began his magic. Drawing from his knowledge of water, he coaxed, more than pulled, at the heart of the storm. Like a beast it raged, spending itself upon the swells of the ocean, as if for some reason it was furious at that which had made it.

A tug, simple and neatly done, turned its attention northward. Like a tap on the shoulder when alone, the beast of a snowstorm knew it felt something. With all its effort it turned northward to find what could have done such.

Tyndall smiled after a time. The winds had changed. By evening it would be here. The bird would fly straight and true. It would be far enough away that it would only catch the outer remnants of the storm, if it caught them at all. Mayhap, the winds coming from the south would help it on its journey north.

He opened its wooden door. The bird cocked its head to one side and then to the other. It peeped twice and then took flight. Circling the castle once to get its bearing it was soon lost from sight.

*　*　*　*　*

"I have something for you," Lady Wenonah said as we walked through the main gate. She was walking slow, and if it would have been proper I would have picked her up and carried her. The guards posted there looked between us and bowed deeply as she passed.

I turned to her and she just smiled. "Go to your room and I will meet you there. I must tell Englay that I have returned."

We parted and it was not long before she knocked upon the door.

In the relative warmth of the castle she no longer wore her cloak. Her long hair lay loosely braided down her back and tied in a ribbon of deep red. She wore a dress of the same color. The hems were wet from the snow.

With her, my gift, was a leather pack that could be worn on my back with comfort. I was just going to use a common sack for my possessions. This was a welcome gift. A haversack she called it. There were ribbons of blue and green tied through a small loop of leather attached to the top. It landed with a heavy thud as she placed it on the table.

"I have placed several small sacks of coins there for you. You will need it along the trail. Spend it wisely, for the road is long and you don't know when you'll need it. The ribbons will help other travelers identify you as someone from Croskreye. Wear it so others may see it. You may find some companionship that way," she slid the pack over to me and then sat down in a chair. I took the haversack from the table and placed it to the side. I would look over it later. She lit another candle to brighten the room. I went to stand near the window.

"Thank you for the gift," I said as I cleared my throat. "I was wondering if the potato sack I have would have been able to keep me for long. Well, with what few things I have I didn't need much. You speak as if Tyndall will not keep me company along the way."

She shrugged her shoulders. "Tyndall is always distant to me. He will keep you from harm. Do not stray from the path he shows you. I know you feel all excited about traveling and adventure that you are about to embark on, but please understand that it's not as easy out there as it may seem. You've lived a very protected life in these walls."

"And I shall return to these walls again. The Gathering should not take long," I said. "I promise you. I will be back in time for the spring festival."

"Are you really happy about leaving?" In the candlelight I could see the sadness in her eyes. "I mean deep down in your heart do you want to go?" As she asked this she bowed her head and folded her hands on her lap before her.

"My feet itch for the feel of the trail underneath them. I doubt I'll get any sleep tonight I am so excited about going."

She sighed and stood quickly. Her voice faltering slightly. "I must go, my mother will be returning and I have some things to ready for her. You know Marc of Nowhere, once you set your mind there is no chance to change it. Go then, find the answers to your dreams. Stay focused on your goal. Do not stray far from us for the road back is twice as rough and thrice as long. And do not let the old fools at the Gathering goad you into things you do not wish to do. Do you have any weapons to take with you?"

"Beyson has given me a dagger and Tyndall has given me a walking staff made of ash." I brought them both from the corner where I placed them earlier. Wenonah did not look at the dagger. She did not care for weapons.

The staff she gave special attention. Her finger tips traced the engraved wolf head several times.

"It is warm," she said holding it in both hands to her chest. "Did Tyndall tell you what these carvings are of, or who made them?"

"He did say the letters carved there are spells. One for protection, one for swiftness, and a third for good health. How did he say it . . . to give you warmth when the nights are cold, to bring fire under your feet so you spend little time in one place, and so you have fire in your veins. He told me at night I can use it for a source of light. Here, watch."

I put out the candles with a simple spell.

"Do you still see?" With the sun set, and the candles out, the room was very dark for me.

"I can see, it is as bright as the candlelight."

"Hand it to me now." As she placed the warm staff in my hands the room brightened and I could see her clearly. Her eyes were wide in the light. She blinked and it looked very unusual. To her, the room was dark with nightfall. The magic only worked for the person holding the staff. With a second simple spell I lit the candles again.

"He wants it back when I return with him from Land Streth."

"And come back you must."

"I shall. I promise. These gifts I have been given should suffice. I have a new heavy cloak and fur-lined breaches and tunic. Comfortable and well made. I wish you the best of luck with your father and Clendenin."

"Oh, he knows," she looked away.

"About Clendinen?"

"Yes. I do not know how. I must have been careless," she smiled weakly. I knew she must have been in trouble with her father. "In a way he agrees. It is hard for him to accept, but he does. My mother may see it differently."

"What happens will happen. You'll see to it that Clendenin will be your husband. I am sure."

"I know." She cleared her throat and stood straighter gathering her strength. "I'll leave you then. I have grown fond of you Marc. No matter where you go always remember that this place was your first home. Here you will always be welcome." I reached for her and held her for a moment, unsure if it was correct to do so. She returned the embrace, kissed me lightly on the cheek, and was gone.

She could not hide the tears.

Chapter #11

The oath I gave Duke Almonesson was a simple one. All that was required was for me to speak a few words in his presence. Thane, the Chronicler, then penned the words we spoke on the edge of pages closest to the center of his book. I was then told to prick my finger and rub the blood across the lettering. Thane cast a spell upon the book as the words dried. The ink, with my blood, became smeared and the words were no longer legible. Some pooled and ran down the paper to the center between the pages.

"Duke Almonesson has accepted your vow and it is now binding," said Tyndall as he stood nearby. "If there is a call to arms, it is your obligation to return and fight. This is where you now hold allegiance. If another approaches you, dismiss them. You must hold the needs of the Kahshgrance Territory above all others."

"I understand," I said.

"Very well, now go gather your things." Tyndall said turning. "I'll meet you at the base of my tower," he had in his hands the book he had loaned me earlier which I had returned. It was interesting to read, but I would not finish it. Some of the spells were very complex, far beyond anything that Davlyne taught me to understand.

I nodded to Duke Almonesson and Thane. The duke shook my hand, which was completely out of character for someone of such status. I noticed that Thane did not write this in his book.

With nothing else said, I left the gathering room.

In my room I wasted no time and took all that was given to me. The books and pens I placed in the pack and synched it tight. A large leather flap on top protected its contents from the weather. The dagger went on its own belt around my waist. The over-cloak was loose and the straps of the pack went over my shoulders with only a slight bit of difficulty. I picked up the staff, spelled out the candle, and smiled at the cat on the wall. The cat was now in a shape contently licking its paw.

I had hoped Rouke would have been there to say good-bye one last time. I had spoken with him earlier in the day and had kept him from his chores for almost an hour.

The snow was coming down very heavy when I crossed the inner courtyard. With only a little wind blowing it was cold and bearable. Night had fallen well over an hour ago. It was dark, but I could still see well enough with the walking staff. It created a glow that made it possible to see a few lengths in front of me.

"Tyndall?" I said looking up the stairs of his tower.

"A moment, please," he said coming down. When he closed the door at the bottom, he spoke a few simple commands. "The tower is now locked. None will be able to gain entrance and menace with my possessions. Walk quietly behind me. Say nothing to no one as we leave the castle. We do not wish to call attention to ourselves."

I nodded.

"Here," he reached out for the staff. I gave it to him and he wrapped a piece of cloth around it. "Hold on to it here. We will need its magic, but not right now." I took the staff back and raised my shoulder up to readjust the weight to the pack. I was not accustomed to all the heavy clothing and the pack was a little heavier than I intended.

Holding the staff with the cloth stopped its flow of magic. Suddenly dark, I saw only his silhouette and heard his footfalls as he walked away.

The portcullis was up and the main gate was open. There were few tracks in the snow. Most were around the gatehouse door. The four torches kept the night at bay.

In the village I saw no one on the streets. The heavy snowfall kept them indoors. In the darkness it was easy to imagine that they ate their evening meals and huddled around their fires. They would wake to find a thick blanket of snow on the ground.

We soon passed by familiar posts that marked the loading docks. The sound of our footfalls changed as we walked on one of the piers. Tyndall stopped so suddenly at the end of one, that I almost bumped into him.

"Marc," his voice held low even though there could be no one near. "I am a sorcerer, you know this. I specialize in Stirewalt, the magic of water. What I am going to do is something I have only done four times before and have always been alone. You will have to trust me on this," he turned back to face the Applegate Straits.

Taking his staff he reached down and dipped the tip in the water. Bringing it out, he tapped it twice on the dock. He began to recite spells.

Snow gathered on the water before us. It collected and bobbed much like the chunks of ice I saw during my time with Nathel's ghost.

Twelve spells total, by time he finished. Breathing deep he let his breath out in a long slow sigh.

"Be sure to follow close. Do not stray far from the center of the aisle.

It reaches to Denhartog, and will for a while, it is only the width of a mans height. If you no longer feel snow beneath your feet, I hope you can swim." He waited for a nod from me and took a step off the pier to the newly formed path of ice and snow.

* * * * *

There was only one horse in the common stables in Denhartog.

"I am sorry, Marc. I thought there would be more. One more at least. Would you mind riding behind me for a while until we find another?" He shook the hood of his cloak free of snow. The horse stood tethered in a stall. His ears perked up and he whinnied at us.

"I do not mind," I said seeing no other way. "Is he strong enough to carry both of us?"

"He is." Tyndall had dropped his pack and placed his staff against a beam. Placing the saddle blanket on the horse he patted its back with one hand and rubbed its neck with the other. "I have used him for many years. The sable master has taken very good care of him for me," he brought the saddle over and began to work the tack.

It was not long until he finished.

He secured his pack on a strap of leather on the saddle. I handed him his staff after he was up. Taking my hand, he helped me on.

"Place your staff across your legs," he said. "Hold on to it with one hand and with the other hold on to the back of the saddle. The road will be a bit rugged at first. Avoid from slipping off."

The horse took my weight easily enough.

"Is it proper to take the horse with no one here?" I asked.

"I am the only one the horse will let ride," he said as we exited the sable. He went a short distance before he brought the horse around. He spoke the sing-song words of a spell and I actually saw the falling snow change direction and strike the door. When the door closed the snow fell normally.

"How was that done?" I asked.

He tapped the horses stomach with his heals and we started again.

"I asked the wind and snow to strike the triangle plate upon the door. If you are here again, look closely, and you will see a matching plate on the other door. When the door closed the two plates touched to form a square. When they did, the spell was complete. Simple magic."

* * * * *

The first day was the longest. We traveled through the night and when the dawn came it took with it the last remnants of the storm. Still, we did not rest. Tyndall spoke very little.

The skies cleared steadily until mid-day when there were only a few wisps way up. When the sun started to set, we came across a small hamlet and here, at last he reined the horse. I almost fell off feeling exhausted.

People came forward, took the horse and began to brush it down and remove the tack. It went to a stable where they would feed and water it.

We went to a small inn and servers brought food. I was thankful they were quick. My legs and thighs ached, my back hurt as did my hand where I was holding the saddle and the other where I held the staff.

Seeing how tired I was, Tyndall dismissed me and told me of a room upstairs.

The beds were no more than rope tightly woven across two thick boards with blankets and cloth. It was warm enough and I stripped down to the just a heavy undershirt. Everything I owned, I placed in a pile in the corner.

Sleep tugged at my eyelids even as I pulled the blanket up to my chin.

* * * * *

The dream startled me, if a dream it was. I heard the hoot of an owl and felt the wind in my hair. I was very tired, still. Dismissing him, I willed him away from my thoughts. The king's commander could wait another night. Letting my mind drift back towards sleep, I heard a whisper, barely audible above the wind and the night noises.

"Marc," said this wisp in the night. "You need to come north."

The darkness claimed me. I felt the tug of his magic weaken and finally disperse. Like the relief of an itch being scratched, the dream was soon only a memory.

* * * * *

Carrying no provisions, we were dependent on the coins we carried and the hospitality of the people we met. Tyndall seemed to know everyone.

For a week we traveled as best we could. There were times that we had to walk up long hills to save the horse. In each town, village, or hamlet it was the same; there were no spare horses. He did his best in bargaining, but the price was always too high or the horse too old.

The first day was the longest. The reason we traveled so long, he said, was because it was better to find a place that was large enough to shelter the horse. Being a sorcerer he was a welcomed arrival at most places and was not very peculiar about where he slept. It was the horse that was the issue. There were only certain people he would let feed and tend to him.

I could tell, though, that he had hoped the storm had covered our departure. If people watched the castle, they would not have seen us. The waves would have pulled apart the snow and ice bridge across the Applegate Straights to Denhartog. It would have vanished by time the snow stopped falling. With few people knowing of my departure he may have gone as far as to spread a rumor and speculation that I was still involved in my studies.

Even though I rode behind him exhausted that first day I did notice that he turned several times. He would watch the trail behind for a moment and then turn the horse northward.

After the first day, the journey took a simple rhythm. We would wake, wash, eat and ride the rest of the day. The inn keepers would feed and tend to the horse, as we were tended to in the evenings, and then to sleep.

This happened for over two weeks. Tyndall spoke little as we traveled. I thought that he would assume the teachers roll, and I, the student. I had expected him to reveal the wonders of his magic. Perhaps, bringing me deeper and deeper into his world and how it worked.

This was not the case. He spoke to the townsfolk and other travelers. He worked magic for them when he could and gave them answers to questions when they asked. He had no potions or powders for me to fetch, I held his staff from time to time, but this was all. I was given the simple chore of tending to the horse and more than once he degraded me in front of others. I knew this was to keep the appearance of a master and squire.

Before I slept one particular night, when his words by day had been notably harsh, he spoke a single word. If Tyndall traveled with a simple farm boy or servant, people expected such comments of shame. It was a ruse to show that Marecrish, the man who had fallen through the mirror, must still be in the grand castle of Croskreye.

That night before sleep pulled me under he spoke a single word. "Sorry."

I raised up to look at him, smiled, and then lay back down. Nothing more needed said.

* * * * *

Two days later, after we finished our morning meal, he sat in his chair and did not make a motion to move. We were in a town of Eilenburg. It was one of the bigger villages, almost the size of Croskreye or Westrick. The hall we ate in was large and could possibly seat over fifty people. There were traders, common workers, and laborers going about their business. Most had a sip of wine or mead to start their day. A practice I saw was common in the larger villages.

A serving girl came to clear our crockery. Tyndall paid her and still we sat. Usually he was the first to rise and I followed snatching a few morsels from my plate to eat on the way.

"Is everything all right?" I asked eventually. He nodded and leaning back, he placed his foot on his knee, and waited. I sat back and softly drummed my thumbs on the thick oak tabletop.

Had there been more people waiting for a place to eat I believe we would have been, politely, shooed out. As it was, the morning crowd was starting to thin.

A group of merchants entered. In finer clothing and neatly primed, there was a way about them as they walked to their table. Like a rooster in a pen of hens, they all strutted as if on display. I watched them for a time as they folded their napkins and cleaned specks off their table.

Turning I noticed Tyndall was watching me. Presently a second server came over and wiped our table with a damp cloth.

"Are we waiting for someone?" I asked.

"In a sense, yes. I am waiting for someone," he folded his hands upon his lap.

"Is it someone important?"

He looked at me and sighed. "I am waiting for you. It has come time for you to make a decision. We are sitting in a village that is, in essence, a crossroad. Travelers, when they leave here, have two choices to make. They can take the road west that will take them directly to Land Streth. On horseback it would take a little over three weeks. Or, they could choose to take the northern gate. If they did, their travels would take them to the border of the Kahshgrance Territory to the people of the horse, the Delfuri Territory. The same route, if taken, then goes directly across that land, through the Kear Forest and to the Wiladene Territory. You can reach Glenhelen and Ihrhoven then."

"You've never told I had a choice to make. I was going to return to Croskreye after the Gathering and prepare for that journey. We need to get to the Gathering, you've said."

Leaning forward he spoke softly. "I know what I said. Others, and not only those who study magic, would be upset if I do not bring you there. You are expected. You have bound your word to Duke Almonesson, what better way to keep it than to remove all forms of temptations. They may stop at nothing to get you. They have done unsavory things and dismissed them in the past. I think that even with you with me it may get dangerous. There is only so much I can do to protect you."

"Really?"

"Marc. If one duke sees you as a way to strengthen his cause then that will be a threat to, not just one, but two of the other dukes. Duke Almonesson did not wish to use you in this manner. Taking you with me to the Gathering was a risk. He allowed this, because he knew, given the chance, you would go elsewhere."

"Won't they look for me? I mean, even if we part and I go north." I whispered. "If someone tries to take me, I can use the dagger, haphazardly. I would likely cut myself."

"Few know of your dream and visits with the king's commander. Go to him. It is what he would have wanted."

"It is what Commander Nathel would have wanted?"

"No, Kalendeck. Remember, above all else, you need to find out the truth about him. You still seek the answers to your questions," he said.

I looked at him for a moment and nodded my head.

"I have enough to purchase a horse, if I can find one."

"Save the coin," he held up his finger in caution. "Save it for when you truly need it. It is winter, stables cost and grain costs. You will no longer have the generosity others give me. If you walked, not an easy task, but not all that difficult, those that might be watching you will not suspect it. They will think you just another simple traveler and dismiss you."

"A simple traveler I am," I said and leaned forward to hear him better.

"If we part ways this day and you go on this journey it will be a year, at least, before I see you again."

I nodded and shrugged my shoulders. Excitement was building in me.

"As you travel," he went on locking his fingers together on the table before him. "You will tell people who ask that you are on a mission for Duke

Almonesson. You have books, pens among your possessions. If you tell them that you are a scribe searching for some answers on the duke's behalf then almost everything you can explain away. Do not give this information straightaway."

"I must only tell them if need be?"

"Yes. If you appear overly friendly then suspicions may arise. Stay distant from others. The more you listen, the more you will learn. It is what I tell my students."

"Here," From a pocket he pulled out a piece of metal a little larger than a coin. "This is a seal given to travelers on business for the duke. He gives it to people he can trust. You can apply it in this territory to get meals and shelter. Stay to the common halls, not the inns. Use it sparingly. Do not over use it in one place or some proprietors may become suspicious. If someone is traveling with you keep it hidden. Return it when you can."

"Thank you, Tyndall," I said catching his hand in mine as he gave the token to me. I had wanted my freedom, but not with so much generosity.

"If it were not so important that I go to the Gathering, don't you think that I would be there with you? This is a riddle I would love to see the answer to."

"And you may still," I said.

"Also, I have had my suspicions about this ghost. To me it does not sit right. There is something amiss. Do not tell him that you are on your way to see him until you are almost there.

"And when you reach the Kear Forest, mind the kear trees. They flower year round with large white flowers with many layers. Those that have come into contact with them learn to stay away. Their vines grow outward many lengths away from their trunks. If you disturb them, they coil back to the tree. Barbs on the vine will bring you with it. More vines will entangle you until a solid egg forms. It would mean your death. Stay on the well-traveled paths and do not stray."

He stood and gathered his cloak and staff. "Now, go boy," he said in a gruff voice that was louder. He swung the cloak over his shoulders. "Fetch the horse. Don't dally."

I gave him a knowing wink and took up my own pack, staff, and cloak.

"Near the stables turn right," he whispered. "The street with the markets will take you to the road north. Find it and be gone. Return when this tale is over."

Pretending to fix a strap on his cloak, I embraced him for just a moment, breathing deep his scent. With nothing else said I left.

* * * * *

By the end of the first day on my own I was very tired. The road was well-traveled and the ground was frozen. As much as I did not want to, I brought out the token that Tyndall had given to me when I reached a town near twilight. I was given a place in the common hall at no cost to myself. Like stalls for animals, these were simple places that provided a place in out of the weather for those traveling. The straw and reeds were thick on the floor. Children ran back and forth in a large central area that the stalls ringed. From an alcove near the doorway they gave me a bowl with weak soup. It was so watered down, but even with just a little stock, the broth was still good and flavorful.

I opened my book to the next blank page and in the lantern light I began to write. When I finished I had only written a few lines. It was all I had the strength for. It would have to do for today.

I would miss Tyndall. Strong and resilient in his own right, I wondered what he did this night, which common hall he slept in, or whose table he eat at. Slowly, I was leaving everyone I had met since I arrived here until I was alone. I did not mind it. It was a welcome thing.

Riding on the back of the horse left me sore. Even after two weeks there was no ease, no feeling that my body adjusted to the day long torture that I had put myself through. Walking was a welcome relief. I could deal with tried and sore feet better than I could the aching back, cramped legs, and stiffened joints.

Placing everything back in my pack, I lay back and used it as a pillow. I watched light from the fires dancing on the rafters above me. In my head I went over the names and faces of those I knew. There were things that I wanted to ask the ghost. If he brought me to the shoreline, this night I would ask him. I closed my eyes and waited.

* * * * *

I found that traveling with small groups of people was a lot better than walking alone. Each morning I would wake and listen to those in the common hall. The people heading north would ask on the conditions and layout of the road ahead from those that were going south. We exchanged information.

At first I did not understand why they walked at a slower pace. I could, on days that were clear and crisp, travel a bit faster than most and make it to the next village well before they did. But these days wore on me and I was very tired by their end. If it were warmer out, I could continue on and sleep somewhere in the countryside. Now, however, I had no choice but to stop in the villages at the end of the day. It would be the death of me if I tried to continue in the winters chill.

Twice I tempted fate. One evening, stopping in at the common hall, I found it crowded. I did not mind the conditions of some, but as crowded as it was thieves could take my possessions and be gone before I knew. I enjoyed having my own space, small as they sometimes were, when I slept.

These two nights when the moon was near full, I ate the simple meal offered and did not stay. The staff I had with me, the staff of ash, gave me light to see and also created some warmth.

When dawn broke I was at the next village and slept fiercely. Waking well after midday I took off again. The next day at sundown, as I prepared to leave, a storm arrived and in the wind and ice it would have been folly to journey on. For a day and a half it raged. I watched with others as the snow piled deeper and deeper. When it was almost knee-high, the weather changed. Although the storm was over, the falling snow only lessened. It continued till morning.

This was a good time. The people had grown bored just sitting there and waiting. I mentioned to a man who this is what happened at the battle of Thumwood and his stories began. Others chimed in from time to time and by the day's end I had many new insights on that battle.

Davlyne told me that the in the days before the fall of Carfrae Kalendeck had killed many Drenthen soldiers in a fierce battle just before a heavy snowstorm settled in the village of Thumwood. Had Commander Nathel traveled elsewhere the storm would have caught them unsheltered. Because of Kalendeck many Drenthen were dead and they were close to shelter. When they left the found the village of Carfrae had fallen and Duchess Rachael perished.

This is where Commander Nathel had come upon Lord Almonesson in the quarters of his wife, Lady Lowy. I knew this, but did not say a thing to the others. If I did I would have betrayed Duke Almonesson's loyalty.

I was up late listening to the stories.

The next day when we traveled, the trail was just a pathway and we followed the tracks of horses which had gone ahead.

I stocked up on supplies because I was in sight of the border. My pack was practically brimming with dried or salted meats. It was the last chance I would be able to use the token that Tyndall had given me. I used it wisely.

It was on this day, well after I heard the midday bell peal over the countryside, that I crossed under the archway in the border. This massive wall, as high as the one that ringed the castle at Croskreye, was all that marked the boundary between Duke Almonesson's Kahshgrance Territory and Duchess Bessa's Delfuri Territory. The gates were open and there were no guards posted. People and their goods were free to travel back and forth across the borders without any type of hindrance.

* * * * *

Kalendeck and Nathel were great heroes of the kingdom, and the people told many tales in honor of their name. Like a shadow, Kalendeck was almost always at Nathel's side in battle. Blood-brothers brought together by the stroke of an enemy's sword, their deeds were legendary. But, they were not the only two that fought.

In his command there were many men and they spoke highly of Sablich, Laensey and Hansgrohe. Their names and deeds were almost as legendary.

Sablich fought bravely with Nathel until the second year of the war. He was then pulled aside and given his own men to command. They saw some of the fiercest battles. Sablich is still living and is now the king's commander, the position Nathel held until his death. He lives in Land Streth with his wife and several children.

Laensey was a commander from a territory to the west that traveled unseen past the enemy to Ihrhoven and destroyed their ships. Tyndall spoke to me of his deeds. His bravery and courage of his ordeal were often praised. He lives still. After the fighting was over, he returned home and to this day commands the troops in that territory.

Hansgrohe was with many men as they traveled in the mountains near his home. With their skill with the bow and arrow he and his men were able to hold the Drenthen from their village and keep them from the summer pass.

There were many more. Each village and hamlet had their favorites.

Evenings, when I rested, I would sit a while before I ate and write in my book the tales I heard that day. Usually just one page, sometimes two.

While waiting for the ink to dry I would eat my meal. Writing often brought stares from other travelers. I came to realize that many of the people of the kingdom did not read or write. In this I was different from them.

* * * * *

Traveling the road was difficult at times. Days passed and then weeks and it was difficult to keep track of time. The chill of winter was finally broken and one day it was warm enough to travel without the heavy coat. Three days later the snows melted completely. The warmth of spring, still weeks away, had not begun to take hold yet.

The dreams with Nathel would come and go. Usually they took me by surprise. I counted the days between my visits to the shoreline and it was never the same. Once I was there two nights in a row. Another time it was over three weeks between dreams. I would tell Nathel the stories I heard. He would let me know the truth behind the tales. Some of them seemed far-fetched and almost too fantastic to hold true as if people made them up purely for entertainment.

More than once my morale was so low I was about to return to Croskreye. A warm bath and clean cloths would be much better than the road. How was Rouke doing? And would Lady Wenonah be going off to see Clendenin this day or not? With the weather getting warmer, I was sure the castle could not contain her. I missed our conversations together. I tried to count the weeks that I had traveled, but the time seemed as a blur and I could not remember how long I had been gone.

Tyndall would be back from the Gathering by now. An escape for him in the winter time, his chores around the castle would have almost returned to normal by now.

I stopped on the side of the road once when I felt my strength was lost. On a tree stump I sat, my pack placed on the ground beside me. My boots had chaffed my feet, this made them swell a little, and my knees ached. I leaned heavily on the staff of ash. Feeling my body rest, and my mind wander, I sat there and watched the travelers move in both directions, not wanting to get up and move north-east. I set it in my mind that when I stood again I would travel south.

"That's a pretty song," said a passerby loudly to his traveling companions.

"Hmm?" was all that I was able to say. I brought my eyes up from the dirt and mud of the road and looked vaguely at the four men who had just happened to pass by.

"Can't you hear that song?" The man said turning to me. They all stopped and looked in my direction. His smile broad and warm, his voice was cheerful and light. "I can hear it as clear as daylight."

I listened and could barely hear a flutist playing a melody ahead in the distance. The notes of the song fluttered through the trees like humming birds searching for nectar amongst spring flowers. My spirits lifted suddenly as the sun came from behind the clouds and I could not help but to smile back.

"Come, young man," said the man reaching out to help me stand. "If we don't dally we can see the minstrel playing. One is playing just up ahead." His voice was full of happiness. As fate would have it, they were heading north.

I stood and grabbed my pack as they waited. Now numbering five we traveled that day always hearing the flute being played in the distance ahead. Never much closer, but never further away. The four men I traveled with this day were very comical and merry despite the mud caked on their shoes.

One man surprised me by being able to juggle four stones at once. Each of a different natural color, but all were so smooth from use they looked polished. Red, blue, gray, and green. People walked with them and talked to him as he juggled. His feet never missing a step, his hands never losing rhythm.

One of the other men became entranced in the spells carved on my walking staff. He traced them with his fingers over and over again, balanced the staff in the air with the tip of his finger and twirled it. He held it for so long that I was beginning to believe that I was not going to get it back. When he did return it, I was sure it was warmer than before, but this was due to the brightness of the sun and the length of the day. Often the sun warmed it as I walked.

The third man talked more than the rest. He engaged me in conversation as we walked. Leisurely and without apprehension, the way he spoke seemed to invite more dialogue. So easy it was to talk with this man. Never once did they question where I was from, or who I was. They asked me my views on many things and it seemed as if I could give no wrong answer. He brought up subjects and spoken briefly of, before they went on to another. Like stepping stones in a stream, the words carried me along.

The fourth man was the quietest. His cloak of a rich deep green billowed behind him as he walked. His long legs and great strides gave him the sense of power and strength. He smiled and laughed with the others, but rarely spoke.

I enjoyed being with them greatly. So much so that I soon forgot about the troubles of the road. When I woke in the common hall the next day they had moved on without me, but I did not mind in the least. They had given me the inspiration I needed.

The Writer of All, this mythical being Duke Almonesson was fond of mentioning, must have wanted me to go on, and that is what I did. The ghost of Nathel would be there when I reached the sea, and Nathel could help me with my troubles and worries.

Anything was possible.

* * * * *

Messilla ran down the corridors of the guild house. The sandals on her feet slapping the stones loudly. Hints of sweat began to cover her brow and she felt drops forming under her tunic. She found the door to the study room and entered. Doing a quick scan of people eating and reading, she spotted the man she was looking for.

"Kopernick, Kopernick!" she whispered loudly waving her hands in the air. She went to the table and stopped. She was so out of breath that her voice did not carry over others.

"I believe I have seen the one you are waiting for. He's here in the village! I ran all the way from the common hall."

"Already?"

"Yes, a young man, his beard not yet thick. He carries a pack with a ribbon of blue and green and uses a carved walking staff made of ash. He has visited the shops, bought some ink, and last I saw he rests in the common hall."

"He'll be off by morning then." Kopernick stood and began to collect the loose papers on the table before him.

When he received word of this mans departure from Croskreye, Kopernick worked harder in his classes and at his tasks. He had told his teachers of the task that was given to him by Sorcerer Tyndall. The timing was off a little. The man had walked faster than he judged. He was just about a week too early. Kopernick wished he was a bit later as there were still some things at the guild house that still needed closure. Normally he would be in his classes another month. His year of studies would be over and he would spend a year with his family in their home in Glenhelen. They would welcome his earliness.

"Has the guild master been told of this?" He asked pushing his chair in. Without goodbyes to those around him he stood and started to leave. Messilla followed closely at his side.

"As of yet, no. I did not know if you wished to leave right away or wait. If you wish we can go to the common hall and see him. It will give you a chance to see him from afar before you meet him," she wiped her brow with the cuff of her sleeve. It was warm early again this year.

"Yes. That would be wise. I have my things packed and ready in anticipation. Once you show him to me you must return to your duties here at the school."

"To be true? You don't want me to stay with you?" she asked. There was excitement in her voice and she wished to play the cat and mouse game further.

"No, I am sure you have other things to do. Besides, there are some young ladies who were sad by the news of my early departure. They will be upset to see me leave. I have to pay them each a visit. I should have rested, the night is a long one." Kopernick winked at her. He saw her blush. She turned her head in embarrassment. She was young and he should not tease her so. He put his arm around her for a second and she laughed.

"You have young ladies desiring you?"

"Oh, heaps," he said triumphantly. "I have to stay in my studies lest they entice me away from the guild house."

"A day anything keeps you from your studies is a day your wits leave you completely."

"To be true," he said. They exited the guild house and headed in the general direction of the common hall. Walking here in the outer part of town there were few people out. As they neared the center, towards the market street, it would steadily get busier.

"You have four years left, Messilla?

"I wish." She chuckled without mirth. "I have five. So much left to learn. I want to do like you do. There is so much you can do with the talent you have. When you finish where will you go? Land Streth? Carnshaw? Welteroth? Any one of these places will pay well for an apt apprentice.

"Who is to know? Perhaps I'll stay in Glenhelen. What is your spring task this year?"

"Ugh," she groaned audibly rolling her blue eyes to the sky. "Don't mention it. They have tasked me to create a tunic of chain mail using three types of metal. The final piece should have a uniform hardness created by magic. It has to stop an arrow."

"Will you wear it when they test it?"

"Only if they are tossing the arrows at me." They both laughed.

"You'll do well, I'm sure. What weave?"

"Four in one. A simple weave," she said pausing to let a man on horseback pass on the narrow street.

"Easy enough, time consuming though. Harden half your metal to form the closed rings and then soften the ones you need for the open rings. If you use a table to lay your work on you can do at least a hands breath before you must cast a hardening spell on all you have done."

"I've never thought about that. Normally you do the work on your lap. You have to cast a hardening spell every few links or they'll split."

"That's the way they want you to think."

"We'll miss you here when you go home till next year. I'll miss your classes." The four gables of the common hall roof came into view.

"I'll be back. I have still one more year of instruction I must give and one I must receive before I become a full adept."

"That will be no problem for you."

"Oh, you think it gets easier as you get closer to the end. I beg to differ."

"Beg, beg," she jested and jabbed him in the arm.

The street door was right before them and he explained to the keeper that they were just looking for a friend.

Families, sparse few for this time of evening, had arrived earlier and settled in before night fall. Near a hearth of hot coals, evening meals were cooking or being warmed. A baby cried in need of changing. A small family dog went from group to group sniffing what it would. There was laughter and a few were drinking.

And there, sitting on a bit of straw, behind it all, sat a man with a simple pack and blanket. Dark hair, his beard not yet full, clothes of a common traveler and haversack to his side. He cradled a book on his crossed legs and he read quietly, oblivious to what was going on around him. The blue and green ribbon could be clearly seen.

"He can read. I think I like him already. You did well, Messilla."

"Who is he?" she asked.

"Tyndall did not go into detail in his note. He said I was to escort him north-east. How far along and to where he didn't say. Did you meet Tyndall when he came two years ago?"

"I sat in and listened. He has a way with words."

"That he does." With one last look Kopernick turned to go. He would return in the morning.

*   *   *   *   *

I was sitting under the shadow of an old oak tree. The leaves were coming in near full and it would not be long before the warmth of the summer sun completely woke the land out of its season of winter slumber. A breeze came by and the young grasses, who were already beginning their push upward, swayed in its wake.

I ate an apple harvested last season and then stored in a venders hickory barrel. I was minding my own thoughts, not disturbing anyone, when I noticed someone had left the road and was walking through the grass toward me. Generally, when someone openly approached you they wanted your coins or food. I did not appreciate this when it happened. Twice I had chased vagrants off. My pack and staff were close to me, so I did not reach for them, making my thoughts known. I could be quick if need be. This mans clothing looked well-mended and he seemed better off than most.

"Do you mind if I sit here and eat?" he said as he drew nigh.

"By all means, no," I said politely as I swallowed a bite of the apple. Two loaves of bread lay in my pack as well as a bit of cheese. I intended to finish these off with no help from the man who had just arrived.

The man, seemingly only bit older than I, but with wider and stronger shoulders, had a small pack of his own suspended over his shoulder and a sword hung at his side. He placed both on the ground and sat down beside them. There was a scar that ran down the length of his forearm. It looked old, nearly faded into his skin, and he may have had it since he was a small child.

"Oy, that feels good. To be off of ones feet and on to ones hams, that's what I say. I haven't sat all forenoon. I don't like to blather mind you, but this road is difficult. Very hilly, and rocky. Give me a valley to walk through any day." The man swept his long red hair away from his eyes and opened his own haversack to peer in. "Then again a person learns more on the harder trail. On the easy trail the mind is left to wonder. What luck! A bit of cheese and two loaves of bread," he rolled his sleeves up further in the warm daylight and began to eat.

"This is good weather for traveling. I've never seen a spring this early. Of course, they say that after a bad winter the summer is always good. Wouldn't you say? Where do you fare from?"

"I am Marc from Croskreye, on Ross Island." I swung my pack around to show him the ribbons. I flicked them a little, so he would note them. Now somewhat tattered and frayed, but still the colors held. He gave me a puzzled look before he went on.

"Oh, forgive me for not introducing myself earlier. I am Kopernick originally from Glenhelen. My parents named me thus after seeing my hair."

He did indeed have red hair that curled at the tips. As his name suggested, it was almost copper in color.

"You're from Croskreye, very seat of Kahshgrance Territory itself. Have you ever seen the duke's daughter, Lady Wenonah? I hear that she is very beautiful, but I've never traveled that far south and so have never seen her."

I nodded. "She steps out of her castle every once in a while. I believe I have seen her on the streets from time to time," I said. I did not wish to call attention to myself. It was better to travel as a commoner, a simple freeman.

"They say," he looked around to see if anyone was about. I thought he was going to tell me something secretive. "The man who fell through the mirror, the one with the flaming dagger, and the book of secrets, they say he still lives in Croskreye. Duke Almonesson has him imprisoned there. The lost one, this Marecrish, is a man taller than most. Women swoon over him, but like Kalendeck, he is bound to someone else beyond the kingdom."

"Imprisoned?" I asked trying to keep the look of astonishment on my face.

"Yes, if he were to cross the water. His flaming dagger would be forever extinguished. Marecrish must stay there to keep the flame alight."

"Where are you coming from again?" I asked. From experience I found that people generally enjoy taking about themselves.

"I am returning to Glenhelen to visit my family. I've spent the last year in Milhematte studying." Kopernick broke off some of his cheese and bread and ate them together.

"I passed through there last week. It's a nice village. What did you study there, magic?"

"Of course magic. What else is there? I've tried to get this thing to hold an edge," he patted the long sword that lay in a leather sheath at his side. Oddly, he had wrapped the hilt in a dark cloth hiding it completely. "I spent my last five days there working on this, trying to finish it, but I just can't do it. The cursed thing just stays dull. I'm not sure if it's me, or if I am using the wrong spells, or what. It should hold and edge that is as sharp as glass by now."

"May I look at it?"

Kopernick again looked around as if to see if any other travelers took interest. The road was empty for the most part in both directions. He pulled on the strings and removed the cloth from the hilt. Drawing his sword from its sheath, he handed it lightly over to me hilt first.

Its design was very odd indeed. The hilt was of two snakes coiling their bodies around each other. When they reached the blade their necks arched out in a steep curve and their heads were thrust back inward as if they were ready to strike each other. If alive, they would have looked at each other with the beginnings of the blade between them. The snakes were of two metals; one was copper and the other silver. The blade itself was from a metal that was as black as darkness itself. A lot of time must have gone into its making. The craftsmanship was beyond compare.

It was in a dream I remembered from my time in Croskreye. When I told Commander Nathel of it, he said that it was not a woman I saw in my dream, but a sword. She had braided hair of two colors, copper and silver, and a dark dress. I was so taken in by the sword that I barely heard Kopernick talking.

"There are only four or so of these in the kingdom. It's a replica of the sword Steelefyre, the one that he used during the wars. I am going to display it at home with my father's sword. I keep the hilt covered so I do not bring attention to it. A thief could get a high price for such a replica."

"He?" I asked unsure of who he referred to. "Who was the one who used a sword such as this?"

"Kalendeck," he said slowly.

"You've seen him with it then?" I asked without thinking as I reluctantly gave the sword back.

"You dolt," Kopernick said, and then he laughed as he replaced the sword in its sheath. Carefully he worked the other cloth on and secured it with a thin length of leather.

"I'm too young to have seen him. Surly you have heard the stories of his sword. From that look, I guess you haven't. What did your parents do with you, keep you locked up from everything in Croskreye too?"

"No, of course not. You study Tymchak then?" I asked anxious to change the subject. The name of the creator of stone and metal magic had eluded me for just a moment.

"Yes, that and a bit about water. Stone is my favorite. Two opposites, but somehow with me they just click."

"Could you look at something for me?" He had shown me his prized possession; I felt obligated to show him something of my own.

"By all means."

I reached into my pack and pulled out the journal I used to write my notes. It was work I penned by my own hand and I always wondered how another, besides Tyndall, would view it. I undid the leather straps holding the cover tight and handed it to Kopernick. Before he took them, he wiped his hands on his pants brushing the food crumbs away.

He flipped through the papers that I had completed and it was several moments before he spoke.

"This is very odd writing. Did you think this style up yourself or were there others involved?"

"I did it alone," I said somewhat defiantly. There was little, if anything, I carried with me from my life before the kingdom. My speech had changed to closely mimic the people who lived here. All I had left were my words and how I wrote them. This they would not take from me. This is something that I owned and I would not let it go.

"From what I can make out, parts of this read much like the book of spirit magic written by Abshagen?"

"Yes it is." I was thankful that the pages had turned to that particular place. I realized, too late, that they could have easily turned to my notes on Sorcerer Tyndall, Duke Almonesson, or Kalendeck, or Commander Nathel for that matter.

"I thought that Sorcerer Tyndall had that book."

"He let me use it for a time."

"So you know him?" Kopernick leaned forward looking at me askance.

"Well, yes. Why?"

"I've only talked to the guild master once, and that was very brief. He is a very hard person to see and usually only the adepts are able to hold a discussion with him. We novices never get to see him, well almost never. When he comes north to the king's castle in the winter, we sit around at the Gathering for several weeks talking. It's a great way to get information about what is happening in the kingdom."

"Have you been to any of these gatherings?" I asked hoping my voice conveyed naivety.

"I missed the one this last year. I have too much to study and learn in the guild house and could not get away. I may get the chance to go this year if I am not busy with my studies or helping my father."

I was relieved by this. If Kopernick was at the Gathering this year, he undoubtedly would have heard the truth about how I arrived in the kingdom. It was good that he believed that the person named Marecrish was held in the Croskreye castle. I did not need, or want, that kind of attention.

"May I see your dagger?" he asked noting the weapon I wore.

"You want me to hand you my knife?"

"Yes. I mean you no ill will, I just want to test its strength. Besides, if I wanted to run you through, I could have done it already with my sword. Well, dull as it is, I could have taken swats at you."

"Odd way to put it," I said. Seeing he had a sense of humor, I felt he did not wish me any harm. I handed the blade to him, hilt first and he examined it closely. He rubbed the edge with his thumb, balanced it on a finger and tapped the blade on his boot.

"Hmm. Fine metal, indeed. Some magic, but wrought mostly by a skilled hand. The design here on the pommel shows that it's over four generations old. A fine blade for you," he handed it back and I placed it back in the basic brown leather sheath. Tyndall had said it was a simple dagger. He never explained more than that.

"Your staff."

"What?" I looked down and could barely see the silver as a lay beside me in the grass.

"Is ... is that a fire drake?" He said pointing to my staff of ash.

"It is. Would you like to see it too?"

"May I be so brave as to ask?"

I hesitated just a moment before I gave it to him. He could've taken everything and ran off. I was sure I could chase him down and it would not have made for a fun afternoon.

When he held it he touched the head of the fire drake gently.

"There is magic here. Deeply embedded, this is very powerful indeed. I believe this was crafted by Nel. He was a master at our school when I arrived years ago."

"It was a gift from a friend to help me along my journey. It's helped me several times."

"Then it was a gift well given. I was going to use fire drake's on my sword, for the guard. I tried to get the design down on paper many days and had many that I could have used, but they just didn't seem to work right. I couldn't get them to curl back inward and so I opted for the snakes."

He handed it back to me and I lay it once again by my side.

"Did you carve the snakes for your sword?" I asked.

"That I did. The carving took almost a month during this winter last.

I great way to spend your time when it is cold outside. Warm fire, candlelight. Hammer and chisel in your hand gently tapping the metal. I could have spelled the metal to make it much softer, but I think that this takes away from it eventually. The Masters could tell how it was made and if I used this method it would have lessened my grade. Yes, all my work is done by hand."

"The sword is beautiful." I said. "Did you receive high marks for it?"

He looked at me and smiled. "You see that it it dull. I would never give it for review as such. Kalendeck's blade, Steelefyre, the original, was sharper than you could imagine. It may sound as a boast, but it was a very well tooled weapon that never dulled."

"Who made it for him? One of your masters?"

He shook his head. "It was made elsewhere and he brought it here with him. He never spoke of its creator."

Both of us had finished our meals and now I stood. With a groan Kopernick did the same taking up his sword and haversack. He had a solid frame and I was not sure if the groan were real, or just something done as a show of sympathy.

"How far is Ihrhoven from Glenhelen?" I asked as I brushed stray bread crumbs and apple bits off of my pants.

"It's not terribly far actually. Stay on this road," he nodded to the north. I followed his gaze over the hillsides and distant mountains. "You will have to travel through my village of Glenhelen to get there. Eight weeks until Glenhelen. Ihrhoven, village on the ocean, will take you a week and a half beyond that. You've business there? In Ihrhoven?"

"Yes, I ..."

"Good we'll travel together along the way," Kopernick said quickly before I could finish my sentence.

We took to the trail together.

* * * * *

There was silence for some time as we walked.

"You've not told me of your business in Ihrhoven. Is it to help with the castle being built?" he asked.

"No, not actually." Thinking quickly I added, "I wish to work on a book of the history of those in the kingdom. Gathering stories and putting them to pen and paper so others may learn. I feel there will be much to learn from those in Ihrhoven. Also, I've heard much from those on the road.

Things that are over looked by those in Croskreye."

"Ah, I see. Interesting. To think of it, it is true. I do not believe such a book has ever been written of our past. At least not of that time."

"This is my purpose in going to Ihrhoven, to learn of the past." Truth, but not completely. Tyndall's ruse, but not completely.

"Well, if you wish to hear of the wars, I would be happy to give you some tales. My father has told me much. He met Nathel and Kalendeck on their way to fight the Drenthen. He had to leave the village because of the battle that followed days later. Where should I start?"

I looked up to him and smiled.

I soon found it hard to believe a person could talk for so long. One week passed and then two. In the village of Corristone I had to purchase a new book and a new tip for one of the wooden pens I carried. I did not grow weary of my friend's voice, rather I soaked up the knowledge as the cracked and parched earth gathers in the spring rain.

*   *   *   *   *

During the second week I traveled with him I saw, off toward the west, a range of hills so high that I considered them mountains. From one of the center-most peaks, two towers of stone could be seen distinctly above the distant tree tops as they rose into the sky.

"What you see was once a seat of power for this territory. Duchess Bessa governs from there, but it is not the same. It was once the grand city named Carfrae; now it is the humbled village of Carfrae," Kopernick stated, following my gaze as I was looking toward the mountains.

"The Drenthen destroyed it," I stated.

"Yes, once four towers stood. They ravaged this territory. Men have begun to rebuild there; bringing it back to its fabled beauty will take some time. They want to rebuild as many villages as they can in the north. Just in the event of another encroachment. It was a shame though, that she had to fall," said Kopernick nodding toward the mountains.

"Who fell?"

"The lady. The lady from the mountain. Lady Rachael. Delfuri is the only territory with a long tradition of having a woman overseer. Duchess Bessa continues this tradition. You've not heard of Lady Rachael as well?"

"Just a little," I said and kept my expression blank.

Oldest sister of Lady Bessa and Duchess Lowy, she was Lady Wenonah's aunt. Nathel had spoken with me at length of Lady Rachael as I dreamt. Unknown to most they had been lovers. Had not the wars brought chaos to the kingdom, he had plans of asking the king for a leave of service. He would now be here helping her govern her lands as her commander. Their deaths were both tragic.

We continued on. Kopernick letting no detail slip by. When I sat and wrote at night he offered more insight. By the week's end, we entered the vast expanse of the Kear Forest.

Chapter #12

We finished eating our mid-day meal near the ruins of a once formidable keep. Here the trees were not as thick and sunlight, pure and bright, streamed down from a cloudless sky. A welcome gift after the near twilight that seemed to cling to the undergrowth of the Kear Forest. Along the road we had found a wall with a carved head of a lion from which fresh water trickled into a basin. Kopernick, looking up from getting a quick drink, saw some early berries growing in a thicket well away from the road. The sun was hot on our backs as we walked through the tall grass with briars pulling at our clothing. In the sunlight near a stone wall they grew their highest. Briar and ivy vines claimed the entire side.

I heard a traveler approaching on the dirt road below and looked up in time to see an elderly man walk under the remnants of the stone arch. He used a walking stick and a sack was slung over his shoulder. From where we were this traveler could not see us. I watched him walk only a few paces when I heard Kopernick cry out in pain. I thought a thorn had dug itself too deep and laughed. The cry grew in pitch. The curses became loud as Kopernick struggled on the ground.

I yelled for help. The traveler, dropping both staff and sack, ran through the high grass.

"Don't remove the snake," he yelled as he ran. "Hold him still! Do not let him remove the snake!"

"He's in pain," I pleaded, my dagger in my hand. I was about to cut off the snake's head. The man was at Kopernick's side kneeling.

"I'll do it. Hold him still." Deft hands reached in. Bringing the snake's head back in an arc, he pulled it off of Kopernick's leg with no more poison entering the wound. The serpent wrapped around his hand and arm as he grasped its head firmly right behind its jaw and skull.

"If I let it go, it will search the scent of its venom again. It will follow us as far as we go. These things have been known to travel for days to find the one they have bitten. Bring my sack. We must keep the snake away from him until the danger is away."

Once I fetched the sack the man quickly placed the snake inside and tied it off with a strand of leather. It hissed and spat, refusing to remain subdued.

"Carry this, hold it away from you, I'll carry him." With more strength than I thought he had, the man picked up Kopernick and carried him to a safer place.

"Once the snake bites . . . " he said, straining from his effort, "the venom starts to work on the body. The sufferer cannot move . . . at first, and after two hours . . . the blood begins to grow thin. This . . . is what the snake feeds on. Milking the body as a . . . baby calf feeds from the mother. I have . . . to cure him before his blood starts thinning."

Turning away from the road on to a dirt path, we traveled as quickly as he could carry him. I saw smoke from a chimney of a thatch roof cottage through the trees. A young woman working outside had seen us coming and yelled to someone inside. An elderly woman opened the door for us.

"Deanna, they are here."

I was not sure, it may have been the exertion the man put in his labors carrying Kopernick, but I thought I heard pleasure in the man's voice.

*   *   *   *   *

"Is he awake yet?" I ask.

She came from the room in the back and placed the tray on the table near the basin. She shook her head without saying a word and began to place the powders, herbs, and potions in a cabinet which held many.

She had long hair which was slightly touched at the sides and the back with the oncoming gray of her elder years. She was thin and tall. When she placed the items on the higher shelves, she had to raise on the tips of her toes only slightly. In the warmth of the day she wore only long loose clothing. Her feet were bare.

Her daughter, of whom I had only seen a few moments, looked much like her mother. She had rushed out of the house when we brought Kopernick and the snake in.

I watched her, Deanna, for a few moments and turned to look back out the window. My arms folded before me, I sat on a stool and was lost in my thoughts and my grief.

"He will wake when he is ready," she said. With her task now complete, she brought me a mug of warm tea and sat on a matching stool beside me. A hand rested on my shoulder for a moment's reassurance. She blew on her tea and sipped.

"There is honey and other spices in your tea. It will help calm you, all you have to do is drink it." To make her happy I drank a little. Smacking my lips once or twice, I tried to remember where I had tasted a tea similar to this. Not finding an answer, I sipped once more. The memory faded and a new one formed.

She had handed me a sheet of paper which was encased in a glass. What once sat upon their sill, and I now held in my hand, was an outline of the events of their recent history. There were markings across the top of the paper. With the sun in one corner and the moon in the other, these slashes signified the passage to time. I counted time backwards as each one represented a year.

The death of Kalendeck and Commander Nathel were noted on a line. They both died in the same year. The death of Sorcerer Cinnaminson, depicted by his symbols, was on a line further to the left. My arrival, oddly enough, was signified by a crude drawing of a rose on the upper portion of a mans leg and a circle of blackness. This was the glass that was in my leg and the gate I had fallen through. Someone had known I would be here.

On the next to the last mark there was a symbol of a snake and near it the person had written the symbols of the ingredients needed to cure the bite. Above the line were the magical symbols used in metal magic to signify copper and nickel. Hence, they received forewarning of a man named Kopernick being bitten by a snake.

All told just over twenty-three marks lined the top of the page. In the center was a crude map. From where and to where I had no idea.

"With this paper," she said. "Edmeston predicted many things. Be thankful that we knew of the snake and were able to prepare for it. We would not have had any of the medicines needed to heal him without this knowledge before hand."

I had held it for the little time, searching for more answers and finding none, before gently I set it down on the sill.

"Ryeson will heal him. Take heart in knowing that. Had Edmeston known of Kopernick's death, he would have told us that as well," Deanna said patting me on the knee. I looked at her and managed a weak smile.

I saw movement outside and a moment later their daughter returned. Deanna rose and went to her.

"I found them, Mum. They were where he said they would be." Deanna took an object from her daughter and handed it to me. I returned the dagger to its sheath. I had dropped it when the snake bit Kopernick. She placed my staff of ash, and her father's staff, near the door next to Kopernick's sword.

"We will cook Marc. There has been a separate room set aside for you. You may take your things there and wash up if you wish. There is fresh clothing for you."

A good cooked meal would be better than anything we had in the last week. I was hungry, but I shook my head.

"I cannot eat now."

"You must keep your strength as well. Hurry, and when you're finished please come out and tell us all about your friend and your journey."

*   *   *   *   *

Because I was to meet the great Healer Ryeson I scrubbed completely. The water was slightly scented and I could not believe how dark it was with dirt when I finished. Had it been so long since I bathed? When you travel on the road, the days just seem to blend from one to another. I dressed in the clean clothes they provided for me. Both the shirt and pants were larger than what I expected, but not uncomfortable. Not knowing what to do with my other clothes I left them in a small pile and went back out.

I took a seat on the bench at the table and sat as the mother and daughter prepared a simple meal. They cleaned potatoes, chopped onions and salted meat for a stew. The aroma was mouth-watering. The stock was much thicker than any they served in the common halls.

Once I started talking, it seemed as if a well-spring had opened and could not be stopped. They knew of my arrival here, so I did not have to pretend about my origins. I told them of the people of Croskreye, of Sorcerer Tyndall, Davlyne, and Lady Wenonah. I spoke of how I met Kopernick and how our friendship had grown. Somehow everything had just clicked together for us. For over a month now we had traveled north, through the hottest sun and the darkest forest, alone or with others, we continued on.

Kopernick's wealth of information on the art of metal magic was vast. Some of the spells he had told me were simply incredible. To think you could make chain armor as easy as knitting, or forming armor to a mans shape by making the metal as pliable as cloth, laying it on his body, and then hardening it again. To learn skills such as this was truly unique.

I told them of his knowledge of the wars. He explained one battle after another to me. Some in great detail, some not so. I soon had all the information I could get.

"I see," said Deanna looking up from chopping spices. "Did he tell you of the Lament of Cinnaminson?"

"He did, as did Tyndall, Davlyne and Duke Almonesson. Kopernick explained it to me so well, I cried that night trying to pen it on paper. One of the saddest things I have ever heard. When he heals and is able to speak he must tell you his version."

"Yes. It was tragic," she said looking up at me with a smile. "Did he tell you at all about the battle of Thumwood?"

"Yes he did."

"Tell us then what you know." The preparations for the meal now complete, mother and daughter sat at the table and began listening to my story.

"Well, to begin," I rubbed my chin thinking, trying to bring it all back without the book.

"Kalendeck and Commander Nathel learned by messenger of a large group of Drenthen soldiers who had just raided a small village. Knowing he would put other lives in jeopardy, Kalendeck slipped away in the middle of the night and went to their camp. He put a spell on the guards to make them sleep. Such a man was he, that he would not kill a man as he slept. No matter the hatred he felt for them. And then he crept from tent to tent taking weapons from the Drenthen and hiding them. When they woke that morning, they saw him standing by a tree. Only five swords could be found, and none would go near him without a sword, so he fought five at a time. When these five fell, Kalendeck would move away, five more would pick up swords and die. He killed all forty men that way."

As I finished, I saw a movement in the corner of my eye and turned to see Ryeson had come into the room. He may have stood there a few moments and listened. I was not sure.

"How is he?" their daughter asked.

"He lives and he will regain his strength. The pain is over, the healing now begins."

Ryeson went to the well bucket and with a ladle drank some of the cool water.

"We must eat and rest. I will watch over him tonight just to make sure. Healing someone who is snake bitten is very difficult. Worse than a cut or broken bone, the poison travels quickly through the whole body."

"Kalista, watch him while I eat." The girl stood and went to the back room without question. Deanna poured soup from the kettle and set the wooden bowls on the table. I took a seat with the two as they passed the fresh bread.

"She has a pretty name," I commented.

"We named her after the warrior. He saved us, you know. The Drenthen did not attack Thumwood, the people abandoned the village weeks before. Deanna and I were traveling through. Had it not been for him they would have found us and surely would have killed us. Let's be quiet and enjoy the meal. I have a long night ahead."

I said nothing more obeying his wishes. The healer ate quickly and when he finished his last spoonful, he stood.

Before he left, he placed his hand on my shoulder.

"You have no idea how good it is to meet you. We have been waiting for you for a very long time. Kopernick will be well, his healing will take time, I look forward to spending time with you."

I was silent and only nodded. I looked between the two. Deanna touched her husband's hand and he smiled.

"Sometimes Marc, we are so blinded by what we think we desire that we lose sight of what we are here for." Saying nothing more Ryeson turned and went back to the sick room.

* * * * *

Kopernick opened his eyes and saw candlelight in the darkness around him. He stirred and tried to sit up.

"Easy, Kopernick. Move slowly or you'll feel the pain." The voice he heard was heavy with fatigue. There was stiffness in his joints when he moved his legs, but no pain. Hands pressed on his shoulders and he eased back down.

"Where am I? Is Marc here? Did he go on?" he asked licking his lips. He heard water being poured and its chill on his lips. They allowed him only a few swallows before taking it away. He doubted the whole bucket could quench his thirst.

"Marc is here, he sleeps now in the other room. You are here with me, Ryeson."

"Great healer, I did not know my plight was so dire."

"Snake bitten. If we had not known forehand how to cure the venom you would have died," Ryeson whispered in the candlelight. Another drink and he spoke again.

"So, the paper was correct then. The two symbols for copper and nickel refer to me. Truth be told, I wish it were another man laying here bitten this night."

"I know it must hurt, I will ease your pain as best I can. But think of it; you, I, and my family are part of the grand circle. The ending is not clear, so this is a very exciting time for us. I enjoy a good mystery. I am happy to play my part and to stand back and watch it unfold. You will have more of a part in the days and months ahead, perhaps."

Kopernick groaned and wanted to sink deeper in the mattress of goose feathers. He brought his arm up and lay it across his eyes blocking out the candlelight. Dim as it was, it still hurt his sight. The retreat to darkness was comforting.

"I made the sword of the two snakes. I did not want to have one bite me."

"Perhaps another one will surface and bite you on the other leg."

Kopernick peered from under his arm and saw the healer was smiling.

"You're in too good a mood."

"Ah, I've been up for a long time. Was hoping for a peaceful day, but you changed all of that. Getting old I guess. Should have passed on years ago."

"From old age?"

"Nay, from a sword. You know the tale of Thumwood, you know how Kalendeck found me. You should have felt the pain I felt that day. I wish Kalendeck had known a numbing spell. I would have fared a lot better."

"Please keep your good mood. You sour when you dwell in the past. Does Marc know that you and I know each other?"

"Nay, again. To him you are an ordinary traveler who happened on my doorstep as many so often do. I think it is best we leave it that way. You have given him a good lot of information." In the candlelight Ryeson was quiet for a time as he dabbed the area around Kopernick's leg with a cool damp cloth.

"Has he told you who he is?" Ryeson asked.

"He is a learned man from Croskreye. As a service to Duke Almonesson and Sorcerer Tyndall he is on his way north to scribe stories from people who lived during the wars. For being so learned, he seems simple enough. At times it were as though he was a mooncalf and naïve about the wars."

"You say this meaning that he may not actually know of the wars."

"I think it is a role he plays to encourage more information from me. I told him, falsely, of the battle at Lanedorf. It is a common tale and many know of darkness Lord Nikkinen had in his heart. Marc, playing his role, now believes that Lord Nikkinen was the kindest person. Also, I told him of King Talmadge fighting in battle. A man by the name of Crider saved the king's life by taking an arrow in the chest. If you ask this is what he'll say."

"Crider?"

"A name I made up."

"Mayhap, he does not know, Kopernick."

"How could he not?" Kopernick looked at him again and made a sound on a different day with more strength could have been a snort.

"Sorcerer Tyndall wants you to help Marecrish, to guide him." Ryeson said simply.

"He wishes that I now travel back down to Croskreye to help Marecrish?" Kopernick almost sat up on his elbows.

"No Kopernick. I met with Sorcerer Tyndall at the Gathering. Much to the dismay of most there he did not bring Marecrish with him. Duke Lysaght and Duke Curwin were highly upset. Tyndall and I are close. Equals in our chosen fields of study. The information he gave to me in the highest confidence. If I did not trust you so thoroughly I would not reveal this to you and let you go on blindly believing what you do. Sorcerer Tyndall holds your trust just as high or he would not have asked you to do this task.

"Kopernick," the healer looked at him intently and then said another word. "Think." Ryeson leaned forward in his chair, his hands gripping the wood of the seat. "If Marecrish is from a different culture, brought here to the kingdom as Kalendeck was, would he know of these battles in our past?"

Kopernick shook his head.

"Marc is Marecrish."

Kopernick tried to laugh, but it came out as a rough croak.

"He is not. Marecrish is much taller, I've heard. And years older. Like Kalendeck he knows things others do not."

Ryeson shook his head. "He is learning what he can of the battles. When he arrived here his head was hurt and his memories lost. A word he remembers from his past is the name of Kalendeck. Mayhap Kalendeck was a great fighter where Marecrish, Marc, lived and grew up. Marc is traveling north to gather information from those in Ihrhoven."

Kopernick looked at Ryeson out of the corner of an eye while squinting the other.

"You are telling me that, like Nathel in his time, I am watching over someone who could be the savior of the kingdom. If the Drenthen arrive, I am not sure if I can fight. I have never had the proper training. In making swords, yes, in using them, no. What if someone attacks us upon on the road? The Wiladene Territory is no place to travel lightly … "

Ryeson held his hands up. "For the time being he has been given to you as a guardian. When Sorcerer Cinnaminson brought Kalendeck here the Drenthen were soon to arrive. I believe if they were coming they would have been here by now."

"No wonder his writing is so odd." Kopernick closed his eyes and lay his head back.

"I will nudge it a little and we shall see how things go."

"Ah, give him a Seed? This is what you call a simple nudge?"

"As I was given a Seed many years ago? No, I will talk with him. He is already on the right path and in good hands. Treat him as you always have. He must go alone to Ihrhoven. When you return to your family you must stay with them while he continues on. There cannot be any distraction in his gathering of information there."

"That is something I would enjoy being part of."

"And I as well. But we are already." Ryeson stifled a yawn with the back of his hand. "Above all you should not let him know that you know who he is. To those traveling you are just two common travelers on your way north. Tyndall and Duke Almonesson have planted many false paths that Marecrish may have taken. This is a path no one will suspect." Visibly more relaxed the healer sat back and folded his hands upon his lap.

"I have been to Ihrhoven a time or two." Kopernick nodded. "Small place on the oceans' edge. I shall not die before day break, great healer. Go to Deanna and get your rest. Marc will wake with the chickens and not stop asking of me till noontide."

"Yes, I shall." Ryeson stood and stretched. "He does love his questions, doesn't he? Good evening, or morning then. Sleep well."

* * * * *

Ryeson and I sat outside under the morning shade of an old oak tree. It was one of the few about. The forest about his home was mostly hemlock.

Ryeson said earlier that he enjoyed sitting under the oak rather than sitting under the pines. There was less sap and it offered more shade. I could hear a stream nearby coursing its way through the ground in which held their roots. His daughter, Kalista, had bought drinks earlier and regularly checked in on us to see if we were comfortable.

He looked weary and in need of rest after the healing he gave Kopernick the day before, but he brushed their concerns aside and chose to sit with me under this tree. It was relaxing enough as it was.

He was a thin man who sat stroking his goatee, gone white with age or worry, and held quiet for long moments lost in thought.

"I do not know where to begin," he said at last coaxing a mother cat to his lap. "There is so much I have wanted to talk to you about, so much I wanted to hear from you. When I heard that someone had arrived from somewhere else I knew it was you. Actually, I felt the ripple of magic that brought you here. It was distinctive, you had to know what to feel for. When I learned that your mind was as a clean slate, I grew disheartened. When the Seer Edmeston gave me the paper, the line representing your arrival, was one meant for a messenger. You are here and you have no message. How odd. But you are here. That is all that matters."

"And I have no message," I said. "It disappointed Duke Almonesson also."

"Ah, perhaps it is something you will learn which others cannot in the time to come."

"May I ask, you met Kalendeck?" I asked leaning forward.

"Yes," he chuckled. "Yes I did. Just the once after the battle of Thumwood."

"What was he like? Not the battle or anything, but the man."

Again, another long pause before he went on.

"Tall man, wide in the shoulders, heavy in the arms. I watched him fight. Men fell before him like shafts of wheat to a miller. Ah, but you didn't want to hear about the fighting did you. He wore his dark hair long, beard and mustache cropped short, and spoke with an accent that resembled one of someone to the west. It was after the battle I spoke with him. He was sore and stiff and had his share of ale, but still had his wits about him. Very intelligent, very easy to get along with. We spoke for a short while before he needed rest."

"Seer Edmeston knew of his arrival forehand?"

"He did, and he also knew of the arrival of the Drenthen." The cat on his lap stirred watching a butterfly and was content when it was out of sight.

"So they were ready for the Drenthen when Kalendeck arrived."

"No, not exactly. You must know that in the seers guild they teach the students that they must, in no way, interfere with what they envision. If, in their mind, they see a child is to fall from a tree and strike his head, then they cannot change it. When they experience a true vision, they must let it come to manifestation."

This confused me. What he was saying was nothing at all what they told me thus far. "Who, then, warned the kingdom of the Drenthen? Did they wait until the fighting started?"

"That task, unfortunately, fell upon Kalendeck himself. None believed him. If you, yourself, would have said something of great importance to the survival of the kingdom when they found you in the castle at Croskreye, everyone, from the king to the loathsome beggar would have taken action. With Kalendeck they believed him a raving mad man at first. The week after he arrived in Glenhelen the fighting started. The rest is history."

I nodded my head. Having it down in my book I knew the story from there on.

"Your part in this is the survival of Kopernick," I said. "His role is very important to the kingdom if Edmeston gave you forewarning all those years ago. Perhaps my part which he wrote on the paper is over."

"Hm, I had never thought on it that way." Ryeson sat after a moments silence. "I believe that, although the paper shows Kopernick's fate, it is definitely more concerned with your survival. Perhaps Edmeston saw in his vision the possibility of you traveling alone through the rest of the Kear Forest. Wrought with guilt or unhappiness over losing a dear friend to a snake, conceivably your future could be completely different."

I thought on this for some time.

"Odd, don't you think, that his visions were so accurate, but there is nothing past a year or so from now? His magic allowed him to see the future so accurately, but then suddenly stops."

"Magic is just magic. If we could see everything, or heal everyone what kind of society would that be?"

"True."

*   *   *   *   *

Kalista interrupted our conversation when she brought a man back to where we sat. He held his head to the left as he walked. The stance, I thought, would have made him walk awkwardly, but it seemed like he was not bothered by walking this way. As he neared, Ryeson stood and I did the same.

"Father, he has a . . . " she grimaced and shook both her hands while managing to point to a spot on his neck. "He has a thingy thing on his neck. Eck," she shook her hands, looking at it wide-eyed. Something moved his beard and she jumped back, squealing, her hands now covering her face.

Ryeson looked close. "Ah, a harvest grub. is it painful?"

"Not at all. Just feels funny movin' there and all," the man said. What teeth he did have were nearly black. He wore the clothing of a farmer. Big hands, dirt around the finger nails and old scars on his forearm. The scents of the field plants clung to him.

"Easy enough to get rid of. Kalista, my pack please." Quick to be away, she ran back to the house.

"These things begin with a small brown beetle that lays just one egg," Ryeson explained to us. "Usually happens during harvest. They hide in your beard. Once the egg is lain, the beetle drops off the person. Like a tick, but these leave a present behind. During the course of the winter and summer months the grub forms under the skin."

Kalista was coming back. She held her fathers pack out away from her, as if it was a source of some powerful stench. Only the tips of her forefinger and thumb held the strap. She wanted as little to do with this as possible. She lay the pack on the table and took three steps back.

Ryeson opened the pack and pulled out a pair of pincers with a small barb at the end. Pulling the skin taut, he deftly reached in and with a slight tug the grub was out. He tossed it in the pine needles some distance away. For Kalista it was all she could take. She squealed once more and ran as fast as she could towards the house. The loose braid of her long hair caught in the wind.

The man stood, smiled and rubbed the spot.

"Keep your fingers out and keep it clean, very clean, for a few days. It left a small hole which will heal closed soon enough."

"Thank you. Haven't had my head straight fer weeks. Not since the misses found it."

"Well, take care of it and it'll be fine. Comb your beard next harvest."

"How much do I owe ya?" he asked slapping a small pouch tied to his belt.

"For what?" Ryeson asked looking confused.

"The grub."

"What grub?"

"The one on my neck," the man looked back and forth between us.

"You have a grub on you neck?"

"No, you took it out."

"Well, if its out don't worry about it."

The man stood there confused for a second and gave us a toothy smile. He bowed and shook Ryeson's hand. Turning, I watched as he walked away. He had to correct himself two times before he made it past the house. With his head no longer held to the side, he favored traveling to the left.

"The way he's going he'll be back before nightfall." Ryeson said with a smile.

* * * * *

"We'll need a water skin each and don't forget to bring your staff," Ryeson told me. Although I had spent some time walking through the Kear Forest, I had never seen a kear tree up close. Ryeson, knowing of a copse of them nearby agreed to take me there that evening.

With her chores complete, Kalista wanted to follow. She was always an interesting person. Slightly older than Rouke she had the same boundless energy. As we prepared to go, she redid her braid taking out the looseness and a few stray twigs that managed to get tangled in her strands.

Odd to see her out of her sandals and in actual boots for the walk.

Ryeson brought the pack which he always carried. When I tried to carry his water skin, he nonchalantly shooed me away willing to carry it himself.

Kopernick had awakened earlier in the day. He had taken a measured amount of herbs and powders before falling back to sleep. Tomorrow, Ryeson assured us, he would be up walking. Stiff and sore, but healing nonetheless. Deanna stayed home in the event he woke before we returned.

Grabbing a large brim hat from a peg near the door, Ryeson called to us to leave.

* * * * *

The trees were bigger than I thought. Tall with white leaves, not in abundance, but scattered about the limbs haphazardly. The clearing, a perfect circle around the tree, was free of any kind of scrub brush. Thin blades of grass grew, and a few smaller flowering plants, but this was all. I pointed this out to the others.

"The ivy like parts of the tree create this," Kalista said this while prodding the ground with a stick she found nearby. I saw movement in the grass. She pulled away and it stopped. "If you look closely at the grass, you can see them. Touch one and it begins to slowly curl. It's not terribly fast, but there are so many."

Around the base of the tree there was a group of boulders with a distinctive leaf pattern on their gray surfaces.

There were about twelve to fifteen trees here in the valley. We had walked along a wooded and grassy isle-way that ran through the heart of a natural grove of the white barked giants. All widely spaced and very little if anything between them. I could see some natural rocks back a distance from where we stood.

"The vines roll up around whatever disturbs them and form the eggs. From what is known the vines harden and new ones grow out and replace those that have formed the egg."

I picked up a stone and tossed it towards the tree. It hit one egg before coming to rest at the base of the tree.

"Ah," said Ryeson slowly taking in a deep breath. "Marc, don't do that. The clearing marks the limit of their vines, but they are at rest and relaxed. If given cause they can stretch further. Be still a while. Everyone."

"Are they alive?" I asked keeping my voice no louder than a whisper. "I mean, as an animal is alive."

"No, do not think so," Ryeson whispered. Clearly what I had done upset him. He explained further. "Perhaps the vines are only used as protection. Keeping harmful things away. The flowers attract little bees and the trees get their nourishment from the soil and rain water. Once the eggs form they are no longer part of the tree. On some hills, where the ground is steeper that this, they have been known to roll."

"A type of magic?"

Ryeson nodded. "The younger trees hold some healing powers. The smoke produced from burning the wood of a very young tree helps seers with their craft."

"And when they are older?"

"Just a hindrance or death to the unwary. Bones have been found in the eggs when cracked open after the tree has died. Bird, deer, bear, and people. The eggs have some magical uses with metalworking, but this depends on age and size."

We stayed a bit longer, but there was not much more to see about the tree. It is true that many other types of trees grew in the Kear Forest. These trees, white-flowered, white limbs, with sensitive vines, were the most notable ones in this wilderness.

* * * * *

"Now, wait until you see the drops of blood on the wood." I put the knife down on the stone of the hearth and tried to remove myself from the pain. The small knife sliced my finger. Not terribly deep. If left to heal on its own the scab would form and it would scar within a week or so.

Blood ran the length of my finger from the laceration and formed one large drop at the tip. First one drop fell and then the next splattering a small area on a piece of firewood.

"Almost there. I can heal you easily enough, but I want you to do it. Say the words in the order I taught you. If you feel you cannot go through with it, then stop for a moment and the spell will cancel."

I looked away from my cut finger to his eyes. His sincerity gave me strength. I nodded and began to utter the chant he had taught me. Speaking the last word, I felt a tingle in my chest and on my finger. Ryeson smiled and nodded his head in agreement.

"Good. Very good. A little more enunciation to keep the syllables separate and you have it."

"I can heal myself?" I said looking for even a hint of a scar. There was none. Even the pain was gone.

"You can heal yourself and others to a certain extent. You cannot grow a hand back, but you can slow the loss of blood. Any wound much bigger would naturally leave a scar."

"Interesting. I can see where this is useful, but the other spell you taught me, modified Bone-Rite, to heal or change bones, what can I do with that?"

"I taught that to you just to let you know the diverseness of magic. The people who created the Bone-Rite did so after many failures. If you spend time studying the spell, there are ways to modify it. This is how our magic is as diverse as it is. Davlyne taught you a great deal. Once all of this settles down, you should go back to her and learn more."

"I will give it some thought. I would find it interesting."

"Will you write those spells I just taught you down in your book?"

"Yes, I will." I looked at the healer sitting on the other side of the hearth. Always the teacher. The four of us sat around the evening fire relaxing. Deanna and Ryeson had cushioned wooden chairs while Kalista and I each had a large straw pillow to sit on. She loved her father's work and watched all he did with great interest. With all she knew, it was easy to assume that she would be a healer when she grew older. There were three guild-houses for healing. With her fathers backing, she could be accepted at any she chose.

A large kettle hung on a hook with the rest of our meal. It was rabbit soup with mushrooms picked in the wild, not in Deanna's garden.

"He writes everything in that book."

We turned to see Kopernick in the doorway of the room rubbing his head with one hand and sleep sand from his eyes with the other. He yawned and took some stiff steps forward favoring his good leg. His red hair was pulled back and tied with a small length of leather cord.

"Kalista, bring him that large pillow."

She did and he sat in a place close to Deanna. His leg was stiff and he winced in pain a number of times. I got a bowl and spoon for him and a mug of water. Kalista served him some soup. She stirred more water in so it would last longer.

"You are feeling well?" Ryeson asked turning Kopernick's head to the left and right looking into his eyes.

"Better than before. Much better. It's a bit stiff and there is a bruise where the snake bit me, but I'll live for a time longer I believe," he blew on his soup and sipped it.

"Your hunger has returned?"

"It woke me up. Couldn't sleep for the smell of this soup."

Deanna smiled and touched his shoulder. "I hope that is a good thing."

After his third bowl he pushed it away contented. A quiet burp to show his satisfaction and he leaned back on Deanna's chair.

"I would like to tell you two that it has been wonderful having you here. Almost a week has passed since you arrived on my doorstep."

Both Kopernick and I looked at each other. He nodded to me and I bowed my head knowing of the direction of Ryeson's thoughts. Our time here, although pleasant enough, should soon be over. I had to get north to see Nathel and I was sure Kopernick was anxious to return home as well.

"Can he travel?" I asked. "His leg may still be too weak."

"For walking, yes, he is still too weak to travel. I have made arrangements for you. A wagon will be along in the morning. The driver will take you past the Wiladene Territory border to Glenhelen. Oddly, if you leave in the morning and travel by wagon you'll arrive there about the same time you would have if you were walking.

"There has been some trouble." Ryeson looked into the hearth as he spoke. Deanna leaned forward, as we all did not wishing to miss his words. "Duke Lysaght is pressing a difficult issue with Duke Almonesson. It would seem that Kahshgrance Territory and Obfelden Territories are up in arms again. Not war, not between territories, not yet. Doubtful it will come to that. Duchess Bessa vows not to get completely involved. She does not have the men or the resources to keep up any kind of front. It will take many years of ruling for the people to feel loyalty if she were to give a call to arms. For her neutrality, at this time, is best. Others see this as a sign of weakness, others see it as strength."

"What do they argue over?" I asked. This was the same argument I had heard when I talked with Davlyne, Tyndall, and Duke Almonesson. The other dukes would be upset at Duke Almonesson. I lowered my head and worked a small twig out of a seam in my pants.

"Marecrish," he said simply. I had to fight to not instinctively look up at the mention of my name. I raised my head slowly, keeping my face free of expression. Still, my fingers worked at the twig. I had to will them to remain still.

"The one that fell through the mirror?" I asked.

"Yes. Duke Curwin and Duke Lysaght were waiting for him to arrive with Sorcerer Tyndall when he reached the Gathering. Alas, he was not there?"

"Where did he go? How could he have escaped?" asked Kopernick. The rumors of this myth had grown in his mind until the person he envisioned Marecrish as was a grand majestic man. Some of the stories he listened to in the common rooms as we traveled made him out as a man of large stature and incredible strength. He would hang on to every word Ryeson spoke about the man. I found it difficult to believe that someone so knowledgeable about the ways of the world would give these far spun tales any credence. I did not have to worry that he thought I was the one we spoke of.

"I heard in the village months ago, after the winter snows receded, that Marecrish struck out on his own. They believe that he traveled to the west to the Obfelden Territory. There have been sightings of him there in one of the larger villages. Some believe that he is traveling from territory to territory to see which one he best enjoys." Ryeson sat back and folded his hands on his lap.

"He is traveling the territories, you can bet," said Kopernick slapping his good leg. "Maybe there will be a chance that we will see him."

"If he is taking the route through Obfelden Territory to the Chisemore then his journey will be a long one," said Ryeson.

"Either way," Deanna tapped Kopernick on the head. "They are searching for him and you know the mind set of soldiers once they set about to do something. The sooner you both are in the Wiladene Territory the better. Duchess Bessa can extend her reach in that territory only a days ride. I would hate to see you both in trouble from a misunderstanding."

Ryeson looked us both over. "If what I hear about Duke Lysaght is true, he will not back down. He feels at times as though he is mightier than the king himself. However, be that as is may, it is beginning to become a very bad time to traveling. There are currents in the river we cannot possibly see. Do you understand?" he looked at me directly and I bowed my head nodding.

"We must hurry then?"

"That would be safest," Deanna said. "Do what you have to and get back to where you belong. Kopernick, your guild is in Delfluri Territory and even though your home is in Wiladene Territory you might be asked to swear loyalty to Bessa. Marc, Duke Almonesson may call his people home. You are a scribe. Little matters in war, but you could be a courier, or a Chronicler for some event."

"Should I return to Kahshgrance Territory now? My oath to Duke Almonesson is binding." I said.

Deanna gave Ryeson a startled look. She began to stumble on her words and Ryeson spoke for her.

"If you have business in the north, then your return can wait. Kopernick needs to rejoin his family in Glenhelen. I'm sure they worry over him. Your travels, Marc, lay in the same direction. I know you are from Croskreye, that is a very long way from here. It would be a shame to have come this far and return because there is a hint of war. Please, do what you have to do, this task of finding the information for Duke Almonesson. When it is complete go where you will. If you see a call to your homeland posted in a village, then return. This is the way that things are done."

I thought for a moment and breathed an inward sigh of relief.

"I must get my book, if it is all right. I need to pen some words before I forget and it gets too late."

I stood and a moment later returned with what I needed.

* * * * *

I helped Kopernick into the back of the wagon and waited for him to settle in. His shoulder pack and sword, still with its hilt in wraps, lay on the floor of the wagon beside him. We were given two blankets and they brought some pillows for cushioning.

I placed my haversack in the back once he was comfortable and tucked a blanket underneath myself. The surface of the wagon, still damp with morning dew, would dry off soon enough. Sunlight threatened, even now, to begin shining through the high lofty clouds and the tall full trees. We sat side by side with our backs against a wooden chest waiting for the driver while he gave the horses and their tack one last check.

Deanna wept openly and Ryeson held her close. His mood was a somber one. Kalista came running from the house with yet another small cloth of fresh-baked rolls. She climbed quickly over a wheel and handed them to Kopernick.

To my surprise she kissed him on the cheek and held him close for a moment. She then came to me and did the same. When she left the wagon, she stood beside her mother and, holding each other, they wept.

"Please dry your eyes women. Do you want their last sight of you as such?" Ryeson spoke leaning heavily on his staff possibly still tired from the late night we spent talking.

"Marc, Kopernick," We each shook his hand in turn. "Well met. If either of you pass this way again please do stop in. I will be happy to learn of your travels since our parting and I know the women will be happy to see you as well."

The driver finished with his task and came around to the back.

"Clay, you take care of these two."

"I shall," said the thin man brushing dust off his arm and straightened his shirt. A scar, very faint, almost hairline, ran from his ear to his chin.

"As far as the main crossroads at Glenhelen, but I must go elsewhere after that."

"And so elsewhere you shall be. Friends, I do bid you good travels."

Anxious to start off to Glenhelen and then on his other errands, Clay quickly took his seat and snapped the reins.

* * * * *

In two days we came in sight of the wall dividing the territories of Delfuri and Wiladene. The stone archway of this break in the wall stood adorned with heavy wooden doors. They were open now, to admit travelers, but could be closed if need be. Soldiers in light armor, in the dark blue colors of the Delfuri Territory, milled about the gatehouse. Their pikestaffs leaned against the wall, swords hung from their belts. Kopernick waved and politely called greetings. They motioned us forward, granted us permission to pass through the archway, and did nothing else to interfere with us.

I felt easier when the wall was out of sight in the trees. The joyous, or carefree mood I so often felt from other travelers was now more subdued. In the evenings when we stopped and rested there were more whispers and more rumors of war among the people. Kopernick seemed more distant and quieter. His mood had deepened. In the evening after stretching his legs and walking off cramps, he would return to the wagon and sit and think in quiet contemplation. I wondered at times what he thought and what he and the great healer had spoken of.

I left him to his thoughts.

*   *   *   *   *

Three weeks after the wall we came across a curious sight. The road had been empty for most of the morning with just the normal people we had come to expect. The usual traders, some on horse back, farmers and some others walking. There was a noticeably less people traveling north as we were. On this particular day, we were the only ones. I saw some broken crockery laying in the middle of the road.

This I pointed out to Kopernick and Clay. Just a bit further on there was clothing and some more articles that seemed as if they were suddenly tossed aside. Our horse began to act up, but Clay was able to coax the animal on. Presently, we happened upon a family gathered about a wagon and a dead horse. There were large gashes along its sides and blood on its neck.

"Wolves," said the elderly man as we helped his children into the back of our wagon. His son came into view carrying a pelt of one.

"I chased them off, but for one," he said holding his trophy up high, his arms covered in blood up to the elbow.

"She was a good ol' horse. Lame, her was, a bit in one o' her leg, but good all the same. If I would ha'e knownd she was a going to get her kilt today I would not have a feedin' her thi' morn," said the man standing beside his wife looking at the dead animal. "Well, no needin' to let her go to waste. Would ah you like the heart or the liver?" he spoke past his one and only tooth.

Clay thought for a moment and then stated that some off the flank and rump would do nicely. This would suffice payment if he was going to take the family onward towards Glenhelen.

"Marc, your dagger please. I shall cut my own." Clay hefted the blade for a moment, testing its balance, and then began cutting and chatting with the man and his wife. They already had the animals belly open. He held the knife and his wife was pulling on the entrails. They cut the meat, sliced, salted and wrapped with efficiency that could only come from practice. The elderly man and woman chatted amongst themselves the whole time.

"Here, here and here," she said showing him where to cut as his knife and able hands brought meat away.

The whole process took most of the afternoon. Kopernick and I did not help in the butchering. We gathered what we could of the families possessions and placed them in the wagon.

We all finished about the same time. Clay and the others went to a small stream and washed off the blood and gore before Clay took up the reins again.

The younger children of the family were mostly shy and quiet, where as the parents and the oldest son talked almost continuously. The boy worked on cleaning the pelt. He worked well even though the wagon ride was not smooth. For three days we traveled with them, our bellies full in the evenings, and on the morning of the fourth day we parted ways with all of them. We had arrived at the crossroads near Glenhelen. Just a half a days walk from Kopernick's home.

*   *   *   *   *

Luck was with us until I felt the first drops of the storm. I halted Kopernick by grabbing him by the arm.

"I felt a drop of rain," I said.

Kopernick held out his own hand and looked to the sky.

"Damn," he cursed. "I didn't want to get wet this day, and this close to home too."

Just outside of the village of Glenhelen, we started to walk faster. Kopernick surprised me when he picked up the pace a bit more to a trot. His leg must have felt much better. Our feet pounding out a steady pace on the packed dirt road that still had more dust than mud. I looked at him as we trotted. He wore the sword across his shoulders this day instead of around his belt. He was running with one hand over his head holding the hilt of the sword while his other reached downward and held the tip. The sheath guarding him from any sharp point the weapon might have. I held the staff of ash tightly in my grip.

We trotted like this until we were at the very edge of the village. Kopernick let out a whoop and we slowed to a stop.

"It's best not to . . . kill ourselves . . . before we arrive," I said between gasps.

"True . . . it is as if . . . I was not bitten . . . at all," he smiled at me and we continued to walk.

The river began to mist over on to the land, adding to the fog and the smoke from open cooking fires that already lay there. This condition, along with the thickness of the trees, made the landscape a disheartening one. These were just my thoughts, it seemed. Kopernick was very excited to return home and was in very high spirits.

I put my hood up to keep the slight rain off. The cottage, he assured me for the fifth time, sat with some others on the west side of Glenhelen.

The village itself was larger than I expected. It was very reminiscent of Croskreye. Here they were far from the sea and had massive oaks, maples and hemlocks around the perimeter of the village. These were kept at bay by the constant need for firewood. The castle which once housed a noble family now lay in a tumble of stone and brambles. People had removed stone to help build the cottages, but made no effort, as of yet, to repair the ruins of the main keep or its walls.

The odor from the lamps in the shops could be smelled even in the street. There was a baker, two shops selling fabric and one selling jewelry and spices.

"Careful of the next place," Kopernick advised.

It was a brothel. Two ladies stood under a wide awning watching people pass by in the rain. The smell of perfume and incense was very suggestive and stirred something inside of me. In all my time in the kingdom, I refrained from women unconsciously. Not that they were not pleasing to look at or not satisfying in conversation, it's just the situation never presented itself.

Inside the place it was dimly lit on this overcast day. I heard laughter and knew they were entertaining someone.

"Hello," one called to us showing us a modest portion of her thigh. "My, my, my look at the red hair, bet he could give me a tumble," she had her arm draped over the shoulder of a woman companion.

"Does his manhood match the sword on his back, I wonder?" said the other toying with the long curls of her hair.

"We have a nice warm bed for the both of you."

"Just a few coppers each and you'll stay till morn."

Kopernick just shook his head and motioned them away. Before we were around the corner, they could be heard enticing someone else. I looked at him and he gave me a nervous smile.

"Never been to one, and don't plan to start now."

"Same."

We made our way down the now muddied streets of cobblestone, and found the cottage well before the clouds broke overhead.

The door to the house opened and a young boy left carrying a bucket. In a moment he passed through the gate of a stone wall that marked the property boundary. Even though his bucket was empty, he leaned slightly to the side as if it were heavy. Kopernick nudged me with his elbow. Keeping his voice low, he spoke.

"He's grown. This is my youngest brother, Dan'l. He'll be almost ten years now. On his way to fetch water, in my youth it was my chore." I expected him to call out, but he did not and the young boy went off, away from us, to do his chore. Dan'l kept looking at the dark skies, but did not look back.

Kopernick's walk slowed and I saw him smile. This was his homecoming, a moment to savor. He breathed deep and there was contentment in his eyes.

"Aye, this does a man good, like looking into a woman's eyes just before the kiss."

I saw a woman reach out to close the shutters on an open window and she paused. She squealed and I saw her point our way.

"Mother," said Kopernick with a laugh. "She's alerted the village that I am home. Come," he said tapping my arm.

As we entered, a clamor of greetings went up by all. He went from mother to father and then to each of his two brothers and two sisters. They embraced him with warmth and kindness. When his younger brother returned from fetching water, he was a bit shy at first, but soon warmed up to Kopernick and from then on would not leave his side.

Kopernick introduced me and it gave me strength once again to feel as family. They accepted me with little explanation or reservation. If Kopernick welcomed me as a friend then I was thusly welcomed in his home.

I was quickly put to work tending to the cooking fires and stirring soup. Corva, his mother, plump with thick curls of long hair, began to make bread and rolls. They cooked a large meal, which was quickly gone once it reached the table. I have to confess that I ate my share without regret. It had been many long days we sustained ourselves on the salted horse meat. I was glad for the home cooked meal.

He showed them, several times, the wound on his thigh left by the venomous snake. All that was visible were two small red spots quickly healing to nothing. His father, Lindergren, gave the wound a casual glance, content his eldest son was healthy. Corva poked and prodded it telling us that she was noting how fast the color came back after she applied pressure. When she was content, she nodded approval and went about other tasks.

After the evening chores were complete and a tour of the village smithy was given, the children washed themselves and sent off to bed as the night was getting on.

Lindergren lit up a pipe, and together the four of us sat around the table talking. The candle flame carried the smoke up in the air to the beams and thatch of the roof. The sweet smell of the burning leaves soon thickened the room and Corva stood to open a window. It seemed so much like the time we spent with Ryeson and Deanna.

Kopernick demonstrated, again, a little of what he had learned this year at the guild house. How to bend metal with the little bit of heat from the fireplace. He could also change its properties slightly. His studies at Milhematte were over for at time, now he would stay here and work with his father until mid-winter. Their responsibilities as village smiths included getting tools ready for the harvest. As his mother darned a stocking, she joked about several of the young ladies that would be glad that he was home.

I was, at first, tempted to show them some of what I knew of magic with fire, but I decided against it. This was his homecoming and his time to reunite with his family. I would wait until I developed my skill before I showed others openly.

It was much later that night, after several tankards of a bitter ale that grew in flavor after each one, that I excused myself. I washed my face and arms. Taking a blanket I went to a designated corner of Kopernick's room and lay down on a mat. In the outer room the others continued to talk in the firelight and the thick sweet smoke from the pipe that hung in the air.

*   *   *   *   *

I opened my eyes and found I was again in a dream at the edge of the world. Looking out over the ocean, I could see the waves as they thundered up and down the shoreline. Light from the quarter moon fragmented countless times off their crests. Wind pulled warmly at my hair and I could feel it in my beard.

"Nathel?" I said into the night knowing that the ghost must stand near. My voice slurred a bit from the ale and my vision wasn't the sharpest. Without thinking I searched around my feet for the staff of ash and realized I no longer carried it. It was leaning on the wall beside our boots and under the pegs that held our cloaks to dry. In the dream, I remained dressed as I was when I went to sleep. The blanket, thankfully I mused, did not come with me.

"I am here beside you, as always. Your presence here is strong. Are you close?" Nathel was standing, but presently sat upon a rock beside me. His clothes remained the same, the ones that he had died in. The sheath upon his back was barren of any sword.

"No, I'm not far away at all," I said as he settled down. "I am in the village of Glenhelen," I pointed in some direction away from the ocean. Whether this was the true direction to Glenhelen, I was not sure.

"Marc! Why did you not tell me?"

"I wanted to surprise you."

"Had I known you were on your way here I would have had you bring some items. What do you have with you?"

"Um, a change of clothing, some food, two books and pens."

"Ah," he stood hands on his hips. He was clearly frustrated. "There are some things in that room with the horse with no nose that you could have brought. You are so close."

"They say that I can get to the coast in just over a week, maybe less. Then I will be here. Only one more week." My finger wavered as I held it in the air.

"Is the ale too strong for you?" I guess he must have sensed I had a bit to drink.

"Please forgive me," I said closing my eyes and forcing myself to focus. Of all things in my life, this was important. Breathing deep, I could smell the ocean with its salt and seaweed. Here also was the smell of jasmine, faint and unmistakable, being carried on the night breeze. He said nothing but sat quietly listening to the sound of the waves breaking on the rocks below.

"It has been a while since I have last seen you. I thought you had forsaken me," I said finally breaking the spell.

"Never." He sighed deeply. "Bringing your spirit here while you sleep draws strength from your being too." The ghost folded his arms on his knees and looked back out to the sea. His hair moved of its own accord in a wind that was not in my world.

"So, tell me what you have learned. I thought you were continuing your studies." he said speaking so I could hear him over the surf. "Truly, there is much others have told you about my life."

"I have heard much about your battles along the way. I have learned much about Thumwood, Rivenburch, Lanedorf . . . the people of the kingdom are very grateful to you for what you have done. They sing of the time Sablich and others were held back in hiding until after the Drenthen line passed over. They fought them from the rear and killed many more than your number. They've made a wonderful ballad in his name. Do you know he is still alive and the commander of the garrison in Land Streth?"

"He is?" The tone of his voice was genuine.

"Yes."

"I am sure he is well into his years by now. I remember when he was just a young soldier. A noble in my guidance, waiting for his turn to rule his father's land. Head strong and full of fight. We all were at one time, I guess. Do you hear the truth in what they say?"

"I have heard it enough to know it is as close to the truth as I will get. Words can bend and change, but underneath the story stays the same."

"Like working with metal," Nathel said and for a moment I wondered if he knew I was with Kopernick. When we last talked I was traveling alone.

"It is like working with metal. No matter what you make, nails or plows, underneath it is still the same."

"Do these stories leave you with questions?" he asked.

"They do. There are some things I would like to have more clarification on, but no one that I talk with knows, or cannot remember the real truth. It can get frustrating at times."

"Ask me and I'll help if I can."

I was silent for a moment thinking. I had so many questions before, but now none would come to the surface. The ale clouded my mind and I fought through it.

"Ah, here's one." I held my hand up. "I heard of a story of you and Kalendeck becoming blood-brothers. Everyone knows this as a fact, but few, if any of them have any idea how it happened. Can you tell me?"

"That is a good one." Opening his hand, he ran his finger along a scar. It was almost straight across the palm from fore-finger to the outer edge. "There is an ancient ritual that is deeply rooted in my heritage. If one man holds a grievance with another, there is a way to make amends of what has gone wrong. A dagger is drawn across a palm of each mans left hand. The hands are then tied together so their blood mixes. From this day on they cannot raise a hand in anger against one another for they have become blood-brothers. Honor now binds them together."

"What made you so angry at him to do such?"

Nathel took a deep breath before he went on. It seemed some wounds carried on even after death.

"He was too bold. The man was very brazen in his actions. He never feared for his own life, but in doing so he placed several of my best fighters in danger. Some were lost. Not just men, but good men. Fighters I hand-picked to fight in my command. With a foolish move, a grievous error in judgment, they were lost to save that one man. I do not wish to speak of it now."

"I understand." There was a pause, long and silent, before I spoke again.

"Do you remember Hansgrohe, and Laensey?" I asked.

"Yes I do, they were fine men. We saved this land. Laensey, I knew personally. Together, we commanded our men when we fought beside each other in Lanedorf. It was he who led the men around the Drenthen and came here to Ihrhoven. He destroyed their guards and burned their ships. You've not heard the story of Ashe have you? I think you have her staff. There is not enough time tonight. Be that as it may, they completed their work in the dead of winter. When they were here, it was during a tragic storm of ice and snow. From there they traveled with much haste to south and brought down the Drenthen when they could.

"Hansgrohe was a great fighter who died with much honor. He was an archer who held off many men. They say a cut gave him sickness and he died in bed."

Nathel looked down and touched the wound that was in his chest just above his heart that continued to bleed. There were other open wounds marked by a crimson taint of blood, but this one appeared to have been the one that was mortal. Several other scars could be seen upon his arms and shoulders.

"The anger I had against Kalendeck was great at one time." he said and I could hear regret in his voice. "Few blades ever touched him. None mortally so. He always had his honor. When he died and fire thundered through the halls of Welteroth, he brought over two hundred souls with him. None of them were from this kingdom. He died with great honor. No man living could have asked for more."

I looked out over the water and thought about this for some time.

"Do your wounds still hurt?" I asked. I turned to Nathel and saw that the blood would drip down to the ground and disappear in the grass.

"I do not feel the physical pain, from this wound, or any of the others I have suffered. That type of pain left me when I left my body. I do feel an emptiness in my heart everyday that I am here. My love waits for me on the other side. When my time is over, and I have the right articles, then I can go. We have waited a long time to see each other."

"Does she know you'll come for her?"

"Aye, she does." There was silence as the waves carried through to the shoreline. There were storm clouds out over the water. Lightning flared several times beyond the horizon, but no thunder could be heard. The rainy season was about at the end. Soon the low storm clouds would lose their purchase of the land and return to the higher air.

"What articles do you need?"

Nathel sighed. "The things that I need are in a locked room in Croskreye Castle. I've got the only key to the door there. You'll need that."

"Couldn't the door be broken down?"

"The door is protected by magic. I have the counter-spell. You have to know it or it's pointless. Had I known you were coming I could have told you the counter-spell, the door could have been opened, and I would have them."

"I still have more to learn." Time, distance, and the ale muddled my thoughts. I would probably only remember the faintest wisps of what Nathel said to me.

Water, as well as wind, pounded against the cliff that night. In the silence that followed a woman could be heard singing. It was a beautiful voice that was high, soft, and pure. I though at first that she stood in the trees behind us. I turned around and searched for the source, but could not find it.

"The lady sings for us tonight," Nathel said.

"Where is she?" I asked turning back around to face the sea.

"You will see her down on the shore line. She arrives usually around midnight on the water . . ."

I looked over the cliff and there she was. On the ocean it looked as if a woman was walking on the water. She wore a white gown was a bit torn and frayed near the edges, but other than that it was not damaged. Her light hair lay in one long braid over her shoulder.

She was beautiful, my breath caught in my throat seeing her.

Walking on a crest of a wave she came. Closer, the white cap brought her gently to the shore. She sang her song until her feet rested on the sand. She took several steps away from the ocean and then looked to her left. She looked along the beach for a moment, and then turned right, searching the ground as she went and kicking at things that were no longer there. She could be heard humming softly as she searched.

"I have heard tales about the ocean's daughter. That this is she, I am not sure. She looks for something here, but I do not know what it is. She will be back this way shortly and search among those rocks there, as she does every time. Then she will leave the same way she came. Odd that she chooses this exact place on the beach below."

"You cannot talk to her?"

"I wish that I could . . ." Behind us the bells of Ihrhoven chimed. I realized it was my time to leave.

"I'm leaving," I said as I saw the moonlight start to fade.

"Be safe," was all that Nathel could say before the night faded and all was black.

As I woke, Kopernick came in the room. He tiptoed across the stone floor and lay in his own bed. Pulling a coarse wool blanket closer around me, I slept well until morning.

*　*　*　*　*

I heard laughter in the outer room which woke me.

"Good morning." Kopernick greeted me as I came out from the bedroom.

"Good morning to you," I said with a yawn. Most of the children were outside. Kopernick and his parents were sitting and chatting. I nodded good morning to each of them in turn.

"I haven't slept that well in a while," I said scratching my stomach under my light shirt. "I want to thank you for the mat and a dry night."

"It is no problem, it is our honor to have you here," said Lindergren. He had soot on his cheek and the tips of his fingers were black. Already, this early, he worked the forge.

Honored. It struck me as an odd thing to say. To them I am a just common traveler. A scribe on a quest for my duke. Did they hold someone so highly? I stood there in the door to the bedroom puzzled.

"I see I have some explaining to do," said Kopernick seeing the look on my face. "I was studying my trade in my school in Milhematte when I received word of you. It was a message by Sorcerer Tyndall to watch out for a man named Marc from Croskreye going to Ihrhoven. A common enough name; two cousins, one on pa's side and one on ma's, share this name. I was to help you as much as I could. I know that being a scribe you may not have the training and be well versed in weapons. You could be harmed easily enough. Tyndall just wanted me to assure your safety north. Our meeting along the road was by no mere chance.

"Until the snake bit me, I thought nothing overly special about you. It was Ryeson who informed me of whom you really are. No, don't be alarmed," he said as I looked about. The look in my eyes must have given me away. I didn't want it to end like this, so close to meeting Nathel.

"Please, sit," Corva offered. "We will keep your secret."

"I am nervous, I will stand," I said, politely declining her offer to sit with a wave of my hand.

Kopernick went on. "I saw that Ryeson was correct. You were not only Marc from Croskreye, but also the man that they refer to as Marecrish, the lost one, Marc-from-nowhere. There is a slight essence about you that I have not seen elsewhere. Also, after a time, you did not try to hide your naivety about the kingdom. At first glance, one may not see the difference between you and the people of the kingdom, but after some time I could tell. My mother has some powers in healing-spirit magic. She can see into people and she knew who you were when you walked in."

I stood in the doorway looking back and forth between Kopernick and his parents.

"I don't know what to say," I said at last. "Do not be angry at me for not telling you the truth about my past. When we traveled together you never really asked. I did not lie to you, Kopernick, I am going north to collect information as I have said. I am glad you treated me as you did and not like an outcast, as others might once they learned who I really am."

"It's been no difficulty at all," Corva said as she stood. She took my hand in her own, curling our fingers together to make one large fist. Her plump fingers were very warm to the touch. She held my hand this way for a few heartbeats and with her other made small circles above them. "You have a very strong alliance with spirit magic. Did Tyndall train you at all in this?"

"No. Davlyne gave me training."

Kopernick sucked in his breath.

"Davlyne trained you?" he asked. "Usually she trains none of the common people. Her skills are so that only the higher lords and ladies are able to afford her services."

I nodded. "Tyndall was going to work with me over the summer, I believe, but I left too soon."

Kopernick whistled low. "To turn down being schooled by Sorcerer Tyndall himself. My word, there are plenty of people who would love to have him train them."

I shrugged my shoulders and nodded.

"At the time this was more important to me. We were going to the Gathering when he offered me a choice."

"You'll need some training in what you're closest to," Corva went on quickly. "Makes the world of difference once your skill opens up to you. You could be very strong in spirit magic if trained properly. You see things that others cannot, don't you?"

"I do. I have had very vivid dreams and I believe spirits seem to seek me out." I had not spoken of this to Kopernick and he gave me a quizzical look.

"Just one ghost?" she asked raising an eyebrow in query.

"Yes, just one." The dream of the sword, of the woman walking in the deep grass, was outlandish and I did not wish to humor them.

"More than one thing calls to you. Search your dreams. spirit magic is not always being able to communicate with those that have departed. It is also strengthening your own spirit. Enhance this skill and any of the others will be easier to master," she said as she lowered my hand and went to the kitchen. She began to clean crockery humming to herself as she did so.

"I have made a promise to someone I must fulfill. I'll be going to Ihrhoven as soon as I can. I will spend time here on my return."

"You'll be well, won't you?" Kopernick asked.

"Yes," I nodded. "I wish to leave early so as not to waste the day." I went to the corner of the room and retrieved my belongings. I opened my pack and pulled out my first book. It was a bit older and had begun to show signs of wear. I brushed it off as I had done many times and handed it to Kopernick.

"If you wish to understand me read this. I started writing this journal within my first month here. I filled the pages with all I learned and I had to buy my new one in Corristone to keep up with the stories you told me. There are some things written there about the royal family of Kahshgrance that need to remain private. Please honor my wish to have it so."

"I shall."

"Another book," said Lindergren slapping me on the back. "We'll never get him to finish his chores now."

I slipped my tunic over my light shirt and began to put my boots on. Kopernick, already looking through the pages, seemed completely engrossed in the book. Staff, dagger, haversack. After placing a few small treats in my sack, I was ready to go.

I would be able to spend time with Kopernick and his family when I returned.

After we said many good-byes, I left from the cottage and then out of the village to the road heading north.

Chapter #13

I stood in the middle of the broken shale road as it found its way down into the valley. It was not wide here, just a wagon trail through the woods that was overgrown with weeds and brambles. Spider webs were frequent. In this particular place, the road sat in a saddle-back created by two hill tops that were bare of any trees on the north side. This was the first time, since I left Glenhelen, that the trees had thinned enough to see what lay beyond. The Kear Forest circled the hill tops around me like a sea of green. A doe and her fawn, which had not yet seen me, continued to nibble on the high grass that grew in the sunlight. Looking further on, I saw the ruins of a house sitting just outside the edge of the forest. Vines had covered most of the outer surfaces blending the structure with the trees.

The sun was warm on my shoulders as it reached its peak in the summer sky. I continued on after a short break. Feeling a sense of urgency at being this close to my destination, I hurried. It was my third day from Glenhelen and I would be in Ihrhoven by the week's end.

*　*　*　*　*

That afternoon the road started to go through some tougher ground. I paused at the crest of another hill, not to take in the sight of the valley below, but to catch my breath. I looked back behind me and wondered how a wagon could have made its way up that.

Continuing on, I stopped at the bottom of the hill to drink from a stream. A bridge must have graced the road at one time, but that was all but gone. The stone foundations for its support now lay in ruin on either side. Moss and grass covered much of the stone work with only the stubs of wooden planks still captive in its grip. Years of travel by men and animals had worn deep ruts in the dirt on both sides.

As I drank, minnows swimming in the water darted about. The water was clean and pure, so I drank deeply. The forest was especially thick along the water's edge and allowed only a little light in making it cool. The banks of the stream were clear of thorn, brambles and golden-rods.

It was then, as I knelt on my hands and knees, head down to the water, that I heard a growl. I didn't move at first, thinking that it was not a beast of any type, but my stomach, or my imagination. To my dismay, I heard it again and it was neither.

It was the growl of a wolf, the noise somewhere beyond my view in the trees. As I looked up water dripped from my beard to the stream.

On top of a knoll I saw the back of a large wolf as it tore at the remains of a carcass near the edge of the road. Had I not stopped for water I would have walked right up to it. Had I splashed onward through the stream I would have been heard. The wolf was growling at a second wolf that was trying to grab a morsel of this kill. They snapped at each other.

I was quite a distance away and not presently in any danger. The wolves had not noticed me yet, both intent on eating the kill. There must have been enough for both, for they stopped their fighting and began to eat the meal together. I eased myself out of the kneeling position and moved backward slowly. Retracing my steps, I put a respectable distance between myself and the two. I did not go as far as to put them out of sight. Climbing on the back of a boulder, safely above the ground, I was just able to see them on the knoll. I watched them for a time until they finished.

*   *   *   *   *

The sun was just beginning to set when one of the wolves stopped eating and perked its ears up. I stopped breathing hoping that it had not caught my scent. The other looked up also, but then continued to eat. The first one sniffed the wind, and took a step or two down the trail away from me. It licked the blood on its jowls.

From a distant hillside came the bay of a third wolf. At this, the wolf that was still eating stopped and cried out as if to answer. This sound was so close it put a chill up my spine. My hand tightened on my dagger and I rolled my eyes upward. This was going to be a long night.

Wolves generally traveled in packs. With just these two feeding here, their pack would not be far behind. I looked at the boulder that I sat on and realized that if I could get up here they could also with enough determination. Several trees around me looked easy enough to climb if I had to. Feeling somewhat secure, I watched the wolves from atop the boulder and did not retreat.

Another howl was heard, more distant than the first and the two wolves below stopped their eating and took off through the woods. I listened intently until they were gone, not daring to breathe lest the sound of my breath betray me.

Still I did not move. Thoughts raced through my head. I did not fear these two wolves. If I heard them coming, I could return and be safe. But there were other animals that would be brought here by the smell of blood. Bears and panthers would find me an easy meal. They could be attracted to this place by the scent of blood, and so it was my final decision to get off the boulder and away from there before it was too late.

Making my way down from the boulder, I quickly went back to the stream. Hearing no animal of substantial size, I continued on quickly.

I thought to pass the area of the kill as quickly as possible, but as I passed the carcass my curiosity rose and I looked to see if I could identify what it was that they had brought down.

* * * * *

The leather sandals were well-worn, so much so that the toe on the left side had begun to curl up, and a hole was clearly seen on the right sole. Her dress was that of a common worker. She had darned and patched it in several places without regard to the color of the parent material. Her ankles and calves were smooth and white.

Even though the sparkle had left her eyes, they still held the color of a stream of water at midday. Light blue. Like a morning sky just before the sun rose from behind the hills to touch it. Several strands of hair, as fair as a field of golden wheat, glimmered as the wind shifted them across her brow. A heavy braid tied with a faded red ribbon lay over her shoulder.

On her lips was an expression that couldn't be called a smile or a frown, but rather that of contentment. It would seem that a great burden was lifted from her shoulders, the burden of life.

* * * * *

I could move no further. My knees buckled and I collapsed there in the dirt. As the evening steadily darkened, I did nothing and looked at the body as it lay. There was very little left of the chest and stomach. Entrails, torn and twisted, lay in dirt, grass, and twigs. They gnawed her upper thigh and buttocks down to the bone. The insects had already found her.

Not wanting the wolves to hear me, I beat my fists upon the ground. They took a life, a human life. I was too late! Had I been faster, had I not stopped to drink I may have saved her! I screamed my anger through clenched teeth and stood and kicked in frustration at the brambles and bracken.

I paused in my anger. My mind raced and I knew it would do no harm and at the same moment I knew it would do no good. I began the chant for healing, the spell Ryeson taught me, and the words came to my lips as if on their own. She was dead I reasoned, but the words still came. A cut was one thing, but to heal death . . . ? I let the spell build. For one breath. For two. It began to tighten around me. Twisting in strength like unseen rope around my chest. Fearing to let it go further, in a cry of anguish, I spoke the last word.

I collapsed on my knees on the ground beside her. Taking deep breaths of air, I paused once more when the dizziness faded. She was the same, she had not changed. I had expected her to, but knew these were wisps of fancy. I turned her head, touching the cool unblemished skin, and brushed some dirt from her forehead and hair from her eyes.

I stood after a time. The spell had drained me, but I could not stay.

It was obvious that she had not died here, for blood covered the trail for a short distance. Just beyond it's beginning, I found her walking staff and a small bundle of cloth. Picking up these, I cradled them tightly to my chest.

Even though my heart hurt for the young woman, I could not mourn for her. I was stricken, truthfully, but tears would not come. Perchance, if I had known her, I would have wept with ease, but now I just couldn't. Anger and disgust replaced that. Perhaps there will be time for grief later after the shock wore off. The threat of the wolves coming back was still on my mind.

Of course it would be wrong to let her stay here in the woods. I had heard that the Kear Forest was no place to die. I would chance it and bring the body with me this night. I could carry it on my shoulder, and still make it with little discomfort. She had been of a slight build when she was alive and with this much of it gone it would not be heavy. Tomorrow I would surly see someone along the road that would be able to help me.

I rolled her on her back and using the remnants of her long dress, I was able to wrap it around her chest and waist containing what threatened to tumble out. As such, I could carry her.

I placed the bundle of cloth and the walking staff on her chest. Her head rolled to the side and the blank eyes stared past me to evening air and the branches of an old oak that stood nearby.

I was about to pick her up when I heard someone sobbing quietly behind me. It startled me at first and I froze where I knelt. For the first time, I realized that there may have been two people. One that hid while the other tried to fend off the wolves and finally became the sacrifice.

If the person had been this close, the wolves would have sensed them, I was sure. Wolves killed for the sport of it.

I turned on my heels and saw a young woman squatting there with her arms wrapped tightly about her chest. If she were a real person, I would have heard her approach. Ghosts don't make noise when they move.

I sighed and looked toward the heavens. By now the darkness was becoming complete. From the stream, bull frogs croaked amongst a quire of pipers. An owl hooted downstream while other animals could be heard beginning to move about. Wind stirred the upper branches of the birch and oak trees making them creak and groan in their effort. The stars came out one by one, needle pricks in the vast canvas of darkness.

Her form shimmered in the night. Her hands covered her glowing face as she cried openly. I went to comfort her, but found there was little I could do. As I knelt beside her, she looked up.

"I'm dead!" she exclaimed.

"I know," was all that I was able to say. My mind raced for something else to say, but I found nothing that was comforting. I was silent and let her to her grief.

"It hurt," she said. "Oh mother, it hurt," She held her arms to her chest and rocked back and forth.

"Do you want to talk?" I asked. It would be awkward if I left or if I stayed. Either way I was uncomfortable. She said nothing for a while, but just sat there rocking.

* * * * *

"I remember when I was young and people from my village died of a sickness that came in the water. I helped the people who were tending to the people with the sickness. I saw a man die and wondered what it was like. What was that man thinking when the end came? That man had done one thing that I never did. In an instant, he left his body and the beating oars of the Skye Boat replaced the beating of his heart. I always wondered at my death, what it would be like. I did not want it to end like this," she dried her eyes with the palm of her hand.

"What do you remember?" I asked. I listened to her, but also kept attention to the other noises around me. As of yet, there was nothing to cause alarm. In the starlight I watched for movement on the trail. The staff of ash lit the forest for some distance. The broken shale of the wagon trail was lighter in color than that of the forest.

"I was walking along the road, when I saw them behind me. I started to run and they gave chase. With one I might have made it, as they are generally afraid when they are alone. With two or more they get their courage up. They would snap at me and retreat, snap and retreat. Finally the bigger one jumped up, grabbed my throat, and bit. I was helpless to do anything, but fall," she paused for a moment before she went on.

"I was laying on the ground and they were biting into my stomach. I tried to beat at them with my fists, but I was weak. There was a numbing pain and I could see their backs. I began to feel numb all over, and as I looked at the trees above, I felt very peaceful.

"The next thing I saw was you kneeling over my body," she began to cry again and I let her. Time passed slowly and she stopped crying and became still. I wished not to stay here. It would have been foolish of me to stay the night so close to this kill.

"As a ghost, are you still afraid?"

"I don't know. There is no more pain, but I would rather be alive. I feel attached to this area somehow. I don't know if it's because my death was here or if it's because my body is here. They say that the Kear Forest is no place to die."

"I was planning to take your body and belongings with me tonight," I said thinking of nothing else to say. "This would not be the place to bury you or to leave you. If I left it here tonight, who knows what might have it by forenoon."

She was silent for a time.

"I understand your thinking and I thank you. I can also see that there is a feeling of fear around you. is this because of me?"

"No," I said with a nervous laugh as I looked at the woods around me. "I fear that the wolves may return, or something worse. A bear perhaps. If I am to take your body would you be able to come with me? Could you follow?"

"I feel more comfortable here I am afraid. It will get lonely here. Will you be coming back from Ihrhoven soon?"

"I will. This is the only road to the south. I may stay in Ihrhoven only one night or so to conduct some simple business with a friend and then I'll be coming back this way."

"If you must leave, take it with you," she was standing next to me, and motioned down to her body. "I have no need for it now, and do not wish to see it rot into the dirt. Before you arrive in Ihrhoven there is a huge elm tree on a hillside. Rest my bones near there, that's where my mother is at."

"I shall," I said as I stooped down and gathered the bundle that was her body in my arms. I held her legs tightly in with one arm, while her upper body lay over my shoulder. Something wet and sticky traveled down my forearm. I tried not to shudder It was easier to carry her over my shoulder this way, like a sack of grain, and as I shifted I turned to her ghost.

"I will be careful," I said at last.

"What a gentle man you are," she said and, on an impulse carried over from her living days, she stepped close to embrace me.

* * * * *

I saw the stars above me as I lay upon my back. The leaves in the upper branches of the trees swayed in the night breeze and tipped with silver from the moon that had just risen. Fireflies flickered on and off as they traveled near the ground.

Another wave of dizziness came and I tried to steady myself as the world spun beneath me. There was a weight on my shoulder that I was unsure of. I reached out with my free hand and touched it. Something in cloth, damp in places.

How did I get here? I wondered. Shouldn't I be somewhere else?

{Where am I?} Came a voice from inside of my head.

"Lady, where are you?" hearing her voice started to bring it all back. I began to remember the events that just happened. I shoved the young woman's body gently off of my shoulder and sat up. Bringing my feet under me, I stood with unstable legs. I looked about, my boots loud on the shale, but there was no one here. She was gone. Where was she?

{Marc ...}

"Yes I am here, where are you?" I asked again.

{I am here with you.}

"I can hear you, but I can't see you." I looked all around again for the glow of her form, but found nothing. Dizziness almost brought me to my knees. The Kear Forest at night was very dark.

{Marc, listen to me.} She said softly. {I am with you. I am seeing through your eyes now.}

"This cannot be . . ." I paused. This was terrible, I thought. How could I get her back out? I didn't want to take her to Ihrhoven to see Nathel. It just wouldn't be right. Could Nathel do the same? My head began to pound with pain and I lost my train of thought. I staggered down the path a few paces with my hands clenched tightly to my temples.

"Can you get back out?" I pleaded. "Please you must try."

{I think I can. It's just that your body is like a heavy skin or a blanket around me. It feels so warm in here.} I felt my arm twitch.

"Can you get out?" I repeated my question with more force. My leg went out and I went down painfully on one knee.

{Do you want me out?} she said mournfully. {I would much rather stay here it feels so nice. I feel almost alive again.}

Thoughts raced through my head as it throbbed. I brought my hands to my forehead again. The dizziness started to subside. I tried to shake it from my skull, and found myself face down on the road.

Distantly I heard the bay of a wolf that cut sharply through the night.

{Wolf!} She began to speak in my mind. {Try not to think about it now, we have not time to waste. Just pick up the body and your things and get out of here. We can talk about my being here later.}

In a stupor I stood again, and slung her remains over my shoulder in one motion.

{Leave my staff, take your own.}

Ash was warm in my hand. The presence of this familiar object in my hands helped me focus. Breathe, just breathe.

Somehow my body movements did not feel my own, but I kept going regardless. Something damp and sticky brushed against my cheek as I took my first step, and this I dismissed absently.

* * * * *

Whether or not I passed anyone else that traveled along the road during the night, I was uncertain. The night left the last valley of the Kear Forest slowly. The light from the moon died away as early dawn approached. Morning came with a murky gray fog that brought a heavy dew covering everything. At the end of the forest, the trees grew to fantastic heights so that they disappeared into the gray nothingness above me.

I continued on, keeping my mind free of thinking, of giving away secrets I meant to keep. My mind sought to only put as much distance on the trail this night as I could. I rested briefly as the sun went from a hollow disk hidden in the fog to its full brightness in the morning sky.

At a boulder some distance from the trail, I lay her body gently to the ground. I did not look at the remains as I tried to keep my thoughts and eyes diverted to more pleasant things. Leaning against the large boulder, I swung my arms in large circles to relieve the tension from the night. With the rock still to my back, I leaned against a plum tree in the knee high grass and raised my head to the forenoon sun.

The warmth of the sun was wonderful as it touched my face. I could sense its brightness through closed lids, and its warmth made my face glow. I brought my elbows to my knees and sighed. is this the feeling, this glowing in the sun, she felt being inside me?

{Yes.} came her voice again.

"This is a bad time for you to stay with me," I said softly.

{Don't make me leave.} she pleaded. I could feel her anguish.

"I will not make you do anything. If you leave me, then you will have to do it yourself. Although I did not invite you here, you are welcome. I will support you for the time being, but I want you to know that you must leave sometime." What I was saying reminded me of what Lady Wenonah had said to me once about being here in the kingdom.

{I understand.} She was quiet for a length of time before she spoke again. {This land is not a forgiving one. If you make a mistake it can snuff you out like a candle. I have learned that, still and all, I learned it too late, I suppose. If, by chance, we happen upon a body that is near death, I will leave you and enter it, however, this body must not be wounded beyond the hope of life. Such as mine was.}

"I agree." I breathed. I was exhausted.

The road had followed the stream throughout the night so water was always near at hand. Possibly it continued traveling to the ocean. I ran my tongue over the roof of my mouth and felt the roughness there. I was thirsty, but not extremely so. My stomach was too empty to grumble. Having been on my feet since the sun rose yesterday all I needed was sleep.

{Do not sleep now. Wash yourself and change your cloths.}

"But, I need rest."

{Sleep then. I will do it for you.}

I was on my feet before my eyes could open. I reached out and grabbed the plum tree to steady myself. The numbness that had come quickly to legs left as I willed them back to my control.

"Please, don't do that."

{I want to Marc, let me move again.}

I was suddenly too tired to resist her. Slowly my body went numb and I sat inside of my skull looking out through my own eyes. Things seemed different as she began to move my body about, but I did not try to fight it.

Giving in to the basic needs of my body, I rested.

*   *   *   *   *

I felt at first the images that I saw were dreams, but they lasted to such a length, and were so sharp and clear, I was sure that they were memories. Shifting from one scene to another, I caught glimpses of places that I had never been to before. As a young child, I was being given a bath, the water was warm, but the air inside the small room was cold with ice on the windows. The scenes changed suddenly and I was working in a field of corn. The corn and their stalks chaffed my hands with their roughness. It continued like this for some time. At last I realized that the road I was looking at was not a memory, but I was awake watching the land pass by with my own eyes.

I heard her humming a simple tune softly in my own voice. They were not my memories at all, as I had first thought, but they were hers.

{Hello.} I thought out to her.

"Hello, and good evening," she said with my voice, and continued humming a tune I never heard before. I looked for the sun and found that it was close to setting on the horizon. The road was a bit wider here and I saw several other travelers dispersed before us at varying distances. The Kear Forest was well behind us and now only scattered strands of birch and popular doted the fields and grasses. I was quiet for several moments as I watched and felt about me.

{What happened today?}

"Not much. I rested my bones at the bolder where you stopped. There is no sense to carry it for three days. The stench would be too great, and it would draw suspicion. Flies were already starting to gather. We don't need to become slowed down. Besides, it was already growing stiff with death. There were many stones nearby and it was not difficult."

I thought on this for a considerable amount of time and then chose my words carefully.

{I mean you no malice when I say this, but it is what I would have done also. I am sorry I promised you different. At the time I did not realize the scope of the task.}

"I understand. Blood and dirt covered the left side of your shirt and your pack was a mess. I couldn't keep the flies away," she continued on. "I washed your shirt, and put the other one on. They fit you well."

{Did I eat any?}

"Yes. We passed a patch of blackberries and raspberries earlier today. Also, there was some biscuit bread and an apple in your haversack."

{I am coming back.}I stated, and she knew what I meant. The feeling reminded me of a flat stone being placed on a surface of water in a cup and then settling to the bottom. I shifted from above and as I sank downward her soul pushed upward.

The transition was not as smooth as I wished. I stumbled when she pulled herself out of my left leg, and I was not ready for it. I regained my stride with only a few stares from the other travelers. A man with two donkeys in tow laughed loudly.

{I am familiar with this area. The road you take is not the straightest or the shortest. I know some side paths and we may make a little better time. Tonight we will stay in the Red Raven Inn, and by tomorrow evening we will be able to see the ocean.}

"And Ihrhoven?" I asked.

{A day and a half if we really push it. But I don't think that you should. That may harm you. Take it easy, we have made a lot of time as it is. A few more hours to rest will not hurt will it?}

"No, it won't," I said thinking of Nathel and then quickly pushing the thought aside. "We are almost there then?"

{Yes.}

"All this," I breathed, "and I don't even know your name."

{I ... I am Brembry.}

*   *   *   *   *

{You've got a bit of change in the pouch you carry and a token from Duke Almonesson. Are you noble born?}

"No, I am just a commoner. Please let me enjoy this meal in peace," I said with my mouth half full of chicken. Brembry grew quiet.

Finding the Red Raven was not difficult, getting the room was. It had cost me more than double the price of anywhere else. That was the trouble with these places. They had no set rate and the price depended on the mood of the keeper of the inn. I suppose I was getting too used to common halls and their simple meals of soup. It was just something more to add to the irritation and fatigue of the day.

She tied a new ribbon to the leather loop on my pack. Beside the blue and green ribbons there was now a red one. It was longer than the others. Taken from her hair as she placed stones to cover her body.

"I saw some of your thoughts while you were in control of my body. Are my thoughts open to you?" I asked her.

{I can see some, but I do not see anything of your younger life. I have seen images of you talking closely with someone you identify as Lady Wenonah. Along with the skill to write, read, and the gold you carry I naturally took it as you were noble born.}

"It is a long story I will have to tell it to you later."

{Are you on your way to Ihrhoven to visit someone?}

"This is another long story. If you are with me I suppose I shall have to tell you before we get there. Now please, no more."

I ate my meal in the common room of the Red Raven Inn. The tables were dark with a deep stain that almost resembled the color of the walls. Beneath this room was the wine cellar. Whenever someone ordered ale the young serving lady went down the stairs and returned in a short while. A dog lay before a fire that crackled in the hearth to my side. I had tossed him chicken bones as I finished them. The fire had been lit more for the need of light than for the need of warmth. Over ten candles lit the counter area and five lanterns burning with a foul pungent odor that wafted throughout the room.

There was little talk about the tension to the south. I listened and heard Lysaght's name brought up at least twice. Mostly they spoke of the festival in Ihrhoven for the coming of the summer solstice. The Day of Turning was just days away. I expected to in Ihrhoven by then.

{I had hoped to go to Glenhelen for the festivities.}

Fireflies flickered outside, and children chased after them. Men on the far side of the room bargained with others for goods that lay under canvases on their wagons.

I stood. My body was bone weary from two days and a night without sleep. The sleep that I had neglected was quickly catching up with me. I gave a bar maiden the coins that was due for the meal, and then went up stairs.

"I did not mean speak harshly. I am sorry if I have hurt your feelings." I said pushing my door open and placing my pack on the floor. I gave a half-hearted chuckle thinking of how I should pen this in my book. It could wait.

{You need sleep, we both do. Tomorrow when you've rested, you will be a better conversational companion.}

"I believe I shall be at that."

Sleep came very easily that night.

* * * * *

I was walking past a set of wagons that were having a bad time of it getting up the hill. I would have stopped to lend a hand but they had plenty of help. Men had gathered around and were working as hard as the horses.

{... so she is in love with Clendenin then? He is a blacksmith and not farmer?}

"Yes, You've heard about that way up here?"

{Everyone in the kingdom knows.} she giggled in my head. {Duke Almonesson is a distant cousin to King Trahune himself. Gossip from the royal families is always good to hear. When something new is heard we chat for days.}

"I thought it was a great secret though," I said. I turned and looked back at the way we had come. The horses that pulled the two wagons strained under the load. Men placed wooden stops under the wheels when progress was made. The wagon would not roll back down and ground lost. They took the hill at a snails pace, and would make it eventually. The wagon master should have been embarrassed to have his horses put through this.

Open fields of crab grass and timothy lay in all directions. Storm clouds had gathered to the south near the horizon. Above me, the sky was clear and blue. We would make into Ihrhoven dry.

Ihrhoven ... thoughts raced through my head. I tried to suppress them. Half a year lay between where I was now and when I started.

"Why were you given the name of Brembry?" I asked changing the subject. "That's the name of a tree." There was a bit of laughter in my head and it was good to feel her in a happy mood. My mood was better as well.

{When I was little I kept getting into everything. You see? Once I was out of sight for just a few moments and they found me on the other side of the village near the cliffs. The elder Ryn once called me Brembry and it caught on.}

Brembry wood came from a tree that germinated from seed, grew to a height twice that of a man, and died within one turning of the moon. The seeds of the tree were light and the wind carried them easily. The brembry trees would make forests that would travel where the wind willed them. The rotting wood was very good for crops, and the mulch was valuable on land that was mostly stone. Such as some of the areas on the western side of the kingdom.

{That's because it's hard for the trees to grow there, otherwise there would be no market for the mulch.} Her voice took over my own thoughts.

"Can you read my thoughts?" I asked more in awe and curiosity than anger. I was not used to have what I thought narrated in a feminine voice.

{In a way, yes. You were doing the same, I believe, when you saw flashes of me when I was younger. This is how you see your thoughts. Just now you were thinking about the time when Tyndall had you look in the fire of brembry wood. It was then that he told you the properties of the wood.}

I reached the crest of the knoll a short time later and looked out over the wide breadth of land that lay before me. The land rolled gently to a band of sand on the horizon touching the blue-green waters. Trees grew in plentiful thickets crowding themselves below.

{We'll be there before nightfall, Marc.}

Chapter #14

The people of Ihrhoven were busy as the last hour of daylight came. The first structure that I came to was a fortress that was well back from the village and the ocean. Men sweated from the weight of stones as they carried them two or three at a time inside the structure. Buckets of water and sand were constantly going in and out. Maidens in white aprons readied a long table with food for the workers. The wagons I had passed earlier would arrive late tonight.

The stronghold was being hastily built. The stone being used was much smaller than those used in the castle of Croskreye. The structure was still very sound.

{This is here in case the men from the north come again. We will be ready this time.} Brembry said with all certainty. I could hear the pride in her voice.

"Shouldn't they build it closer to the ocean. Its purpose should protect the village. Here the enemy could go through the village first."

{The stone near the cliffs is not as sturdy as it is back here. The foundation would not be as strong and it could not support the tremendous weight. The castle is a watch tower, mostly, the Drenthen would see the castle and attack here first. Our people would then send word south.}

Soldiers wearing colors from other territories were working about the castle. With the tension to the south, I thought they would have returned to their home lands.

{Soon they will, Marc. If word reaches here tomorrow, they will have to abandon all of this and leave it for my townspeople.} I felt her sigh in my head. {They work fast just in case. They are working on the eve of the Day of Turning when they should celebrate the day.} Suddenly controlling my arms she flung my staff in the air, clapped twice and caught it.

Thankfully no one turned.

{Brembry!} I scolded her.

I skirted around the outer side of the work area and avoided a crowd that had gathered to unload a wagon. Brembry yearned to call out to others that she knew, but I held her back. I had no need to talk with others here. I wanted to keep my business to myself.

In Ihrhoven itself I stopped at a bakery and meat shop and refilled my haversack. I called the shop owners by name and they looked at me oddly. I ate a small meal of jerky, goat cheese, and barley bread. This I finished off with a long drink from the wellspring basin in the middle of the village. Drying my mouth and beard on my sleeve, I picked up my haversack and continued to the ocean.

Clearing a large copse of trees, I neared the cliff that I had seen a score of times before, and sat down where I always had, but only in my dreams.

{Um, we should go away from here.} she asked and I could hear a warning tone in her voice. {I don't like it here, I never have. A powerful spell curses this place. If anyone should see you here, they might be suspicious.}

Turning to look behind me I saw no one. The village itself was hidden by thickets of trees and the townspeople were busy with their own daily matters. Only the lone gable of the town belfry could be seen where as the four towers of the fortress were still too small. I have seen this area here so many times, but only at night, only in my dreams. It was good to see it during the daytime with my own eyes. I watched as gulls crossed over the land to fly out over the ocean. The smells and the sounds filled my senses. Even though I was about to meet Nathel, I did not feel tense at all. I felt a peace I had not known since I left Croskreye. Being here and feeling the sunshine and wind felt wonderful.

{You've been here before?} she asked reading my mind.

"I have dreamt of this place many times," I explained simply. "There is someone I need to see. This meeting is very important. Please be quiet. Let's watch the sunset this evening."

{It is deceiving I tell you. When we were young the elders told us to never come here. This place is evil I say.} Brembry shook slightly and my body shook with her.

"Please stop that. This place is as safe as the king's own bedroom in his castle. There are no demons or such here. All is safe."

"Hello Marc," Nathel's voice was near. I am not sure if it was me that jumped at its sound or Brembry.

"Hello," I replied and stood.

"Look to your right and you'll see a path that leads down. Please take it and be quick. The sun sets and you may lose your step."

I looked toward the sound of the voice. The day was still too bright to see any form. I felt, for a moment, as though I should introduce Brembry, but I held my tongue silent. Perhaps it was better to keep quiet on this and not complicate matters.

{A voice with no body in a place that I say might be cursed, hmm.}
I shushed her quietly.

Taking my haversack and staff I slipped agilely between some jutting rocks and followed the steep path downward. Twice I had to lower myself down with my arms. I stopped when I came to a cave set back under a natural outcropping of rock.

The mouth of the cave lay shielded from view from above by a shelf of rock that protruded from the top of the cliff. Sea moss and ivy hung in large clumps on the rock wall. I pulled some strays from the straps of my haversack and let the green leaves fall towards the beach.

Standing deep in the cave the shimmering form of a man could be seen in the near darkness. As I watched the shape dissolved like smoke caught in the wind.

"I'll return when the darkness is complete. Peaceful Day of Turning," he said and I returned the greeting.

I looked behind me out to the sea and the setting sun which started to touch the horizon moments before. The staff of ash and my pack I left on the rock ledge. I hesitated only a second before I went in the cave.

With my legs crossed I sat upon the floor just inside the stone archway and waited. Moments passed and the cave grew steadily darker in the evening twilight. For once, Brembry was silent as well. It was a relief to have her still. I wondered if, in her fear, that she left me completely.

Time passed and still he did not return. Well after sunset and as the sky changed from hue to darker hue, Nathel was there again glowing dimly in the shadows as I always had seen him in my dreams. Glowing as Brembry had when she died.

"I am glad I am here," I said.

"I'm sure you are. How was your journey? I wish I could offer you better comforts than this. A soldier would not mind." His long hair caught some long forgotten wind and the strands that were not tied in his warrior braid shimmered.

"This does not bother me. My journey was long indeed."

"Again, had I known you were on your way I would have had you bring the vials from the room." Nathel said absently as his form knelt in the sand beside me.

"Would you want me to get them for you?" Spoken as a jest I could see that it was weighted question.

{Yes, yes. Oh please, yes.}

"Your journey would have only just started. Let me think on his. I will tell you what I have to gain by these vials and you can judge.

"I cannot leave this place, Marc. For some reason it is different for me somehow. I have heard of ghosts lingering, but I do not think it was meant to be this long. I've waited so long to see my wife and my family again on the other side. I grow very anxious as time goes by." He brought his hand to his forehead as if in thought. "I'll make a bargain with you, if you prefer. There will be a reward for you once you return with the items I ask."

"What type of reward?" This roused my curiosity.

"Of gold, or perhaps, since you like books best, it will be books. Not just one or two, but several."

"Books of magic?" Questioning him further, I sought to see the breadth of his generosity. The cave went deeper into the rock wall. There was little likelihood that he could have almost anything of value here.

"I know where you may find some. There is one book above all others that you seek out, don't you?"

This surprised me.

Was he playing a game with me? A deception? A ruse? The whole time he led me to believe that he had the answers I needed. He now turned things around and dangled another carrot before me. Should I react as he asked? I could accept or decline this task of my own free will. The reward of gold or books would be pleasant, but it was not what I desired most. I wanted answers of my past life.

"The book you speak of, is it the book of 'Kalendeck'?" I asked.

"It is."

"This book actually exists?"

"If you have seen it in your mind before, I am sure does. I will search. It will be my task for you while you are completing mine," he held out his broad hands before him and smiled.

"I must tell you, honestly, that I am a little disappointed. I had the understanding that you had the answers I sought."

{It will be an adventure, Marc please. The places we'll see!}

I shook my head.

"Think on it before you decide."

{I will gladly do it!} Brembry spoke with my voice. Her enthusiasm was not contained. To my ears the sound that came out was more womanly than I cared for.

"Ha!" Nathel raised an eyebrow. "Then it's settled."

"I will return when I can," I grumbled to the ghost nodding my head. I scolded Brembry and willed her silent.

Nathel smiled.

"I came here for answers on my past and you give me another task. Will there be more after this one?"

"None that I give you. You see, it has been a very long time since I have commanded troops. I am not used to making bargains to get things accomplished. Men respected my command. When I spoke, they did my bidding. If this task does not suit you please let me know."

"As I said, I will return when I can." I tried to hide the irritation from my voice. "I had to deal with winter snows, chaffed feet, snakes and wolves to get here. Who knows what the return trip will bring."

He laughed once more. The sound was lost in the surf. "Lad, you should have seen what I had to get through to get here myself!"

He stood from where he sat and went to the back of the cave and knelt. His booted feet made no noise on the stone. The dust was not even disturbed as he walked. In the light of his form a set of bones in a moldered brown tunic could be seen laying on the floor. I stood and went over. I knelt also being careful not to shift them in their resting place.

The hair lay about the skull in a thick layer matted with dust. In the dimness of the light it was hard to see if it was black or brown. Drawn back from the face it lay tied in a thick braid well past the shoulder. The tunic and pants were of a light leather that was common for hunters and woodsmen throughout the kingdom. There were a number of places where the fabric was coming apart as nature took its course. In other places it was apparent that the rends were from blows from a weapon. Here also dried blood had made dark stains.

Nathel's scabbard was empty of any sword. My thoughts went for a moment to the replica of Steelefyre that Kopernick was working on. Such a scabbard would be too small for such a large sword. I had never heard if Nathel's sword had a name.

{Ah,} Brembry thought to me. {If Nathel was fighting near the cliffs it was likely that his sword fell to the sea.} I looked down to the bones again and she let my thoughts be my own once more.

I cleared my throat and spoke.

"This is you?"

"Yes," Nathel sighed. "I have been here for the longest time watching my body grow less and less. My blood slipped away into the sand, and then my skin became dry and turned to sand itself. I went from a man with strength and health to this pile of bones. Do you know what that does to one's soul?"

"I can only imagine. No one has been this way? None came to this cave, or the shoreline?"

"No," he shook his head in grief. "No. This place has never been popular with the people of the kingdom. All of the items I died with lay where I dropped them. No one looted them. Even the rancid black bugs that I have seen crawling over the dead as they lay in the field did not come. Nathel, the once powerful champion of the king, lay here dying and dead and no one knew. If Kalendeck were alive at the time, he would have come."

I rubbed the cloth of the tunic between my fingers and then let it lay. There was no stench, just remains. "Tyndall had said that you killed the last of the men from the north. Some farmers had seen you, but they didn't see your body after it fell."

"The story is the truth. I must have landed among the rocks and found my way here. When you are mortally wounded, your instincts take over at the end. Wounded rabbits may find their way back to their hole and die there," Nathel laughed half-heartedly. "I have called myself a lot of things over the years, but never a rabbit. Now, we must do some work, if you would be so kind as to reach into a pouch tied to my side."

I found the pouch on the belt and tugged softly at the leather strings which broke in my hands. The pouch ripped down its length and a brass key tumbled out to the ground.

"There is a room in Croskreye castle with the door of the horse with no nose. You have not seen it yet. It's in the far west tower and down beneath the ground. This is the room which I spoke to you of. You can open the door with this key and a spell I'll teach you later. In the room, locked away, there is a vial made of dark blue glass. Bring that to me and your tasking will then be complete. This is all I ask of you."

I though for a moment committing as much as I could to memory. Had I kept my haversack nearer I could put this all to pen before I forgot.

"What will it do? This blue vial?"

"When you sprinkle the contents on my bones, they will be as dust and blow in the wind. My connection will be gone. I will leave this place finally. I hear the Skye Boat from time to time, but never closer than the village. This will bring it to me, on the oceans shore, and I may leave."

"Wouldn't we be able to just scatter your bones?" I said raising my hand as if to do so.

"Don't speak nonsense," Nathel cautioned raising his own hand to stop me. He laughed nervously and smiled at me. The fear in his eyes was apparent.

"That wouldn't be magic, now would it?"

"I guess not." I lowered my hand.

"My skin and innards are already as dust. Do you think that the presence of a persons bones keeps his spirit here on the ground? I have missed my call to ride the Skye Boat. The potion in this vial will bring it back to me."

I nodded my head in understanding.

"On my left hand there is a ring. Do you see it there?"

"Um . . . yes, it's there."

"Take it off mine and put on your own hand. Carefully."

As I raised the ring from the dust, I disturbed the bone. I placed the ring beside me and replaced the bone as close to its original position as I could.

The ring was of gold with a band of silver around each side. Across its face the word 'Kalendeck' lay engraved. No other mar, or blemish, could be seen on its surface. Brembry took control and placed it on my hand. She then held my hand out and admired it.

"He gave me that ring. Just before we went to Welteroth. Knowing he would die, I suppose. He wanted the ring to survive the end."

"He destroyed Welteroth, they say, killing himself, the opposing commander, and two hundred of his troops," I said quoting what Tyndall, Davlyne and others had told me. Actually, Nathel and I had talked about it a number of times.

"Yes, but there was a bit more than two hundred. Kalendeck died in that tower. He was a great man." As Nathel replied his voice trailed to a whisper as if his thoughts wondered distantly. I looked up into his eyes and thought I saw a tear fall from his cheek, but I was unsure.

"We must not discuss his death now," he said as he regained his composure and cleared his voice. "Not yet anyway, We have much to speak on before the sun rises. It is known well throughout the kingdom, that the man who once wore this ring also carried the name of Kalendeck. You have told me in your visits past that you come to this place with no name. Kalendeck is gone. His name is becoming a myth they sing to children around hearth fires at night. You searched for a name and you chose Marc. Marecrish, the lost one. Wear his ring and take Kalendeck's name as your own . . ."

"I can't!" I stood suddenly. Jumping up as if I had been struck. I searched for something to say, but was too shocked to speak. I walked to the front of the cave and then came back.

"Sit down. You don't have to use it openly, my friend," he pleaded. "To do so may cause you unwarranted trouble. There will be a time in the future that you will have to draw strength from his name."

"I can't . . ." I started again as I sat down where I was before.

"You can, and you will."

"He and I have nothing in common."

"Ha, I say. You and he have more in common than you know. Two people brought to the kingdom by no known means. He came here just before a war started with peoples we never knew existed. Some say Sorcerer Cinnaminson had a hand in it. Others say, even though I do not place complete faith in them, that the Brothers needed a protector for their kingdom. Only the Writer of All knows.

"Be that as it may, you are the second one to arrive here. Perhaps another war is brewing. With the tension to the south trouble may spread. They will need you. You were not brought here without reason.

"You say that you have not used his name in the past, but use of his name, and of who he was, has helped you in more ways than one. You've told me of the training you have received from the graciousness of Duke Almonesson. They did this because they do not know who you are. They feel that you have it in you to become like he was. In this you have, unknowingly, used his name."

"Nathel," I said after a pause. "I understand this. I do not feel at this time that I am worthy enough to carry his name with me. Truly, he was a greater man than I ever will be. His name was his and his alone. You have no right to give it to me. I have no wish to use it. I have a name I am comfortable with and I am going to use it." I looked at him, his faint glow in the darkness. He frowned at me and shrugged his shoulders.

"You are stubborn young man." He took a stance, folding his arms across his chest. "I'm not afraid to say it, not now, but Kalendeck was the same, you know. Once he got something in his head, he would not let it go. Don't you see the resemblances that are between you two that cannot be over looked? There is something very special about you, Marc. If you don't see it now then you are blind and never will.

"Do you know how much energy it takes for someone travel from one world to another? The resources used with that type of magic are phenomenal. If the common people of this world knew the effort involved that brought you here, they would surely fear you. That the Writer wanted you here that bad means that he has very good reason to. Something awaits you in your future. Only the Writer knows your fate."

"It might be because you are not of this world, or perhaps it is your lack of memory. I don't know which one applies or if they both apply to enhance your existence here. Your lack of memory was by no means a mistake, you are not to know of your past life. Hear me, my young friend, and let it be known to you, that the Writer of All smiles brightly on you.

"Harm may come your way, but it will never catch you. Please, don't get careless. There is the gift of protection that parents give their children, but that protection has boundaries. Fire is still fire, a sword will always be a sword. Heed these words," he knelt in the light layer of dust that covered the stone floor of the cave. His arms open as if to embrace me as he pleaded with me. The scar on his palm was plain to see.

"I hear what you say," I said looking at his pale bluish form. "But I don't understand why the Brothers chose me to come here. I have nothing I can offer this place. I am sure they could have done better."

"Kalendeck was a fighter, lad. This is why they chose him. Your talent, or gift, may soon be found."

I was quiet for sometime as I thought on this.

"I understand the logic behind your reasoning. The ring and the key I will keep. Both I will tuck away in a place safely held until needed," I said drawing a circle in the sand with my fingertip. I heard the waves on the ocean below and we were both silent for a time.

"Kalendeck gave you the ring?" I asked at last to break the silence and to move on to a new subject.

"He did." Nathel sat back and smiled seemingly more at ease. "In an upper room of the smaller keep in Welteroth, he called for me. He had collected a large amount of things that he needed to do his magic and was preparing them there. At the time, I had no idea what he was going to do. If I had known the outcome, I may have argued with him. I doubt it would have done any good.

"The water in the village was becoming foul. The men from the north had not arrived yet. We were very elated having just received word of Laensey. He stopped me from my work and asked me to take his ring and the key. He carried these with him always. He said that he no longer had a use for them. He asked me to never let them out of my possession.

"He then gave me the knowledge to do the spell that brought your soul here while you were sleeping. At the time I didn't understand the spell, but I trusted Kalendeck. The spell served me well. I never thought I would be dead when I used it.

"Bah, I've tried it hundreds of times. Always waiting for the whisper of a soul to arrive, but you were the first to come. In this, I know you're special."

Nathel stood and went to the mouth of the cave. Brembry looked at the ring on my finger again and smiled.

The day was gone and the night replaced it with a vengeance. It was windy, as windy this night as it always was here. Just like I remembered. A cool breeze from the ocean stirred the wisps of my hair. I looked at Nathel and was sure that the wind had no effect on his form. This was something I still could not get used to. Above us, the full moon of the summer solstice was half way to its zenith. I looked up and saw clouds pass before its face and then continue on into the night like whispers of a dream.

"Nathel, will I ever find my home?" It was a question I asked those of knowledge, who also knew of my plight.

"I'm not sure. Perhaps you will find that this is your home and all the other places you've seen were but an illusion." This sounded something like what Tyndall or Davlyne would say. "As king's commander I had a place in Land Streth, but rarely used it though. Always something kept me away." I thought that Nathel was about to continue, but he stopped with his ear to the wind.

"Shhh . . . " he paused for a second holding his hand up so I would remain silent. "She comes tonight!"

"Who comes?" I looked up towards the top of the cliff to see if anyone was there.

"The lady, young man. The lady from the ocean. Can you make it to the shoreline to meet her? She searches for a ring she once owned. It lays wedged beneath the rock there and she does not know where to find it. Move it for her."

"I can try," I said. As I began to scramble down, I could hear her singing softy to herself. I hurried the best I could in the moonlight and was careful not to fall or slip. With only slightly scrapped hands and a bruised knee, I found my way to the narrow stretch of sand.

The two of us made it to the shore at the same time. She did walk on the water. On the crest of a wave she came. The white froth of the water churning at the hem of her dress hiding her feet entirely. I saw her form appear from the nothingness of the night. By the look on her face, I was sure she knew I was there. She looked surprised to see me.

{She is real?} whispered Brembry.

"Hello fair maiden," I said, and trying not to show that I was out of breath. I looked into her eyes which seemed somewhat wild in the moonlight. She paused for a moment before she spoke. Oh, she was so beautiful. Feeling my cheeks grow warm I felt slightly embarrassed and looked at my feet in the wet sand.

"I've not seen another soul on this beach since I've died. I was here with my love when the men came. They saw us and we had no chance," she caught her breath and shivered. Her feet sank beneath the sand, but the sand lay smooth without breaking.

"Lavan and I were to marry on the night of the summer solstice, the Day of Turning. I fell from the cliff there . . . " she pointed to the cliff and I saw she pointed to the area were I always talked with Nathel above the cave. Nathel had fallen from the cliff as well.

At the cave I could see him standing. She looked back at me and I realized that she couldn't see the him at his cave there.

"Such a tragic place. No wonder people feel it's cursed," I whispered quietly.

{I've told you.} Brembry piped in.

"I lost our ring someplace here and have not been able to find it. That is why I come back time after time. I can still feel its presence. It was a gift of love."

"Tonight is the night of the summer solstice. At mid-day tomorrow the Day of Turning begins. I will help you find your ring," I stated. She smiled warmly at me and together we turned.

*   *   *   *   *

"She will not return now, you know. She's gone forever," Nathel said as he saw her depart the shoreline and return to the ocean. Fog was beginning to roll in blocking out the stars and the moon. Such was her song also, fading into the night as if it never was, and never would be again.

"I know. We talked before she left and she said the same. Is it right that the dead should stay on the earth?" My feet were cold from the sea water that could not be avoided. I shook what I could from each boot and put them back on.

"That is not for us to decide. The dead have already returned to the earth. It's their spirits that rise. It would seem as though someplace the Writer has a plan, or an idea of how things are to go. We are just here. Living our lives, dying our deaths."

"You put a lot of faith in this Writer," I said.

Nathel just shrugged his shoulders and watched the ocean.

Behind us the bell of Ihrhoven rang twelve times and then was silent. Above us, high above our heads, the moon crested to its peak and slowly sank. It seemed as if time held still for a moment.

The music began. Somewhere in the village someone played a string instrument that was slightly off key. Cheers went up and the celebration for the Day of Turning began hours early.

We sat a while longer and Nathel taught me the spell that I needed to open the door in Croskreye. It was a form of healing magic. This type of Alden magic placed a barrier around an object so strong that nothing could penetrate it to cause it harm. When he was confident that I memorized the chant, he went back into the cave.

Nathel stood to the side of the cave in an area that I had not seen before. There was another bundle there. It was a book. Had Nathel completed his task so soon? I voiced my question to him.

"No," he said shaking his head and smiling. "Here is a book written with the uses of the magic of stone. In particular, the use of iron. Take it with you to read and study. You look disappointed. Do you know the value of this particular book?"

"I had thought it was the other book. Wouldn't a book laying in a cave this close to the ocean rot over time?"

"It has a spell of protection upon it. Nothing could harm it."

I began to reach for it, but Nathel held me back.

"Reach close, but do not touch it."

I did this and could feel something the closer my hand went to the book. Like a layer of moss or blades of unseen grass stretching out to my hand.

"You can feel the magic, can't you? Now, repeat the spell I taught you. Concentrate on the book this time."

As I spoke the counter spell, I felt a slight tingle in my chest and fingertips. I paid the price of magic.

I picked up the book and looked at it for a time before I put it in my haversack.

"Tell me more about him," I said sitting with my back against the stone wall. Out of my haversack, I took my pen and journal. It was barely light enough to see, but I could write, and it was necessary to get this information down straightaway. The spell could be written as long as I broke it apart. I needed to pen it down and with it written on paper I could practice it more later on.

"Kalendeck?" he said looking surprised at my request.

"Yes. You gave me bits here and there on what he was like and who he was, tell me more. Possibly something else will click in my head, and I'll remember something I forgot."

He rubbed his beard and thought. Twice he was about to speak, but stopped.

"Should I put the book away?" I asked recapping the pen.

"No, it is just that I never had my spoken words down on paper before. Penned, I think is the proper term. I shall try. You may write," he said scratching his head.

And with that he began telling me of the times that he and Kalendeck were together. A hard man to understand at first, but once people knew him, they tended to like him. When he had finished speaking, several hours later, I had managed to fill almost ten pages. There were times that the moonlight was hidden by clouds. I brought the staff of ash closer and it gave me light.

*   *   *   *   *

"You must leave now, as you always have. There is nothing more that I need to tell you. I will search for your book when I can. Do not be upset if I do not contact you again before your return. I need to save my strength as well. This visit has taken a lot from me," he said and rose waiting for me to do the same. I went back outside the cave and he followed silently.

"I will return then," I said as I stood in the dim moonlight again. Above us, well above the lip of the cliff, a sandpiper called into the night, hunting for insects. I gazed at the cliff I would have to climb to get back to Ihrhoven, and turned back to Nathel.

The staff of ash making the ledge of the cave brighter and his form dimmer. I placed the staff over my shoulder and tucked it in between the straps of the haversack. This freed up my hands for the climb upward.

In these last few parting moments, I felt the need, the deep desire, to shake the man's hand. This was not possible and never could be. I told this to Nathel.

"If you wish us to clasp hands, my dear friend, shake your own. Your hand is much more solid than mine," he laughed lightly and waved. At that I waved good-bye and scrambled back up the cliff to the cooler air above. As I made my way through the thicket of trees, my thoughts were so distant I almost failed to see two of the soldiers who slept there. It looked as if they wore deep blue colors of Delfuri or the black of the Spruill Territory.

Possibly revilers, drunk and passed out, sipping the ale a bit early for the Day of Turning.

* * * * *

The mist grew thicker as I passed through the village. I noted that all of the stores and shops were not open this late at night. However, I saw candle light coming from one shop, and in passing I saw a woman sitting on a stool reading a book. Her long dark hair covered most of her features. I did not disturb her, did not wish to startle her if she looked up and saw me looking in.

{This is the Chronicler,} said Brembry. {They have been very generous to me,} It was Brembry who reached out and tapped the pane of glass.

The woman looked up. She quietly marked her page with a ribbon and stood.

"Thanks," I said softly to Brembry.

The Chronicler picked up a candle, came to the door, and stepped outside. The woman was tall. Older than I, but not by much. She must have been very sure of herself to greet a stranger in the mist of the night. She wore all black and as she cupped the candle flame to keep it alight, I saw the sun had darkened her skin.

"Peaceful Day of Turning," she said.

"Peaceful Day of Turning," I replied with a smile.

"So early, it will be dawn soon. Are you traveling?" she asked warily. She looked at my pack and the staff sticking above my shoulder. Her eyes lingered there a moment and when she looked at me, she smiled.

"I am heading south. I came to see the ocean," I turned slightly, motioning towards the ocean, and the water in my boots made an odd sound.

"Did you happen to go in the water?" she asked.

"I did, actually," I said. "I have heard about it and seen it in my dreams. I was curious about something so large."

"And now that you have seen it, you travel back?" she said. I could hear the merriment in her voice. She was possibly a little drunk from the celebrations that began early.

"I came to see what I had to see and now I travel back. Yes." I nodded and turned to go.

"Forgive me," she reached out and touched my arm. "I am the

Chronicler. I tend to ask questions so I do not write down anything false."

{There has been a tragedy along the road.} said Brembry suddenly through my voice. I pulled back and let her do what she willed to do. If I would have tried to stop her, it would have looked very awkward.

"Oh?"

{I was, I mean, Brembry was, taken down by wolves. She did not make it to Glenhelen as she had planned. She was hoping to spend a festive day with friends.} As she spoke the woman brought her hand to her chin. She placed the candle on the stone window sill and leaned back on the wall.

"Brembry was a very good young woman," she said, her voice was unsteady with sadness. "My grandfather and I will miss her. She was a true bit of happiness in a place so secluded from the rest of the kingdom. Were you with her when she died?"

{I came upon her and the wolves right after they attacked. After chasing them off, I held her as she died. That is when she spoke to me of her journey. She told me that you had always treated her well.} It was Brembry's story and I let her speak with her imagination.

"There are many passages I have in the Chronicles of Ihrhoven that speak of her. She will always be remembered."

I began to weep. Not of my own accord, but by Brembry. Drawing back almost completely I let Brembry control my body. She dried my eyes with my sleeve and looking at the Chronicler, who now openly wept, she reached out and embraced the woman with my arms. To my amazement the women embraced us back.

Her touch was very warm. Even through the numbness of being where I was I could feel it. She held me tight for some time and when I thought Brembry was through crying, she began anew.

This woman must have known Brembry all her life. This parting was different from the true parting of life and death. Here, Brembry could say her goodbyes and farewells a final time. Like a casual onlooker, I waited as their grief took its course.

Brembry released the woman and stepped backward.

{Forgive me.} she said wiping my eyes.

"There is nothing to forgive," the Chronicler said softly. She stood back and picked up her candle off the sill. The melted wax must have fallen because the flame burned higher. Even in a slight breeze the flame did not flicker.

"She was a good woman and it is very sad to see that she is gone. I will tell others of her passing. Was her body left by the wayside?"

{It was left near one of the large boulders on the hill two days from here. If you wish to search for it there is a plum tree growing on the lee side. I buried her there so the animals may not find her. He, I mean I, did not leave her in the Kear.}

"Thank you," she reached up and again with her forefinger brought a stray lock of hair back behind her ear. "I must rest now. I will tell my grandfather the sad news when he wakes in the morning."

{Rest well.} Brembry said even as the door closed. She must have put out the flame straightway. Through the window no light could be seen.

In the darkness we turned, Brembry granting me possession of my body once again. I left Ihrhoven that night, stopping only to drink again from the wellspring basin in the middle of the village.

"I will not come back this way for a long time," I told her.

{It is just as well.} her voice was solemn and quiet. Suddenly, she perked up. {We're going on an adventure though!}

I signed. "It's not really an adventure, it's just walking." I reached over my shoulder and pulled out the staff of ash and was thankful for its familiar tap on the ground.

The music still played, not as loud as before, in the fortress. Torches hung on the walls of the inner bailey. Their light could be seen on the higher stones of the unfinished tower.

I was well within the first grove of trees when Brembry spoke to me.

{You know, we won't make Glenhelen this night no matter how fast you walk. Are you going to stop?}

"In time. I want to get away from people and think. Walking helps me think. If I sit, I will fall asleep," I said, but moments later I knew she was right. It had been a long day full of expectations and excitement. Finding an alcove between two large rocks and some tree roots, I settled down for the night. I pulled out my second cloak and used it to cover me.

{I can still smell her on you.} said Brembry bringing my hand close to my nose. {She smells slightly of soot or ash. Always has.}

"It is the candle you smell," I whispered.

The cloak was dark and if it wasn't for the sound of my breathing I would have blended in perfectly with the night.

In the morning I woke well after the sunrise when the cloak grew too warm.

I stopped the evening of the next day to see that Brembry's body still lay undisturbed, and added a few more rocks to the pile. I continued on.

As I entered Glenhelen just under a week later, it began to rain again.

Naturally.

*   *   *   *   *

She watched him go. Her face so close to the glass that she could feel the chill that it had collected from the dampness and the night. She heard the curtain that divided the rooms shift aside as her grandfather came in.

"Is he gone?" her grand-pa asked. She knew he could see her silhouette against the glass.

"Yes. He is leaving the village now," she sighed before she spoke again. The weight of the news was heavy on her shoulders. "She is with him."

"Ah, that was him crying I heard."

"I think she was crying for him. I did love that woman," she said backing away from the window. After a moments pause, she snapped her fingers and two candles sputtered and spat to life.

"She was beautiful and friendly. The red ribbon she wore in her hair is on his pack. There is much in her that he can use. When she moves on, she will take some of him with her." She folded her arms across her chest and bowed her head. "I will miss Brembry, grand-pa. Her sacrifice will be difficult."

"Was your sacrifice an easy one? Or mine?" he asked. She looked at him in his simple nightshirt. This man who was growing more and more frail as the days left him. She could only shake her head.

"Come," he said turning. "We'll talk of things to come over a pot of tea. They will be busy in the tower today. It is more shoring up to do before the stones arrive."

"There will be no work done on it today, grandfather. The Day of Turning. Remember?" she said simply arms folded across her chest.

"I must find those drunk soldiers in the grass, is it?"

She nodded. "The rumors must start." Even with the loss of Brembry she could not keep the excitement from her voice. The planning for this day had been over many pots of tea. After this day was over, they could sit back and watch the flowers of their labors blossom.

Chapter #15

It was a gentle wind, a whisper in the early hours of the day, that woke Almonesson as he slept. He looked at the ceiling of his chambers and wondered what had changed, what had stirred him from his sleep. The few candles alight gave an adequate glow to see by, but the room was still.

Not disturbing Lowy as she slept deeply, he slipped a summer robe over his shoulders and rose from his bed. He paused a moment before he left the bedside and she still dreamed. He longed to reach out and caress her long hair, but he knew if he did so she would shift and wake. She was beautiful now as always.

The servants still slept. They would not be roused for their duties for a few hours. Once again he breathed in the quietness of his castle. For a time it would be quiet. He would stay awake for a while and eventually return to bed. The day would begin anew.

With a brand from the fireplace he lit a candle and removed it from the mantel. He smiled slightly at the face he had carved in the stonework. It brought back a rush of memories of his youth.

The Day of Turning was two days past. The after effects of the singing dancing, wine and ale, had worn themselves off. His son, Farnstrom, had bested him at a game of knife throwing. It had been a number of years since they had played and his shoulder ached from the effort. But it was good. The family, his family, were back together again.

He went to the small podium that held the book that Marc had unknowingly brought with him through the gate. It had been a few weeks since he had glanced over the words. It was an interesting book to read. Whimsical and at times seemed so fanciful that he wonder if the writer had drunk much as he penned the words.

He pulled the stool out and sat.

He had come to believe that this was the message that Kalendeck had spoken of. Marc was inconsequential. Marc could do as he wished and it would not matter. The book mirrored Marc's actions almost perfectly. Well, nearly so. It was a book of stories that the writer intended for enjoyment. It held true to a number of facts, but the text held a few falsehoods. A person just had to know what to look for to sort them out.

There were few, if any books in the kingdom that told actual tales. All were for the exchanging of information and the studying of knowledge.

This book was the first in many ways.

For all he knew of Nathel, the book spoke of a different man. Almonesson knew him personally. He had fought with him in many battles and was with him when he left Welteroth and Kalendeck died. A strong man and sure of himself, even when he was wrong, Nathel had confidence in everything he did. The book, this tale that the storyteller dreamed up, told of someone completely different. Under-handed, weak, there were thoughts brought in by the ghost that reeked deceit and treachery. Oddly, the person Marc spoke of in his dreams before he left had none of these qualities. Had he not known better Almonesson would have guessed the ghost in the story was someone else.

There was news of Marc and Tyndall going different ways in Eilenburg. A sorrowful separation of a student and teacher. Tyndall had since returned from his travels and had spoken with him on the two separating. There was truth in those passages.

Marc encountered a snake much further on that almost killed a traveling companion named Kopernick. The snake was nearly the length of a man long and twice as thick as a forearm. Although Marc thought quickly and killed the snake it was the quick thinking of an elderly man who drew the venom from Kopernick and healed him. After a few pages the writer revealed that the elderly man was none other than Ryeson the great healer.

The name of Kopernick begins and ends with the same letter. Almonesson mused time and time again that it was just was the Writers way of getting the reader to think of Kalendeck. Although he knew, for a fact, that Kalendeck did not have red hair and was never gifted in the magic of metal. According to the story in the book it was not long before Ryeson healed Kopernick and they were on their way once more.

On a map, Almonesson had been tracking Marc's progress northward. By now his journey would have taken him to the ocean, or nearly so.

It was very interesting to read the world through the eyes of the storyteller. Through these eyes he could sit around a campfire at night, wave to a farmer in his field, or catch fish in a stream. Vicariously, he could talk with strangers along the road and hear their stories.

And still there were no further words. With a sigh he pulled back the black cloth. He traced the letters of Kalendeck's name once and opened the book to the page with the marked ribbon.

There was more pages written. He gasped. More of the story was told.

He looked once to check on Lowy. Seeing she still slept soundly, he turned back around and began to read eagerly.

* * * * *

"Tyndall," Duke Almonesson happened upon him as he sat in an alcove reading. The day was warm and with the window open, the sunlight streaming in, the alcove had beckoned to him for a visit. In a quiet part of the castle he had anticipated some time to sit and study. Duke Almonesson was the first person he had seen pass by since he started reading. The duke doubled back and looked about the corner.

Tyndall swung his feet around and was only able to give him a quick bow before the duke sat. He was excited about something. His mood, Tyndall sensed, was light and not due to wine or ale.

"In a weeks time we will receive a message from King Trahune," Almonesson said straightaway.

"We will, my lord?" He marked the page and placed the book placed aside.

"We will. He will inform us that I am expected to leave here by the harvest moon and arrive there, in Land Streth, by the moon following." Almonesson scratched his beard and leaned back. Taking a moment he looked at the inner bailey for a time and breathing deep, he turned back to Tyndall. "I truly enjoy this time of year," he confessed. "It's not because of the warmth of the day, or the breezes that cool the island, it's the scent of the spices that are in need of harvesting. To my nose it is like the sweetness of flowers to a young girl. Ah, my mind wanders."

"You spoke of a messenger." Tyndall said clearing his throat.

"I did. That I did."

"This is interesting. I will have to prepare. Almost before the snows arrive we will be there, you say. I will arrive to the Gathering early this year," Tyndall mused. "To many this will be a surprise. How did you come by this knowledge?"

"Tyndall, it is with regret that I have to say that you must stay here."

"My lord?" He almost choked on the words.

"I am to take Nayoor. The king will ask that I bring my commander and no other advisers. I will need you here to assist the duchess in the event of anything arising?"

Tyndall paused a moment. He searched the dukes face, but there was no hint of deception or deceit. The duke was still in high spirits.

"Why would the king wish just you and Commander Nayoor in attendance?" Tyndall asked.

"I will not take just Commander Nayoor, there will be a handful of others, soldiers mostly. In this I will not question the issue, nor will I bring you to temp his anger. Abide in what I have said and this year rest here in Croskreye."

"I will do as you ask, I am bound to, but I must say that I cannot see the reasoning behind it." This would be only the third Gathering that he had missed.

"Also, there is a second matter." Duke Almonesson looked at him somewhat nervously. He fidgeted with his hands just enough to make note. "There are rumors that I have heard that are yet to come across to your ears. I will not repeat them to you. More than that, I know the truth of the matter and the rumors are far from what has actually happened. You will hear about them soon enough. I sense your ire now and when you hear the rumors they will trouble you further. But trust me when I say that they hold no merit. The rumors are just that."

Tyndall scratched his head. "To make clear what you have just said; you've heard rumors, and I will hear them in due time, but you cannot tell me the rumors." Tyndall sniffed the air, but smelled no hint of wine although the duke was giddy.

"Yes, exactly." Duke Almonesson smiled broadly.

"When I hear them I am to dismiss them?"

"Yes!" Duke Almonesson tapped him on the chest with a finger.

Saying nothing further, Duke Almonesson stood and departed. It was quite some time before Tyndall became settled enough to read again.

*   *   *   *   *

"This is old," Kopernick said from across the table. I did not think I would miss this man. Today his red hair was bound back from his eyes with a length of leather. I had found him near the forge at about midday working on casting horseshoes. Gone were the loose fitting cloths he traveled in on his way north. The thick leather vest and shirt were tight at the shoulders and wrists to keep the clothing from trailing in the fires or hot coals. Now it was well after the evening meal, his father had closed down the forge, his mother had cleaned the dirty crockery, and washed the younger children. Still he sat looking over the book.

{I like her candle holders.} Brembry said in my head.

I shook my head hoping she would stay quiet.

"Where did you come by it?" Kopernick asked after a little time.

"There is a cave next to the sea," and he smiled at this. "It was there bound with a spell of protection," I said softly hoping that he would not think of the place where the Drenthen first came to the kingdom. If common people thought that place cursed, what would they think of a book from the very same area? Thankfully, Kopernick was too involved with the book to think about anything else.

"From him?" He asked making the connection to Commander Nathel I had hoped he wouldn't.

I nodded my head, sighed and looked to the floor. "He gave it to me. An offering of sorts."

"Scribe Cothren wrote this ten years before the war." Kopernick began to flip through the first few pages. He had scrubbed his hands for several minutes before he picked up the book. It now rested on a cloth on the table. I watched him in the candlelight and saw how he looked at the book with a sense of reverence.

"It says here," Kopernick enthusiastically said as he thrust his finger in the book to the desired line, "that the text of this one was from a book much older. This is a fantastic find. Do you mind if I read it?"

"No, of course not. I thought that you might like it."

"You dolt, of course I like it." Kopernick punched me lightly in the shoulder. He smiled at me and then returned to the book.

"How long do you think it will take for you to read it?" I asked.

"I could have a guild house of my own just based on the writings in the book. There is a lot of knowledge here. Scribe Cothren wrote several books during his life. The one of his we use in Milhematte is about only half this size. That one is for seventh and eighth year adepts and for some of the truly talented students. If you only knew the treasure that you have here."

{Let him have the book.} Brembry offered so unexpectedly that I almost dropped my own cup.

"Why?" I said softly under my breath. Kopernick was too involved with the book to notice.

{You will have to come back this way soon. If you carry the book around the whole kingdom, it will do little use for anyone.}

I sat there for several moments thinking. Corva came by briefly and refilled our cups. "Oh, I see we have a second visitor," she said nudged my shoulder and said no more. I tried to give a look of puzzlement, but we both knew. I could not hide it from her. She wiped the table and returned to the kitchen humming.

{I love these mugs, too.}

"I will let you have the book until I come back up in the winter," I said straightaway, but the other didn't hear.

"Kopernick?"

"Hmmm?" He looked up from the book, but still kept his finger on the line he had last read.

"I'll be back in the middle of winter. You may have the book until then," he looked at me a moment, smiled, and went back to reading.

*   *   *   *   *

Kopernick, and his parents, sat around the table that night listening to all I had done with Nathel on the cliff. Some secrets, specifically the ring, I kept to myself. If they knew of these, word could spread easily with the slip of a tongue. This is something that Nathel warned me keep silent at all cost. Even though he and Kalendeck were dead I would not betray them.

All of us made a late night of it. When I woke the next day, I realized that the day was starting on its second half. Corva said I was weary from my journey and had not bothered to wake me. However, the morning was lost. If I started on my trek south, with what remained of this day, I would not get very far before the darkness of night stopped me. If I was fast enough, I could make it to the crossroads, but possibly no further.

I decided to stay one more night in Glenhelen. I had made it from Ihrhoven in quick enough time and so there was some time to spare. I had to catch up on some writing. I went back through the notes from the cliff and rewrote them to make them more legible.

Kopernick had woken up quite sometime before me to read his book and to help his father when he needed it. Into the third hour after mid-day Kopernick put away the book and his father excused him from chores at the smithy. The fever to read had claimed Kopernick's being and it would be some time before his home was back to normal. I knew what that feeling was like.

We spent the rest of the afternoon walking through the marketplace getting items for my travels.

Later, just before dusk, we climbed a small hill a short distance from the village. From the ruins there we could see the village and all that lay beyond. It was very peaceful and relaxing here with the sun on its way to setting behind the great trees to our backs.

"A great family used to live here," Kopernick said waving his arm out over the crumbling stonework. Standing on some rocks that had been clearly been cut by man he could survey the land and his village. He picked up a small stone, turned it over a few times, and then tossed it to the ground. The whole place looked as though people picked over it. Grass grew on the stonework and people made paths were they walked.

"They hired my father when he was young as a metal smith. He says the doorway to his fathers forge was just over there where the tree now grows. When the men from the north came, he fought beside the men from the village. He would have died here, but it was better to draw back where there were others. If we would have fought as we were, the Drenthen would have taken us as easily as a maiden plucking roses from a garden."

"Did you know the family here?" I asked.

"No, I was not born until after the war. None have come back to reclaim what was theirs. They have all died, I believe. Not that there is much to come back to." Again he made a motion toward the ruins.

"If a rightful heir could be found alive, they could claim the Wiladene Territory."

"That they could. Time passes, however. They must make a new linage."

"Kalendeck fought here?"

"He did. My father saw him several times. Once before and then after. Whenever Kalendeck and Nathel rode into town, those that could fight stayed. The young and the old scattered with all they could carry because they knew that their arrival meant a battle was right behind. Yes, Kalendeck fought here. The man fought everywhere."

I poked at some stones with a stick I found.

"Watch out for snakes," he said and smiled sheepishly.

We talked for some time before we waded through the knee-high timothy grass and returned to the village.

* * * * *

Lindergren was a bit late for the meal that night. While we were waiting, Kopernick returned the book I had loaned him. It was the book with my notes that I had written on my time in Croskreye. With it back in my possession, I breathed a sigh of relief. I knew I could trust him with it, I just felt better having it. I saw something else in his eyes when he looked at me. I feel that he presently considers me an equal to him, or very near, and this means a lot. No more was I the bumbling chum heading out on some fool errand. They understand my motivations and ideas.

He went back to his reading book, and to pass the time, I showed the younger children how I could light a candle. This was a simple thing for me to do. The whole time I did not feel the tingling sensation that I felt at the cave. I paid my price for this several times before. Tyndall said that the more you use a magic, the more your magic grows with it. I think, in this, I have grown.

When Lindergren finally did return, he had a somber look on his face that I could not read. He took his wife aside before we sat down to eat and talked with her at length near the hearth.

The evening meal was a bit more quiet that night than usual. Everything seemed normal, but still there was a slight tension in the air.

After the younger children were to bed, we all sat around the fire. Corva, had picked up a pair of breeches that needed mending, and Lindergren found his pipe and lit it.

"Unsettling words have reached Glenhelen," he said taking a long draw on the pipe. "Two soldiers working on the castle in Ihrhoven saw a man vanish up along the coastline. As if he never were there to begin with."

That's odd, I thought silently to myself. I wondered if Nathel had anything to do with it.

{Some one may have drank too much and slipped over.} was Brembry's reply to my thoughts. She giggled at this.

"Did they say who it was?" Kopernick asked from his seat near the fire.

"Well, to remain honest with you, they say it may have been the mysterious Marecrish. The story they told the Chronicler was that a man of large height, long hair and broad shoulders went to the shoreline at sunset. Right before the very eyes of the soldiers, he just disappeared. Poof. Vanished," he said without expression and went back to his pipe.

I looked around at the others and they were all looking at me. Corva continued to sew, and Kopernick still held his book, but their complete attention was on me. I brought my cup down and looked in the fire as if I could find my answers were there.

{Trouble! Let's get out of here. We must leave.} Brembry said.

"No," I said aloud. She made my leg twitch and I had to will her to stay still.

"Yes. One moment this person was sitting near the cliff and the next he was gone. Did they make a gate? Had they sprouted wings and flown over the ocean? The soldiers looked but could not find him. These were soldiers of Duke Tominson and Duke Lysaght."

"I did not disappear." I pleaded with a low tone. "I had climbed down to a cave. I've told you all this yesterday."

"Oh, don't worry," Lindergren went on laughing softly. "My family and I don't care where you were. It doesn't matter. We know the truth. The soldiers just didn't see you leave and got scared that's all. The story, so far, has it that they saw you had red glowing eyes just before you vanished," he said with a chuckle. Kopernick laughed also.

"What you need to fear, Marc, is that word is spreading quickly and that you are here in the Wiladene Territory. Once word reaches the dukes of the other territories that will only give them more of a reason to try to occupy this territory. If the territory is open then they will claim they need to station people here for the protection of the kingdom. The two soldiers who saw you will be returning to their home territories soon. Word has gotten around that you traveled almost the length of the kingdom and did great magic like that in an evil place. Things might be rough for you in times to come."

"For Marecrish." I stated. "They will search for him here. I didn't do any magic then. All I did was climb down the side of the cliff to a cave there. They must not have . . ."

"That is not how they see it," Lindergren said pointing the stem of his pipe at me and then placed it back in his mouth.

"I will leave in the morning."

"You don't have to go so soon. As a friend I ask you to stay," Kopernick said. I saw the genuine concern in his eyes.

"I must I'm afraid. I am bound by what I have to do. I've told you I have to get the vial and give it to him. I will not waver from this task. I'll be back this way around midwinter."

"You shouldn't go to Croskreye. They may see you there. You cannot travel as fast as a rumor, not in the kingdom. Did he tell you what this vial contained?" asked Kopernick.

"No. Something magical is all I know." I just shrugged my shoulders and drank again from my cup. "A potion to call the Sky Boat so he might be free and see his family once more."

{You're frightened out of your mind, aren't you?}

I said nothing but stared in the fire.

* * * * *

I did not leave the next day, but rather late that night after the moon had set. Brembry was very nervous and would not let me rest.

Kopernick had drawn a map for me on the hearth with charcoal that explained to me there was a shorter route between Corristone and Eilenburg. It was a course that tended to go more directly south. It was not as widely used as the trade route that I traveled coming north. I would be able to make up a week or more that way. There would be less of a chance of my identity being discovered if I traveled alone than in a group.

With a handshake from his father and a hug from his mother I left. Kopernick walked with me until the edge of the village. No clouds or moon kept back the brilliance of the stars this night. I heard an owl off on a hill to my right. Frogs croaked and crickets chirped. Ground mist was beginning to form, but by the paler color of the crushed stone I was able to barely see the road south. The staff of ash made the path easier to follow.

"Rest assured your secrets are safe with us. If there is something my family knows how to do, it is to keep silent," Kopernick said, his eyes wide in the night. His red hair was easily seen. He could not see as well as I could. I believe he could only see my silhouette in the night. We had traveled months together and I would miss him greatly.

"I never had any doubt. Tyndall chooses those he trusts wisely."

He shrugged his shoulders and laughed. "If you see him before I do, which you shall, tell him of all we have done together. Also, speak to him of the book I have."

Even though he could not see it, I nodded.

"Traveling at night, keep your dagger ready. There are those that hunt at night. You would make an easy target."

"I shall be alert. Kopernick, well met. I will miss you and your stories, honestly. You have given me a wealth of information."

"Well met. Like a brother," he said and we clasp hands. I knew it would be a long time until I saw him again.

Shortly thereafter I took the trail alone.

* * * * *

I found, as I continued south from village to village, that the rumor that started about my night in Ihrhoven was getting more and more out of hand. The rumor changed from me arriving as a hero to help save the kingdom to one that I was a master sorcerer from the Drenthen and that I had come to the kingdom as a spy.

I wrote almost a page in my journal about the grand castle at Edelstone. Whoever designed the place must have enjoyed towers. There were buildings that were round towers and not squared off like the normal fashion. From what I could see, and what Brembry speculated, everything in the castle was circular. The roof tops were graced with the red standard of the territory. Catwalks covered with bright flowers and ivy tied them together. We tried at each gate to enter the castle, but with no real business there they would not let us enter.

It was here where I learned that The-Lost-One towered over normal men and could almost carry a mule with the strength he possessed. On the night that I went to the cave I blinded the two soldiers with lightning from the sky, and then flew off out over the ocean on demon wings that suddenly sprouted from my back. Of course, there was no one able to say that they actually saw me fly away. There were other variations on this theme, but this one was the most wildly accepted.

The tale shook up the entire kingdom. More and more men traveled the road I was on making their way to the wall dividing the Territory. If armies of the other Territories were to arrive, they would make sure there was no trouble from them. Leaderless, they still would not just openly give their lands away.

Those that stayed to defend the villages could be seen in the drilling fields with swords, pike-staves, or bows. They were busy gathering stone and building fortifications. The metal smiths were pounding out swords and shields, and the women were at work making or mending clothes for the troops to wear.

As I left Edelstone with it tall towers and high spires, I shook my head, and smiled.

All of this for me, I thought toying with the ring on my finger as I kept my hand in my pocket.

{Lets hope that you make it to and from Croskreye in one piece. I've grown used to your body. I'd hate to have to find another because they take your head.} Brembry said.

"I like my body the way it is also. I have no intentions of getting myself killed."

*   *   *   *   *

Sometimes, as I was walking with my mind set on things I must do, and things that have happened, I would suddenly start humming bits of songs that I never heard before. Although the words were seldom lost, Brembry was not a good listener of words, she knew the tunes and how they went. For many of them, she made up her own words and this I found comical.

Brembry proved a talkative companion as well. She did not talk about the kingdom, or the legends of the past, or the life she literally left behind. She would just talk on whatever agreed with her at the moment and was enjoyable.

There was an expression I heard on a few occasions. People would say "You have one bird." When they said this, they meant that the person's mind would flutter as if they had a bird loose in their thoughts. This is exactly how Brembry felt to me.

Often I would find our conversations interrupted when something would catch her attention.

{Oh my, did you see the sparkle on that stone?}

"No, I missed it."

{Here, stop. Pick it up.}

"This one?"

{To the side. No, not that one, the other side. There, the one above that one. Yes there. Turn it over in the sunlight as you look at it.}

It glittered slightly, but was nothing more than a common rock. I held it for sometime, feeling its roughness in my fingers and holding it close so she could have a better look.

"Are you done?" I asked her.

{Yes.} she said and I dropped the rock without a second thought.

We rounded a bend in the road and came to a place where the briar and brambles were thick. I recognized the place when I saw the stone ramparts of a keep that had once stood here. Part of a tower still endured. Vines claimed the sills of what remained of the windows. Much of the roof, wooden beams and shingles and all, had collapsed years ago leaving it open for nesting birds.

"I remember this place. We are close to Ryeson's home now."

{This is where the snake bit him?}

She made me tiptoe and held my hands up and out to my side to keep my balance. After a few steps I bid her to stop.

"Yes, just up there by the wall, near the fountain. We will be in the company of a great healer. I know you must have heard of him. Please be still when he is about. I do not wish him to think I am mad."

{Yes, yes, yes. Don't do this and don't do that. You get all the excitement. I wish only freedom and to live again.}

She flung my arms in the air and made me twirl where I walked. I was thankful there were no other travelers about to see me.

* * * * *

"You," said the healer looking up from wrapping a woman's arm.

This was not the greeting I expected from Ryeson, but it is the one I got nonetheless. He sat on a rock near the path of his house tending the ailments of some people who had come to pay him for a visit. They were all sitting on the ground and turned to look at me in unison when Ryeson spoke.

"Hello again, I have returned."

"I see that. You were ill last time you left." A quick wink and I knew there was a part I had to play.

"Um, yes. I am, er, was once. Can I rest? It has been a long journey thus far."

"Under those trees and you'll be fine. I'll be with you shortly." And he went back to work on the woman's arm without a second look.

{Ah, a rest before nightfall, this is a welcome event.}

In the shade of an old oak tree I sat.

* * * * *

"What have you done, Marc?"

"Like tossing rocks at a kear tree, I had no idea of the full effect of what I started. I guess just standing still and breathing softly will not keep me from getting tangled up in this one." We sat once more in their home eating rabbit stew. My humor was lost in the dire mood of the family.

"Hmm," said Ryeson barely touching his meal. "I wait for the duchess's messenger to arrive in the village any day now. Lady Bessa will call upon the men of her territory to gather for its defense. I am sure to receive a calling to Carfrae if they feel the threat of battle."

"Who would oppose Lady Bessa?"

"She will side with her uncle and Duke Tominson, if it came to war. If they won the control of Wiladene Territory as well, that family would have domination of three of the six territories."

I ate some bread and was silent. Even Kalista was quiet in her moods.

"When this is all over, I shall go to King Trahune and present myself. I shall explain to him my actions."

Deanna looked at her husband and he nodded.

"You say Nathel's ghost wants you to return with some vials? Well, then once this is complete return here and I'll take you to Land Streth myself. My voice he will trust."

We spoke little else during the meal.

Had I given them advanced warning of my arrival, Ryeson could have provided a horse. As it was, there was little they could do to help me. We sat around the fire that night and were silent for the most part.

I began a discussion on the ghost of Nathel, what he was like and how he looked, but the conversation was not as lively as I imagined it would have been.

They allowed me to stay the night. Dawn came too soon. I quickly dressed and gathered my things. I gave them more apologies than goodbyes for doing what I knew as right. Leaving this time was altogether different. I was sad this time, but for different reasons.

{You did not bring any harm to them.}

"I know. This is something I thought these people would appreciate."

{Ryeson and Deanna?}

"Everyone. Now they treat me as such."

{Don't be disheartened. When they see the outcome, it will be better. A hero you will be.}

*   *   *   *   *

I stopped to rest. When I was in the forest, on days like today, I would climb on a boulder to eat. This gave Brembry peace of mind and kept her from twitching my head around at every noise she heard. She was still wary of wolves.

Taking my pack off, my staff laying beside me, I wiped the sweat from my brow and brought out my meal of a few plums and a small portion of sliced bread. This slice I took from a loaf spiced of pepper and butter made from goats milk. It was getting stale now having been bought at a shop just over a week and a half ago. The plums, I had picked from a tree, not in an orchard, but wild grown along the roadside. They were very abundant this year.

Thinking of more to write, I took out my book, opened the pen and began to write. Wind blew lightly through the branches causing their shadows to play across the words I had written the day before. The explanation of a spell Ryeson had taught me was giving me a hard time.

As walked, I would toss the words of different types of spells about in my head. Committing most of them to memory occupied my time. Some of the longer ones took more time to memorize, naturally. I had to keep reading these until I had their rhythm down.

I sat, this day, in the sun and shade thinking how to get my thoughts on this spell exactly how I should write it on paper and began to daydream.

The words were just beginning to fit in my head, when my eye caught something unusual.

"Look there." The shape of a boulder was odd. Just inside the line of trees of the forest to my left there was a boulder that stood out from the rest. The others, like the one I sat on, were flat with rough, jagged edges. This one, although it had almost the same color as those around it, was round and very even. It was partly blocked by several trees, but the sun was shining on it at the right angle and gave it a smooth glossy look. I looked back up and down the empty path before making my decision.

I recapped my pen and put everything away. Climbing down from the boulder I jumped the last bit and heading off toward it.

{What is it?} Brembry asked, she still had not seen it.

"The rock doesn't look right, I want to look at it. It'll take just a moment."

As I drew near it confirmed my suspicions. It wasn't a boulder at all, but an egg. It was a kear egg. Looking around, I did not see the white flowers of the tree. It must have died some time ago, because not even a stump remained.

Both Tyndall and Ryeson noted there were special magical properties of dust from a kear egg. If I had the powder from such an egg, it would be a much prized and valued possession.

{It would not be wise to touch such a thing. Not something I would do.} Brembry said being ever cautious. {To break the outer shell would unleash whatever it contained if it was still alive. Let us leave this place altogether. If a kear tree made an egg this large, it must have been a very large and probably dangerous animal.}

"If something was bound by a kear tree, then it is bound. I do not wish to crack it open completely, I just want to take a bit off and look at it. Perhaps a scraping of some off the side," I said in a whisper.

Twice she used my left hand to smack my right as I reached for my dagger. I willed her still, but did not reach for my dagger again.

I walked closer, Brembry brought me up on my the tips of my toes to be as quiet as possible even though this was completely unnecessary. The leaves crunched under my feet regardless. Drawing near as I dared, I was careful not to disturb it. I touched the surface tentatively with the back of my hand.

The shell was warm to my skin, and being this close I could tell that the surface was porous. The color amazed me; it blended in almost perfectly with the surroundings. You could actually see the patterns of the kear leaves and vines on the surface. Leaves and twigs of other trees lay on the egg's top and some piled around its base.

I tapped it once and then twice with my knuckles to test its strength. It was very solid. The term of 'kear egg' was very miss leading.

First with one rock, and then a larger one, I attempted to chip some small piece off. Even the hardened point of the dagger had no effect on a surface that seemed so frail. Hitting it with sticks only numbed my hands with the shock. Frustrated, and knowing I did not have the upper hand in my task, I gave it one last shove to unseat it. With its great weight it remained still and unmoving.

"Eh, so be it, Brembry, no wonder the dust from such is a valued possession."

As I brought my hand away the ring Nathel had given me slightly scratched the surface.

{It could be demon spawn, a nightmare. Let us leave this place.} she insisted.

"We'll go then," I said to her. My sample of egg dust would have to wait.

As I turned to go, I must have stepped on a twig because I heard a snap, but my foot felt just the smooth ground of the forest floor and nothing else. I turned on the ball of my foot and looked back to the egg as a crack ran from the top to the bottom. The simple pattern made by the vines and leaves broke.

{It wakes. RUN!!!} Brembry screamed in my head.

I fought with all of my might against her emotions and actions inside of my head. She tried to take possession of my legs once again, but I gained them back as quickly. She bruised my shoulder from hitting a tree. This made me stumble and I fell awkwardly to one knee. Instead of running I drew my dagger. Still crouched down on one knee I watched as the one crack shattered into thousands across the once smooth surface.

{What's the matter with you? Get out of here! Are you daft?}

"Listen, the tree is long dead. There is nothing inside but the dry bones of what it caught." I held fast in my stance and her scream trailed off to nothing.

For several seconds the egg sat motionless as if the cracks across its surface meant nothing. Then the two halves fell inward, and a great cloud of dust rose as they collapsed. I watched, wide eyed, never taking my eyes off of the dust cloud. No wings of a demon flapped, no roar from the throat of any type of animal broke the solitude of the forest.

The dust began to settle.

"I guess there was nothing. As I said probably just bones now." I relaxed, and the tip of my dagger dipped a little. I breathed deep, and the dust in the air made me cough. Brembry had made me nervous.

It was then that something stirred. Something was there. Only a little could be seen. The beast that had lain flat lifted itself up on its two front legs. Its entire form, as well as its mane, lay covered with the white dust from the egg. The creature did not stay hunched on its four legs like a wolf or a bear would. With its hind legs coiled beneath it sat up back and brought its hands up to wipe the dust out of its eyes. As even more of the dust settled from the air, it blinked at me with brown eyes. Eyes almost human.

{It is a woman!} Brembry exclaimed. She was giddy in knowing it was now harmless.

Something gold in color fell from the young woman's neck to the cleft of her breasts to the ground below. I saw it drop but was too absorbed in her beauty to notice.

She coughed, and sat up so she was on both knees. I stood and went forward. As I approached, I lowered my knife and offered her my hand. She grasped it firmly, and stood on legs that were not steady.

"Have you chased them off?" she asked.

"Whom do you speak of?" I asked after looking about.

She took small steps away from the pile if dust. "There were men chasing us. Dre-nnth-een." This word was hard for her and she spoke it slowly. Dust fell from her hair and shoulders. She shook and brushed herself off. The dust enveloping her once more until the light breeze carried it away. The whole area lay covered in a thin layer of this powder.

{Ah, it sparkles in the sunlight. Look at the colors!}

"I believe that they are gone for good now. I've seen not a sign of them this day." I noted that as she took her first steps away that she was, indeed, naked. She noticed this at the same time and covered her breasts with her arms. I brought my pack from the boulder, where I had dropped it, and pulled out my heavy shirt and breeches, but I did not give them to her straightaway.

"After you bathe. I can hear a stream down the path." I turned to show her the way and she followed. Because she had nothing to cover her feet she took her time getting to the path. I waited for her there, and then led her to the water keeping my head turned out of modesty.

"What is your name?" I asked hearing her just a few steps behind.

"Chay. Ow, sharp stones. Chay is my name. You have more people?" she asked.

"I am traveling alone. I am on my way back from northern towns. On my way to the village Croskreye."

We could hear the stream louder now, even though we were several lengths from it. The late summer rains had swelled it some.

"There is fighting there? You fight? They came to my home. Melsha helped me. I ran, I did. My town of Eil-enn-burg saw fighting. The village had fallen . . . I ran . . ."

She did not finish her sentence, but began to cry. Hearing the sob, I turned, and watched as her tears mixed with the dust and carried it down her cheeks. She did not try to hide them, nor did she try to wipe them away.

{Do something. She needs comforting. Her mind is that of a child.}

I was not sure what to do and stood there. Feeling slightly awkward, to say the least, I went to her. Brembry took control of my arms and held her. Chay returned the embrace. Thankfully, there were no other travelers upon the trail to witness this. An odd sight for their eyes, no doubt.

{Like this. Just hold her.}

I willed my arms back. One tear still lay on her cheek. I kissed a tear away on the right and then on the left. I breathed deep and found that the aroma of the egg powder numbing my senses. I saw her smile as she backed away. My own cheeks grew warm and I turned away and continued walking to the stream.

{Well, I would not have gone that far.}

Chay must have ran from the fighting when they tried to take Eilenburg. The town is about a half of a days walk from here. To be trapped in that egg for that long . . .

{She doesn't know that any time has passed.} Brembry said softly, her thoughts echoing my own. {She may find it very difficult to handle when she finds out how much has changed. Break it to her gently.}

"Thanks," I thought back at her.

We had slowly worked our way down to the stream. In these tall ancient pines and oaks, there was no bridge across the stream. Stepping stones had been placed in the stream. I crossed and waited for her.

As she entered the water, a trail of white rose from her feet and traveled with the current downstream.

Like a linen sheet in the wind, I thought.

"Ah, it's cold," she said and splashed some on her face. When she looked back my way she smiled, and the whole world seemed a bit brighter, more alive. She did not try to cover herself now. Her nakedness seemed not as important as getting the egg dust off of her.

"Have you any food?" Chay asked. She took small sips of water, milky-white with the egg dust, from her cupped hand.

"Hmm?" I said taking my eyes away from her. "Umm, not much now, I was going to get some in Eilenburg. Hungry?"

"Very," she sat on a rock in the middle of the stream and let the water rush over her legs and lower body. I noticed goose bumps on her arms and thighs. She splashed about to get the rest off.

"Ah, I'll be back," I said as I rose from my place near the stream. I walked until the water was out of sight and then began to gather wood. Sticks snapped and broke under my boots. I was sure to make enough noise to assure her I had not abandoned her. The vision of her body clouded my thoughts and I had to push it aside and concentrate on the task at hand.

Moments later I cast the spell of fire upon a small portion of the firewood. When the smoke was strong and steady I added more. I then set to the task of finding apples and plums from nearby trees.

{You'll have to ask Tyndall if the kear dust has any other properties he has not told you of. Marc, I believe you are suddenly smitten.}

"My 'smitten-ness' is not due to egg dust. And I am not smitten."

When I arrived with an armful of fruit, she was already dressed with my extra breeches and heavy shirt. Water hissed on the burning wood as she wrung her hair out over the fire. It would seem that the whiteness of her hair and skin was not an illusion brought on by a covering of egg dust. Washed and cleaned she was as still shockingly pale in color. All but her eyes. I placed the fruit on the ground next to her.

"Thank you," Chay said as she looked over the apples searching for the ripest one. She stiffly sat down cross-legged in the warmth of the fire and began to eat.

I dug through my haversack once more and pulled out my over cloak.

"The nights are getting cooler, the leaves will be turning soon. You can have this to keep you warm."

She wrapped it around her legs.

"You are weak?" I asked.

"I feel ... tired ... empty."

I looked to the sun and knew there was no real hurry. I would wait for her. As long as it was needed, I would wait.

"We'll stay here. I'll get more fire wood."

"Is it safe?" Chay asked looking about.

"It is."

"Stay we must," she said smacking her lips. "I do not like it at night. I get scared," she said and shivered. "The baby sheeps were getting big. We left them. Melsha tells me just last morning summer has come," she paused, and took a bite from her fruit. Speaking with food in her mouth, she went on. "You say nights are cooler. Summer end must be here. How long have I...?"

She brought the question to light so quickly. I was going to delay it some. Forcing my hand, I had no choice but to answer her now.

When I did, I looked into her eyes hoping she would know I was telling the truth. Outlandish as it may sound to her, I did not want her to think I had lost my wits.

"You say that we are only half a day from your village. You have traveled much farther than that. There is no war, not anymore. The people of the kingdom drove back those who came from the north. The last one has died. The last battle was fought roughly twenty years ago," my voice trailed off.

"How many is a twenty?"

I held one palm open, then the other, then both again once more.

The only noise was that of the fire. Even though she had not spoken or said a word, she suddenly looked drained, a shell of her former self. I saw the sorrow in her eyes, but no tears were shed. A flake of ash from the fire landed on her cheek and she absently brushed it away, in the same motion she pulled a pale lock of her hair over her shoulder. She threw the core of her apple into the fire and it hissed.

"This is a long time?"

"Well, yes. Um, It is as long as I have lived," I said.

"You go back to my home?"

"Yes, and then back to Croskreye. I will take you home if you wish. I would enjoy your company." Eilenburg is where Tyndall and I parted last winter.

"I am so big though," she said touching herself over her legs and her chest. "Is this magic? I want to become my size again," she all but pouted.

"You were young when the egg formed?"

"Yes. I have only seen this many summers," she held up two fingers. "This is all the summers I remember. I am not this big. Melsha is big, not me," she began to cry as a child might. Brembry made me stand I and went to her side. Sitting on the ground beside her, I cradled her lightly in my arms. She clung to me as though she thought I was going to let her go or abandon her. She cried loudly at first, muttering names at times.

Brembry grew sad as well. I had to deal with two emotional women.

Then, as the fire died down and the evening turned to twilight, Chay stopped crying, and just held me. Moments later, I leaned back to look at her. Her eyes closed and she slept. Small flakes of egg dust clung to her forehead and hair and I slowly took them away.

I brushed her hair away from her eyes once more and touched her cheek softly with the palm of my hand. One kiss, and then another lightly on the forehead, for comfort, then I let her down to lay on the ground.

*   *   *   *   *

Taking the small pouch that Wenonah had given me, I dumped the coins left into my haversack. The empty pouch was then tied around my belt. Looking around the camp once more, I departed, but not before building the fire back up a bit to keep her warm.

At the trail I went to the area where the dust of the egg lay. Even though the wind was gentle that day, it was enough to take most of the egg dust with it. I found that a good bit remain trapped between the spaces of the other rocks and collected there. It was here I knelt and began to scoop it up and put it in the coin pouch.

"What am I to do, Brembry?"

{About what?} she said softly seemingly as distant as always.

"You know, about the girl?"

{Take her back to her home to Eilenburg. Continue on till you finish the quest Nathel has given you.}

"That might be bad for her though. Her parents might be gone, brothers and sisters grown and may have children of their own. She will have no home or no one with her. I will bring her to Tyndall and we'll see if he can reverse the spell. She is too much a woman to remain as young as she is, also she is too young to become as much of a woman as she is."

{I see you really noticed how much of a woman she is,} she chided.

"Hush," I said as I felt my cheeks blush. "I am not as simple and as homespun as you might think." I could feel Brembry laughing inside.

The pouch was as full as I could get it so I stood and looked over the area once more. In the spot where the egg once stood I found the remains of her clothes. The leather of the small sandals leather were deeply weathered and cracked. The brittle soles crumbled in my hand as I held them. The clothes were in shreds after all this time.

"Did she undress?" I asked.

{You are homespun.} Brembry said laughing.

"Why do you laugh?" I asked with a bit of irritation in my voice.

{I'm sorry.} she said, and after a she giggled more she went on. {When the vines wrapped her she was just a young girl. She grew as time went on and her cloths fell from her. I think that there was no spell cast on her to make the young girl into a woman, she just grew to that size with the natural course of time.}

"If she was two and the Drenthen have been gone for nearly twenty years she would be about that now. Twenty. She looks much younger."

{She said that she was only able to remember that many summers. Does a babe remember their years?}

"She might be older?" I asked.

{I think she is about your age more or less.}

"Well, yes. She would be about my age. I still want to check with Tyndall though. He might be able to make her as she was before."

{Is that what you want?} Brembry asked.

I said nothing, but continued to sift through the cloths. I found a locket laying just off to the side. It was gold with the remains of a leather cord. When mended it would have hung by way of two small openings in the back of the metal. I placed this into my pocket and stood.

* * * * *

I woke at dawn to find her gone. The fear that she had left in the night made me yell her name out through the woods. I saw movement in the trees and her voice returned my call. Her stark white hair unmistakable in the brush around her.

"I had to go," was all she said for an explanation.

"I am sorry. I thought you may have left in the night. I didn't want to lose you here in the wilderness." I turned and began to kick dirt over the near dead embers of the fire. "I am not staying in Eilenburg. I have business further south. We can look for family or friends of yours. I should not stay long, however." I said with my back to her.

"My family might still be in Eil-enn-burg. I will stay with them. My friends might still be there. Melsha will be old, and Teahasha will be a mommy now," she said as she gathered my cloak around her shoulders. After being out for so long in the elements the changes in weather did not bother me as they had before. I had not seen the cloak in many months.

The sun was just up, but its warmth had not penetrated the woods yet. Within an hour we would be warm enough with the heat our bodies made while walking.

I searched my pocket and held out the locket that I had found the night before.

"I found this last night near where you were," she took the locket from my hand and held in hers. She looked upon the charm with such force that she seemed enchanted for a moment. A tear touched the corner of her eye, and in one quick motion she kissed me and wrapped her arms fiercely around my neck.

I held her also, and it seemed forever that we stood there. I was sure we would have stayed rooted to that spot until the sun set, had it not been for the stag that startled us. We stood so still that when the animal ran through the woods several lengths to our side I was sure it had not see us. The spell broke.

With everything packed and the smoke from the fire next to nothing I helped her to the trail. I carried my staff of ash.

{Marc,} Brembry's voice coming like a soft wind across my thoughts. {I think you have found someone.}

Chapter #16

We arrived at Eilenburg on the evening two and a half days following. We did not cover as much distance as I would have liked on the first day or the next. Chay's legs were still not as strong as needed for such a journey, and she had nothing to cover her feet.

The weather was good for this time of year. The days were clear and the last couple of nights the sky was overcast with clouds without rain. It was getting colder out, but not drastically so. Just outside of Eilenburg the trail that we were on rejoined the main road coming from Taberham far to the north.

We rested on some rocks under an old elm and watched as people passed us by. From nearby trees, children gathered apples that were at such an abundance this year they almost broke the branches with their weight.

I picked several and brought them back to the rock. We ate quietly. Her weariness was beginning to show. She was hungry, and it was clear that the fruits were not nourishing her nearly enough. Eilenburg had several butchers and bakeries. I made a promise she would eat well there.

There was a commotion on the road as people moved their wagons to the side. A column of troops was coming by on horseback. They traveled under the standard of Duke Almonesson. With this many troops heading north, the garrison would be all but empty.

"Why would the duke be going north this late in the season?" I asked.

Brembry, naive in such matters, said nothing, and just shook my head.

{This is the duke? Oh, goodness. I have never seen royalty before.} She began to pat my hair down and straighten out my tunic.

As they drew near, I could begin to make out faces among the group. Riding beside the man with the standard was Duke Almonesson and someone else, possibly his son, Lord Farnstrom. Behind them, I saw the gleaming armor worn by a slim man who carried himself well. This could only be Commander Nayoor, someone who Tyndall and Rouke had only spoken briefly of. Ah, now this was his element. The sweat, smell of horses and dust of the road was his milk and honey.

Duchess Lowy would be governing the affairs of state while the men were gone.

"We must bow our heads. Just do as I do," I said seeing the quizzical look in Chey's eyes.

A dust cloud rose from the earth as they passed. When the last horse was past we gathered our belongings and continued south. Fortunately, I was not recognized by any of the soldiers or the duke himself. I was just a common traveler. I looked at Chay and smiled. Well, just a common traveler with a young woman my own age with hair and skin as white as snow. No one seemed to notice and I breathed a sigh of relief in their passing.

"It is strange," I said. "To have the duke and his soldiers traveling north this time of year. They should be with the others gathering the harvest."

"The war is over?" Chay asked looking at my eyes to see if I was telling the truth.

"Yes. There's probably some other kind of trouble. Eilenburg will be fine though," I assured her.

* * * * *

As we walked, I told her about the ocean. I explained how at places the forest and waves were just a few lengths apart. She was saying that she'd like to go there, when we rounded over the last knoll of the road and before us sat Eilenburg. She gave pause.

To me it looked like most villages I have seen in my time here. Thin wisps of smoke could be seen from most chimneys in the afternoon sun. The paddle wheel of the gristmill turned a stone that crushed corn or wheat into flour. The miller would live and work here. Two towers stood and the north and south end of the village with a wall about a man's height circling it. Now that I stopped and really looked at it, the wall seemed more to define borders, than for any means of protection. Much like the wall around Westrick. A third tower, ringed by scaffolding, sat in the center of the village obviously being repaired and saved from ruin. Distantly, I heard the sound of hammer and anvil from the blacksmith, and also the steady rhythm of some one beating a mat to free it of dust.

She stood there for a moment, eyes wide and awe struck. Her smile faded to nothing and she brought her hands up to her mouth, as if to hold back a scream.

But she held quiet, and her inner turmoil remained unspoken. Tears swelled in her eyes and she sobbed silently. Had I not been there for her support, she would have fallen where she stood.

* * * * *

"You'll not believe what happened today," the baker said to his wife as he was eating his late dinner. He dabbed away soup from his mustache.

"What happened, dear?" She asked scooping out the last bowl of soup from a small pot near the hearth. She leaned in too close and soot from the chimney got on her sleeve. Disgusted, she rubbed it off with a scowl. She returned to the table with her meal, her plumpness made the joints of the wooden chair creak in protest.

"A woman came into m' store followed by a man. She just stood there wide-eyed and all just lookin' all about."

"Lookin' at what?" his wife said as she ate her soup with a wooden spoon.

"Lookin' about the shop, woman. Her condition was not the best mind you. White as flour all over, hands, face, hair, longest hair I've seen mind you. I thought my death had come to claim me. Her feet were bare and by the looks of it, she had on his cloths. Those were a man breaches she wore, I tell you," he paused to chew on a bit of bread that he broke off of a roll. Only five of his teeth remained. The sixth had fallen out by eating a tough piece of bread last year. Sweets and sugars had claimed the rest.

"Go on then, what happened?"

"Well, she just looked about the shop and got all weepy. Her eyes started crying and what not. The man just stood there behind her and watched as I was. Then she asks me if I had any dough that had not been baked yet. I says yes and brought her a pinch out of the back. When she eats this she rushes out. Meanwhile, the man tosses three coppers on the table and says thanks for the dough," he said licking his lips.

"These people coming to this place are getting odd I tell you," said his wife.

* * * * *

I showed the owner of the inn the coin Tyndall had given me and although they gave us a fine meal he said he had no rooms available. I would have to find a place elsewhere. I drank an extra mug or two of ale with the meal and Chay drank juice from crushed berries and we were content.

The tailors shop was shut as was the shop of the cobbler. I could not get her new clothing or shoes. She said that she did not mind.

In the common hall we were given a stall and it was here that we slept.

The twinge came in the early hours of the morning. I tried to dismiss it, but it would not let me be. Easing my arm from under her I paused a moment. I left slowly to make certain that she had not woken. I walked bootless over the straw and thrushes that covered the floor and into the night.

I knew that when such feelings woke me they also woke Brembry. If she were the first to wake, she would be upset. I kept my thoughts to myself and was sure that she still slept in my mind.

As with most of the common areas there was a place around the back where people relieved themselves. There were booths with curtains set aside for privacy when they sat. I did not need one and relieved myself in the water which ran down the gutter.

The weather was slowly turning. I looked to the skies and saw no stars. So thick the clouds were that the full moon did not show through. I saw the dim flash of lightning as it struck somewhere distantly.

Before morning it may rain.

Completing my task I turned, jumped a puddle, and walked back.

The guard slept at the door. His feet were resting on a piece of firewood and his hands folded over his stomach.

The candle's sconces set deep in the stone of the walls offered enough light to see by. Set as they were the wind did not touch them.

On the balls of my feet I crept back to where our place was. I tried to stay noiseless as I returned. There was a nook that was empty except for a pack and a few other things. With a start I realized that this was our place.

She was gone. I looked about, but could not see her anywhere. Her hair, long and white, was easy to see in the night.

I slapped my face and there was a moment of dizziness as Brembry woke up.

{What?} she asked. There was definitely a tone of irritation in her thoughts.

"Chay is gone," I said still looking about.

{Where?}

"I do not know," I whispered. Besides the snores of others the night was quiet.

{Leave your things, they will be safe.}

I listened to Brembry, but thought it best to bring the staff. It felt warm and comforting in my hands. It would give me light to see by.

I went back to the open door and looked outside. I called her name, but this only woke the guardsman. He looked at me, smacked his lips a few times, and returned to his slumber.

I went further out into the street and called her name louder.

{Check around back. She probably had the same urges you did.}

I ran to the back, but there was no one there.

"She could not have gone too far," I whispered. "I hope nobody took her from the common room."

I went back to the street and looked in both directions. Listening I could not hear the sound of footfalls or hooves. In the whole village it seemed as if I alone were awake. I felt a drop of rain on my cheek and looked skyward.

That is when I saw her. At the top of the scaffolding, perched on the edge of the stones, she stood. My cloak was barely visible about her. It whipped in the wind that also thrashed her hair about her head creating a pale halo against the storm clouds above.

{She'll fall.} Brembry's words were just a whisper of a thought. I ran, my bare feet thudding on the slick cobblestones and dirt. The door to the keep was before me, the scaffolding to the side. Trusting I would find the steps easier to climb, I ducked beneath a timber and slammed the door with my shoulder.

Three times it took before the wood splintered.

"Don't do this Chay," I whispered in the darkness. "Don't do this."

For a heartbeat I stood in the doorway letting the staffs light penetrate the night.

{Move Marc, the stairs are right before you.} Brembry used her will on my legs and I stumbled forward landing awkwardly on the stone steps. My legs and arms were mine once more and I scrambled upward as fast as I could.

In the time that it took me to reach the top the skies had opened up and it rained heavily.

She was gone.

I ran to the edge and looked, but could not see where she had fallen. I did not see her on the ground or the scaffolding. Calling her name brought only the howl of the wind. I turned to go back down when I saw her.

She had climbed back from the edge of the wall and stayed here at the top of the tower. Against the rock she knelt with her arms folded tightly across her chest. She was crying and in the dim light I could see she was cold. Her hands shook.

"What are you doing here?" I asked her hoping my voice did not give away my emotions. I was almost afraid my words were lost in the wind and rain. Kneeling beside her I did not touch her. Rain fell from my hair. It was at that moment my heart went to her. Perhaps Brembry had planted this idea, this strange romantic notion, that Chay and I should be a couple, however I did not need encouragement from her. There was a deep feeling which I felt and I could not stop the torrent of emotion that welled up inside me. Brembry was right; I had found someone, someone like no other. She was like me in that she should not be here. The kear tree sealed her fate years ago and she should have died a child. But she lived. And I saved her. I released her from her prison.

She did not speak. Her lips trembled and it was only when I placed a hand beneath her chin that she looked into my eyes.

"I wanted to jump." The words came from her as a sob. "I am alone here. No one is here anymore that cares for me. Everything has changed."

"I care for you," I said. The staff left my hand as I gave it to her and the night was suddenly dark. She needed the warmth more than I did.

"And when you leave?" Her lips formed words that I did not wish to hear. "You travel. Your place is not here." Her tears mixed with the rain.

"I will not abandon you," I told her. I though she had known of my intent. When this was all over I would settle with her somewhere. It would all be behind us and we would move on with our lives.

"My friends are gone, Marc. I miss them," she cried some more and I went to her slowly taking her thin hands in my own. Cold and so frail. The rain robbed her of warmth. I held her for a long time and the night slowly passed us by. She clung to me desperately and still shivered.

"I am afraid to die. Life is too painful to live," she said from the folds of her cloak.

"Would death be better then?"

"That pain won't last," she whispered.

I leaned back and brought my hand up to her chin. The half moon broke out through the clouds and I could see it glow in her eyes. It was then, it was that night that I knew I loved her.

"Don't hurt yourself. Please? A promise? A vow I want to give you. No matter where you are, I shall always be with you. If ever we part, I will find you. This I promise you," I said. Then with a motion that I was not even conscious of and seemed so natural, I bent my head down, and we kissed.

* * * * *

I talked with her for some time before we descended the spiral stairway together. We had no drier clothing to change into so we lay down in the straw still damp from the rain. She held the staff of ash close and this warmed her.

Although it was the same number of candles that burned in the sconces of the walls in the common room, the place seemed brighter. A child cried out in the until its parents quieted it. An owl could also be heard ever so often somewhere in the night shrouded forest.

She slept with her head laying softly on my shoulder.

* * * * *

She looked to Marc as they walked. He was in the middle of a story and it was good to hear him talk. She felt an ease when she was with him. When they left the town that was once her home Chay remembered the moon was less. As they traveled the moon turned full and still she walked with him. Waking every morning she was glad he was at her side. She smiled as he finished his story, not sure exactly what it had been about, but she was happy nonetheless.

Chay smiled to herself as she walked with Marc. She did not look back. She did not say good-byes. The place where she once lived was gone. None of her friends had been found. There were new families in the homes she remembered. Seeing this, feeling a strange pain in her chest, there was no reason to stay.

She loved him. Since the time he broke her free she had felt it. Slowly at first, but now she knew. Like he some how pulled her to him.

Her mind was changing. Growing. Her body had changed. Her mind was busy catching up. There was pain in her head from time to time. This she hid from him lest he grow angry at her. She would always go with him. He gave her food and shelter now. His promise she remembered. He had said he would not leave her.

A place called Croskreye would be seen in two days. He was very happy talking of it. People were there that he knew. People he remembered.

* * * * *

Chay looked up seeing him come through the door.

She watched him move. Taller than her, but just so, he was pleasant to look at with his long hair and light beard that scratched when he kissed her.

As he came close, she smiled, but he did not smile back.

"What is wrong? Did you get the food?" she asked.

"Pack our things quickly. There is trouble. We must leave this place," he said taking up his cloak and other small items she had taken out of his pack already.

"What is wrong?" she whispered. His emotions confused her. Other people were near and she did not want them to hear.

He came to her side and brushed her hair away from her ear.

"I was in the shops getting some bread," he whispered to her, "I over heard a traveler talking about Croskreye. Lady Wenonah has been ill for over four days now. She has not eaten and they do not expect her to last more than another day or so." She squeezed his arm in alarm. This woman was important to him.

"We must find a wagon going there tonight then," she said.

"It will take too long so I've bought a horse. It's in the stables waiting for us."

* * * * *

"My king," The herald bowed deeply. The long curls of her hair covered her face momentarily as she went to one knee, and she straightened only when he spoke.

"Are they all here?" King Trahune asked looking up from the paper he held in his hands.

"Adding to the compliment of the sons of Duke Tominson, and Duke Curwin, we now have the last two dukes. Duke Lysaght arrived earlier this morning and Duke Almonesson is setting up his camp at this time."

Young King Trahune just shook his head. "A meal will be given tonight and we shall begin the audience in the morning."

"Doubtless they will not wait that long," said Counselor Wroe scratched his head. He then ran his fingers through his thinning hair. "It surprises me that they are not here tonight. They'll be arguing this evening. Make sure you secure the ceremonial weaponry on the racks in the Gathering room. We need not have anyone injured if fighting breaks out."

The herald nodded.

* * * * *

In the Gathering room in the castle of Land Streth servants busied themselves. Dusting, cleaning and polishing. They took away old floor rushes and fresh ones brought in. They checked the upper corners of the room for cobwebs a final time, and replaced the large candles in the wall sconces with newer ones. The thick table and chairs where generations of men created treaties and alliances was thoroughly polished no less than four times and dusted again as evening arrived.

On a wooden trivet with black velvet lining and legs of dark metal, sat the Coin of Truth. The Coin had flipped silver to the last given question and so remained until the next inquiry. Out of fear or respect for it, no one touched it.

A servant paused in the dusting of the table. Thin cloth in hand, she looked at the Coin nervously.

"Be on with it and we'll be finished," chided one of the four others. They paused in their work to watch her.

"They say if you look away it helps," whispered another.

With a quick sigh of determination, her hand darted out and the Coin and the trivet it sat on were quickly, but thoroughly, dusted.

She held the cloth out at arm's length and gave it a sharp snap. Everyone breathed again.

* * * * *

The population of Land Streth had almost doubled in just over two weeks. First to arrive were the sons of Duke Tominson from their fathers north-west territory of Spruill. He was an aged man and the snows came early to his lands. Catching a chill he bid his sons take his place at the gathering. Their men encamped well outside the great village in the north-west corner.

Duke Curwin and his troops arrived on the evening of the next day. Haggard and looking worn out, their camp was hastily made and they rested. They had traveled the farthest.

In a rousing herald, trumpeted by his own men, Duke Lysaght's troops emerged from the edges of the forest and began to promptly erect tents.

Last to arrive was Duke Almonesson.

* * * * *

It was a bit painful riding. Muscles so used to walking, ached trying to keep me steady. I remembered now why I wasn't fond of riding one.

Once we started, I didn't want to stop. Chay made small conversation at first, but neither of us was in the mood for talking. As the ride drew on, she grew quiet and I believed she now slept. The horse seemed to have no problem seeing in the darkness. I held the staff of ash against its neck knowing this would help. It snorted from time to time perhaps wondering why it was still light at this time of day.

Chay moaned softy. I felt her warmth to my back and was glad the horse was generating a good bit of heat itself while it galloped along.

The moon was full this night and the sky was cloudless. As the night grew darker, it began to get colder. It was the time of the season for the first frost. The leaves would change their color then and winter would be soon behind.

I shivered thinking about the winter to come. I would be on this road soon heading back north to Ihrhoven again this year. Kopernick would not be with me in my travels, but still there in Glenhelen. I would be thankful to see Nathel. When this task was complete, I planned to rest a while.

{Do you think you can do anything?} Brembry asked. Her voice quiet and secluded this night. I could sense sorrow in her mood.

"I don't know. We have to do something. I would like to see her again."

{Don't you think that the Sorcerer Tyndall has already tried all that he could think of? Perhaps he has found an answer and what you heard was a rumor. Perhaps she is awake even now and this ride is for nothing.}

"Anything is possible. I just want to see her again."

{That's understandable, but how are you going to get yourself inside the castle?}

"Rouke will help me."

With that, Brembry was quiet again. An hour before dawn we reached Denhartog.

* * * * *

"Money is not the issue really. I must sell her."

"I am glad you don't care much for your money. It's an old horse and I'll have to give you little as it is. She has about two more good years left in her though and then it's to the kitchens," said the stable hand checking her teeth. A younger boy was looking over her hooves and shoes. Tapping each one with a small hammer. Chay leaned against a short stone wall.

"I am just asking enough for passage across the channel, a meal and a room for this evening." Granted I could use the token to obtain these, but it may rouse suspicions. Why would someone use a token, given by the duke just outside his walls? There were rooms in the castle and plenty of food.

He looked at me for a moment with his one good eye, squinting the other shut.

"What else ails her? Is this all she is worth to you?"

The horse twitched her ears and tapped the bare dirt of the stable with her hoof. The young boy held tight to her reins.

"Honestly, there is nothing. I do not have enough for passage for a horse across the Straights. I give my word."

"The saddle?"

"I would not take the saddle if I had no horse. It goes with her."

He looked me over once more before reaching in his pockets and took out several large coins which he gave to me. The young boy took the horse away for brushing.

"Thank you," I said taking my pack and staff from the ground.

* * * * *

In Croskreye, Chay leaned heavily on my shoulder. She was weak from hunger. At an inn called Shaye's Hostel I gave a young kitchen hand five coppers to fetch Rouke for me from the castle while we ate.

Chay's appearance still brought looks from people, and as we sat, others moved to find different seats. She was not as gaunt as when I first freed her, but with her white hair and very thin features she stood out from others. Weary and hungry, I barely noticed them.

* * * * *

It was good to see Rouke again, taller than I remember, his hair was a bit longer and he showed the first signs of a beard. His arms were more fit and his shoulders were broader. I nudged Chay in the side, she looked up briefly and then began to eat again. I was very hungry also, but this was a joyous sight. Our last meal had been yesterday's breakfast.

I watched him as he entered the dining hall of the hostel. He looked in our direction, gave Chay a second look and continued to glance about the room. On his second glimpse over the room his eyes met mine. I smiled and nodded. Rouke lowered his eyes and quickly walked to our table. Chay looked up between mouthfuls as he came near. I grabbed him by the shoulder as he sat down. We clasp hands for a moment and then I introduced Rouke to Chay.

"Damn it's good to see you alive, Marc." When he said my name his voice went to a whisper. No others had heard.

"Yes, and it's good to see you also. I wish the circumstances would be better."

"What do you mean by that?" he said in a hushed tone. "Lady Wenonah's illness or the fact that you have the kingdom scared out of their wits and all of the king's men gathering for war?" Chay sat next to me and held my hand in hers. She was quiet now, finished with her meal, and listened to us talk.

"I did not know the rumors had reached such a height. You know I mean the condition that Lady Wenonah is in. Is she as bad as they say?"

"Tyndall says that if she comes out of it before the sun sets tonight, there is hope. If she comes out of it after, then it will be very difficult to save her. She has not taken nourishment in several days. By dawn her soul will be too far gone and she will probably die regardless."

"Is there any way I can get in to see her?"

"They are to allow no one near her room except those closest to the duke and duchess. She has guards posted at the doors. I have tried to go there with food for her, but they refused me entrance. Tyndall takes the trays in for her."

"What medicines has Tyndall tried?"

"What medicines you ask? He's tried all that he knows. Of course medicine is not his best magic. A healer from a village to the west arrived, but nothing has worked and the lady still sleeps. Bischof the healer is tending to her as well."

I thought on this. "Is there a way that I can get into the castle itself?"

"I do not see a problem in that. Gifts and favors have arrived from land barons. I cannot say that security has been overly lazy, but it does lack in sharpness. The more experienced of his host went with the duke to Land Streth."

"I need to get to the far west tower. I've learned about a room there that I have to get to."

"It's been all but abandoned. is this the room that Tyndall was talking about before you left? The one with the horse with no nose. I found it. No one could open it."

"Yes, I know," I nodded. "I need you to just get me there."

* * * * *

"Your business?" the guard asked. They wore heavier armor now. Possibly from the rumors they heard from the north, possibly with everything that was going on with Duke Lysaght to the west. They would not let me pass just on the word of a castle servant.

"I am here to see Tyndall, Sorcerer Tyndall."

"He's busy." The guard began to turn away.

"I am returning a book I borrowed from him. He had sent an urgent message yesterday that he needed it. It may have a cure for the lady." I reached in my pack and brought out my journal.

He took it from my hands forcibly. Opening it, he flipped through the pages. These were my own personal writings and had not expected him to call my bluff. I knew in a moment I would be found out. He looked at me and began to read.

I looked at the book and smiled. What I had written on the pages I could read perfectly. Even though he had his finger on a line, and his lips moved as he was reading a passage, the book itself was upside down.

"A book of spells?" the guard asked closing the book.

I nodded, and he handed the book over wiping his gloved hands even after it was back in my haversack. He looked at the leather of his gloves in distaste.

"Pass," he stood aside and let us enter.

* * * * *

Rouke reached the top of the stairs and knocked on the door there. Tyndall opened the door as Rouke leaned against the wall trying to catch his breath. The sorcerer looked very tired.

"What is the meaning of this? No one is to bother me. You know I need rest at this time."

"Sorcerer Tyndall . . . I'm sorry, but . . . he is back."

"The duke?"

"No, Marc."

"What? How could . . . he's returned? Here, in Croskreye?"

"Yes. He's waiting for us . . . at the base of the far west tower. The room that is magically locked. Horse with no nose. He says he has a key to the room. There is some writing there we think you should see."

Tyndall left to return a moment later with two candles.

"We already have candles, sir."

"I would like to bring my own. Close the door," he said as he brushed quickly past Rouke.

*   *   *   *   *

Chay had set her candle on the floor and sat with her arms around her knees for warmth. She looked down the hallway. Marc was there carrying a candle. The light made an orb of light around him. He was walking away from her now looking at the writing there. There was a door at the end of the hallway. Marc shook the handle, but it didn't move. He said that his key would open the door as it had just opened the one behind her. She rubbed her hands over the flame to ward off the chill she felt.

'I shall stay with him', she thought to herself and smiled watching his back. It had been an interesting time since he had found her in the egg. He had spoken to her of wondrous things in the world. Ideas that she could not grasp as a child, but as an adult their understanding was easier. Her mind grew as well. He had told her that he was in awe at what she had learned. The simpleness that she once knew was no more.

She brought her hand up to the locket that she wore, the one that he had found, and realized it was warm. She must have leaned too close to the small flame.

There was a slight breeze, and the flame flickered in the darkness. She heard a noise up above them of doors being opened and she called out to Marc. He returned and knelt down beside her with his arm over her shoulder.

"I love you," she said softly.

"And I love you too," he kissed her.

*   *   *   *   *

Tyndall saw me as he reached the last few steps of the downward spiral of the stairway. He looked at the door in wonderment. I stood and motioned to Chay to stand beside me. She took the candle and held it before her. I was smiling broadly. It could not be helped.

"Is there someone beside you or am I so weary with sleep that I see illusions?"

"Yes, she's real. It's good to see you, Tyndall," I said as I held out my hand in greeting. Tyndall ignored it completely.

"If the duke or duchess knew you were here they'd have you bound to a stake. You wouldn't make it that far. The soldiers would have an arrow through you before you could draw a breath. There is talk that you flew off over the ocean and were last seen leading an army through the darkest of the Kear."

Rouke reached the bottom of the stairs now and stood beside Tyndall. He peeked around the corner at us.

"I have heard the rumors that men have started, and I want to tell you that things are out of control. They must have seen me go to the cliff edge on the ocean and then I went down a small path to a cave below. I believe they thought I disappeared as if by some form of magic. I am on an errand for Nathel, that is all. Again, it seems that simple men get confused by things that they do not understand."

"And this girl?"

"Her name is Chay. I found her in a kear egg. It trapped her since the men of the north tried to take Eilenburg."

"She would be as old as a hag now. Nothing has ever lived once inside a kear egg."

"I am . . . I was a little girl," she said with a bit of defiance in her voice. "Two months ago I was a young girl. My body was much smaller at that time."

"Looking at her I thought she was a ghost." Tyndall did not touch her, but touched his own hair and skin. "I'll take it from you that she is real. The spirits seem to attract to you somehow, don't they?"

I felt Brembry laugh inside me and could not contain my own smile.

"I have as much dust from the egg as I could carry at the time in my haversack. It will come in use with sword making. Kopernick has taught me much on the way north. I thank you for having him find me."

"Ah, so he did find you." There was obvious relief in his eyes. He sighed and looked upward. His hair had more gray than I remember. "I knew you would need a helping hand in the forests of the north. He seemed like the best choice,"

"The door," I motioned to the door he and Rouke stood at. "I opened up with a key that was given to me by Nathel. I saw his bones, and the key he had tied about his belt in a pouch. He also taught me how to remove the protection spell that was on the door."

"This door was never locked, Marc. The spell secured it. The key that he gave you probably belongs to the door at that end of the hallway. Men have tried for years to open this door. Key or no key, it would not budge. An axe could not even scratch it. The spell was a powerful one because we couldn't figure out how to counter it. Tell me this spell as he taught it to you."

I spoke this spell to Tyndall, broken apart in segments, so it was not cast, and Tyndall nodded.

"I see. Pardon me for my rude tongue," he said, running his fingers through his hair and holding back a yawn. "I've had but cat naps over the past five days and the duchess has been after me like hounds on a hare. I am glad to meet you Chay and it is good to see you again Marc. I see you are no longer that young puffy man who left here. Those scars that are not scars are beginning to show."

"As I have said, it is good to see you too," I said with a smile. I stepped forward and closed the gap between us. I held out my hand, but Tyndall refused it a second time and for a moment he embraced me as a father would a son.

*   *   *   *   *

"What does it say?" Chay asked. I realized that she could not read. I made a note to teach her when I returned for her from Ihrhoven.

"It gives a symbol for something and the words read 'will save her'." I read for her. In darkened ash the words lay scratched on the wall. Several sticks of brembry wood, with burnt and blunted ends, lay scattered and covered with dust on the hallway floor. Smoke stained the stone of the ceiling above them. It must have been from the torches used long ago.

"I don't understand," Tyndall said reading the words to us for the fifth time. "The symbol that they used is the one for a type of wood. A half-moon with a leaf. This is the symbol of brembry wood which has no healing powers that we are aware of. It lives and dies so quickly that it's hard to study its exact powers. It's not a magical wood though, great for holding magical properties, but not magical in and of itself. Perhaps it's used to enhance something. I do not know."

"So it reads 'Brembry will save her'?" Rouke asked.

Tyndall nodded.

{I think it is for me.} Brembry said.

"What are you saying?" I whispered softly.

{Marc, we can do it!}

The remark came with such force from the voice in my head that I lost my balance. I fell backward to the floor causing the wind to leave me. Chay came into my field of vision and Rouke was there also.

"I . . . can save . . . her," my lungs heaved as I hugged my ribs.

"Sit him up he's talking nonsense," Tyndall said.

With help from Chay and Rouke I was able to stand. Leaning against the wall I spoke.

"I know what the writing means. Someone place it there for me to read. Someone knew I would be in this hallway when this illness occurred." I gestured to the charcoal scars on the wall.

"I must get to her room. I can save her, Tyndall."

"But how?" Rouke asked.

"I'll tell you when I return. Tyndall, something has happened that I have not told you about. I will tell you about her on the way."

*   *   *   *   *

"It's all right, he is with me," Tyndall said to the guards that stood at the top of the stairs.

"Another healer?" asked the guard.

"Yes. He is from a village to the west."

"Should we call for the duchess?"

"Let her rest. She was up all night."

"You may pass then," said the guard. He was a young recruit. The more experienced had traveled to Land Streth with the duke. Those that stayed could have had no more than two or three years in service.

The leather of his armor creaked as he motioned to the guards at the other end of the hall. We would be granted entrance without hesitation.

We walked to the end of the hallway in silence. The door was quiet as the guard opened it to let us pass.

The room was about the same it had been that last time I was here. The curtain that divided the room into two sections was gone, and there was an earthen bowl with incense burning. That night when I bore the blunt of the dukes anger seemed so long ago. I had learned so much since then.

The door closed behind us and we went to the bed to see Lady Wenonah.

The mid-day sunlight came through the slats of the shudder on the eastern window. She was as beautiful as she was when I left. Her hair was a bit longer and I noticed that her complexion seemed to have lost some of its youthfulness, but that might be due to the illness. She seemed pale and weak.

"Spend as little time as you can. I do not wish for the Duchess to return with all of us here." Tyndall said to me.

"I'll be quick."

{I am ready Marc, just hold her hand.}

"I will miss you," I said softly as I took her hand.

{Don't worry I'll be here. We can talk later.}

"Leave me then, Brembry."

And so she did.

* * * * *

Brembry opened her eyes. The two loomed around her like trees in the woods, and she smiled weakly. She breathed deep, and for the first time that day she heard sparrows outside the window.

"I am so hungry," she said.

"Of course you are," Tyndall said touching her brow with the back of his hand. "I will have food brought shortly. Quickly, Marc, leave the upper area of the castle and go back down to that hallway. I will call for the duchess once you leave. I will send word north to the duke. Tell Rouke if he has any duties to tend to them, although I am sure that within a very short time they will not note his absence. Since she will not perish this day, I believe the Duchess would favor a feast. I'll be down to see you there in the hallway when I can break away."

Marc squeezed her hand once more and left. Tyndall stayed behind with her.

"You are not to harm the Lady Wenonah." The word of warning clearly heard in his voice. "Do you understand?"

"Yes," she said. "Some water please, my throat is dry."

From a wooden bucket Tyndall brought a ladle of water to her bed. She raised herself to her elbows and drank. She wanted more, but Tyndall would only allow her a little.

"When Lady Wenonah returns you will give her full control of her body. There are ways of magic to remove you if you grow violent. It can be quite easily done. I do not wish to do this as you are now saving her life."

"I understand."

"What was your status when you were living?"

"I was a worker. No given status. I cooked, scrubbed and mended clothing of others. I would give soldiers water as they worked on the castle," she rubbed the sleep sand from her eyes.

"The new castle in Ihrhoven?"

"Yes, Ihrhoven."

"Were you given?" he asked cocking one eyebrow higher.

"No," she hesitated. "My virtue stays untouched. Marc can vouch for me. Lady Wenonah will remain chaste," she spoke in a voice just above that of a whisper. "The soul of Wenonah is still here," she pointed to her chest. "I can feel her. I can feel she has a strong soul, but something troubles her that I do not understand. This that bothers her is dark, almost a shadow. We will survive now. I will help her conquer this thing. In time, I think, her soul will grow strong also."

"In time." Tyndall turned to go, but she stopped him with a motion of her hand.

"Be kind to Marc. I was with him before he talked with the ghost of Nathel. I have listened to the rumors that had started when we went to the shoreline, and they have made me angry. Marc is innocent and just trying his hardest to do what is right. Deep inside, he just wants to know of his home."

Tyndall had turned toward her, but now looked toward the window with its closed shutters, and rays of sunlight filtering in through the slats.

"I believe you," he said with a sigh. "I was forewarned of these rumors and see them simply as that. However, I am powerless to quell them."

*　*　*　*　*

Their candles were still bright as I entered the hallway below the castle again. I told them at length what had happened. Chay had not known of Brembry, it was something I did not think she could grasp. She nodded and smiled and I believe she understood, but I was not sure if she comprehended the true depth of it.

Rouke was very happy to hear of Lady Wenonah's awakening. From the stairs we could hear a clamor build in the hallways above as news of this spread. Rouke made no move to go.

"They will not miss me. I would rather spend this time with my friends."

We sat on the floor for some time. Rouke told me of things that happened around the castle in my absence. The disappearance of Tyndall and I caused a bit of an uproar among some. There were people assigned by the other dukes watching us. When we left, we had several days head start. The channel was virtually closed after the storm Tyndall created. It was a time when neither ship nor man on foot could cross.

Things had calmed down until the call to Duke Almonesson to go to Land Streth. In the same order, the king called the other dukes. A meeting was being held, once again, on the decision of the Wiladene Territory. There was a rush to get there before the others. This would show the king Duke Almonesson's eagerness to see the situation through. Albeit, many said that Duke Almonesson arrived last.

There was other news, but this is what I found interesting. Soon it was clear that Tyndall would not be down for a while. I picked up a candle. We went to the door that blocked the back end of the passage.

"I wonder if the spell of protection you used worked on both doors?" Rouke asked his eyes wide in the flickering candlelight.

I held my hand before the door and listened. If it was quiet enough, I could feel the magic. There was none.

"I think," I said after a breath, "that when I removed the one on the door with the nose-less horse it may have removed the one here also." I twisted the key in the key hole and the door swung open silently.

"It seems you did," Chay said.

*　*　*　*　*

I was the first in the room and was startled at first by the presence of others. Raising the candle, I realized it was our reflection in a huge mirror straight on. Chay and Rouke came in as I spoke a soft command and candles around the room lit up. There were ten sconces, but only nine candles lit. One, close to the doorway, curiously, was empty.

None of us uttered a word, or dared to breath, it seemed.

On a table just inside to the right sat three small vials of liquid. One of these would be the one that I would have to take north to Nathel. I would either have to make a choice of which one or take all three.

Beyond the table and chairs a set of shelves stood so large that they went from the floor to almost the ceiling above. Books filled the length of each shelf.

To the left there were more shelves and a wooden chest. Straight on the huge mirror sat back from a series of stone steps. It nearly covered the wall.

"They say this room was once used as a storage room. Wheat, grain or something," Rouke said. "These books might be from Land Streth, or somewhere, for fear it would besieged and the books taken."

"Nathel had said nothing of this. Wait until I see him again." I tried to make my voice threatening. Shaking my fist in the air, they laughed.

"The Tyndall man will know where they came from," Chay said. "He will know who brought them."

"No, I don't think anyone knows who brought them. Think on it. If a boat brought them here they could not hide it. The sorcerer before Tyndall would know they were here and would have passed the knowledge to Tyndall. They were snuck in, through the mirror." Rouke's eyes lit up. "Sorcerer Cinnaminson was here because there was gate travel used." Rouke motioned towards the mirror.

I moved forward and rested my hands on a chair still looking in awe at the books there.

"What all do you think is here?" I asked Rouke.

After a moments hesitation and a shrug of his shoulder he replied "The lost magic of the kingdom, of course."

Chapter #17

It was the chest and not the books, or the mirror that held Chay's attention. Marc and Rouke were busy looking at the books, so she walked over to the chest and looked at it more closely.

It was stout, at least three arm lengths long and two high. She ran her fingers across the wooden surface covered with bands of metal and smiled. Gifts, this was a room of gifts. She called to Marc and Rouke.

"Should we open it?" she asked.

"I think we should wait for Tyndall," Rouke replied his eyes shining in the candle light. "We do not know the magic of the things here. We may open something unwanted."

"Nathel left us the key. The room of books is a good thing. There would nothing harmful in the same room," said Chay with a pout on her lips.

Marc touched her on the arm. "I say, as well, we should wait. We'll have our time to look through it later." He brought his hand up to her shoulder and they held each other. Presently Rouke, more interested in the books, went back to the wall.

Chay caught their image in the mirror and smiled at herself. She looked a bit odd. White hair and skin, the clothing she wore, and still she had no sandals. Having nothing to cover her feet did not bring her much notice. Others working their daily tasks wore nothing on their feet.

She stepped closer.

She was dirty though. A bath in a stream was all she needed. If the castle had a place for bathing that would be very pleasant. She had grown used to the way Marc smelled. A slight hint of cloves from the sachet he wore around his neck. Sweat, grass, dust from the road, all together.

Rouke called to him and after a kiss, he left her and went to the wall of books again. She looked and saw herself in the image of the mirror. Alone, she stood and studied herself. She felt a chill and brought her arms across her chest to keep warm.

Of all that was in the room it was the mirror that she liked the least. Something about it seemed odd. The light coming from the mirror looked wrong.

Again, she stepped closer.

In the candlelight there seemed more colors swirling on the surface than should be. The clothes she wore, even her hair and skin, went through color changes. She stood as close as she dared. So close, that she was actually looking deep into her own eyes. Her breath misting the glass.

What would it be like, she wondered? What would a person see in that last step, that last whisper between one place and another? Is this the one Marc came through? If it was, then his world, his home, lay just beyond this mirror.

The colors began to change again, reds and then greens. The prettiest blues passed between her and her reflection. "*Will he pass through this gate again and leave me here, or will he take me with him and we both leave this place?*" She knew he did not wish to leave, he just wanted to remember, but would the temptation be too great?

The mirror sent people away. It was large enough. She looked again at its height, she had to bend backward to see the top, almost losing her balance.

She felt it was colder here than near the chest. She brought her hand up and stopped just a hair's width from the surface, like Marc had done to the door. The colors began to dance near her palm and around the reflection of her finger tips. What would the colors do if she touched it?

Something grabbed her. She shrieked. Marc had his arm around her waist pulling her away from the mirror, laughing.

She fought against his grip and pushed him away.

"What's wrong?" he asked unsure of her mood.

"Oh, nothing," she looked at him and then shook her head. "I was just thinking."

"You are shivering. Cold?"

"A little. Will you ever leave me Marc?" She turned her head a little to the side as she asked.

"No. I will always have you with me. A promise I made that I will not break."

"And if you are able to go to your home can I come along?"

"I do not wish to go home now. You must know this. I will be here with you. With all of these books and all that is brewing, there is so much to do and learn. There is plenty in these books that the kingdom can learn from."

She kissed him on the cheek quickly and they held each other.

"Listen, we are hungry and Rouke is going to get us something from the kitchens. Remember those stairs at the end of this hallway? They go up higher in the tower above the castle. There is a room up there that we can have to ourselves without being bothered. No one will come here."

"I'm so tired," she said leaning on his shoulder.

"I am too. It will be good to have a rest for a few days."

"A bath first. Soap would do you no harm at all."

He sniffed the air and then wrinkled his nose. "You're right. Rouke, find Tyndall and tell him what we have found. Chay and I will be in the tower above after a bath."

"I'll bring the food shortly. Do . . . do you think I could ever become a magic user Marc? I have been thinking on what you have said before you left and scrubbing linen is not what I wish to do till the end of my days. I will learn fast, you'll see."

"We can talk to Tyndall about it. He should tell you."

* * * * *

Rouke brought a tray of food, and a flagon with wine. He could not stay long. The smell of wine clung to him and he burped twice. I was sure he drank from that which he had brought us. There was a great dinner being prepared that night in honor of Wenonah's awakening and he had to get back to help.

"I have told Tyndall about the books, but the duchess commands his attention now. I also told him where he could find you. All he said was that he would be here as soon as he could. He may not have understood what I was saying, I think he was a bit slushy, being caught up in the celebration. The island is in very high spirits this day and all were a little drunk. I must get back though."

"Have a drink for me too," Chay called down the stairs after him.

I returned later from the bath house and found Chay was back from her bath. Draped only in a shirt of mine, one that was large on me, she stood near the open window. She was watching people below. From this height we could see over the outer wall and the village.

I had to pause. Chay was beautiful. I was in awe that this woman loved me. As she leaned on the sill, I saw the shapeliness of her hips and the sensuous curves of her thighs. She was standing on the balls of her feet, almost on the tips of her toes, and shifting her weight from one to the other.

Since that day I had first found her, I saw no more of her skin than her face, neck, hands, and feet. This was something completely new. Perhaps it was something that Brembry had done to me while she was in me. I loved Chay. During our travels south we had held each other during the night and kissed endlessly, but never any further. I never thought it could be anything such as this.

We had never been alone. Even on the road or in the common rooms, there was always someone there or nearby. Brembry knew me more intimately than anyone else. I wonder if the ghost in me kept something dormant. The act of lovemaking had come to mind several times, but because of Brembry I refrained. It might be selfish, but I did not wish to share it with another with her still in my mind.

"Everyone is dancing. Oh, this is wonderful," Chay said as I came to her and hugged her from behind. I glanced over her shoulder and saw minstrels playing their music on the inner bailey street below. People danced and were merry everywhere. It was a good time for all.

She turned her head towards me. I caught the hint of wine on her lips as I kissed her. Breaking away, I saw the sun had broken through the clouds and glistened off her hair. There was color there. Deep in the strands were several shades hidden amongst the pale locks.

Unbuttoned, the neck of the shirt fell from her shoulder. I ran a finger over the fine smooth skin. I reached down and gently brushed her thigh with my other hand. I kissed her shoulder. Moving the shirt away, I kissed the textures of her back as far as I could.

"Come." I took her by the hand and led her away from the window.

* * * * *

In the morning there was no one awake in the kitchens. Chay prepared a large tray of food, and carried two sacks of elderberry wine over her shoulder. We spent the day being together and resting in the upper room of the tower. The view from the lookout at the top of the tower was breath taking.

It was noticeably colder in the evening and so we ate down in the room where the books had been left. The table and chairs that sat there so long unattended were now covered in dust. We brushed them off before we ate.

"These things are so old. Rouke said that if most of these books came from Land Streth then they must have belonged to Sorcerer Cinnaminson. Most would be over five generations old."

"That is a long time?"

"Five lifetimes," I said holding up my open hand.

"There are answers that you look for, Marc. Do you think that you'll find them here?" she said and it astonished me how well her speech had improved. The simple sentences that she once used had grown in complexity. It was like she was aging faster than she should.

"I don't know, it's anyone's guess. I wanted to go home, but now I don't. When I first saw you, I thought that we could get you back to your younger smaller body. This is what you wanted at the time. Things change."

"I have you and that's all I want," Chay said as she reached her hand across the table took mine.

"I am happy also," I paused for several heartbeats thinking about how I would word the next sentence. Without finding an easy way to phrase it, I went on.

"For a short time, however, I must leave you. As soon as I talk with Tyndall about the books, I can go north and give Nathel his elixir. When that is complete, I can return and we will be together."

"Let me go with . . . " Chay began, but I held up my hand and silenced her.

"It's all the way north," I said. "It is much farther than the journey we just took. It has not been easy for you, and with winter coming it will be cold and dangerous. Winter is well on its way," I said as an afterthought.

"I do not want you to leave me here," she pleaded.

"I don't want to leave you either. In this place, or anywhere else. But here you will be well-tended to. That I promise."

"I'm going with you," she said folding her arms across her chest.

"No." I laughed slightly at her fortitude, knowing she was no match for me. "You're not going."

* * * * *

It went like this for two hours. In the end Chay, close to tears with frustration, only pouted and it was I to give in. I could not argue with some one so beautiful.

"I am a man with a weak heart," I said finally. "How can I have people look up to me if I have a weak heart?"

"Your heart is anything but weak. That was quite a fight you gave me."

I was about to kiss her again when we heard the noise of the doorway opening at the top of the stairs.

"Hello?" A woman's voice called to us. Light and musical, the sound echoed down the steps like water.

"Ah," I whispered to Chay. "She is here."

Like a vision from a dream, Lady Wenonah soon entered in a gown made of white silk and inlaid with diamonds. Her hair, which she always left to fall as it wished, was now in a tight bun bound by bright ribbons. Her lips were beet red and her face was heavily powdered.

On the stairs behind her stood Clendenin. He combed his hair back from his face and appeared lightly oiled. The white shirt he wore had stains in several places from wine and food. Doubtless they had just roused themselves from the feast upstairs. However, they looked wonderful. It was very good to see them both.

Chay and I stood and offered them our chairs.

"Will you join us, lord and lady?" I asked.

"Ha," said Clendenin. "Imagine, Lord Clendenin." he placed his hands on his hips and looked down at us as if we had bad airs.

"We're not interrupting anything are we?" Lady Wenonah smiled and winked. She slapped him lightly in the stomach and he dropped his posture and laughed.

"Not at all. Marc was just telling me that he would like to have me along when he goes back north."

Lady Wenonah sat and laid her head on the table. Clendenin stood behind her with his hand on her shoulder.

"I am so tired. They kept at it till dawn I tell you. I look a mess. A bath and a large pillow are all that I need." I could see now that the powder was rubbed off her face in places. There were several streaks running down the length of her face from her temples where droplets of sweat had formed.

"We heard the music from here in the west tower," I said.

"It woke the hounds in Westrick," Wenonah said and we laughed.

"It is good to have her back," Clendenin's voice was somewhat hoarse. "Thank you, Marc. I do not know what I would have done. She means the world to me."

"Your voice, are you well?" I asked.

"Well? You should hear my love sing." Wenonah touched his arm. "He has a wonderful voice. Sang every song he knew twice if they played it or not. I would like to tell you that my father is very pleased with him. They meet after you left, Marc. What the dukedom needs is a man of strength." They laughed, still feeling the effects of wine. Chay and I laughed as well. Wenonah made a face at Clendenin, who made one back at her. They kissed deeply and with much longing.

"However," she said when they broke away, pecking Clendenin on the cheek once more. "I did not come down here to make small talk with you, Marc and Chay. I want you to know that what you did saved my life, and for that I am eternally grateful. I do not know the nature of my spells, but I know that I will not have to fear them anymore. You have found a true friend for me."

"Ah, so that is you Lady Wenonah, and not Brembry."

Suddenly Wenonah's eyebrows lowered to a dark line across her brow, and the muscles in her cheeks twitched.

"I am still with the lady, Marc," her voice had changed somewhat. "I am glad I am here with her. I miss being with you, but I was a woman at one time and I feel more comfortable here. Once a common worker, I am now a lady." She waved her hands in the air.

"As long as your happy, and Lady Wenonah is well, then I am happy. I always wondered how I looked when you took over my body."

Her face grew slack again and her eyes closed. A deep breath and when she looked up it was Wenonah once more in control.

"I cannot forget what you have done for me, Marc," she said slapping my arm. "Do you know what it is like waking up and finding yourself standing before a mirror and people are dressing you?"

"Um, she has done the same with me on occasion. She will have to tell you about the boots I almost lost."

Wenonah laughed.

"She laughs in my head. Wait," she held up her hand for silence. Her head tilted to one side as if she were trying to listen to some distant music. She burst out laughing again.

"The tree branch hit you?"

My face reddened. "Yes, the tree branch struck me in the face waking me up. I ran barefoot thinking it was something else."

I was sure the laughter could be heard in the hallway above.

"This reminds me somewhat of an outing I took with my family and there was this horse named Rada. I will have to tell you when there is time. Brembry's handled herself well," said Wenonah once she regained her breath. She placed her hand upon her cheek and sighed expressing her fatigue. "So far, I have talked with her and found her very pleasant. Over the past few hours, Brembry and I have grown close. In some ways she is almost like a sister to me. I wish I could have met her while she still lived."

"We will not let you forget what you have done also. Yes, I will tell him." Obviously, Brembry had spoken. "I do not feel that this is no small deed, it is a great one and I will reward you. King Trahune has called the dukes to Land Streth to solve the issue of governorship of Wiladene Territory. Whoever they chose will oversee lands from Glenhelen, where the seat of power was originally. The castle which the Drenthen destroyed will be rebuilt shortly."

"I cannot govern!"

Lady Wenonah and Clendenin laughed. Chay looked between the two with a smile on her face. She was still mostly naive about the positions of caste and rank. Wenonah paused and then burst out laughing again. My face reddened and I knew they could see.

"Duke Marc, she says." Wenonah laughed pointing to her head. "She has a sense of humor. No, Marc, I am sorry we don't laugh at you. Don't be offended. You are correct in saying that you cannot govern. They will find a male of royal parentage to reign."

"One of our many contributions is to provide them with a scribe. Each village has a Chronicler, someone to keep an accurate record of the events of the castle. There is a bit of power and stature in this position. Your living quarters will be given to you and they will see to your meals. There are so many details that I have not the time to go over them today."

"Your parents, the duke and duchess ..."

Lady Wenonah did an odd thing then. Standing, she went behind Chay and placed her hands on Chay's shoulders. She smoothed her hair down and began to comb through it with her fingers. Straightening out the wayward strands as she went. Chay closed her eyes and seemed at peace. Like a mother tabby grooming a kitten.

"They need not know. I have asked my father and to him it is a trivial thing at best. He has contributed far more by going north for the past few years and having his men work there. You will not have to deal with him at all. Once a year you will have to gather information about the territory and report to the Chronicler in Land Streth." Having completed her task, Wenonah divided Chay's hair into four parts and began to weave a complicated weave. "Marc, it's what you do. You have helped me out and once word reaches my father he will sway those that need swayed."

Clendenin spoke up in his hoarse voice. "It is no small task or undertaking, Marc. It is a very high position to hold."

I shook my head. "There is this threat of war that the dukedom and the kingdom are preparing for. If I go there now and just show myself, there questions bound to arise."

"I have thought on that," said Wenonah touching my hand holding the strands of hair between the fingers of her other hand. "Do you think I'm completely homespun? I believe that they will soon see their folly in believing the rumors. It may take a half a year to a year, but they will see. Your quest shall be fulfilled by then and you will truly be a freeman. You and your lady will travel to the north this time with horses. I wish no arguments about you walking this time, Marc," she gave me a harsh look. "Do you wish her to walk? Ha, I think not. You will be carrying papers with my fathers seal. This will entitle you to better food and lodging than that given in the common halls. All will be well." Clendenin pulled a green ribbon from Wenonah's hair and placed it across the braid. The end was gingerly tied and she lay her hands on Chay's shoulders.

"Tyndall has given me a token with such a seal to use."

"The papers will be good beyond his borders. Use them as you see fit."

"Don't fear," Chay said with a smile that could not be contained. "I'll have no trouble talking him into taking the horses."

"Do so quickly then, because I must have my answer before the both of you leave."

"Leave for where?" I asked.

"What are you here for?"

"I am to get the blue vial and return north."

"And what else?"

I searched for an answer, but as the heartbeats went by I could not find one to suit her question.

"Well, I don't know. I'm not sure," I stammered.

"There is nothing here holding you back. Brembry and I have talked and she is still wondering why you two are sitting here on your hams when you should be gone."

"I need to tell Tyndall about the books."

"I will tell him when his ale wears off. Nathel is waiting. The once great and powerful king's champion. I have requested that four horses be standing in the courtyard saddled and ready for travel by daybreak tomorrow. Three with saddles and the other for supplies. You will not have Nathel wait another day longer than necessary."

"You must hurry, my friend," said Clendenin his large hand ruffing my hair.

"Three, but there are only two of us."

"I wish to assign you a traveling companion. I should have had this done before you left the first time." Hands on her hips it looked as though she was going to shake a finger at me. "We have never been able to spare anyone. There is a general helper and stable hand that knows much about the kingdom, but is mostly absent in his duties here. When he does get around to doing these things, they are never concluded, and as always, someone has to go around to check his work. Frankly, I say that he's more trouble than he's worth. It would be better if he chummed around the kingdom with you two. He's of no use to us here."

"Why?" I demanded. "Why are you going to assign someone to us? We do not need them. I have been to the end of this kingdom and back with little help from anyone. I assure you, Chay and I will be fine by ourselves."

"Who is it?" Chay asked ignoring my protest completely.

"Rouke," Wenonah said with a smile.

"But . . . I . . . oh, good choice," I said and they all laughed.

*　*　*　*　*

It was a knock at the door, in the hours before midnight, that woke us from our sleep. I said the spell for candle light and there was suddenly light about the room.

"The door is not barred, please come in," I said. Chay had slept on my chest and I moved her aside as I sat up rubbing my eyes. Tyndall came into the room and shut the door. He placed the lamp he carried to the side on the floor. He came to the bed and sat on its edge.

"Bless you for what you have done. If you knew the scope and fullness of your deeds, you would be in shock," Tyndall said in a hushed tone as if he did not wish to disturb Chay. His breathing was heavy and I realized that he must have run up the length of the stairs.

"What are you talking about? You've already thanked me for curing Lady Wenonah." I looked at Tyndall and the mans face was so full of emotion it seemed he was about to weep. There was a faint odor of elderberry wine and other ales that clung to his clothing.

"The books! Have you seen how many are there?"

"Oh, yes. The wall is full of shelves."

Tyndall folded his hands together before him and looked up to the ceiling as if he was going to give homage. "He sees a wall of books and wonders not at his findings. Oh, Writer of All, will he ever learn? Get some clothes on and I'll show you all that is there," Tyndall said. He had to use great reserve to keep his voice just above that of a whisper and no further.

With my feet bare, breaches on, and a light shirt over my shoulders I kissed Chay lightly on the forehead.

"We'll be right back. Tyndall wants to go look at the books again," I said to her as she looked up from the bed.

"What is it?" she asked.

"He has just discovered the room downstairs. He said that he has several things to show me," I said as I ran my fingers through her hair.

"Don't stay too long. It's late. We leave in the morning."

"I know." I brought the wool blanket up around her bare shoulder and kissed her again.

Without a thought, I gave the command and the candles in the room went out. Tyndall picked up his oil lamp, which remained lit as my spell did not affect it, and we left.

*　*　*　*　*

"Whoever placed them here did so without regards to their subject. I have found a book of water spells laying on top of a book of wood. There is no harm, after all these are just books, but it would have been nice to have a bit of order. I just looked over the whole thing in a brief glimpse before I came up to see you."

"How long will it take you to get everything straight?"

"Oh, at a glance one, perhaps two weeks. I will know more as I go along." Tyndall brought a book down and lightly dusted its cover off. He wiped his hand on his cloak to clean it of dirt and then opened the book to the first page.

"It's going to take several years to fully understand and develop what has been found here," he read quickly and replaced it where he had found it.

"What of the other articles in the room," I asked as I made a motion to the room around us. "Nathel wished me to bring a vial made of blue glass. Saying that I should take the one I find in the room and now I find three. Which one should I take?"

We went back to the small table and Tyndall picked up each in turn.

All were the same in color and in style. He held them before the light of the lamp and each contained the same thick fluid.

"There is a strong protection spell on all three. If we knew the spell then we could find the counter spell. It would take too much time to try the known counter spells and it might be harmful. You don't mix spells and counter spells. Most do not blend well together, I'm afraid.

"If Nathel wishes you to bring him a vial from this room then I say you bring all three and let him decide which one he wants. That is about the best information I can give you at the time." I helped him put the vials down since I was still not sure of his steadiness.

"I shall take them with me when I leave then. Have you looked at any of the other things here?" I asked.

Tyndall was close to the mirror and that is what he chose to examine next. He held his hands out, palms forward, to the outer edges of the mirror while muttering a spell softly.

It sat, or perhaps leaned against two large posts of wood driven deep into the earth. I could have stood in front of the mirror with my arms outstretched and would not be able to reach both sides at once. The glass itself was as thick as my palm was wide. I looked up and saw, but could not reach, the top of the looking glass.

"It hums, or vibrates softly," Tyndall said as he brought his arms down.

"Is it a gate?"

"Was once, was a gate. The magic that a gate uses needs replenished often or they fail to work properly. That they came into being in the first place was unnatural. It takes great concentration and skill to work one and it is very a risky way to travel. The only good that I have seen of them was to bring us Kalendeck," he looked at me. "And you, of course."

"Do you think it could work again to send me to the north?" I asked. "My task could be accomplished within a week."

"I would not risk such a thing on you, lad. You are traveling there as best you can anyway. Gates were mostly used in times of importance. In a case of urgency," he stepped down from the raised dais the mirror sat on.

"I did not come through this mirror, but the one upstairs in the dinning hall. A way could be found somehow. How could it be that these two mirrors of different sizes work for the same purpose? I don't understand how . . ." I stepped down not wishing to stay near the thing.

"The mirror that we have upstairs is just that. Duchess Lowy commissioned a man in the village to make it just recently. It is not the size of the mirror that makes it eligible to become a gate. Actually, I have heard that you do not even need a mirror to create a gate. A wall of stone or wood could be used. But, that is hearsay, rumor, I have never read any of the texts.

"Sorcerer Cinnaminson was the greatest of his kind in the past few generations, but there were others before him. All tales from the past have not been lost. I shall have to tell you of them when we have time. There is nothing here." Tyndall made a motion toward the mirror. "It is just a mirror now. I, for one, am glad that the knowledge of the gates is gone."

Tyndall turned from his reflection and went to the chest. He examined it, chanting the same incantation as he used with the mirror. When he finished, he stood back for a moment. He brought his hand up to his chin and stood there in deep thought.

"What is it?" I asked.

"Something that I cannot be sure of. One moment," he said and began to chant again. When he finished for a second time, he stood back.

"There are no spells here, and it's unlocked." Tyndall reached forward and tried to raise the trunk's lid. The rusted hinges groaned as he forced it chest into opening. Placing the lamp down I gave Tyndall a hand.

The trunk had not been constructed for looks, but built to withstand abuse. We realized that it was not the rusty hinges that had given us the trouble, it was the weight of the wood and metal used in its creation. The lid fell backward and came to rest on the wall. Dust fell like a sheet to the floor.

Tyndall brought the lamp up to dispel the shadows that could not be reached by the light from the candles on the wall.

Something small and shinny glittered on the pile of clothing.

"A button?" I asked.

"No, a Ravenstone. One of many throughout the kingdom. I have two myself. They are useful to help channel magic. They will hold magic and slowly dissipate it as time passes. Powerful for what they do. You may keep it. I have no use for it."

"Thank you," I said, placing it in my pocket. "What else is here?"

"Clothing ..."

* * * * *

Beneath the clothing was a remarkable find. We found two satchels of gold coins in heavily lined sacks that were commonly used for grain for horses. It astonished Tyndall at the amount there. He assured me that no mention of my name or the coinage found, would pass his lips to the ears of Duke Almonesson. All the duke would hear of would be of the books and the mirror.

"The duke is a great man, do not get me wrong," Tyndall said. "But he would think that by giving you the gold we would be taking away from the dukedom. He would want it to go to the royal coffers. You are a good man, Marc, do not let all of what you have done get to your head. One mistake and the kingdom could be a very harsh place for you to live. We must get you out of here without you being noticed. Then we will have done something great."

We had talked for a great length of time on my travels north and back. Rouke finally broke the spell by coming down and telling us it was nearly time to leave. His clothing was much different from the clothing I had always seen him wearing.

We said our good-byes at the foot of the stairs. Tyndall did not leave the room, but stayed awhile longer to study the finding.

*   *   *   *   *

"Well it does seem to fit you," I said to Chay.

The outfit she now wore was more suited for a lady. Gone were the baggy pants and overly large shirt that I had given her weeks ago. Now she wore a pair of under undergarments made from a cloth with a thick weave. She would wear leg wrappings and a dress over this. It is what she would need for the journey north on horseback in the winter time. The shirt that she wore was thick and tailored to a lady's form. I had tried it on, but the shoulders were too small and cut off the blood to my arms.

I watched her as she sat on the bed and tried on the set of boots that we had found. She stood and walked from one side of the room to the next. From the door she ran back to me and tossed her arms about my neck. We kissed long and with much passion.

"Please we must hurry. Dawn is coming, its early morning," I said between kisses.

"I wish to thank you," Chay said. "I feel so much better," she took a step back and looked me up and down. "Your new cloths suit you as well, my love. Why have we been given such treasures?"

"Tyndall had no use for them. In the spirit of celebrating, he has been generous. I do not question his hospitality."

"But what of the gold?" she asked nodding two the two sacks that lay on the floor.

"They are for us to use once we come back from Ihrhoven. They say that there will be a place ready for us in Glenhelen when we arrive."

Chay dressed and the contrast of her dark clothing and her long white hair, now in one braid, made her beauty more noticeable.

Rouke arrived a few short moments later to help with the loading of the horses. Taking all of our possessions, we left the upper rooms of the tower.

* * * * *

As Lady Wenonah entered the gate house, she startled the young soldier on duty. He was humming a war ballad and was busy polishing his ceremonial armor.

"Oh, I am sorry to frighten you. Should I leave?" she asked. Gone was the elaborate clothing and face powder of the day before and she now wore clothing she was more accustomed to.

"N ... no, Lady Wenonah, please you may stay," he knelt before her until she bid him to raise by tapping him on the shoulder. Brembry giggled softly in her head.

She went to a window that looked out over the village. Dawn was soon to arrive. A cold breeze came from the Applegate Straits and ruffled the tresses of her dark hair. She could smell the sea water. It reminded Brembry once again of home.

"I have lived in this castle all my life, but have never seen the inside of the gate house. Or even how the portcullis works. For all I know it could be magic."

"It's not hard at all, lady. Really," The young soldiers chest practically swelled with enthusiasm. "Do you see this pike ..."

* * * * *

"It has been many days since I have ridden a horse," Rouke mumbled softly as he searched for the straps that would hold the bedroll to the saddle. The stables were empty, but for the three riders and their mounts. Chay held higher a small lamp with the window only slightly open. This allowed Rouke to see what he was doing.

"Do you wish to run beside us then?" Chay whispered back to him. In the dim light she saw him smile and shake his head.

"Finished yet?" I asked from the door.

"Done," Rouke said with triumph as he pulled the last of the straps tight. I looked once more from the door, but saw no one in the early morning light. I was going to use the staff to light my way, but realized that Rouke had synched it to the bed rolls on the packhorse.

Quietly, I pushed and the door opened to my touch. I brought my own horse and the packhorse into the courtyard and the others followed. The portcullis was up and the doors were open as Lady Wenonah had said they would be.

A noise came from the area of the guard shack and I stopped. Chay and Rouke were watching my back and they stopped also.

"Go," Chay said. "She drew the guard away."

Quickly, I made my way across the courtyard thankful that it was mere dirt and not like the cobblestones of the streets. I could barely hear the noise of the horse's hooves and they were right behind me.

It seemed that I was only able to breathe when we all had passed out of the castle.

"She has done us well this night," I whispered to the others. "Mount up and let us be gone of this place."

*   *   *   *   *

Wenonah watched as the three disappeared around the bend of a village street. She felt the muscles in her back release the tension that had risen since she first walked in the gate house.

{I will truly miss him.} Her voice was very mournful.

"We will see him again. In better days."

{May they come quickly.}

"Rouke has been a good friend as well. I will miss him."

The young guard came over with a blanket he had found and a ladle of water.

"No, please I am fine. It was just a spell of dizziness. I feel much better now, really." Lady Wenonah held up her hand and he stopped.

She wrapped her simple cloak tighter about her slim shoulders, and turned to go.

"I hope that you will not get in trouble for having the gates open so early. I think it would be best to close them now, and wait until the proper time. If it troubles anyone, I shall address the issue. Also, I wish you would not speak of my dizziness to anyone. Some tend to worry too much."

"It has done no harm. I shall not tell a soul. My honor, my lady."

"I will mention the gate being open to no one."

"Thank you," said the young guard as he bowed deeply.

Chapter #18

With the horses down the ramp and tied to a railing below the deck there was little else to do but to wait for the small ship to cast off. Rouke stood on the open deck while the others stayed below with the horses.

He looked back at the village that he had called home for all of his life. Both of his parents had died years back, so there was little to hold him to this place. If it had not been for Lady Wenonah insisting that he went with the two, he would still be tethered to the castle and would be so till the end of his days. Such as Fern, the elder servant who had first found Marc. He would miss Rosemary for a while. At the thought of her he sighed deeply. Once they made it to Glenhelen, then arrangements could be made for her passage north. There was the chance she would be with him by summer's end of next year.

As he waited, dawn came and the land came into existence out of the blackness of night. He was able to see the village better.

Activity picked up on the docks. The stalls that sold fish started to open their doors to the brisk morning air. Smoke began to creep heavier from several chimneys. He looked at the castle. Fern and Englay would be going around waking up those who had chores. They would find his cot empty this day.

Would they wonder where he has gone, or just fold it away for someone else? He knew Englay would worry, but she had her cleaning to do. In a few weeks he would be all but forgotten. Perhaps Lady Wenonah would explain.

A team of horses brought a wagon load of goods along side the ship and men began to load the deep hold while others prepared the vessel to leave.

Picking up the feed sack that held all his belongings, he made his way down a ladder to the deck below.

* * * * *

"Trumbull, hurry come here." Trey raced in the door and nearly slipped on the small stones of the cobbled floor.

Trumbull looked up from the anvil, his hammer was resting and was silent.

"Where have you been?" he asked loudly not wishing to hide the anger in his voice. "I had told you last night that you I needed you here early this morning. Not well after sun up, but a'fore."

"Shhh, come look. I found something." Trey quickly went to the window and pushed open the shutter. Trumbull gave him a cautious look and with a low growl in his throat placed the metal shoe in the bed of hot coals for reheating.

"So, the boat is unloading," he said looking out the window with his good eye.

"Look at thems three there."

"On the boat?"

"No, getting on the horses."

"Ah," A fine set of horses they were. Well feed, well groomed, and well housed. "Two lords and a lady going back home after the festivities is all." With a shrug of his shoulders he was about to turn around.

"Look at the woman. Hair is almost white. It is be white, say I."

"She was here before, wasn't she? A few days ago."

"Yes," Trey smiled broadly. "She wore worse clothing then what we have. Him too."

"Do you think they robbed someone?"

"No, possible, but I think not. The third one says as he gets off the boat 'Marc, I've never been off the island, lets alone clear to Ihrhoven.' The fellow he calls Marc says nothing, but just nods as he helps the lady. Marc . . . Marecrish," Trey finished with a whisper.

"Ha, now I know you're a fool. If this is the Marc, the lost one, then you cannot be right. He flew from Ihrhoven on raven wings last Day of Turning. Say nothing more of this and tend to the horses."

Trumbull turned from the window and began to work his iron again.

"But, Trum..."

"Enough said. Let me think."

And think he did. The hammering of the hot metal and anvil helped. Orders came in and tasks were complete. Every time he picked up the hammer the thought process would begin again. Not where it stopped, but his thoughts would begin all over.

They arrive with very few possessions and leave dressed as two lords and a lady. He had to figure this one out first. Every time he thought on what Trey had said, and what he saw, his thoughts got sidetracked.

If they did attack and rob some nobles, they would not travel so openly. To ride about as such with the gold and clothing of another was truly wrong. There was no rumor of such a crime. Only the news of Lady Wenonah escaping death.

And who was the second young man?

Perhaps he poisoned the people as they drank and danced and then took their clothing. And horses too. They could have poisoned the stable hand as well. He would not give up the nobles' horses for any amount of money. Maybe the stable hand is the one that caught them thieving and he was the first killed.

The day wore on.

Trumbull sat and looked at his evening meal too shaken to eat. If this group of three was this ruthless then they would kill anyone without so much as a moments thought. So close to death he had come. Had he not given the man the gold for the old mare they could have disposed him just as easily.

That evening, laying in the straw in the loft of his stables, he could not sleep.

So, since they had so little money it drove them murder. Was it his fault? Had he given them more money for the old mare when they came through they would not have been so desperate.

Now the next thought. He, this second young man, had called the first one Marc. If this was Marc from Croskreye, the one who might be of the Drenthen, then why would he be returning to Croskreye? To kill some nobles truly, but he could have done that anywhere? Why here? Why now?

Trumbull's stomach began to twist in knots.

Lady Wenonah was near death as it was, and she is much better now. Perhaps she was his target. She was under heavy guard and he did not get the chance to get close. Knowing this, Marc had chosen another noble. Probably someone at random.

Marc, and this white-haired woman, used magic and brought the second young man under a spell. He will be theirs to do their bidding until he breaks or is broken. Poor man. What would they do with him once they finished their hideous schemes?

Trumbull barely made it to the corner in time. An hour later, when the dry heaves were over, he lay back in the straw too weak to move. His sides and throat hurt from their own contractions.

How could one man do as such?

They were on their way north now, back to Ihrhoven, undoubtedly. To what end? Meet the Drenthen on their return to the kingdom? Create mayhem as they traveled? From Ihrhoven would they travel to Land Streth?

* * * * *

Trey opened the stable door and found the crumpled form of Trumbull laying face down on the floor.

"Trumbull!" he rushed to the mans side and nudged him. He lived. His breathing was slightly ragged and he smelled of vomit. Trey knew he had not touched the ale in years. Had he gone back to drinking?

Trumbull moaned and Trey got his hands under him and rolled him over.

"Trey," Trumbull said weakly. He coughed and spat. "Think of those three. Tell me what you think they were doing?"

"Um, the three from the boat? Since he did not wish of a lot of gold I think he carried enough with him. A wealthy man not wishing to show others he was wealthy. He didn't want the mare any longer, and was just waiting to get to Croskreye to purchase new horses. Perhaps someone robbed him on the road and his fancy clothing taken and the old soiled ones given in return. It's been known to happen. He could have hired the young man to help find the bandits so they might be punished. I've not really thought about it."

Trumbull nodded weakly and Trey helped him sit up.

"I shall tell you what I think happened." His heavy hands brushed the hair back from his face and he shuddered as if taken a chill. He looked at Trey with bloodshot eyes. Trumbull spent the next few moments giving the details as he saw.

"What should we do? If this is the case then the Drenthen are bound to return," he said looking into the young boys eyes.

"The duke needs warned."

"Yes, and the king as well. Trey, I must tell you, with deepest sorrow, that I cannot travel. I am ailing. Do you know the way to Land Streth?"

Trey nodded. There were only two roads leaving from Denhartog. North-east to Eilenburg, or north-west to Land Streth.

"I have coins saved. Take what you can to your family, tell them nothing of what has happened, just tell them you must go. I bid it. The coins are for your journey and for the wages lost while you're gone." Trumbull hugged his knees and rocked back and forth.

* * * * *

Clendenin stepped off of the boat to the loading dock. His boots sounding heavy on the planks as he paced back and forth waiting for his horse to be brought up. Moments later with its reins in hand he walked it to the cobblestone streets of Denhartog.

It had been many years since he had been away from Ross Island. Once he had to travel to a village north of here for a new hammer for the smithy. This journey would take him much deeper in the kingdom. It would be exciting to see Land Streth and all its peoples.

Still walking, he found the shop of the blacksmith of Denhartog.

In the early morning shadows he saw two people huddled on the floor. As he came closer, one stood and the other turned.

"Good morning. Trumbull, what is wrong?" Even though he rarely made it far from Ross Island, he knew every blacksmith within two days walk from the island. He had known Trumbull for years. It was always good to see him, but not like this. He helped the man stand on shaky legs.

"Clendenin? You're here? Looks as if you'll be traveling," His voice wavered slightly as he nodded to the horse tied to the hitching post outside.

"I must leave for a time. What has happened to you?" He looked into the blacksmiths bloodshot eyes. Trumbull took a step or two backward to the wall which he put most of his weight on and rested.

"He has a sickness," said the young boy. "Happened upon him last night. Must have taken a chill."

"Ah." Clendenin went over to the forge. In a matter of moments he had the coals warm again and the temperature of the room grew more comfortable.

"Bring him close so he may get warm." When Trumbull sat on a stool near the forge Clendenin spoke once more. "I was in Croskreye last night when they received word that Duke Almonesson wishes more of his blacksmiths there. I believe if fighting breaks out they will need all they can."

There was an audible groan from Trumbull and he looked as though he was going to black out. Clendenin held out a hand and steadied him.

"Trey," Trumbull nodded to the boy. "We spoke."

"Um, Trumbull and I were speaking about important matters. Things that need his attention."

"His?"

"I have a need to go to Land Streth to see Duke Almonesson," Trey said somewhat nervously.

"So you'll go in Trumbull's place? Will you be up for such a journey?"

Looking between the two, the young boy just nodded.

Clendenin warmed his hands over the coals. "Someone this small will not need his own horse. He can ride with me. Once he delivers his message, I shall send him back. If war is inevitable, it will be no place for a boy so young."

"Thank you. I shall tell his family," said Trumbull after a moments hesitation. He was obviously relieved.

"I will tell them." Trey spoke up. "I shall have to go home and gather some things. If you can wait for me, I will not be long. I wish to say goodbye as well."

"Be quick." Clendenin nodded. "The duke would not have called upon us if he didn't need us. Tell them you'll return by winter's end."

* * * * *

We stayed in Eilenburg only one night. I was thankful that it was almost dark when we arrived. If Chay saw the village in the daylight it may bring back memories again and her mood would turn sour indeed. We passed through the gates and she took little notice of our surroundings.

Again, as it was before, there were no rooms available and we had to look elsewhere.

She found an area for us to sleep in the common hall as Rouke and I took the horses to the stable. We returned with the bags and placed them on the straw where she lay sleeping.

Later that night, something nudged me on the shoulder as I slept. I turned and saw the snout of a piglet not two hand breaths from my nose. The piglet stopped rutting through the straw and sniffed me. It began to squeal as a young boy grabbed it by its hind leg.

"Sorry sir," whispered the boy as he held the runts' mouth closed with his hand. He walked around others that were sleeping in groups and placed the piglet back in its cage. It squealed a bit more, but finally settled down to sleep.

I turned back over and realized that Chay had been watching me.

"You are very tired tonight?" I asked in a hushed voice. I spoke next to her ear and when she spoke I moved my head away and she whispered softly.

"Yes I was. It was colder this day than it normally been, I guess it was hard on me. Did you have any trouble unpacking the horses?"

"No. We did fine. It warmed us up after riding all day. I think Rouke broke a sweat. He is very happy to get away from Croskreye I believe."

"Will he be with us in Glenhelen?" As she whispered I felt her breath on my ear.

"Yes, although I do not know what he will do yet."

"Surly, he will not clean the place as he did in Croskreye."

I smiled at this, my cheek touching hers, and then spoke. "No, he will more likely find something better to do. He is very creative. There will be something for him to do I assure you."

"And what of myself, Marc?" she asked hesitantly.

"You will be my bride, of course. I was hoping to have a wedding in the summer."

"You've made nothing known to me." she softly punched me on the chest.

"I am sorry. I thought that you understood. I love you Chay, I do not wish to leave you. Do you think that I have brought you along to set you down in one place and myself in another?"

"No, my love," she said as she kissed my temple softly. "You have never made your true thoughts about the future known to me. That's all."

She moved closer and we held each other for a long time. I was sure that she was sleeping when she spoke again.

"In what village do we stay tonight?" she asked.

"Why, we are in your home, Eilenburg."

"Would it bother you if we leave as soon as possible in the morning? I do not wish to see the place again."

"Of course," I said and kissed her.

The next day as we left Eilenburg she stayed beside me as Rouke traveled on ahead with the packhorse. I looked over to her as she brought her hand up to her cheek.

"Are you well?" I asked.

"I am fine," was all she said. When she looked at me, I saw she was crying. I reached for her, but with a motion of her hand she waved me off. Pulling my horse away, I left her to her silence.

*　*　*　*　*

"This is the place?" Rouke asked reining his horse.

"Yes, I found her there among the rocks and we camped the night in the trees there." Looking around the forest, I could distinctively see the rock on which I sat on that day and also the place where her egg had been.

Chay sat with her bare hand resting on her leg and held the reins of her mount with the other. With her dark cloak and heavy dress she blended with the bark of the trees behind her. The locks of her hair she wore long this day. It helped keep the chill off. Her horse pranced nervously, and she calmed it with a rub on its neck.

Rouke wore his deep green cloak and hood. He normally wore it so his face was hidden in its shadow. I believe this gave him a feeling of being secretive and mysterious. This was something that was completely new to him, so I let him be. It was amusing to watch at times. A pointed cap and thick mittens of rabbit fur hung from the belt at his waist.

My horse whinnied and it brought Chay's thoughts back around.

"It is too cold to stay the night. We will rest the horses?"

I swung my leg up and was off the horse straight away. Rouke followed. As we came to the ground, the dusting of snow made small clouds beneath our feet. Rouke steadied her horse and held her hand as she climbed down.

"We'll take them to the stream for fresh water. We'll be back."

"I'll be there soon."

*   *   *   *   *

"Is there something wrong with her?" Rouke asked.

"You know the ladies. Always getting sentimental about things. She will probably look through the snow to see if there is anything left of the things she wore when she was little. Perhaps there is something I didn't see," I said and began to chip away at the ice with the tip of my dagger.

"Ah, seems like good weather to ride in, if you don't mind the chill, but it won't last. Snow will come. More than we have now." Rouke said kicking at it. If I had thought the trail we were on was desolate in the warmer months, now that it was cold, there was almost no one. There was no sign that anyone had been this way since we left Eilenburg. I kept an eye on the animal tracks we came across. Mostly deer or elk. Rabbits were especially abundant this season. We saw very few traces of predators.

Rouke stood on the bank with two of the horses. He looked around at the woods as I worked chipping the ice. From where we stood we could see very little of the valley that we had just crossed. The wind blew in the higher branches of the trees often causing the dusting of snow to flit to the ground. The giants creaked and groaned. Before long the wind subsided and they stilled. A small band of chickadees chased a crow from their territory, but other than this, the woods were silent.

Well, there I was with the dagger. Every time I struck the ice a plume of flakes arced out. I kicked the ice a few times and it cracked. It was going on the noon hour and my stomach rumbled.

"It is different being away from Croskreye," Rouke stated in the silence and I looked up at him. "I want to thank you for giving me the chance to get out of there. There is so much to see."

"Look well. Once we leave Kahshgrance Territory the land of Lady Bessa is grassland. Except for the Kear Forest. Once in Wiladene that's all we'll see. The Kear is a big place."

"I should have left sooner, do you believe?" He placed a helping of grain in a sack for the packhorse to eat as he waited.

"I was under the impression that you could not have been given the title of freeman. If I had known that getting you away would have been as simple as asking the duke or duchess, you could have traveled with me last time."

I finished the hole in the stream which was now big enough for the horses to drink one at a time. Rouke brought the lead horse ahead and as it began to drink its hooves broke through the ice and it reared back. We settled it down and I chipped a hole closer to the bank. It was easier this time due to the cracks made by the horse.

"I knew the rest of the dukedom would be exciting, from the stories people tell of the places they have been. It is like a tapestry coming to life. I was biding my time."

"An improvement?"

"Oh, much better," Rouke said with a laugh. "I am not always being sought after. I am free now and can make choices about all kinds of things. Of course I miss the meals and the warm bed every night, but the work there is not for me. I wish now I had left sooner."

"And you would have gone . . . Where?"

Rouke shrugged looking about.

"It is good to have you along. You know that Lady Wenonah has only . . . assigned I think is the right word. She assigned you to us only until Glenhelen. After that you are free from all obligations and may go where you wish."

Rouke brought the second horse forward.

"I think I will stay with you in Glenhelen. I thought that is what you planned from the start." There was a slight hint of puzzlement in his voice that caught me off guard.

We looked at each other from each side of the horse as it drank. Again, I had assumed I had known the thoughts of someone who I cared about. I looked at Rouke and knew he was a good friend. He would be a good man to have around if anything wrong happened.

""You, young man, can do as you please." I said with a smile. "I won't chase you off. It will be my honor if you stay and I mean that. Glenhelen is a nice area and from what I have seen, it is mostly quiet, desolate, and peaceful. There are ruins there that they will undoubtedly try to rebuild. There is still the issue of governorship, but whoever they agree upon we'll have to put up with. You could become an apprentice tradesman. Find a craft you're comfortable with. We'll get you into something better than what you've seen. Don't expect riches, however. A small village will always be a small village. I guess what I am trying to say in a round about way, is that there will be much to do there."

"A round about way? Naw, I'd call it rambling," he laughed and I laughed with him.

The horse finished and Rouke brought another forward.

"I understand," Rouke said. "I do not know if you realize it yet or not, but you are still the same person who happened to come to this world through our mirror. Things happen around you that are not of your own doing. Commander Nathel's ghost, Brembry, Lady Wenonah waking up, the books in Croskreye. I do not think that the simple life of a Chronicler will suit you at all. Not now at least."

I just looked at him and did not know what to say. It would seem that Rouke's thoughts mirrored Nathel's at times.

"I have Chay now. Also, I have the task of being the Chronicler at Glenhelen. I will soon have a home and a family. Who could ask for more? Look at all the villages that we have been through. Those people are happy. We will be as they are."

"Is it for you, Marc?" Rouke asked taking the third horse away.

I didn't answer.

* * * * *

With the last horse watered, we could smell smoke on the wind. Going back to where we left Chay, we found she had built a small fire from some dry kindling. She sat in the nook between a tree and boulder that the egg once occupied.

I helped bring over the sacks with food for our meal. Rouke brought another one with more grain for the horses. I brushed them down while softly talking to them. Rouke checked their hooves when I finished and all was well.

"Do you have bad memories of this place?" Rouke asked Chay as she sat quietly. I could tell her thoughts were distant.

"No. Not many," she said looking up to him. "I am like Marc. My younger life faded away. The life I knew before I saw through the eyes of a little girl with no understanding of the things around her. I yearn for that time, but know I cannot go back."

She had come so far in so little time.

"Umm, I do remember coming up from the village with others." She smiled and brushed her white hair from her eyes. "Through the valley below we traveled and then we ran, hiding, in these trees. We were running from the attack on my village. I wanted to get so far away from them that no man could find me," she spoke her words slowly.

"I saw a handful killed. Their hiding place was found out. We were the mothers and the children, but it didn't matter to the Drenthen."

Her chin trembled slightly, but other than that she held herself well. She had learned to control the young emotions of her childhood. She was growing stronger.

"I remember coming to . . . about here. Here was a place I could hide," she said as she stood and moved near the boulder. She kept looking to the stone and to the forest around to make sure she had the distance right. What difference it made, I was unsure.

"I stopped . . . and looked up . . . and the white flowers of the tree were so close . . . and then they were gone. Marc was there helping me stand, by taking my hand."

She blinked coming out of her daze. She looked about her as if unable to see her surroundings. Then she saw me, and as our eyes met, she smiled.

* * * * *

"I came into my apprenticeship in the year after my beard began to grow. That was two years before the time of the wars. Life in Land Streth was beautiful then. I spent long hours in the service of Sorcerer

Cinnaminson, but soon realized that magic was not my trade. I had no gift for its use, I guess you could say it like that. Though I studied and studied, little was to become of it. I began to tell stories to the others with me, and soon that's all I did. Story telling became my magic."

The speaker stood before the hearth in the center of the common room. The tavern was large and boasted two such hearths. As he told his story, he paced back and forth. The people that he spoke to sat at their tables and ate and drank. Some sat in a half circle on the floor for the warmth the fire provided. The elderly man, the speaker, the storyteller, was almost completely bald having hair just around the sides of his head. It was so white that it was almost silver in the candle light. His blue and green robes were long enough that they hid his feet from view.

The crowd was thin this evening due to the chill in the air. There had been fewer and fewer travelers on the road north as the snows had started two weeks past.

I made my way gingerly around the tables and benches as I brought my bowls of broth and venison to Rouke and Chay. They made room for me and I sat on the bench between.

We listened to the man speak.

"I was practicing my trade in Rivenburch, the third year after fighting had started, when word came by horseback that King's Commander Nathel, Kalendeck and his troops would arrive in one days time. Outnumbered and haggard, they were pulling back from the battle of Oldroyd.

"Within hours the whole village began to fortify the town in which they lived. They built stone walls without regards of mortar, it would have no time to dry. Men worked outside the village. They were busy with digging pits into the earth and then covering them with thin branches and then straw and leaves. Troths were also dug into the ground. These would do little harm to men, but could bring down a charging horse with ease. They loaded wagons and made ready for those that would withdraw the women, the children, and the old.

"The people of Rivenburch knew that with these two on their way the men from the north were soon to arrive. These men did not lack their wits, they knew that there was a chance they were going to lose the town. They slaughtered their animals, and cooked a great feast. Many would die, but at least they would be able to slow down this hoard that was trying to take the heart out of the kingdom. If they were to die, they would die as men of honor.

"First we saw the cloud of dust and then the foremost riders of the king's army came into view. All told over two hundred on horse passed along the road and waited outside the gate. Many were the king's men, some were just farmers and woodsmen. We took their horses and tended to them. We brought food and people consumed it in huge quantities.

"Men had time to relax and tend to their wounds as they had just fought a battle of four days. Kalendeck had said that the men from the north would be here in two days time. There would be no dispute about this. If Kalendeck said that they would arrive in two days time then they would. No sooner or no later. It was a time for the men to sleep and prepare.

"That night before the battle I sat around the camp fire as did many others, listening to what the men had to say. Many told many tales that night and I would be here till dawn telling you of them.

"Kalendeck was there, but he was silent, lost in thought. He listened to tales told by others and about the deeds they have done. I watched him as he listened. Kalendeck's eyes searched around the fire until he saw me and his gaze stopped.

"You are a man who tells stories?" he said to me although I had told none. At the time I was young and awe struck that a man this great would talk to me. I only nodded in agreement. He said to me 'When this battle of four days is over and done with remember what has happened and tell it to others. Do not forget there is a story to be told. Always, there is a story'.

"I told him then that if I lived to see the sun set another day I would be thankful. If I saw it four days hence then I would tell my story. He smiled and gave me a coin of gold." The old man reached into his breast pocket and withdrew a thin coin half the size of palm.

"What is this for? I asked, and he just smiled. I placed it in my pocket. As I did so a messenger arrived at the fire and told us of men in great number moving through the trees. Kalendeck left before he could answer me. The soldiers and the people of the village kept busy the rest of the night getting ready for the attack.

"I would soon have my first glimpse of the men of the north; the invading Drenthen.

"At dawn I was on the rampart with many others. We did not have to wait long for as the first spark of sun light touched the distant hills a horn sounded. The trees came alive with men and horses galloping across the fields. Fierce they were. Screaming as if to drive us away. But we held. The trenches and pits that were dug brought to death more than four score of men. The horses traveled so close together that once a pit opened up those behind pushed those in front into it.

"As the sun completely crested the horizon, the men from the north came in distance of our arrows. When the day was one-quarter gone, they reached the base of the walls of our village. Anything that could not be of use inside the village we tossed over to stall them further. Broken pottery, furnishings, scraps from the metal smith all sorts of items. I had the honor of dropping three honey buckets, and I must tell you they all found a mark."

Everyone in the common room laughed at this. Chay nudged me in the ribs and asked what a honey bucket was. I was laughing and would have to explain later.

Laughter died, and the room went silent as the speaker went on.

"We did not go without causalities. They had bowmen also. They did not use them at first because a village this small should not put up any fight. They wanted to make the village fold under their numbers. Against all odds, Rivenburch stood.

"That day, they managed to get ladders on our walls and by noon we had enemies within our stronghold. We tried to hold them at bay, but it was of no use.

"Men fought near Kalendeck and they asked him why he laughed. His reply was 'Now we have them where we want them'. It was then that I heard the song of Steelefyre for the first time. Kalendeck had drawn his sword and brought death to more enemy than could be counted that day. He was a sensation to watch.

"A group of ten men climbed over the wall. He ran to the street to greet them. As they saw him advance, they slowed and stopped. Getting ready with their weapons. He ran to the group and did not stop until he had passed through the other side. His sword danced in his hand. The wings of a hummingbird could not have been as fast. The men fell to the ground like dead trees, rotten to the heart, caught in a summer gale.

"He did not slow or stop there. In a moment he was gone to another group.

"Nathel was there also. His bravery cannot be forgotten. He was careful about those he chose to kill. He singled out the leaders and those men around the leaders. These he slew with a certain style or grace that would seem odd coming from a man so strong and so well muscled. Blood mixed in the streets and before nightfall the gutters would be full of it."

At the mention of Nathel, I smiled. If these people only knew how closely I knew this man they would be shocked. I looked at my gloved hand and could feel the weight of the gold ring on my finger. There was a comfort in this also. My attention drew back to the speaker.

"As the sun set, we chased the last of their kind down within the walls of the village and slew them as they tried to flee." The people clapped their hands and yelled with enjoyment. They had quieted back down as the speaker raised his hand to silence them.

"As I watched the last one fall, I felt a pull on my shirt and a sudden thrust as something struck me there. Reaching down I could see an arrow had struck me in my chest. I wondered why it did not go all the way to my heart. I should have died. As I plucked the arrow from my shirt, something fell out. It hit the wooden floor and rolled around me twice before it came to rest by my feet.

"It was this coin, people," he held up the coin in the candlelight again for everyone in the room to see. "The coin Kalendeck had given me had a slight dent in it, but other than this there was no damage. It had saved my life."

"I did not see him again because there was much to do. We thought we had destroyed the army of the men from the north, but we had not. Those that had died were just one part of its army. As we buried our dead and burned those of our enemy, Kalendeck slept when he could, and fought to drive them back. The battle lasted three more days.

"As we know now, Rivenburch still stands. not because of the bravery and deeds of one man, but of all who fought there. The Drenthen attacked it again a year later, but Kalendeck was not there at the time. He was fighting in Lanedorf where the bulk of the hostile army was. I was elsewhere, in Land Streth, when I heard the news of the second besiegement of Rivenburch. It withstood it quite well.

"I have kept my promise with Kalendeck and through the years have told this story over and over again to the people of the kingdom. What I say in my story is true and it honors the spirit of the man."

* * * * *

I watched as the man bowed slightly to the room of people and step away from the stones of the hearth. No one stirred until he was gone from the common room. Most of the people broke of into small groups for the night and going back to their tables. Many talked with excited tones. Children with sticks did mock battles in the candlelight. When they struck each other, it was laughter that was heard, and not screams of pain.

I sat and wrote in my journal while the tale was still fresh in my mind. I did not wish to lose it. He had a lot of information, and it would have been nice to talk to him further, but I did not wish to stray from the others. It was a long time before the people in the tavern were quiet enough for anyone to sleep.

Rouke snored quietly in the spare bed, Chay lay with me as in our room she always did. She pulled the blanket covering us closer to keep in the warmth. Her head lay on my chest, and her hair tickled my ear.

My thoughts were very distant this night. Although I looked up to the rafters, it cannot be said that I saw them.

It worried me that I had no dreams of Nathel since I left Ihrhoven almost half a year ago. It would have been good for some response, but there was nothing. Had something happened to the ghost, or was he just saving his strength and waiting for my return?

I missed having Brembry in my head. She was surely much better off with Lady Wenonah, but my thoughts seemed so empty, alone, all mine. She, at times would make me see things differently, and this I missed. When the trail or the night was lonely she always wanted to talk. Like Rouke, there was very little she had seen of the kingdom. For her anything and everything beyond Glenhelen was a wondrous thing. I am sure she was keeping Lady Wenonah busy.

Chay moved slightly and I the softness of her body distracted me. My hand ran down the light cloth of her nightshirt. Feeling the warmth of her skin under my touch.

My mind was then filled with thoughts of her as I held her gently, and I did not care in the least.

Chapter #19

Trey stood outside the tent of Duke Almonesson and shivered. His legs shook and the cold was not completely to blame. He saw a group of riders, a few moments ago, leaving through the eastern gate of Land Streth. One rider carried the unmistakable standard of Duke Almonesson. If the duke saw him this evening his task would be complete, and he could return home. If not, then the only thing he could do is stay in the camp, wait and hope an audience tomorrow.

He wiggled his toes in his boots and stomped his feet a few times to try to keep the chill out.

The camp, small as it was, sat on a hilltop well any from any trees or stone wall where shelter might be found. The biting wind seemed a living entity this day and had sought him out since he woke, but as evening drew on it must have found someone else to chase after. Best not think on it or it would hear his thoughts and return to torment.

The old gray cloak he wore from Denhartog made him look too much like the commoner that he was. The duke would not listen to just a commoner. Ugh, more horse hair. He wiped his sleeves down a fifth time. Brushing and shaking the cloak worked well for the more noticeable gatherings of horse hair, but there was always more. If the man did not believe his word when he told him he worked in the forge and not the stables how could he believe his story about Marc?

Trey shivered. If any name made him shiver, it was Marc. Again he shivered at its thought. When he was younger, his parents used to tell him stories of a man named Frimpstin. Even though he knew the name was possibly made up it still scarred him. What kind of man would do that to children who didn't fall sleep right away? Hearing stories like that made him stay awake even longer and his chores would suffer in the morning.

Frimpstin was not real. Marc now, well he had met Marc.

When he shivered this time, he left new tracks in the snow.

There were shouts which roused the men of the camp. He brushed himself down and waited. In short time the riders entered the camp and dismounted. With their horses taken away Duke Almonesson stood with his son in the circle of men. There was little laughter and many exaggerated gestures. The conversations were low and hushed as they talked with others, as if the wind could carry the spoken sounds off this windy hilltop. Some looked from time to time in the direction of the other camps.

Even with all the fine leather and polished light armor, the man looked weary. He carried himself well though. As Trey searched his face, he could see the fatigue that was there. He had spent the day with the king and other dukes deciding the fate of some territory. With a gesture and quick word from the duke, the circle of men broke up. Seeing the duke and his son come closer, Trey remembered his position and went to one knee.

"Tend to her well and I'll be out shortly with an apple." This was the duke's voice yelling to the stable hand. "Ha, yes, some soup," he said to someone closer still. Trey could hear their footfalls in the snow coming near.

"Some soup as well. Two loaves this time." Lord Farnstrom said this. "We'll take some wine too, eh father?"

"Warmth better than fire. Who's this?" the duke spoke as they stopped right in front of Trey.

"My lord, I have news," Trey said when no one else spoke.

"News. From whom? Please stand."

If the wind caught him again, it would certainly knock him down. Surely saplings were more steady. He could not bring himself to look at the man's eyes.

"My lord, I am Trey from the forge in Denhartog, Trumbull is my mentor, and I bring news."

"We understand you are bringing us news. Whom does it involve?" Lord Farnstrom asked stepping forward. Trey quickly glanced his way, their eyes met, and he hurriedly glanced to the snow.

"I . . . We . . . I think Marc has returned."

"Marc?"

"Yes, lord," he said and bowed with his head keeping his body rigid.

Someone was walking closer and the smell of beef soup was unmistakable in the crisp air.

"While we eat please tell us this news. Ah bugger, what has he done this time?" Slapping his gloves on the palm of his hand, the duke went to the tent.

Trey was the last one to enter.

* * * * *

It was warm here. The thick canvas held the heat and kept the wind at bay. The duke took off his cloak and stretched his arms. The servant placed the meal on a small table and then quickly departed. Trey immediately knelt as he had in the snow outside. Finding a place to look at on the floor, he never let his eyes waiver.

"What news then do you bring from Denhartog, boy?" the duke asked taking a seat.

"My lord," trying not to quiver his words he went on. "I work with Trumbull in the forge at Denhartog. One morning, when Lady Wenonah had taken ill, a man stopped in from the north and sold us his horse. I witnessed this myself. He traveled with a young lady with the whitest hair I have ever seen. The money we gave him for the mare was just enough for passage across the straits.

"Some short number of days later he returned from Croskreye with the lady and a boy a bit younger. My lord, I must say that their clothing was much finer than any that he could have purchased with what we gave him."

"What did they wear when you first saw them?" Lord Farnstrom asked unbuckling his light ceremonial armor and letting it fall to a heap beside his bunk.

"My lord, at first his clothing was well-worn, mended in places. Her clothing looked too big for her. She was a thin woman to begin with and the larger clothing looked odd. Trumbull jested that she wore his clothing."

"Did he carry a pack of any kind?" Duke Almonesson asked.

Think, think, think.

"Yes my lord, he did."

"Were there any ribbons on this pack?" Wind picked up making the canvas snap and candlelight flicker. His eyes went to the candle and Duke Almonesson's possessions beside it. A black cloth covered an item tucked away. He heard the two begin to eat.

"Yes, yes there was. A green, a blue and a red one." Trey smiled at himself for remembering this.

"Ah, that was Marc. I know of the green ribbon and the blue one. I have no idea the meaning for the red. What would he be doing back in Croskreye?" Duke Almonesson asked.

"He may have been the one to help Wenonah," Lord Farnstrom stated. "Healers were helping her, but as of yet few succeeded. Perhaps the message he carries is a cure for her. I'd lay a wage to that."

"Could he make it to Ihrhoven and back? Five . . . six . . ." the duke counted on his fingers and scratched his head. "Well, I would guess he could make it back. It has been a whole year now since he's left. Perhaps, as you say, he could have found the answer in Ihrhoven. So, you say, boy, he was back in a short time with better clothing?"

"Yes my lord. After your daughter came out of her spell, three of them came to Denhartog and continued to travel north. In passing the boy said that it would be exciting to see Ihrhoven. Also, he called the man Marc. This is the news I swore to bring you. I have told no one else along the way knowing it would be your will to judge it first."

"You've done well, but this only brings more questions. Why does he go the length of the kingdom, to return to Croskreye, only then to return to Ihrhoven once again?" Forgetting his meal, the duke began to pace. When his head touched the top of the tent, he turned to take a few steps back over to the other side.

"Were they walking you say, boy?"

"He mentioned horses, father," Lord Farnstrom said around a mouthful of bread.

"My lord, they had four horses among them. No nags, my lord, fine mounts they were."

"When did you see them?"

"One month ago, my lord. More or less. I traveled as quickly as I could with a blacksmith from Westrick."

"Oh, let's see. Could Ihrhoven be had from Croskreye in three to four months time by saddle?"

"I'd say for a seasoned rider, perhaps three. With Marc I'd say more likely four, although he has been known to surprise us before." Lord Farnstrom drank his soup from the bowl and placed it back empty on the small table.

"How soon could we make it? From here, say."

"I'd say the distance through Wiladene Territory is just a bit longer than the one through our own territory, father. We've already crossed the mountains." Trey, who had not lifted his head, could hear the hint excitement in Lord Farnstrom's voice.

Duke Almonesson said nothing. Standing before one of the candles he rubbed his chin and was lost for a time in deep thought.

"If we traveled to the Wiladene Territory, to Ihrhoven, we could question Marc ourselves once he arrived there," he said finally folding his arms across his chest.

"Yes we could."

"We would need the king's permission, and undoubtedly he would want to send some of his own people to travel along as well. So everything could be verified and not taken just on my word alone."

"He trusts your judgment father, but Duke Lysaght may raise

questions."

"He and his men are welcome to travel with us. Would he have answers to questions we need, you think?"

"Why else would he spend this all told, what, year and a half traveling from one end of the kingdom and back? Truly, father, there must lay some answers there for him."

"So it seems, so it seems." Duke Almonesson turned his attention once again to the candle as if seeking direction there.

Without warning he clapped his hands together loudly. The sound making Trey jump and almost fall over.

"I shall go to the king and give him this information. With the coin he can verify all that this boy said. Truly, he searches for a way from our dilemma as we all do. Come, gather your cloak. We'll leave the others to their meals. Just you and I will ride. Boy, you've done well. In the morning there is a wagon heading back. Ride back if you wish."

Without further incident, Trey stood, bowed once more and departed.

* * * * *

King Trahune sat in the Gathering room with his fingers drumming out a simple beat on the table top as he waited with restrained impatience. It was clear that the days activities had stressed him. Being a younger man than the three dukes, these proceedings bored him easily. Negotiating with the others for a peaceful and prosperous outcome brought excitement and a change to the everyday life this winter, but with it a price was also paid. Better to enjoy the quieter moments of the snowy season then to listen to these aging men haggle like hens over a kernel of corn. They seemed tireless. They need to find someone to govern and such bickering he expected. That was why he waited for them to agree on a solution.

He wore no heavy crown this night, just a light circle of gold that fit snugly to his brow. He wore a favorite silk shirt that reminded him of summer, horse back riding, and festivals. The negotiations for the Wiladene Territory during the last two weeks had put a damper on his lively spirit.

To the king's side stood Sorcerer Yahn. Daily he seemed to grow impatient as well. With news of the books found in Croskreye, the old sorcerer wished to go there. Only these negotiations held him back to serve his king. Day after day, as the news spread, many of his brethren would leave their winter duties and travel to Ross Island. It would be a yearly

Gathering unlike any he had ever seen. Yet, he was honor bound to remain here with his king until released. There was a silent understanding by all that things should draw to a close. The sooner the better.

Taking their place to the right of the sorcerer, Duke Almonesson and Lord Farnstrom sat in the chairs they had occupied most of the day.

"I regret that I have called you back this evening, but I have received some information you may find important. I spoke of it with King Trahune and he agreed that you all should hear it directly this night rather than by rumor in the morning." Duke Almonesson looked at each individual squarely and gave no other explanation. The issue of Marc surfaced from time to time during the last two weeks to the regret of Duke Almonesson. It was a sore subject for all.

Commander Sablich sat at the other end of the table with Duke Lysaght to his left and Duke Curwin to his right. He opted to wear a black leather tunic that accentuated his solid frame. This, added with the large belt and dagger about his waist made him seem more formidable and intimidating. He averted arguments by a simple gaze. After the first week, the three dukes rarely looked him in the eye when there was a disagreement. The commander's duty here was purely a matter of protocol. Whenever two or more dukes conferred with the king at once, it was customary to have the king's commander present. He had listened to these men over the past two weeks, as well, and found it odd what simple things they would squabble over.

Duke Curwin would agree to having the uncle of Duke Lysaght sit and govern, but he wanted a guarantee of so much of a percentage of the grain and fruits harvested per year. As the commander watched, these two, mostly, would spend day after day bickering. Duke Almonesson and his son injected comments from time to time, but for the most part they would just stay back and listened. Having called them back from their tents this evening was almost unbearable.

Duke Tominson of the Spruill Territory, held at bay with a sickness, had granted that his sons sit and listen. The men were quiet. Rarely did they speak, but would watch the proceedings intently. As a vulture watches the outcome of a fight between a bear and a boar. They could get scraps no matter what the consequence.

*　*　*　*　*

With a nod from the king a servant uncovered the coin, and

stepping backward, he retreated to his place by the tapestries that hung on the far wall. He held the fabric before him by the corners not letting the cloth fold. When his back was against the wall, he bowed to the king.

Candlelight caught the edges of the coin's gold surface.

"Coin. The next voice you will hear will be that of Duke Almonesson. You will listen to his questions and answer them truthfully," said the sorcerer stepping nearer. He folded his arms across his chest, the fingers of his one hand gently tracing the outline of his mustache. The coin upon hearing this request flipped twice with the gold side upwards. The sorcerer nodded to Duke Almonesson and took a step back.

Duke Almonesson leaned forward in his chair and cleared his throat softly.

"Has Marc been in Croskreye recently?"

The coin flipped in the air twice. When it landed, the gold side was up. The answer was yes.

"Did he have any involvement in the cure for my daughter?"

Gold again.

The sorcerer touched his arm and he stopped the questioning. He whispered quietly in the dukes ear. Duke Almonesson cleared his throat and spoke.

"Did Marc have any involvement in the finding of the books in the vault in Croskreye?"

Four flips in the air and the coined landed with gold up. The sorcerer chuckled rubbing his hands together. This was a very enthusiastic yes. His involvement in finding the books was great.

"Marc is on his way to Ihrhoven?" Gold.

"This is north of Rivenburch?" Duke Curwin asked leaning forward.

Commander Sablich shook his head. "It is just north of Glenhelen. A small village along the sea. If you recall, Commander Nathel died there."

"Is Marc from somewhere else besides the kingdom?" Gold again.

"Marc is Drenthen?" Silver for the first time.

"Now you see," Duke Almonesson went on, "I stated that Marc is not of the kingdom and not of the Drenthen. We do not know where his origins rest. I wish to express that my opinion of the man in the past has not been wrong. I let him go because I did not wish to use him to gain an upper hand against anyone. It is not my nature to use men as pawns."

Even though he formed no question, the coin flipped gold. This caused Duke Almonesson to smile briefly for King Trahune knew he spoke the truth.

"We cannot say that he is hostile to the kingdom or beneficial," Almonesson spoke on. "It is all a matter of perspective. I know I risk ridicule from all present when I bring up again that it you said just last week that my own views are not beneficial to the kingdom. Since I choose to remain neutral in the matter of finding someone to govern the empty territory, I may cause deep divisions between everyone. Marc's existence might be the same way. Because he has not chosen to league himself with any one of us, he has also caused great divisions. I know how I stand and to myself, at this time, it seems best. The same goes with Marc. What man can deny the path his own dreams take him?"

"This clears up a lot of matters, Duke Almonesson," Duke Lysaght whispered harshly with sarcasm.

And then the question was asked. He could have voiced it to calm fears, quell rumors or stop fanciful ideas. It may have been just the fear of the unknown that made him ask the question. Duke Lysaght raised his hand and everyone grew quiet and hushed.

"There has been rumors of late. Some say that he is evil to our lands others say not. I have wondered if he may have signaled to others when he was near the ocean. I would like clarification on this matter.

"Coin. I ask you, will there be an army waiting for Marc when he reaches Ihrhoven?" Again it flipped four times. When it landed it was off center just a bit. Spinning slightly, it rolled on its edge as it settled to the confines of its trivet. It was gold.

No one spoke, no one moved.

Taking a slow breath, Duke Lysaght formed the next question.

"Coin. I ask you this, will the army Marc meets in Ihrhoven be of peoples of the kingdom?" his voice wavered slightly as he spoke the last.

Without hesitation, almost before the question was fully formed, the coin flipped in the air spinning twice. Polished, so shiny they could see the flame of every candle that stood in the candelabra, the coin lay with its silver side facing upwards.

No one breathed.

The leather of the chairs creaked as everyone leaned forward to make sure they saw the coin properly. There was a sound, so slight and so subtle it was almost dismissed as the winter wind outside, as the knees of the servant with the cloth gave out and he slowly slid to the reed-covered floor. Almost as one King Trahune and Commander Sablich stood at opposite ends of the table. The king leaned forward, the palms of his hands flat on the tabletop to steady him.

He cleared his throat and looking at Duke Lysaght, he smiled.

"May I ask a kind request, Duke Lysaght? Please, if you may indulge me, ask your question again, word for word." King Trahune held his hand out in offering. The stress could be heard in his voice. His tone made him seem only mildly interested, but his outstretched hand trembled slightly. Quickly he folded his hands before him before anyone noticed.

"Coin." One flip with its silver side still upwards. Many likened this to a hound sitting upright when it hears its masters whistle.

"Will the army Marc meets in Ihrhoven be of peoples of the kingdom?" Again, without hesitation, the coin flipped with its silver side upward.

Before anyone could speak King Trahune held up his hands.

"Sorcerer, is there anyway that anyone here could influence the coin? If there is treachery in this matter I am not amused."

"My lord, no. There is no magic that will coax the coin into giving a wrong answer. Always the coin has answered its questions truthfully. I must say," he went on without hesitation when he saw the king was about to speak again. "That it is very, very rare that the coin will answer questions pertaining to the future. If I asked the coin about the circumstances of my death, such information is vague and clouded. Say if, after a long series of questioning, I found out my death was not until years from now I could take it upon myself to test the coin's validity. If I suddenly walked in front of an ox cart in the morning and it crushed me the coin's information would show as misleading and false. The information we receive is true to events that have already happened or are happening. I tell you all that we cannot hold much credence to questions we ask the coin pertaining to the future." With this said, the elderly sorcerer took his seat once more.

King Trahune looked at the coin and drummed his fingers on the tabletop lost in thought.

"It becomes obvious, my king," said Commander Sablich motioned towards the coin, "that this information, once given, cannot be ignored. Had your father and brother attained this foreknowledge, even before Kalendeck arrived, it could have saved lives. We could have avoided much bloodshed. How many lives could we save if we had been able to keep the fighting limited to the upper reaches of the Wiladene Territory? It is quite possible that if they had the men on hand, Duke Shindle and Commander Caddoan may have been able to save Glenhelen."

"Your recommendation?"

"It is clear, my king. We must send a sizable force as well. If, by mere chance, the coin is wrong then it does little harm. If the coin is correct then we have the power to avert more damage to the kingdom."

"And you sorcerer?"

"Er, these are my feeling as well, my king. With the Wiladene Territory still as sparsely populated as it is, these Drenthen could land almost anywhere and go undetected for a very long time. I will send word to Lady Bessa to the east and you two must return to your father, Duke Tominson to the north, and report our findings. They can fortify and patrol their borders. If there is an army of Drenthen then we will keep them contained in the Wiladene Territory until they are routed out."

The servant, regaining his senses, shook his head and began to stand. Still holding the cloth dutifully before him, he managed to get his feet beneath him.

Duke Almonesson raised his hand. "My king, may I ask the coin a few more questions for clarification? Some of what the sorcerer has said confuses me. I think the coin may help."

"Yes, please, by all means."

"Does the coin still listen?" Although he directed the question at Sorcerer Yahn the coin flipped once and landed with its gold face upwards.

"Marc will meet the Drenthen in Ihrhoven?" Gold once more.

"If pushed Marc will fight, not just for any single territory, but for the kingdom itself, of this I am completely sure," said Duke Almonesson.

"Coin, will Marc fight these Drenthen for the kingdom?" Four flips with the gold side facing upwards.

"Ah, see. He leagues himself with no one, but he fights for all. Coin, will Marc lead, in some way, others of the kingdom against the Drenthen?"

Again it was gold.

"Much like the true nature of Kalendeck, Marc will do the same. Of this we cannot deny."

"Duke Almonesson, may I ask a question?" Duke Almonesson nodded and Duke Lysaght went on. "Has Marc even been trained with a sword?" Again, although he directed the question to Duke Almonesson the coin flipped gold.

"When he first arrived in Croskreye, we put him through a series of tests. By doing so we determined that he had little, if any, knowledge of magic, and it seems he had never held a sword or other weaponry. The man was good with words, reading and writing, and we let him be at this. He did spend a few months with my armorer in training." Duke Almonesson looked at Duke Lysaght and rubbed his chin wondering where he was leading.

"So, there is a young man going into battle against an army of men who have significantly more training than he has. Duke Almonesson, you must see the inevitable conclusion as I do. Coin, I ask, will Marc find his death in Ihrhoven?"

They noted the hesitation. One heart beat, then two and a third. The coin flipped.

"My word," breathed Duke Almonesson somberly. He sat back heavily in his chair. "The man was a thorn in my side at times. When he was away from the castle, finally, it relieved me to say the least. However, I never wished to see him dead.

"Is there a way we can avoid this?"

The coin had flipped to its silver side.

"No. It seems the coin sees clearly in this matter," Sorcerer Yahn said folding his arms across his chest before him. "We must decide what we will do next, my king."

"We will send what we can and hope that it is enough to hold off the Drenthen for now. If he dies, then he will be another casualty of war. There is nothing I can do here to stop one man's death. Truly, we cannot muster the whole kingdom and be there within a few days. Send word back to all of your commanders and have them ready your men you have here. We'll be there, in force, by spring. Most battles are not fought in winter, as it is."

"Carfrae," Duke Curwin blurted out. Duke Almonesson looked at him sharply. Curwin winced knowing the word was ill spoken. King Trahune nodded and solemnly bowed his head in remembrance.

"Carfrae was lost in the winter because the Drenthen were desperate for a victory that year," Commander Sablich turned and began to pace with his hands clasped behind his back. His heavy boots mere whispers in the dried reeds laying on the floor. When he spoke again, his voice was deep and clear. "Coin, is Marc still on this quest?" The coin flipped gold.

"So he is still under the pretense that he journeys north to see the ghost. It was his being in Ihrhoven in the first place that started this whole thing. If this is the ghost of Commander Nathel and if he is helping the ghost out in some way, then I feel we have the obligation to see this task complete. My king, I served with your father's commander and fought alongside him. I dare say that Commander Nathel and I were good friends and I mourned, as we all did, at the news of his death. If this is the last legacy of his existence, I must see it through to the end. Sorcerer, is there anything in Croskreye that you can think of that the ghost would need?"

Sorcerer Yahn thought deeply for a few moments before he spoke. "I didn't even know the vault of books was there until I heard word of it. If Sorcerer Cinnaminson placed the books there then what else he placed there could be any one's guess. Besides, what is it on this earth a ghost will be in need of anyway?"

"My king," Commander Sablich bowed slightly to the king. "I must travel to Ihrhoven to assist Marc in any way I can. This is the second time that someone has traveled to this kingdom by mysterious means, only to die at the hands of our enemy. We must not sit idly by and let this be."

Weighing all his options took some time.

"I do not want any bickering about my decision amongst any of you. No ruse, no deception. At this time, and I must know right now, is there anyone who objects if I send my commander to Ihrhoven ahead of the main army?"

"I do not object in any way." Duke Almonesson said. "I do ask, however that you allow my son, Lord Farnstrom, to travel with the commander." he nodded towards his son.

"Does he ride well?" Commander Sablich asked.

"My wife is Lady Rachel's sister. Lowy raised him in the saddle."

"I have a man who I would like to send as well," said Duke Lysaght. "I wish to know the answers we all seek. I have the utmost trust for Lord Farnstrom, but I wish to hear what arises from my own man."

"As do I," said Duke Curwin.

Duke Tominson's sons remained silent.

"Agreed," King Trahune nodded. He stood back from the table. The servant came forward with the cloth.

"Take what you will and may you return safely."

The servant covered the coin once more.

*   *   *   *   *

Trey roused from his sleep by a disturbance inside the tent. A man had entered and began to wake the others.

"Wake, wake. I have news." A candle was lit and he began to tell all that he had heard. He was an elderly man, thin and lean, and it seemed the ale removed the stiffness from his joints. Trey listened closely from the cover of a simple blanket as he lay on his mat.

The man spoke kindly of Marc, saying the man was not in league with evil, but the harbinger of war. By using magic the king was able to listen to his news and messages. This time they would be ready for the Drenthen. They would achieve in a year what had taken their forefathers over five years. Thankful to hear that he was wrong about Marc, Trey listened intently to the men talk throughout the night. As the hours crept by and the night deepened they continued on. When talk turned to whispers he could no longer keep his eyes open and he slept.

In the morning Duke Almonesson sought him out and gave him a folded piece of paper sealed with the royal seal. He was to give this letter to Duchess Lowy upon his arrival home. Trey smiled inwardly watching the Duke move on to other men with other matters. Trumbull would be pleased to hear that he was, for a short time, a royal courier.

Chapter #20

I stood on the trail and looked down the small path that led to Ryeson and Deanna's home. The snow was thick in the direction of the house. Other than the occasional tracks of a hare or field mouse the white remained undisturbed. A drift had formed on the lee side.

Had something happened to the family? If they had to go out for food, or if other people stopped for assistance, there should have been a worn path in the snow. Something was wrong.

I nodded to Rouke and Chay and started forward leading my horse by the reins.

The front door had not been opened since the last snowfall. The house was empty. I walked up until I was several paces from the house and stopped.

"Ryeson? Deanna?" I yelled.

"There is no smoke coming from the chimney. I doubt they are here," Rouke said leaning forward in the saddle.

"A paper is on the door, Marc," Chay pointed to a heavy bit of parchment tacked to the wooden frame.

I dropped the reins and stepped closer and read it for them.

"It reads: To whom it may concern, we travel to Carfrae by order of Lady Bessa."

"Ah," said Rouke. "Because of the turmoil, she is pulling her people, the talented ones, to her."

I nodded and was about to turn away when something caught my eye. From the door latch to the door frame there was a weave of hair. The braided lock looked thin and frail and I doubt that it would have stopped anyone who wanted to gain access to the place. A knife could have cut the strands of hair with ease. Around the door latch and a ring of metal on the frame they wound. It looked like Deanna's hair.

"You can't get in, Marc."

"I know." I started to reach out to touch it.

"Marc! No!" Rouke's alarm came a moment too late.

One heartbeat my hand was reaching for the hair and the next, somehow, I was laying on the ground looking up. My horse nuzzled me with his nose. I stood using my right arm to help get my feet beneath me. My finger tips were numb, and my whole left arm tingled from the shoulder down.

I looked at Rouke and he just shook his head. Chay's concern turned to amusement now that she saw I was fine.

"What happened?" I asked dusting the snow off with my right hand. My left hand was still numb. Hopefully I could get back on the horse without further embarrassment.

"You didn't see the strands of hair?" asked Rouke.

"I did. I was going to touch them. Something stopped me."

"Ryeson didn't want anyone to use his house while he was gone. If you look at all of the windows you will see small braids of hair there also. They locked the house, Marc."

I looked at him and it finally dawned on me. Chay smiled.

"Only one person can break the locks. Only whoever the hair belongs to can cut them. You should use caution next time."

The tingling sensation in my arm was beginning to go away. I was able to move my fingers again, slightly.

I got back on my horse, and without a look back, Chay led us out to the trail once more.

* * * * *

Kopernick held his hand steady over the iron and concentrated. His eyes closed, and he took a deep breath. When he spoke his spell, it was with low hushed tones. A pause, to let it build around him, and then he released it upon the metal.

There was an audible popping noise. Rouke jumped where he sat and Kopernick smiled. Chay looked at me and winked.

"It is like cooking dough now," he said. He slid it off of the table on to his open palm. If he held his fingers too far apart, the steel would have slipped through his fingers. It was not hot or warm to the touch. The temperature of the metal stayed the same as Kopernick worked with it.

Holding it so, with his free hand he touched it in the center and applied the slightest amount of pressure. Between the fingers of his hand holding the metal, a piece emerged. As his finger went all the way through the piece fell to the ground almost without a sound.

Gently, he laid the large piece back on the block of wood. Again his brow drew into a straight dark line. He wiped his forehead dry with a cloth, and brushed aside a stray lock of hair. His lips moved, but no sound came as he thought of the spell that was to come. When he was ready, he spoke the spell, let it build, and cast it.

Grabbing his chest, he took several deep quick breaths. The magic took its toll. Although the room held a chill to it, a new film of sweat lay on his arms.

"Stand back," he told the us. "Here's where we see if the spell works or not."

Putting on heavy gloves on, and donning a leather apron, he picked up a large hammer and went to where the metal lay on the wooden block. Twice he smashed the hammer into the metal with all his strength as he shielded his eyes with his arm. It held firm and rang out loudly and clattered to the floor when he finished. He stood back with a cry of triumph and tossed the hammer aside.

"Come see for yourself," he beckoned to us.

Turning the metal over, I could see the outline of his hand with such clarity that an old scar on his thumb came out in detail.

* * * * *

Later, much later in the day, Chay went with Corva to the market for things for the evening's meal.

Rouke and I went with Kopernick and his father to the forest for firewood.

"We would not have to bring this thing back in," the large man motioned to the tree we were dragging. "but Koper has had his nose in the book since you left. Have to beat the boy almost to get him to do his chores. Not that I really mind though. The money that we get with his magic helps out. If he didn't have the knack for it, we would have starved or froze for sure this year. I could try to drag it myself, but I am not the ox I once was."

I looked over my shoulder at him and Lindergren smiled. Kopernick's ears grew red and I was not sure if it was due to the cold or not.

He slipped in the snow once and we all set the log down to rest. I was glad that the house had just come into sight. Lindergren marked the tree sometime last year. He had scored the trunk, taking a palms breadth of bark away from the bottom all the way around, causing the tree to die. By now the heart wood would be dry. If we ever got it chopped into smaller pieces in time, we could cook our evening meal from its heat this night.

"I thank you for the book," Kopernick said for the twentieth time since he woke this morning. A hand on his chest and a bow of his head conveyed his gratitude. He had thinned some since I last seen him. His hair and beard were longer than before.

"I saw you grab your chest after you cast the spells today. Does it always hurt when you cast all your spells?" Rouke asked.

"No, not at all. There is a sensation that is very odd to name. Some people describe it as pain. Feels different for me. I would like to say it is a type of elation but it is unlike anything else I feel. I sense a part of me go into the metal itself. I think . . . that is how you would best describe it."

Lindergren had made it clear that he never really felt comfortable with using magic. He enjoyed benefits from its use, but never took the time to learn the intricacies beyond the simplest spells. His past had been such that he did not have the time or means for a lengthy education and so did not pursue the knowledge as others did. Working in the forge over his life had granted him large hands and thick arms. He was content with the little he knew and preferred to use his own strength and natural heat from the coals instead. That was what he used to bend the will of metal to his liking.

Rouke, I believe, is about the same as Lindergren in the knowing of magic. To him it is something that is still mystifying. I am sure he would sit and study at will if the time is given to him. There was the issue of his education to deal with also. Someone would have to teach him how to read and write.

Of the four of us sitting here resting in the snow, I believe I understood what Kopernick was saying the most.

"I would call it rather like giving to your work," I said and Kopernick nodded. "I have heard of times when a man could tell the stones which he had shaped. One stone out of thousands. Even a man who would know the tools he had made by simply feeling them. The magic that he gave to his work called back to him. They also say when a mother helps her child along with a healing spell, she can tell again if the child is hurt even though they are some distance apart."

"I would hear Tyndall talk like that," Rouke said and stood as the others did. He wiped his hands of snow and stretched his arms.

"Sorcerer Yahn often talked of a certain spell," Kopernick said taking up his length of rope and went on. "It is a spell which our ancestors thought of. I cannot remember the exact way he phrased it, but it was the idea of total magic. Over the years they have tried again and again to create such magic, but as of yet no one has."

"Why have I not heard of this?" I said slinging the rope over my shoulders. The others did likewise and we carried the tree forward.

"There are the main groups of magic; stone, fire, water, and spirit.

Some spells use items just in the base group. Working with stone you use a metal chisel and a steel hammer. There are a few that combine two base groups. To help create rain or snow you would use a wind and water spell. With total magic they take something from each group for one outcome. It is a form of magic combining all the forms of magic into one powerful spell. He had said the spell would take so much from the one casting it. Magic from one group takes a little bit of the person casting. Combining two groups and you can believe it takes a substantially greater amount. Combining all four and . . . Whew . . . look out."

"What would be the purpose of such a spell?" Lindergren asked the question that was on the tip of my tongue.

"That is still unknown. Perhaps there are some answers in the vault of books Tyndall has found. Perhaps Kalendeck found out in Welteroth."

I looked over at him, and he answered me with a simple shrug of his shoulders.

* * * * *

The four of us were able to split and stack the wood by time the evening meal was fully prepared. As I sat at the dining table, I looked around at those around me and realized everyone was in a very joyous mood. It would be a wondrous thing to have meals like this throughout my time as Chronicler in Glenhelen.

Chay and Corva had returned with news and gossip from those at the winter market. There is a rumor that King Trahune was sending a small detachment of men to Ihrhoven. They were under the belief that the men from the north were preparing to attack again. This was the first I had heard of the Drenthen returning. There has been no news of anyone seeing any of the enemy. Those that they talked to, remained vigilant. The king might be forced into this action to quell the rumors that started when I was here last. When they see that there is no enemy they will return to Land Streth and such rumors will be forgotten.

We had a head start on the king's men. I am sure I could make it to the ocean, free Nathel, and get to a place of safety before any of them found us. We had made quick in our time as we journeyed north.

Duke Tominson of the Spruill Territory directly west has taken ill. His men were on alert and in watch towers all along the coast and border. Spruill shares the border with the Wiladene territory. It was heard that Duke Tominson and his men will guard their border against all costs.

Duchess Bessa, they say, has closed the Wiladene-Carfrae border as well. Travelers and merchants were kept within the host territory. When they resolve this issue, they will reopen the borders for trade and travel. We were lucky to cross when we did.

Duke Almonesson, Duke Curwin, and Duke Lysaght are mobile likewise. Bringing their men up from their lands in preparation. This force was much larger and needed more supplies as they traveled. They will arrive here by time the snows melt. By then Nathel's soul would be free of this earth and traveling onward and I will be elsewhere.

*   *   *   *   *

Rouke and Kopernick were talking about some subject in the book of metal which I had given Kopernick. They had tried to get me engaged in conversation earlier, but I wanted to relax for a while. Rouke seemed very interested in the matter and as their discussion went on, they paid little attention to the things happening around them.

Chay worked with Corva in and about the kitchen area. She sliced bread which had been freshly baked that morning. Corva had kneaded the heavy dough with her thick fingers. She had taken a small length of red ribbon and tied her hair back to keep the long curls from interfering with her cooking. She hummed as she worked apparently happy for the gathering of people in her home.

Lindergren was working somewhere out of doors. He was a quiet man at times keeping to himself. I felt that, although he was happy to have us here and that we were always welcome, we took time away from his family. I might be wrong in my assumptions. It could be that he had a lot to work on.

With Chay's riding outfit put away in the other room, she now wore a heavy dress used by peasants for working. The length of it hid her feet as she walked. She washed her long white hair early in the morning and was now done up in one braid which lay across her shoulder. It had been months now since I freed her from the egg and the natural color of her hair was beginning to work its way back through her strands. Like Tyndall had said, her speech, thoughts, and ideas were becoming more complex as time went on. Her mind was growing older faster. Catching up, as it was, to pace with her body. In the egg, her mind was not worked, same with her body for that matter, but where her body grew; her mind didn't.

Flour and berry stains had found their way on to her blouse. The younger children kept coming to the table for bits of food. She would shoo them away and they would eventually come back. She chased them at times and when she caught them, she would tickle them with no mercy. Still, a child herself.

She looked at me once, as I sat near the hearth writing, and she smiled. I could not help but to smile back at her.

"Are you well?" she asked coming close.

"That I am. It's good to see you so happy. The children like being with you."

"They do," she smiled at me again and seemed as if she was going to say something more, but she was silent. She bent down and kissed my forehead. Her slender arms went around my neck. So frail, so tender.

"I have something to tell you." There was a look in her eyes, a fire all their own, and a hint of a smile.

"What?" I asked wanting to know her secret.

"Not now, later," she said and kissed me again. She drew away and held my hand.

"Is it important?"

She said nothing as she let go and went toward the kitchen. I noticed the spring in her step. The exaggerated sway of her hips as she played with me. "You shall see," she said coyly over her shoulder.

* * * * *

The evening drew on and before long the children had found me sitting alone. What began as some playful punching soon turned out a mock fight in the middle of the room.

I was soon overwhelmed by so many small ones that I was helpless. I did not wish to play too rough for fear that one of them may get hurt. Once or twice heads got bumped on the floor, but the children paid no mind and were back in the fun of the tangle of arms and legs in a heartbeat.

It was Kopernick and Rouke who finally came to my rescue. Pulling up one child after another, I was soon free to stand. Out of breath, my ribs hurt from a knee, but other than that I was fine.

"Chay sent them to you. She said you enjoyed being tickled," Rouke said as I dusted myself off.

"Only five children, Marc. You need to learn how to fight," Kopernick said slapping me on the back.

Sometime later after Chay and Corva set the table, the children quieted down, and Lindergren returned from the forge, we all sat down to eat.

* * * * *

"So you'll stay here in Glenhelen then?" Lindergren said smoothing out his thick beard and mustache. He sat back with his pipe and brought his feet up on a low stool near the hearth. His chair was the one which he most favored over three they had. Corva sat in one which had her sewing items near. She was constantly fixing torn or worn clothing. Kopernick took the last seat and Chay, Rouke and I sat on a cloak amongst a gathering of children. The young ones were mostly quiet and sat listening to the adults talk.

"Possibly, quite possibly. We've got the seal from Duke Almonesson stating that I can hold the office of Chronicler. There is also some gold coins to help us along."

"I see. Do you believe that with all that you have done, you can simply take that position and all will be well?" he asked drawing a breath of smoke from his pipe.

"I don't follow you." His tone was hard to comprehend. So relaxed he seemed and yet his words held a sense of urgency. I imagined that he could tell us the house was on fire in the same sort of nonchalant manner. He did the same when he told me that the soldiers that had followed me from Croskreye started the rumor I was Drenthen on my first visit here.

"You have the kingdom in an uproar. Duke Lysaght and Duke Curwin have let it be known publicly that there might be more to your past then what we see. They may have even fueled the rumors that, if you were not Drenthen, then perhaps from the same place as Kalendeck. With a man such as you on their side who would dare oppose them? No one wishes to go to war, but if the people believe that you are as unbeatable as Kalendeck was, such a figurehead would elevate their status to no end. They could put anyone they wanted to in place of control of this territory and oversee them from a distance."

"To their advantage."

"Yes, to their advantage," he went on. "Again, do you think the people would let such a person as yourself become a simple chronicler? You have to blend in with the kingdom more. Perhaps choose a new name and let them forget about you. If such a thing is possible."

Suddenly the ring felt heavy on the leather cord around my neck.

Nathel had said to use the name of Kalendeck if I needed it, but I was not about to bring on that kind of attention. If I thought the name of Marc was a difficult burden now, using the name of Kalendeck would bring untold repercussions.

"Head north and do your business. Nathel awaits. I must ask you politely, do not return. Not for a while. Stay in this territory or even return to Kahshgrance Territory, but keep to yourself as much as you can," he went back to his pipe and all was silent once more except for the fire and the wind on the shutters outside.

"Well, perhaps with the whole of the kingdom in our borders, we could get the castle started. Choose whom they will to govern, they need the castle first." Corva brushed stray threads from her lap and began to sew again.

"They are on their way now, rumor says. The whole lot of them." Kopernick looked towards Chay and me, and shook his head.

"Did Lady Wenonah have anything to do with you getting the seal?" Corva asked.

"Yes she did. We spent some time together when I was in Croskreye. We are close."

"Heard she almost died a bit ago," Corva said placing the garment she was sewing on her lap. "How was she doing when you left?"

"Her health fared much better when we left. It is a long story, but I helped Tyndall and together we finally found a cure for her."

"Well, that's good," she said and went back to her work.

*   *   *   *   *

An hour later, after all the children went to bed, and Lindergren added another log to the fire, Kopernick left the room for a moment and returned with Steelefyre in its sheath. Corva had muttered something about 'men talk' to her husband. Chay left the room with her and they both sat at the kitchen table talking and sipping a berry tea in the candle light. Kopernick passed the sword around for us to look at.

"I hate to say this," Rouke said as he ran his thumb over the cutting edge of the wide blade. "But it is not sharp at all."

"I know, I know. I have tried everything I can think of from magic from the book to a wet stone. Nothing works. The shape you see it in is the way it was cast. If I didn't know better, I would say there was some sort of protection spell working against me, however I feel no magic about it. The adept helping me in Taberham said the metal was just that. It had no other properties that were abnormal."

He handed me the sword, which I held gingerly no matter how dull it was.

"If you wish, we can try to sharpen it again in the morning. I have brought some dust from an egg with me."

"Egg? What kind of egg?"

"I didn't tell you I was able to crack a kear egg in the forest? I have some of the egg dust with me."

Kopernick said nothing, but just sat there wide-eyed and mouth agape.

"You have some dust from a kear egg? Oh, why haven't you told me sooner? This is great. Could I get some from you?"

"Well, yes it's what I brought it here for. Also," I reached in my pocket and brought out the Ravenstone Tyndall had given me from the chest where we found the clothing. "With this you will be able to make your sword the only exact replica of Steelefyre." I told them briefly how we had found it in the vault of books.

"I cannot believe this," Kopernick said rubbing his eyes. "Am I dreaming or what? Marc what is the Writer of All preparing us for, a person can only guess?"

I shook my head and just smiled. "With the armies of the kingdom weeks from getting here, I hope the Writer hurries with something suitable."

I passed the sword to Lindergren. He held it in one hand and brought it up to his chest with the tip pointing up to the rafters. He held his hand there above his heart for a second and then brought it down. I had seen soldiers do this once or twice before. It was like a salute.

"I held a sword such as this once before ..." he began.

"Here we go with the war stories again," Kopernick said softly, but it seemed no one heard him.

Lindergren went on.

* * * * *

"Commander Nathel and just a small band of young nobles came riding up from the south one day. With them was a man not in the uniform of the king's soldiers. The horse the stranger was on had thrown a shoe and they needed a blacksmith to fix it. My father was busy helping others with a stubborn wagon wheel and I was the only other one here and so I went to work.

"He brought the horse into the forge and I began to size up the horse for the shoe I would need. I was young then and had seen very little in the ways of a fighter. When he saw me looking at the sword as it hung from his side, he drew it out. I guess my eyes grew wide as he handed it to me because he laughed.

"Was It was beautiful, just like this," he said running his hand over the hilt and then the blade.

"I asked him what the king's men were doing so far north. He said there was great trouble in Ihrhoven and that it would soon be coming this way. I thought he was joking because I had heard nothing of the sort."

"I finished my work and he paid me with coin. They were gone before I woke in the morning," he finished as he gave the sword back to Kopernick.

"Was this the last you saw of him?" Rouke asked.

"No. He returned three days later with an army of men a day half behind him the likes of which I have never seen before. Half of the men with Nathel were gone and the men here in the village tried to gather their weapons, but it was too late.

"We fought at first. The keep of the ruling family caught on fire and then chaos broke loose and all, death seemed to lay everywhere. Most who were able ran for the woods. The lucky ones had horses and were able to retreat and spread the word of the invasion."

He stopped talking and ran his fingers through his thick hair. He took a deep breath and went on.

"I did not stop running that night. By time I was in Edelstone they were three days behind. I fought there and then again in Kiest. I returned after it was all over and found nothing that was my own still standing. My parents and family were gone."

He grew silent and everyone was left to their own thoughts.

Corva and Chay came into the room a short time later and they all began to get ready to sleep for the night.

"Does it bother you at all?" I asked him, seeing the troubled look on his face.

"No. It doesn't. I fought for my kingdom and we won."

With that we all settled in for the night.

* * * * *

I heard the creak of the wood and saw the far wall light up as a candle shone through the door behind me.

"Marc . . ." a voice whispered.

I turned, and shielding my eyes from the light, saw Kopernick standing there. The red strands of his hair were unmistakable.

"Do you mind if I get the dust?" he whispered.

"No. It's in my haversack in the stables. Is it even near daybreak yet?" I said after running my tongue over the roof of my mouth a few times to dispel the dryness there.

"Soon. Will you be coming?"

I reached out and touched the softness of Chay's long hair. My hand went down the smoothness of her bare back to rest on her hip. She did not stir from her sleep, but slept soundly in the early morning.

"Let me get dressed," I mumbled. "I want to see this."

*   *   *   *   *

I paused just outside the house on my way to the smithy.

The village still slept. Lindergren had three main buildings. The house, the smithy and the stables. Chest high stone walls ringed them and the courtyard between the three was completely inlaid with cobblestones. Now, on this midwinter morning, snow covered everything deeply. From the small parcel of land other houses could be seen through the forest. Trees grew to the south and hid most of the village itself from view. Snow must have fallen during the night because our tracks from the days previous were gone. The skies were almost clear this morning with only a few scattered clouds forming near the southern horizon. The moon had set hours before and stars blazed across the heavens. As I breathed the sharp, cold morning air it stung my throat.

I looked around me once again, drawing my cloak closer, and made my way to the smithy. Rouke was already there trying to light the fire in the forge to heat the place. Kopernick stood near the table with the small bag of egg dust and Steelefyre. He read from the book in candlelight.

"Rouke," I said and the other looked up from his labors. He was striking the flint near some kindling, but with no results.

"I can do this for you, I think," I said. Rouke took a step back and placed the flint back on its shelf.

I closed my eyes for a second, bringing the spell to mind. I would have to put a bit more emphasis on the size of the flame that Kopernick needed because the forge itself was larger by far than any candle. When I had the spell in my head, and knew the strength I would need, I spoke it. It was not a long spell, but as the words came off my tongue I could feel its strength gather around me tighter than any cloak. With the spell spoke, I opened my eyes, and looked at the others, and then at the forge. Pausing no longer, I gave the command of execution and the wood in the forge came to life with light and heat.

The tingling was in my chest and I brought my hand up instinctively. The whole room seemed far away and distant for a moment. I willed myself to focus and the room returned to normal. I shook my head to clear it.

"Are you well?" they asked in unison.

"Just some water please," I said and took a seat on the floor. The door opened and closed as I held my head in my hands. The door opened again and a wooden cup was placed on the floor before me. I drank deeply. By the time I stood, the room was much warmer and my head had cleared considerably.

"I have never done a spell of fire that strong before. The Writer be easy on me, what a shock."

Rouke watched me constantly during the next hour. He would not relax no matter how well I said I felt.

During this time, Kopernick muttered half spells trying to get incantation just right.

Before the sun broke over the horizon, Rouke and I excused ourselves and tended to the horses. As I brought fresh oats, my mount nudged me on the shoulder. Perhaps he was saying he was glad for the rest and hoped we would stay longer. Or he may have felt the place was almost too comfortable and wanted to leave soon.

"We'll spend one more day here and then leave early in the morning," I said as I brushed him down. The horses ears twitched, but other than that he did not move until I had finished. I began to fork the manure into a pile.

"It feels good here, Marc," Rouke said from his side of the stables.

"It seems as though we are one large family. It would have been nice to stay here longer. Change of plans though, eh? Keep the tack close by. We may have to leave in a hurry."

"We'll find a place. Our place. It'll work out.

"Was Croskreye so bad?" I asked brushing the packhorse down.

"No." He looked over the back of the horse at me. "If you were the duke's daughter, or some unknown entity who just happen to have fallen from a mirror and for a while everyone favors you there. Taking linen to the washrooms day after day, it gets tedious. Being out here it is different. It's not just the place, or the people. It's just that . . . say I could have a chance to get a better position and still be in Croskreye. To those there I would always be Rouke the Kitchen Hand, or Rouke One Who Cleans the Privy. Here in Glenhelen or elsewhere I can start off new. You see my meaning?"

"And what is it you would do here or wherever?"

"I'm not sure. It would be nice to study magic I think."

"Lofty expectations, that's a good thing. Glenhelen is not the place for learning magic. Kopernick had to travel clear to Milhematte for that. If those are your wishes, we'll have to send you there."

Rouke was not sure if I was joking or not, I could see it in his eyes when he looked over to me. He watched me for a moment and we both began to laugh.

Before going back to the forge, I went to the house to look in on Chay. She was still asleep, and I did not disturb her. Lindergren and Corva were up and about tending to their morning chores. I told them we were outside with Kopernick working with his sword in the forge.

* * * * *

"If today is going to stay clear, your father wants us to go to the market. If that doesn't take long, there is another tree that he wishes brought here that he would be greatly thankful for now that he has the help." I told Kopernick upon my return to the smithy.

"We'll go shortly. I have the spell down to memory now I think. We can begin." Rolling up his sleeves, he placed the bare sword on the thick wooden table, Ravenstone in place, and Rouke and I stepped back. He spoke a few simple words that were of a metal spell in origin and cast it upon the sword. Taking a step back, he spoke to us.

"That part of the spell is done. The sword will stay the way it is until I call attention to it again by speaking my next spell. What we have to do now is to sprinkle the dust over it in a smooth pattern so one area does not have more or less strength than the rest. If it gets to the sword uneven, it can shatter."

"How is this done?" I asked.

"We need some coarse fabric as long as the sword is with a very loose weave. We sprinkle the dust on the fabric and it will filter through to the sword in an even manner. My mother is up. I shall ask her if she has any."

He left to return a short while later with a small bit of fabric. He unfolded it and spread it over the table.

"I need each of you to catch two corners and hold them up," he rubbed his red hair vigorously. Already disheveled it was heavy with sweat.

We did so. Kopernick lifted the bag of dust up and taking a deep breath, scattered a line of dust down the length of the cloth. It all passed down to the sword except where it caught on the thick thread.

Taking the palm of his hand he gently tapped the sides of the cloth until the last of dust had passed through. He placed the sack with the remaining dust on the window sill to the side. We drew the cloth away.

I was sure there should have been a few flakes of the dust that did not find the blade, but had landed on the wooden table. I was wrong. It seemed as though that the dust was drawn to the blade. Nothing was on the table except for the sword. Kopernick bent close to examine the blade and then beckoned us to do the same.

"What are we looking for?" Rouke asked with his nose just a hands-breadth from the hilt.

"If you have good eyes and look very closely, running down the center of the blade there is a thin line that is the same color as the dust."

"Ah, yes," he said. "There it is." Rouke stood back and I had a chance to see it.

Like Kopernick had said, a faint gray line passed down the entire length of the blade from hilt to tip. No more than a hairs breath in width and in the light of the fire, it seemed a light-gray or silver. "This is what should happen?" I asked.

"Oh yes," Kopernick said. I looked at his face and could see the smile of pride. He seemed to glow, he was so happy. "It is what we were hoping to get. Any less of the dust and it would not be so. It would have all moved to the end by the hilt. The blade would break the first time it struck anything. With the way it is now, the dust adds a barrier around the blade for protection . . ."

"Much like the egg did when it was whole," I stated.

"Oh, yes. Very much so. Now the next few spells are a tad tricky. The first will be to put an edge on it. The second will restore the strength to the metal and the third will invoke the dust to begin its protection."

"And after that?" Rouke asked.

"If all goes well . . ." Kopernick took a deep breath and slowly let it out. "If it does as it says in the book, then the sword will never dull from its original sharpness. It cannot be nicked, cracked, shattered, or otherwise broken. The dust in the blade will not let any harm come to what is inside."

"But the original magic of the egg is not to let whatever is in the egg get out. How can this be reversed and the magic still work?" asked Rouke.

"It's not changing the magic at all," Kopernick said. "It will not let what is in its possession out. This case, it is the sword itself. The magic does not let anything penetrate its protective shell, thereby letting whatever it contained out. Nothing will get in to harm the blade."

"I see," Rouke said softly.

* * * * *

Kopernick fell to the floor as if a hammer struck him. We had been near, but had not known what the outcome would be of this last spell on the sword. I had thought Kopernick had just taken a step backward from the table and tripped.

He fell backward amid a shelf of tools that collapsed under his weight. Before we could react, he lay on the floor unmoving.

"Get his parents!" Rouke shouted as he knelt down. "Marc!" he yelled louder when I didn't move.

I fumbled at the door feeling for the latch. Running across the cobblestone courtyard, I practically tripped over children playing there. I burst in the house with a gust of wind and snow.

"Come quickly. I think Koper is hurt," I yelled. Lindergren grabbed his cloak while giving orders to Corva. Chay looked to me for an answer, but there was nothing I could give her. She went after Corva. I held the door open as Lindergren rushed by.

Rouke had Kopernick half in half out of the shack dragging him by his arms. His foot caught on the door jam and they had fallen. Lindergren picked his eldest son up with one motion and came back across the courtyard to the house. They brought him to his room and gently placed him on his bed. Corva began to loosen his heavy clothing with one hand while feeling his forehead with the other.

"Does he bleed anywhere besides the forehead?" she asked searching for any wounds.

"No," I said. "He fell right after a spell."

Lindergren listened to his breathing while ordering everyone quiet with one thundering word. The children who were crying because of the confusion grew silent within two heartbeats. Kopernick's face was a pale bloodless white, his eyes shone white and his mouth lay open.

"He still lives," said Lindergren softly taking a deep breath himself. "I am going to the village to get the healer." He stood and gathered his boots and cloak.

"Chay get me some linen from the closet." Corva motioned to the far wall. I watched Chay go about her task quickly. Although I wanted the world to hold her in my arms, I just touched her hand in passing. Corva then shooed us all out of the room and shut the door.

When the healer arrived moments later, he had the beginnings of a bruise on his cheek and his hair was a slight tangle. We all gave Lindergren a puzzled look.

"Persuasion helps," he said with a nervous smile. He brought the healer into the room and the door was once again closed.

*   *   *   *   *

"He completed the first two spells with little effect on him. Just the slight tingling in his chest he told us. He waited for a few moments to rest after the second one by reading from the book and drinking some water. When he said he was ready he began the incantation.

"I don't know if the spell needed that much energy or if he put that much energy into it purposefully." As I finished, I placed the wooden cup down on the table top and my hands shook. I clenched them into fists and after a while they stopped.

Lindergren sat beside the window and looked out over the snow. He was about to speak when the healer came out of the room with Corva and Chay directly behind. Corva went to her husband and held him. Chay came to me and stood close at hand.

The healer looked around the room and spoke to the room in general.

"He will be better," he said flatly. "Given two days time he will be back chopping wood. The spell he cast drained him that's all."

"And the blood?" Lindergren asked.

"Just some scrapes on his head. They are healing now."

*   *   *   *   *

Kopernick woke later that night and the whole family tried to gather in the small room. Corva brought him some broth and bread. The children climbed on the bed to sit next to him and he did not mind. We pressed him with all sorts of questions until Corva began to clear the room of children to give him rest.

"I am going to give the sword to you, Marc." Still weak, I thought he had lost his wits.

"But why?" I asked.

"I have searched for a way to repay you for the book, and I think this would be the best way. I was going to give it to you all along. As soon as I was able to keep an edge on the blade, it was yours. Now there is no doubt. I have enough egg dust to see us very comfortable for a while."

Corva wiped some broth from his beard and Chay took the food away.

"I have no use for a sword. You keep it. Display it in the smithy so others may see and admire the work you do."

"Please Marc," he said with such force, he had to reach out to a wall to stop the dizziness that followed. "Will you let someone do something for you without a fight for a change? The sword is yours and that's final."

"But . . . I . . ."

"You can take the sword and do with it what you will. I am done with the cursed thing. Night after night I've worked on that blade and hilt. Now I finally complete it and this happens? Take it with you now or it gets lost in the woods come springs thaw."

"We shall see," I said, but looking at the expression Lindergren's face I knew better than to challenge Kopernick in this matter.

* * * * *

"In all of the confusion today Corva and I forgot to go to the market to get material for clothes," Chay whispered to me as we lay together under our heavy wool blanket. Sleep played with my senses and she helped keep me awake awhile longer.

"You have enough clothes. Wait until we get back from Ihrhoven."

"They were not for us, they are for the baby," she said and snuggled closer. I felt the nakedness of her body against mine and the warmth was heavenly. Her hair, unbound and free now, brushed against my face.

"Wait a moment," I said. "Kopernick is the oldest and has no wife. Her youngest is almost four winters old. Corva should have enough clothing for them all."

"Silly man," she said bringing her head back to look into my eyes. "She is not the one expecting a child."

Chapter #21

We left the morning after Kopernick fell in the smithy and with many assurances from him that he would be fine. The night's rest did him well. Color had returned to his cheeks and he was walking about the house. The weakness was still there and his movements were stiff, but he was greatly improved.

After we prepared the horses, I made my way to the smithy. It was the first I had entered the place since the day before. The forge fire had died down and the place was as cold as it was outside.

The sword lay on the table top where it was left when the last spell was cast. I picked it up by the hilt and studied its detail for a time before placing it gingerly in its sheath. Taking the leather straps in hand, I wrapped them twice around my waist and secured them with a buckle. There was the bit of cloth nearby which Kopernick used to cover the serpentine pattern of the hilt. I tied it on over the snakes checking twice to make sure it was secure. I did not need the kind of attention such a thing would bring.

It felt cumbersome as it hung from my side. I walked from one end of the forge to the next and found it stayed out of my way as I walked and did not make me trip. Hopefully, it was on properly.

Picking up my cloak, I went out into the cold morning light.

*   *   *   *   *

Chay was already in the saddle. She smiled down at me and I could do nothing but frown at her. Her clothing was heavy with a very tight weave to keep out the chill. She said the rabbit hide gloves she wore kept her hands warm enough, but even now the tips of her ears were starting to turn red. She should not go, not in her condition.

Our journey thus far was cold and here she should stay. Corva could have used her help with tending the children. She could be safe and warm.

With her hair braided once more she reminded me of someone I had seen before. This had been an older woman with a braid such of this with silver and gold streaks of color in her hair. I could not call to mind this remembrance and the vision quickly passed. A dream possibly.

"I will be fine," she said again knowing my thoughts, and blew me a kiss. As I swung my leg up and mounted my horse, Rouke finished his last minute checking and mounted his also. Corva and Lindergren were there along with the youngest of the children. Kopernick lay asleep in the cottage.

"One week and a half we will be back through. We will not stay, but be off. I will take your advice, Lindergren. When this blows over like a storm I will return."

"You will always be welcome in our house. However, don't bring so many of the king's men with you next time," Lindergren said holding out my pack. The weight of my books and the vials felt comforting. Although the ribbons faded from the weather and the sunlight, they still held their form.

Corva gave Chay an extra shawl. "Traditionally, you have the right to call yourselves husband and wife now. Make sure he does not leave you and stay by his side. Marc, she is your wife now. Any harm happens to her, we'll find out. I will have no qualms whatsoever in hunting you down." she was smiling as she made this threat. I nodded to her. She knew I would let nothing harm Chay.

"By all means, please do." I said making a jest. "The rest of the kingdom are on my heals." It was good to hear them laugh.

Lindergren took a step forward as I beckoned him closer. He held out a hand, palm open, as I held out my hand. From my closed fist I passed five gold pieces to him. This is more than they would get in one month working the smithy.

"For your kindness, the healer for Kopernick, and for the sword. Take this gold and spend it wisely so you may prosper."

"Yes. Oh, yes. Thank you, thank you very much," he stammered taking a step back.

We said more good-byes. With a wave of my hand, I kicked my heels to the side of my horse. We were off.

*   *   *   *   *

As the sun began to set on our third day out of Glenhelen, we took shelter in an abandoned house. The thatch roof was thinning at one end and the door almost fell from its hinges as we peered in. It was barren of any usable furniture, or shelving of any type. Clay pots lay broken in the dust on the floor.

We barred the door the best we could after bringing the horses inside the structure. They would fare the night better in from the elements. What was left of the small barn would be of no use. It was roofless and a wall had caved in. I also knew of wolves in this area first hand. With the three horses in and a modest fire burning in the fireplace, it grew warm enough.

In the morning we woke to leave, and I was glad the night had passed without incident.

* * * * *

The next day I was able to show them where the wolves had attacked Brembry. I stopped briefly at the old oak and said a short appeal to the Writer of All to see her well. We passed many families heading south. Wagons encumbered with belongings or just people with heavy packs as their burden. It seems they had heard a rumor of the Drenthen returning.

"Is all of this your cause, Marc?" Rouke asked when no others were about.

I did not say anything, not wishing to answer.

We stopped again when we reached a pile of stones near a larger boulder at the edge of the Kear Forest. Brembry's grave lay untouched. A leafless tree, a plum tree if I remembered from before, stood nearby as if guarding her grave. The towering trees had given way to the much smaller ones and the open fields and orchards returned once more. It was a very welcome sight after being in the region of the Kear Forest for so long.

We pushed our mounts and were quite exhausted and cold when we reached the Red Raven Inn late in the night.

* * * * * *

Chay did not eat much and complained of a stomach-ache. I asked if she was well, and she simply stated that Corva said things such as this happened. Corva had brought six children to this world and Chay trusted her experience in these matters. I looked over at her across the table and sensed she would complain no more.

"I knew we shouldn't have come this far, but there are few other places between here and the farmhouse." We stayed at a large stone ring the night before, but it was mostly for caravans. The shelter, just a thick stone wall chest high in the shape of an open circle, did little to keep weather out. It kept animals safe with no protection from the elements at all. We lay, all three of us, close to the fire as we slept. One side uncomfortably warm, the other chilled.

"We had to get here tonight, there was no other way." When I finished I felt my temper rise and realized suddenly how loud I was talking.

Others eating their evening meal or drinking looked at me, but paid us no mind.

"It's not the riding or anything, Marc. Please. These things do happen. You've never had just a stomachache before? If I had felt any pain while we rode I would have told you. She'll be fine," Rouke spoke with a mouthful of bread.

"Bah," I said throwing my spoon to the table top. I knew I was angry at things I had no control over. I sat there brooding for a while, but in time the aroma of the soup brought me back. I found my spoon and ate again.

She finished her meal and left the table early. I watched her as she went up the stairs to the room.

"Does she have any names picked out yet?" Rouke asked.

"None yet," said I taking a sip of broth. "I think it is too early to begin making a fuss with such. I did not want her to come along due to her health. That is what she should worry about. Now she has stomach aches. What if something is wrong?"

"After we see to Nathel, we will make her visit a healer in Ihrhoven. If there is one still left. She cannot be too far along in her term. Riding should have no harm on her now. You should not worry," Even as Rouke pleaded with me, I knew my argument was moot.

"Wait until Rosemary is in such a state. Ha, then I shall be the one telling you not to worry about her aches." I thought to tussle his hair, as I would have done if we were back in Croskreye, but he was older now. When I looked at him I no longer saw the young lad who brought my meals.

At the mention of her name, Rouke got a gleam in his eye. "Ah, can't wait for these snows to leave," he said waving at the window. "Then she will be here and we will marry. Ah, what a day that will be."

"You sent word to her then?"

"The first day we were in Glenhelen."

* * * * *

There had been much work done to the keep at Ihrhoven. Builders still came and went, but it seemed they finished most of the masonry work. The only wagons I saw were the ones with wood timbers unloading before its gates.

Two of the towers were complete with roofs and all. From these, sentries looked over the land and sea.

"You should have seen it this summer," I stated. "A beehive it was."

In the village we found a stable with space for our horses, and I also put a handful of coppers on a room for the night. We would need to have one after we finished our work with Nathel.

From a vender on the street we bought our noon meal.

It was just past the noon hour when I could wait no longer that we made our way to the sea.

* * * * *

From the wall of the castle the king's men watched as the three travelers passed the stone rampart. The young woman with the white hair was easy to identify. There were two other male companions as described by Duke Almonesson. With a fourth horse as a packhorse, it was plain to see that they had traveled some distance.

Commander Sablich bid the others to stand back from the parapet edge so as not to be seen. If Marc and his companions knew they were under such scrutiny they may hesitate in their task.

For the king's men, their fourth day in the village of Ihrhoven was drawing on. The villagers treated them well enough, but it would be good to return to Land Streth.

"Do we go soon?" Lord Farnstrom asked quietly, the steady wind drew his hair back from his face.

"No. We wait." Commander Sablich stood with his hand on his sword. He looked at the three and then gazed at the ocean. "It is what we must do. When I spoke with the Chronicler, she told me not to interfere. He is so ordinary, so plain looking. Marc seems nothing like his father whatsoever."

"And then?" the rough voice of Duke Lysaght's man, Rasp, was unmistakable. "After they are gone?"

"And then wait until Marc and the girl are dealt with. It won't take him long. When it's truly nightfall out, we will visit the cave."

* * * * *

As the bag of gold coins hit my chest, it nearly knocked me down. Steelefyre, strapped on my belt, managed to get between my legs and I almost tripped. The second bag of gold had the same effect as the first. Rouke, who stood just a few measures away on the cliff edge, tossed them to me. However, I was ready for the weight of this one and it did not hurt as much. I set the bag down and readjusted the sword.

The gold was our future and I felt better when it was with us. Not once did we leave it with the horses for fear of someone may take it. Kopernick's family had no idea of the amount that we carried.

Of course, I did feel odd carrying it with us as we walked the streets of Ihrhoven. The townspeople kept to themselves as we went our way.

I had bound the ends of each sack with the same strip of leather so I could carry it better over my shoulders like a yoke.

Chay came down next. Thankfully, she wore her riding breeches this day and not her thick riding dress. She slid the last length on her bottom.

I gave her a worried look, but she stood, brushed the snow off, and gave me a quick smile. Rouke had more balance on his feet and made it down smoothly.

It was warmer here on the rock shelf. The sun shone brightly upon it and the blowing wind failed to reach its surface due to the jutting rocks. The waves below were calm and did not carry the turmoil I remembered the last time I was here.

"Do not go inside. We must wait for Nathel to appear. There are things there we should not disturb."

Chay and Rouke went to the entrance of the cave and looked in but did not go further.

Rouke was about to comment on something he saw there when we heard a new voice spoken softly nearby.

"Hello," said the voice. "Welcome to Ihrhoven everyone." Deep and rich his tone did not seem as troubled as before.

"It is good to finally be here, Nathel," I said into winter air seeing no form to speak to. "Your time to leave has about come."

"That it has," came the voice again and he laughed. "I will not spend another night from my love it seems. My wait is over." The relief could not be mistaken.

"Where is she at?" asked Chay.

"Chay . . . ?" There was a pause of many heartbeats as if somehow the ghost had not sensed her standing there. "I . . . I have been able to see you in the dreams of Marc's at night. I cannot fully see you now and will only at dusk. In your voice, you seem as beautiful as in his dreams. I . . ." there was another pause lasting for sometime before he went on. "There is a barrier those living and those such as myself cannot cross. I have died, but my spirit still lives. Death is a passing or crossing over. Tonight, with the vial that Marc has brought to me, I will be able to cross the barrier and be with my wife once again. She waits for me there and has longed for my arriving. When the time comes, and you listen closely, you will be able to hear the beating of the oars of the Skye Boat."

"Truly speaking?" Chay asked.

The voice that was the ghost just laughed.

"I am not sure if I brought what you needed, Nathel. There were three vials ..."

"And you brought all three." Nathel finished for me and I nodded. "You have all that I will use. Do not fret Marc, you did the right thing. Did you enjoy the books in the vault of Croskreye?"

"Tyndall was very pleased."

"It was during the wars, well before the battle at Welteroth, that we came upon a large cache of books in one of the lower levels of the castle in Lanedorf. It was Cinnaminson who made the gate and we brought the books from there to the room in Croskreye. I had never seen the island myself. I remember the old sorcerer saying that we were in Croskreye. It seems odd, but he told me several times, like I would forget."

"He stammers like you do, Marc," Rouke whispered and I gave him a sharp look.

"The three vials Kalendeck brought from his pack and placed on the table. I forget most of what he told me, but I do remember that the vials were for leaving of the dead. Resurrection I asked, if such a thing were ever possible and Sorcerer Cinnaminson said; No, to take a man's spirit to the place beyond where all spirits go. My spirit must find the Skye Boat to allow me to travel onward.

"I know it may seem I am talking nonsense, but this is what the sorcerer said. I grew angry and very frustrated with Kalendeck that day, if I recall correctly. He had a habit of doing such, however. By and by, I am sorry. My mind wanders. I am glad Tyndall liked the books.

"Perhaps I can find the answers I am looking for there," I said in calm silence following. "The last I heard, adepts from all over the kingdom were on their way to Ross Island to study. Duke Almonesson will have his hands full for a while."

Rouke laughed. "Ha, he likes his island quiet. That will be a sight." Immediately he blushed speaking his mind so freely in the presence of someone of such status.

"Who can this be? Marc, Have you brought the whole kingdom here?" Nathel said in a cheerful voice. Rouke twitched where he stood now being under everyone gaze.

"Someone I have not met yet. Rouke is this you? Your name has also come up in discussion from time to time. I hope all is well with you."

"I am fine," his voice faltered. "Um, what did he say about me?"

"You are a young man in his prime and well before the mid years of his life. Let us look at who your companion is. He arrived here by forces so strong you could not imagine. Do you think the Writer of All has not found the best in companions for him? Be ready for him when the time comes."

"H ... how can I do that?"

"Become who you are. Nothing comes easy."

Rouke said nothing, but looked at us seeking an answer to this. I could think of none and just shrugged my shoulders.

"I thought Tyndall was bad with riddles," he said at last.

*   *   *   *   *

"I still am a little confused," I said. "The magic containment of the egg is one of the most powerful known. How could it have cracked so easily when I did nothing to it but touch it's surface?" We, the living ones, sat together on the rocks. Huddled together for warmth, Chay pulled her cloak tighter about her neck.

"With what hand did you touch it with?" asked Nathel.

"This . . . no, this one," I said remembering.

"What else is on that hand." The sound of his voice seemed to move from the left to the right as if he was pacing.

"The ring of Kalendeck. But . . ."

"The ring contains some powerful magic itself, least you forget."

"Strong enough to dispel magic of that strength?"

"And more." There was stress in Nathel's voice. "When they brought Kalendeck here from . . . Wherever they brought him from, he carried the ring with him. It is known that Sorcerer Cinnaminson brought him here with the magic of the gates. Chances are the ring is not of this world. Have you thought of that?"

"No. I have not. I assumed the ring was from here, made by someone in the kingdom." I looked down at my hand and watched the ring in the sunlight. It fit my finger better now than it did half a season ago. Had it grown smaller, or had I grown into it, I mused? I supposed the latter was true.

Rouke and Chay, who sat on either side, looked at the ring with me.

We sat with our backs to the cave, and the sun to our faces.

"Was Kalendeck of this world then?" Chay asked bringing her knees up to her chin and wrapping her arms around her legs.

"Cinnaminson said no. From another land entirely." Nathel stated with a sigh. "He knew of our ways and customs, but at times he was lost. He told me a bit of his home when he grew depressed, but now I remember little of it. The years have clouded my mind, you see? It was a place not of the kingdom at all. I am not sure I wish to know of it, if it bred fighters such as him. He must have had a difficult childhood."

"He'll be on the Skye boat as well. You'll get to see him."

Nathel again laughed.

"Rouke, you are correct. I shall see him again this day. A good fighter he was and he knew his magic. Of this you can be sure. Cinnaminson brought him here to fight and it is what he did best. If he had known what waited for him on this side of the gate, I have doubt he would want to come willingly. No man can know his fate. No man. If he had known his fate, he may not have died at Welteroth. There were other ways we could have won. Much, so much, was lost that day. I trained on the battlefield. We knew their tactics. It would have been only a matter of time. He did not have to do what he did." His voice was full of sorrow and remorse as he spoke the last.

"Do you wish to talk about it?" Rouke asked.

"Not now, I cannot. I wish to speak no more of the past." There was a pause before he spoke again. "I am very happy because today there is much reason for rejoicing. Let me do something for you and your companions, Marc. I have not left yet, but you all have brought me much happiness."

"What can one as yourself give us but knowledge?" I asked. "In a sense you have given me everything you had promised before. When I was here last, you tempted me with books and gold. I have both and I am as happy as anyone can be. What more is there?"

"My point exactly. Don't leave."

They heard a spell being cast. When he spoke the word of execution a portion of the stone wall grew dark. Color played over the black surface and suddenly it brought back memories I had all but forgotten. The memory surfaced of its own accord. My hand moved about until I found Chay's. She moved closer to my side and in this I found comfort.

"Do not fear," Nathel's voice said very close to my ear almost a whisper. I did not look because I knew his form would not exist in light this bright. My eyes did not leave the darkness of the gate. "The gate will not harm you. Please wait here, I shall return shortly."

First, several books passed out of the darkness and then small pouches made of fine cloth floated through the air to land at our feet. We did not move until Nathel spoke to us again. With a word or two, the gate was gone with a tug of wind as if it never was.

"These are for you. Take them and I shall tell you of their purpose."

"Rouke. The first two books are for you," Rouke stood and went to these lifting the heavy tomes from the ground. They seemed old. Their construction was like most of the books I had seen in the kingdom. Heavy paper protected with soft leather covers bound together with metal binding.

"One is an almost complete volume of the magic of air. The other is one much older and is mostly in the magic of stone," Rouke nodded as Nathel spoke recognizing the symbols on their surface.

"Quite a contrast," I said with a smile.

"Yes, but two very powerful magics. You will find as you study them that you cannot have one without the other. The sky above and the ground below. All else exist between these realms."

"It will take me a while to get these finished. Years actually. You've given books to someone who cannot read."

"Marc will teach you. Take your time. It will be best. As for the last book, it is for you Marc."

I went forward and picked up the remaining book. Bound on its surface was a metal piece in the shape of a sword. I opened it up and skimmed several pages.

"At a glance I cannot tell what it is about."

"It is a book on warrior magic. You've heard of it, they call it the Book of Harms. It is an art of the spirit since it deals with controlling the mind and body to enhance the fighter's abilities. This is a very powerful magic."

There was a pause as he finished and it was a long while before anyone spoke.

"I am to become a fighter then, and not a scribe or chronicler?"

"Did you read the book I gave you on metal working? Have you joined Kopernick in the smithy? You can do what you wish, Marc. This book is not for you, but a token gift for the next ruler of this territory. Give it to them when the time comes. Perhaps a guild of fighters could be founded to ensure the knowledge of spirit magic is not lost from the kingdom. Beyson, the armorer in Croskreye, would find such a book very valuable. And with you also, Rouke. Do not hoard the wisdom as a loaf of bread or a gold coin. There is much to gain from the books by the people of the kingdom."

"I shall do my best," Rouke said solemnly.

"And I will also," I said shortly after. I untied the straps of my leather haversack and placed the book in.

Chay cleared her throat.

"Ah, Chay. The last but not the least. Take only one pouch at your feet and look at it. What one contains, they all do," Chay bent and delicately picked up only one of the sacks. It lay comfortably in the palm of her hand.

She untied the draw strings and looked inside.

"Oh my," she exclaimed and poured part of the pouches contents into her open palm. Sunlight struck the rubies there so that her hand seemed to alight with a soft red fire. She looked at us, and her eyes were gleaming with their tint. Her hair sparkled with red highlights.

She laughed and put them back where they had been.

"They are beautiful, Nathel. Where did they come from? The high king's own chambers?"

"Much was lost during the wars. One such as myself can go places the living cannot. The books were found well beneath the ruins in Glenhelen, and the rubies are from a cache of jewels in Kiest."

"Why couldn't you go to Croskreye and get the vials you need? You sent me to do this task. Why?"

"Creating gates such as this takes much power and concentration. Of that type of power, I have very little left. If I were in solid form, if I still lived, I would have a worse time going through this gate that was just created. Things with no material travel better. If you could have seen my form when I had just died you could tell the difference between then and now. I am slowly fading. What was once my original self, my being, is all but gone. Another two or three seasons and I would be almost nothing. Communication would be very hard."

"Isn't this what you wish?"

"No. Not in that sense. My containment, will soon be over. Do you understand?" At the last Nathel's voice took on a bit of resignation.

"We wish you no ill will and a safe journey," Chay said. "When you leave this place, may you find those you love quickly."

"I have just met you this day," said Rouke when Chay stopped. He cleared his throat before he went on. "I have heard about you many nights during the times they told stories around the fire. All these tales were of a man with great strength and wisdom. I see now they were not false. You are all of these. I am glad to have known you, and I wish you a safe journey as well."

As Rouke finished, they turned to me.

"You catch me at a loss. I did not really prepare for this moment," My voice wavered and I took a deep breath trying to collect my thoughts. "I knew this time was bound to happen, but simply, my thoughts did not dwell on it. I am glad things will be well for you. May you never have to leave your family again. I will miss you greatly. Out of all that I have learned here in the kingdom, I have learned the most from you," I paused for a moment and lowered my head. When I looked back, I was not ashamed of the tears in my eyes.

"Fare thee well, my friend."

"Well met," Nathel whispered. "Well met."

*   *   *   *   *

The sun was beginning to set. I looked about at my friends as we stood on the shelf of rock safe from wind or snow. Shivering, I knew that with the sun setting, our little shell of heat would be gone.

There were no changes to the three vials I had placed on the smooth surface of the stone.

"It seems my time is almost here. I am so nervous. I hope I remember the spells I need. Of course I remember them," Nathel said answering himself. "I have said them over and over so many times since I have been here. I would repeat them over and over again just to pass the day."

Rouke turned his head to this. "This would not invoke the magic?" he asked.

"No. Spells of this nature, without the proper potions, are nothing. I believe it is time we start. It would seem though, I have very little strength to move the vials which you have brought. I need someone to help me with their stoppers."

"I'll do it," Chay spoke up.

"No. I'll do it," I said stepping forward.

"I thank you for your offers, but no. Rouke will help me. Chay, look at your hands. Your shaking because you are cold. If you drop one of these with the top off it would be very disastrous. Marc, take her in the cave where it is a bit warmer. Watch over her there and protect her."

"Why, what is to happen?" Rouke asked with a worried look.

"I was not told what happens as the spell works out. You must sprinkle the contents of the vial on my bones and that is all. Of course this is what I think you must do."

"You think?" I felt an uneasiness grow. I was not about to have Chay here where she could be harmed.

"I am sure that if something very powerful was going to happen when this spell was cast, Kalendeck would have said something."

"Kalendeck gave you the knowledge of this spell?"

"Yes. He was the one who had the vials. The day we arrived in Welteroth he begged me memorize the spell until I could say it to him backwards. Marc, I am sure you remember this. Please all will be well."

Reluctantly, I nodded agreement.

"Gather your things now and go to the cave. There is not much time."

Busy picking things up, I noticed Chay was standing still looking at something to my side. I saw a movement and realized I could barely see Nathel's form shimmering in the twilight. I stood facing the ghost of the king's commander and it surprised me still that this man of normal stature could have commanded the fighting men of the whole kingdom. When I heard tales of him, I often expected to see a giant. Looking at him here, eye to eye, it was easy to see that we stood at almost the same height. His shoulders were very broad, and his beard was long and full. Blood still trickled from the wound in his side. Nathel stood with his scabbard empty of a sword where as mine held Steelefyre.

I turned, Chay blinked and I knew the moment for her was gone. I picked up the two bags of gold and noticed the evening sun was about to set over the frozen expanse of the sea. I helped Chay with my haversack that held the book, my journals, and now the rubies. We paused one final time to look back at Rouke and Commander Nathel.

No more good-byes were spoken as we hurried inside.

*   *   *   *   *

I took Chay by the hand and she led us into the cave. It was difficult to see inside as our forms blocked the light of the setting sun.

"Watch your feet," I said. "There are things here we should not disturb. Straight back some ways the cave ends. We will be safer there."

"It does feel warmer in here," Chay exclaimed. She could not hide the shiver in her voice.

I was watching the ground as we walked not wanting to trip with the bags of gold and the sword. I felt her tug on my hand and this caused me to look up.

In the darkness I saw a deeper blackness that had soft colors lightly shimmering across its surface. Her foot traveled forward and came down on nothing, she began to fall forward. My response to seeing the gate was to pull Chay away, to move her from the damned thing.

But it was too late.

Time slowed.

Suddenly, I came to face the greatest decision I have known. Here I was on the edge. Teetering precariously above this chasm from which I could not see clearly the pathway that lay before me. I was so close now, living to see this last myth through to the end. Abruptly, without warning, a second pathway, an alternate destiny to my future, is given.

No, not given, forced upon me.

I could have drawn away, pulled back from her, let her fingers slip from my grasp, and our love would be over. The gate, this remnant of the last of Nathel's magic or the beginnings of Tyndall's power, would close and she would be lost to me, maybe not forever, but at least for a while. I could see Nathel onward in his final journey.

Or I could hold on to her. Tighten my grip on her fingers and let myself be drawn by her to a new place. This woman I loved, deeply and truly, I should not leave. A child, she was in her mind, carrying a child of mine in her body.

My child.

Our future.

I did not wish to lose her. Not now, not when our lives were going so well for us. And so, instinctively, my grip tightened on her slender hand and her momentum pulled me forward through the multicolored turmoil of the gate.

I yelled for Rouke, but the sound was lost as a gale of wind hit me with such force it took my breath away.

* * * * *

On the rock shelf Rouke watched Marc and Chay seek shelter. He thought he heard Marc call his name, but the sound was lost and forgotten in a sudden gust of wind. Colder now, he waited for a command from Nathel with his hands in the pits of his arms.

"It is complete. Finally. Rouke, take the vial that is closest to the sea. Yes . . . that one. Lift it off the ground," Nathel said the beginnings of a spell and it was cast on the vial. Rouke looked at it closer, but there was no change in its form.

"You can remove the stopper now. Be careful."

Rouke did as told, not spilling a drop. He held the vial in one hand and the cork in the other.

"Now come inside," Nathel said and Rouke followed obediently.

He looked for Marc and Chay, but they must have been farther back because he could not see them. He was about to call out to them when Nathel spoke again.

"In the vial you have a thick sludge. As I cast this next spell, something may happen to the liquid. Do not drop the vial. Please, do not drop it. Understood?"

"Yes."

"Come over to these bones." Rouke could see the pale form of Nathel as he stood in the near darkness of the cave. He momentarily looked to the back for the others, but still could not see them. What he did see made him start.

"Whose bones are those back there?" he asked.

"Please, be quiet. I begin my spell," Nathel snapped.

Not wanting to doubt someone as great as the king's commander, he pursed his lips and stood quietly resigned to complete this task. Perhaps the other vials were for the other bones. Nathel began to chant his incantation. With the spell spoken, he gave the word of execution. The contents of the vial bubbled and ran over the lip of the container. A warm feeling burned the chill from his fingers as the substance spilled over on his knuckles.

"Hold it over the bones and move it back and forth. It has to go from head to toe, and shoulder to shoulder."

Rouke did so obediently, and as it came in contact with the bones sparks began to move over their form. To his eyes, in the darkness, it seemed as though the bones were gaining material, not dissolving. Nathel had said they would become as dust.

The sparks that began as just a few increased in number. The activity grew rapidly. He heard Nathel yell at his side. The noise startled him, so it made him jump. He felt his fingers slip on the vial.

And then a sudden brightness filled his vision . . .

Made in the USA
Charleston, SC
27 May 2016